Oh, help, Claire th... ...here before.

She could still remember the first night she'd kissed Sean Farrell.

The way his mouth had felt against hers before he pulled away and given her a total dressing-down about being seventeen years old and in a state in which an unscrupulous man might have taken advantage of her.

Right now it would be all too easy to let her hands drift up over his shoulders, curl round the nape of his neck and draw his mouth down to hers. Particularly as they were no longer on the dance floor, in full view of the rest of the guests. At some point while they'd been dancing together they'd moved away from the temporary dance floor. Now they were in a secluded area of the garden. Just the two of them in the twilight.

'Claire...' His voice was a whisper.

And she knew he was going to kiss her again.

IT STARTED
AT A WEDDING…

BY
KATE HARDY

Published in Great Britain 2015
by Mills & Boon, an imprint of Harlequin (UK) Limited,
Eton House, 18-24 Paradise Road, Richmond, Surrey, TW9 1SR

© 2015 Pamela Brooks

ISBN: 978-0-263-25127-2

23-0415

Harlequin (UK) Limited's policy is to use papers that are natural, renewable and recyclable products and made from wood grown in sustainable forests. The logging and manufacturing processes conform to the legal environmental regulations of the country of origin.

Printed and bound in Spain
by CPI, Barcelona

Award-winning author **Kate Hardy** lives in Norwich with her husband, two children, one spaniel and too many books to count! She's a fan of the theatre, ballroom dancing, posh chocolate and anything Italian. She's a history and science geek, plays the guitar and piano, and makes great cookies (which is why she also has to go to the gym five days a week…).

To the Harlequin Romance authors, with much love and thanks for being such brilliant colleagues and friends—and for letting me bounce mad ideas off them!

CHAPTER ONE

No.

This couldn't be happening.

The box had to be there.

It *had* to be.

But the luggage carousel was empty. It had even stopped going round, now the last case had been taken off it. And Claire was the only one standing there, waiting with a small suitcase and a dress box—and a heart full of panic.

Where was her best friend's wedding dress?

'Get a grip, Claire Stewart. Standing gawping at the carousel isn't going to make the dress magically appear. Go and talk to someone,' she told herself sharply. She gathered up her case and the box containing the bridesmaid's dress, and went in search of someone who might be able to find out where the wedding dress was. Maybe the box had accidentally been put in the wrong flight's luggage and it was sitting somewhere else, waiting to be claimed.

Half an hour of muddling through in a mixture of English and holidaymakers' Italian got her the bad news. Somewhere between London and Naples, the dress had vanished.

The dress Claire had spent hours working on, hand-stitching the tiny pearls on the bodice and the edge of the veil.

The dress Claire's best friend was supposed to be wearing at her wedding in Capri in two days' time.

Maybe this was a nightmare and she'd wake up from it in a second. Surreptitiously, Claire pinched herself. It hurt. Not good, because that meant this was really happening. She was in Naples with her luggage, her own bridesmaid's dress...and no wedding dress.

There was nothing else for it. She grabbed her mobile phone, found a quiet corner in the airport and called Ashleigh.

Whose phone was switched through to voicemail.

This definitely wasn't the kind of news Claire could leave on voicemail; that would be totally unfair. She tried calling Luke, Ashleigh's fiancé, but his phone was also switched through to voicemail. She glanced at her watch. It was still so early that they were probably in the middle of breakfast and they'd probably left their phones in their room. OK. Who else could she call? She didn't have a number for Tom, Luke's best man. Sammy, her other best friend, who was photographing the wedding, wasn't flying to Italy until tomorrow, after she'd finished a photo-shoot in New York. The rest of the wedding guests were due to arrive on the morning of the wedding.

Which left Ashleigh's brother. The man who was going to give Ashleigh away. The man who played everything strictly by the rules—and Claire had just broken them. Big time. He was the last person she could call.

But he wasn't in Capri yet, either. Which meant she had time to fix this.

What she needed was a plan.

Scratch that. What she *really* needed was coffee. She'd spent the last two weeks working all hours on Ashleigh's dress as well as the work she was doing for a big wedding show, and she'd skimped on sleep to get everything done in time. That, plus the ridiculously early flight she'd taken out here this morning, meant that she was fuzzy and unfocused.

Coffee.

Even thought she normally drank lattes, this called for desperate measures. She needed something strong and something fast. One espresso with three sugars later, Claire's head was clear enough to work out her options. It meant more travelling—a lot more travelling—but that didn't matter. Claire would've walked over hot coals for Ashleigh. She was more than Claire's best friend; she was the sister Claire would've chosen.

She tried calling Ashleigh again. This time, to Claire's relief, her best friend answered her mobile phone.

'Claire, hi! Are you in Naples already?'

'Um, yes. But, Ash, there's a bit of a problem.'

'What's wrong?'

'Honey, I don't know how to soften this.' There wasn't a way to soften news like this. 'Is Luke with you?'

'Ye-es.' Ashleigh sounded as if she was frowning with concern. 'Why?'

'I think you're going to need him,' Claire said.

'Now you're really worrying me. Claire? What's happened? Are you all right?'

'I'm fine.' Claire had no option but to tell her best friend the news straight. 'But I'm so sorry, Ash. I've really let you down. Your dress. It's gone missing somewhere between here and London.'

'What?'

'I've been talking to the airline staff. They phoned London for me. They said it's not in London, and it's definitely not in Naples. They're going to try and track it down, but they wanted us to be prepared for the fact that they might not be able to find it before the wedding.'

'Oh, my God.' Ashleigh gave a sharp intake of breath.

'I know. Look—we have options. I don't have time to make you another dress like that one, even if I could get the material and borrow a sewing machine. But we can go looking in Naples and find something off the peg, something I can maybe tweak for you. Or I can leave the bridesmaid's dress and my case here in the left luggage, and get the next flight back to London. I'm pretty much the same size as you, so I'll Skype you while I try on every single dress in my shop and you can pick the ones you like best. Then I'll get the next flight back here, and you can try the dresses on and I'll do any alterations so your final choice is perfect.'

Except it wouldn't be perfect, would it?

It wouldn't be the dress of Ashleigh's dreams. The dress Claire had designed especially for her. The dress that had gone missing.

'And you'll still be the most beautiful bride in the world, I swear,' Claire finished, desperately hoping that her best friend would see that.

'They lost my dress.' Ashleigh sounded numb. Which wasn't surprising. Planning the wedding had opened up old scars, so Ashleigh had decided to get married abroad—and the dress had been one of the few traditions she'd kept.

And Claire had let her down. 'I'm so, so sorry.'

'Claire, honey, it's not your fault that the airline lost my dress.'

That wasn't how Sean would see it. Claire had clashed with Ashleigh's brother on a number of occasions, and she knew that he didn't like her very much. They saw the world in very different ways, and Sean would see this as yet another example of Claire failing to meet his standards. She'd failed to meet her own, too.

'Look, I was the one bringing the dress to Italy. It was my responsibility, so the fact it's gone wrong is my fault,' Claire pointed out. 'What do you want to do? Meet me here in Naples and we'll go shopping?'

'I'm still trying to get my head round this. My *dress*,' Ashleigh said, sounding totally flustered—which, considering that Ashleigh was the calmest and most together person Claire knew, was both surprising and worrying.

'OK. Forget Naples. Neither of us knows the place well enough to find the right wedding shops anyway, so we'll stick with London. Have a look on my website, email me with a note of your top ten, and we'll talk again when I'm back in the shop. Then I'll bring your final choices on the next flight back.' She bit her lip. 'Though I wouldn't blame you for not trusting me to get it right this time.'

'Claire-bear, it's not your fault. Luke's here now—he's worked out what's going on and he's just said he'd marry me if I was wearing a hessian sack. The dress isn't important. Maybe we can find something in Capri or Sorrento.'

Ashleigh was clearly aiming for light and breezy, but Claire could hear the wobble in her best friend's voice. She knew what the dress meant to Ashleigh: the one big tradition she was sticking to for her wedding day. 'No,

Ash. It'll take us for ever to find a wedding shop. And what if you don't like what they have in stock? That's not fair to you. I know I'll have something you like, so I'm going to get the next flight back to London. I'll call you as soon as I get there,' she said.

'Claire, that's so much travelling—I can't make you do that.'

'You're not making me. I'm offering. You're my best friend and I'd go to the end of the earth for you,' Claire said, her voice heartfelt.

'Me, too,' Ashleigh said. 'OK. I'll call the spa and move our bookings.'

So much for the pampering day they'd planned. A day to de-stress the bride-to-be. Claire had messed that up, too, by losing the dress. 'I'm so sorry I let you down,' Claire said. 'I'd better go. I need to get my luggage stored and find a flight.' And she really hoped that there would be a seat available. If there wasn't… Well, she'd get to London somehow. Train, plane, ferry. Whatever it took. She wasn't going to let Ashleigh down again. 'I'll call you when I get back to London.'

'Please don't tell me something's come up and you're not going to make it in time for the wedding.'

'Of course not,' Sean said, hearing the panic in his little sister's voice and wondering what was wrong. Was this just an attack of last-minute nerves? Or was she having serious second thoughts? He liked his future brother-in-law enormously, but if Ashleigh had changed her mind about marrying him, then of course Sean would back her in calling off the wedding. All he wanted was to see Ashleigh settled and happy. 'I was just calling to see if you needed me to bring any last-minute things over with me.'

'Oh. Yes. Of course.'

But she sounded flustered—very unlike the calm, sensible woman he knew her to be. 'Ashleigh? What's happened?'

'Nothing.'

But her response was a little too hasty for Sean's liking. He deliberately made his voice gentle. 'Sweetie, if there's a problem, you know you can always talk to me. I'll help you fix it.' OK, so Ashleigh was only three years younger than he was, and he knew that she was perfectly capable of sorting out her own problems—but he'd always looked out for his little sister, even before their parents had been killed in the crash that had turned their lives upside down six years ago. 'Tell me.'

'The airline lost my dress,' Ashleigh said. 'But it's OK. Claire's gone back to London to get me another one.'

Sean paused while it sank in.

There was a problem with his sister's wedding.

And Claire Stewart was smack in the middle of the problem.

Why didn't that surprise him?

'Wasn't Claire meant to be bringing the dress with her?' he asked.

'It wasn't her fault, Sean.'

No. Of course not. It would never be Miss Follow-Your-Heart's fault that something went wrong and everyone else had to pick up the pieces.

But he wasn't going to spoil his sister's wedding by picking a fight with her best friend. At least, not in front of Ashleigh. He fully intended to discuss the matter with Claire herself—sooner, rather than later. 'OK. Is there anything else you need?'

'No, it's fine.'

But his little sister didn't sound fine. She sounded shaky. 'Is Luke there with you?' he asked.

'Yes. He said the dress didn't matter and he'd marry me if I was wearing a hessian sack. He says it's our marriage that matters, not the trappings.'

Sean mentally high-fived his brother-in-law-to-be. And thank God Luke was so sensible and reliable. Ashleigh's last boyfriend had been selfish, thoughtless and flaky—and he'd just so happened to be the best friend of Claire's boyfriend at the time. Which figured. Claire always seemed to leave chaos in her wake.

'I could've told you that, sweetheart. Luke's a good bloke and he loves you to bits. Look, I'll be there later tonight, OK? If there's anything you need, anything at all, just call me. And I'm with Luke. Even if you're wearing a hessian sack, you're going to be the most beautiful bride ever.' The bride his father should've been giving away. His throat tightened. If only. But the crash had happened and they'd had to make the best of it ever since. And Sean was determined that his little sister was going to have the wedding she really wanted. He'd *make* it happen.

'Thanks, Sean.' She blew out a breath. 'I'm fine. Really. This is just a little hiccup and Claire's fixing it.'

Yes, Sean thought grimly, because he'd make quite sure that Claire did exactly that.

'See you tonight,' she said.

'See you tonight.'

Sean checked his diary when he'd put down the phone. All his meetings that afternoon could be moved. Anything else, he could deal with in Capri. A quick word with his PA meant that everything would be sorted. And then he called Claire.

Her phone went straight through to voicemail.

So that meant either she was on the phone already, her phone was switched off completely, or she'd seen his name on the screen and wasn't answering because she was trying to avoid him. OK, then; he'd wait for her at the shop. And he'd make absolutely sure that Ashleigh's dress didn't get lost, this time round.

It didn't take Sean long to get to the terraced house in Camden which held Dream of a Dress on the ground floor and Claire's flat on the top storey. Although the sign on the door said 'closed', he could see light inside—meaning that Claire was there, or whoever she'd employed to man the shop in her absence. Either would do.

He rang the doorbell.

No reply.

OK. Play dirty it was, then. This time, he leaned on the doorbell until a figure hurried through to the door.

A figure wearing a wedding dress.

Claire narrowed her eyes at him when she opened the door. Though he noticed that she didn't ask him why he was here. Clearly she had a pretty good idea that he already knew she'd lost his sister's wedding dress and he wasn't happy about the situation.

'I'm Skypeing Ash right now,' she said quietly. 'And I don't want her upset any more today, so can we leave the fight until she's chosen another dress and I've said goodbye to her?'

Claire clearly realised that they were about to have a fight. A huge one. But Sean agreed with her about not rowing in front of his sister. Right now, Ashleigh's feelings had to come first. 'OK.'

'Good. Come in. If you want a drink, feel free to make yourself something. There's tea, coffee and mugs in the cupboard above the kettle, though I'm afraid there's only long-life milk.' She gestured to a doorway which obviously led to the business's kitchen.

'Thank you,' he said. Though he wasn't about to accept any hospitality from Claire Stewart, even if it was do-it-yourself hospitality.

'If you'll excuse me, I have a wedding dress to sort out.' She gave him a level look. 'And I'm modelling the dresses for Ash, which means I'll need to change several times—so I'd appreciate it if you didn't come through to the back until I'm done.'

'Noted,' he said.

She locked the shop door again, still keeping the 'closed' sign in place, and vanished into the back room. Feeling a bit like a spare part—but wanting to know just how Claire had managed to lose a wedding dress—Sean waited in the main area of the shop until she walked back out, this time dressed in faded jeans and a strappy top rather than a wedding dress.

'No coffee?' she asked.

'No.'

She folded her arms. 'OK. Spit it out.'

'Firstly, does Ashleigh actually have a dress?' he asked.

'There are three she likes,' Claire said. 'I'm taking them all over to Capri as soon as I can get a flight. Then she can try them on, and I'll make any necessary alterations in time for the wedding.'

'What I don't understand is how you managed to lose her dress in the first place.' He shook his head in exasperation. 'Why wasn't it with you in the plane?'

'Believe it or not,' she said dryly, 'that was my original plan. I cleared it with the airline that I could put the boxes with her dress and mine in the overhead storage compartments, and if there was room they'd hang Ash's dress on a rail in the stewardesses' cabin. I packed both the dresses in boxes that specifically met the airline's size guidelines. Your waistcoat and cravat, plus Luke's and Tom's, are packed in with my dress.'

So far, so sensible. But this was Claire—the woman who was chaos in high heels with a snippy attitude. 'But?'

'It turned out there were three other brides on the flight. One of whom was a total Bridezilla and demanded that her dress should be the one in with the stewardesses. There was a massive row. In the end, the captain intervened and ordered that all the bridal dresses should go in the hold with the rest of the luggage—even those belonging to people who weren't involved in the argument with Bridezilla. He wouldn't even let us put the dresses in the overhead lockers. The atmosphere on the plane was pretty bad.' She shrugged. 'The airline staff have looked in London and in Naples, and there's no sign of the box with Ash's dress. They're still checking. It might turn up in time. But it probably won't, so these dresses are my contingency plan—because I don't intend to let Ash down. Ever.'

It hadn't been *entirely* Claire's fault, Sean acknowledged. But, at the same time, she *had* been the one responsible for the dress, and right now the dress was missing. 'Why didn't you buy a seat for the dress?'

'They said I couldn't—that if I wanted the dress to come with me, it would have to be treated as additional cabin luggage. Which,' she pointed out, 'is what I organised and what I paid for.' Her blue eyes were icy as she added, 'And, just in case you think I'm perfectly OK about the situation, understand that I've spent weeks working on that dress and I'm gutted that my best friend doesn't get to wear the dress of her dreams—the dress

I designed especially for her. But moaning on about the situation isn't going to get the dress back. I'd rather do something practical to make sure Ash's wedding goes as smoothly as possible. So, if you'll excuse me, I have three wedding dresses to pack and a flight to book.' She shrugged again. 'But, if it makes you feel better, do feel free to storm and shout at me.'

Funny how she was the one in the wrong, but she'd managed to make him feel as if *he* were the one in the wrong, Sean thought.

Though she had a point. Complaining about the situation or losing his temper with her wouldn't make the dress magically reappear. And Claire had spent most of today travelling—two and a half hours each way on a plane, plus an hour each way on a train and waiting round in between. Now she was just about to fly back to Italy: yet more travelling. All for his sister's sake.

Claire Stewart was trying—in both senses of the phrase. But maybe he needed to try a bit harder, too.

'Do you want me to find you a flight while you pack the dresses?' he asked.

She looked at him as if he'd just grown two heads.

'What?' he asked.

'Are you actually being *helpful*?' she asked. 'To *me*?'

He narrowed his eyes at her. 'Don't make it sound as if I'm always the one in the wrong.'

'No. That would be me,' she said. 'In your regimented world view.'

'I'm not regimented,' he said, stung. 'I'm organised and efficient. There's a difference.'

Her expression suggested otherwise.

'I was,' he pointed out, 'trying to call a truce and work with you. For Ashleigh's sake.'

She looked at him for a long, long time. And then

she nodded. 'Truce. I can do that. Then thank you—it would save me a bit of time if you could find me a flight. I don't care which London airport it's from or how much it costs—just let me know as soon as they need paying and I'll come to the phone and give them my credit card details. But please put whichever airline in the picture about what happened to the dress this morning, and I want cast-iron guarantees that *these* dresses are going to make it out to Italy with me. Otherwise I'll be carving their entire check-in staff into little pieces with a rusty spoon.'

He couldn't help smiling. 'Spoons are blunt.'

'That,' she said, 'is entirely the point. Ditto the rusty.'

'You really care about Ashleigh, don't you?' he said.

'Sean, how can you not already know that?' Claire frowned. 'She's been my best friend for more than half my lifetime, since I moved to the same school as her when I was thirteen. I think of Ash practically as my sister.'

Which would technically make her his sister, too. Except Sean didn't have any sibling-like feelings towards Claire. What he felt for Claire was...

Well, it was a lot easier to think of it as dislike. When they weren't being scrupulously polite to each other, they clashed. They had totally opposite world views. They were totally incompatible. He wasn't going to let himself think about the fact that her hair was the colour of a cornfield bathed in sunshine, and her eyes were the deep blue of a late summer evening. And he certainly wasn't going to let himself think about the last time he'd kissed her.

'Of course. I'll get you a flight sorted.'

Though he noticed her movements while he was on the phone. Deft and very sure as she packed each dress in tissue paper to avoid creases, put it inside a plastic cover to protect it from any damage and then in a box. As if she'd done this many times before. Which, he realised, she probably had.

He'd never seen Claire at work before. Apart from when she'd measured the three men in the wedding party for their waistcoats, and that had been at Ashleigh and Luke's house. He'd been too busy concentrating on being polite and anodyne to her for his sister's sake to take much notice of what she was actually doing.

And, OK, it was easy to think of dress designers as a bit kooky and not living in the same world as the rest of the population. The outlandish outfits on the catwalks in Milan and the big fashion shows left him cold and wondering what on earth was going on in the heads of the designers—real people just didn't wear stuff like that. But the woman in front of him seemed businesslike. Organised. Efficient.

Like someone who belonged in his world.

He shook himself. That was just an illusion. Temporary. Claire didn't belong in his world and he didn't belong in hers. They'd be civil to each other over the next few days, purely for Ashleigh's sake, and then they'd go back to avoiding each other.

Safely.

CHAPTER TWO

As CLAIRE WORKED on packing up the dresses, she found herself growing more and more aware of Sean. He looked every inch the meticulous businessman in a made-to-measure suit, handmade shirt, and perfectly polished shoes; as part of her job, Claire noticed details like that. Sean wouldn't have looked out of place on a catwalk or in a glossy magazine ad.

And he was actually helping her—working with her as a team. Which was rarer than a blue moon. They didn't get on.

Apart from a few occasions, and some of those were memories that still had the ability to make Claire squirm. Such as Ashleigh's eighteenth birthday party. Claire's life had imploded only a couple of weeks before and, although she'd tried so hard to smile and be happy for her best friend's sake, she'd ended up helping herself to too much champagne that evening to blot out the misery that had threatened to overwhelm her.

Sean had come to her rescue—and Claire had been young enough and drunk enough to throw herself at him. Sean had been a perfect gentleman and turned her down, and her adult self was glad that he'd been so decent, but as a teenager she'd been hideously embarrassed by the whole episode and she'd avoided him like the plague for months and months afterwards.

Then there was his parents' funeral, three years later. Claire had been there to support Ashleigh—just as Ashleigh had supported Claire at her own mother's funeral—and she'd glanced across at Sean at a moment when he'd looked utterly lost. Wanting to help, Claire had pushed past the old embarrassment and gone to offer him her condolences. Sean hadn't been quite approachable enough for her to give him a hug, so she'd simply squeezed his hand and said she was sorry for his loss. At the time, her skin had tingled at the contact with his—but the timing was so inappropriate that she hadn't acted on it.

They'd fought again when Ashleigh had decided not to join the family business. Sean had blamed Claire for talking Ashleigh out of what he clearly saw as her duty. OK, so Claire had been a sounding board and helped Ashleigh work out what she really wanted to do, encouraging her to follow her dreams; but surely Sean had wanted his sister to be happy instead of feeling trapped and miserable in a job she really didn't want to do? And surely, given that his parents had died so young, he understood how short life was and how you needed to make the most of every moment? It wasn't as if being a maths teacher was some insecure, fly-by-night job. And Ash was a really gifted teacher. She loved what she did and her pupils adored her. It had been the right decision.

The problem was, Sean had always been so overprotective. Claire could understand why; he was Ashleigh's elder brother and had been the head of the family since he was twenty-four. But at the same time he really needed to understand that his sister was perfectly capable of standing on her own two feet and making her own way in the world.

She forced herself to concentrate on packing the dresses properly, but she couldn't help noticing the deep tone of Sean's voice, his confidence and sureness as he talked to the airline.

Most of the time Claire didn't admit it, even to herself, but she'd had a secret crush on Sean when she'd been fourteen. Which was half the reason why she'd thrown herself at him at Ashleigh's birthday party, three years later.

Another memory seeped back in. Ashleigh's engagement party to Luke. Sean had asked her to dance; Claire had been well aware that he was only being polite for his sister's sake. Which was the same reason why she'd agreed to dance with him. Though, somewhere between the start and the middle of the song, something had changed. Claire couldn't even blame it on the champagne, because she hadn't been drinking. But something had made her pull back slightly and look up at Sean. Something had made her lips part slightly. And then he'd dipped his head and kissed her.

The kiss had shaken her right to the core. Nobody had ever made her feel like that with a single kiss—as if her knees had turned to mush and she needed to cling to him to keep herself upright. It had panicked her into backing away and cracking some inane joke, and the moment was lost.

Since then, she'd been scrupulously polite and distant with Sean. But in unguarded moments she wondered. Had he felt that same pull of attraction? And what if…?

She shook herself. Of course not. Apart from the fact that her judgement when it came to men was totally rubbish, she knew that Sean just saw her as his baby sister's super-annoying best friend, the woman he ended up bickering with every time they spoke to each other for more than five minutes. It rankled slightly that he still didn't take her seriously—surely the fact that she'd had her own business for the last three years and kept it going through the recession counted for *something*?

Then again, she didn't need to prove anything to him. She was perfectly comfortable with who she was and what she'd achieved.

She finished packing the last box.

'Any luck with my flight?' she asked when Sean ended his call.

'There's good news and bad,' he said.

'OK. Hit me with the bad first.'

He frowned. 'Why?'

'Because then I've faced the worst, and there's still something good to look forward to.'

He looked surprised, as if he'd never thought of it in that way before. 'OK. The bad news is, I can't get you a flight where they'll take the dresses on board.'

The worst-case scenario. Well, she'd just have to deal with it. 'Then if planes are out, I'll just have to go by train.' She thought on her feet. 'If I get the Eurostar to Paris, there'll be a connecting train to Milan or Rome, and from there to Naples. Though it means I probably won't get to Capri until tomorrow, now.'

'Hold on. I did say there was good news as well,' he reminded her. 'We can fly to Naples from London.'

She frowned, not understanding. 'But you just said you couldn't get me a seat where they'll take the dresses.'

'Not on a commercial flight, no. But I have a friend with a private plane.'

'You have *what*?'

'A friend with a private plane,' he repeated, 'who's willing to take us this afternoon.'

'Us.' The word hit her like a sledgehammer and she narrowed her eyes at him. 'Are you saying that you don't trust me to take the dresses on my own?'

'You need to go to Naples. I need to go to Naples. So it makes sense,' he said, 'for us to travel together.'

She noticed that he hadn't answered her question. Clearly he didn't trust her. To be fair to him, she had already lost his sister's wedding dress—but it hadn't been entirely her fault. 'But don't you already have a flight booked?'

'I cancelled it,' he said. 'I promised Ashleigh I'd be there tonight or I would've offered you my original booking and flown in later. This seemed like the best solution to the problem.'

'You have a friend with a private plane.' She still couldn't get over that one. 'Sean, normal people don't have friends with private planes.'

'You barely accept that I'm human, let alone normal,' he pointed out.

And they were heading towards yet another fight. She grimaced. 'Sorry. Let's just rewind and try this again. Thank you, Sean, for coming to the rescue and calling in whatever favour you had to call in to get me a flight to Naples. Please tell your friend that if he ever needs a wedding dress or a prom dress made, I'll do it for nothing.'

'I'll tell her,' Sean said dryly.

Her. Girlfriend? Probably not, Claire thought. Ashleigh was always saying that Sean would never settle down and never dated anyone for more than three weeks in a row. So maybe it was someone who'd gone to university with him, or a long-standing business acquaintance. Not that she had any right to ask.

'Thanks,' she said. 'So what time does the flight leave?'

'When we want it to, give or take half an hour,' he said. 'My car's outside. I just need to drop it back home and collect my luggage.' He looked at her. 'You might as well come with me.'

Gee, what an invitation, Claire thought. But she wasn't going to pick a fight with him now. He'd already gone above and beyond. It was for Ashleigh's sake rather than hers, she knew, but she still appreciated it. 'Ready when you are.'

He drove them back to his house and parked outside. His luggage was in the hallway, so it only took a few seconds for him to collect it; Claire noticed that he didn't invite her in. Fair enough. It was his space. Though she was curious to know whether his living space was as organised and regimented as the rest of him.

They took the tube through to London City airport. Claire used the noise of the train as an excuse not to make conversation, and she knew that he was doing exactly the same. Being with Sean wasn't easy. He was so prickly. He had to have a charming side, or he wouldn't have made such a success of running the family business—clients wouldn't want to deal with him. But the sweetness of the toffee that Farrell's produced definitely didn't rub off on him where Claire was concerned.

The check-in process was much faster than Claire was used to; then again, she didn't know anyone with a private plane. It was more the sort of thing that a rock star would have, not a wedding dress designer. The plane was smaller than she'd expected, but there was plenty of room to stretch out and the seats were way, way more comfortable than she was used to. She always travelled economy. This was another world.

'Welcome aboard,' the pilot said, shaking their hands. 'Our flight today will be about two and a half hours. If you need anything, ask Elise.'

Elise turned out to be their stewardess.

And, most importantly, Elise stored the dress boxes where Claire could see them. This time, she could be totally sure that none of the dresses would be lost.

'Do you mind if I…?' Sean gestured to his briefcase.

Claire would much rather work than make small talk with him, too. 'Sure. Me, too,' she said, and took a sketchpad from her bag. She'd had a new client yesterday who wanted a dress at short notice, plus there was the big wedding show in two months' time—a show where Claire was exhibiting her very first collection, and she was working flat out to get enough dresses ready in time. Six wedding dresses plus the brides-maids' outfits to go with each, as well as colour co-ordinating the groom's outfit with each set. She could really do with an extra twenty-four hours in a day for the next few weeks—twenty-four hours when she didn't need to sleep. But, as that wasn't physically possible, she'd have to settle for drinking too much coffee and eating too much sugary stuff to get her through the next few weeks.

As he worked, Sean was aware of the quick, light strokes of Claire's pencil against her sketchpad. Clearly she was working on some preliminary designs for some-one else's dress. When the sound stopped, he looked over at her.

She'd fallen asleep mid-sketch, her pencil still held

loosely in one hand, and there were deep shadows beneath her eyes.

Right at that moment, she looked vulnerable. And Sean was shocked by the sudden surge of protectiveness.

Since when did he feel protective about Claire Stewart?

That wasn't something he wanted to think about too closely. So he concentrated on his work and let her sleep until the plane landed. Then he leaned over and touched her shoulder. 'Claire, wake up.'

She murmured something and actually nestled closer, so her cheek was resting against his hand.

It was his second shock of the afternoon, how her skin felt against his. It made him feel almost as if he'd been galvanised. Very similar to that weird sensation when she'd measured him for the waistcoat—even though her touch had been as professional and emotionless as any tailor's, it had made him feel strange to feel the warmth of her fingers through his shirt.

Oh, help.

Sexual attraction and Claire Stewart were two things that definitely didn't go together, in his book.

OK, so there had been that night, all those years ago—but Claire had been seventeen and his mother had dispatched him to rescue the girl and get her safely to bed back at their house. Of course he'd been tempted when she'd tried to kiss him—he was a man, not an automaton—but he also knew that he was responsible for her, and no way would he ever have taken advantage of her.

And the times since when their eyes had met at one of Ashleigh's parties...

Well, she'd normally had some dreadful boyfriend

or other in tow. In Sean's experience, Claire's men were always the type who'd claim that artistic integrity was much more important than actually earning a living. Sean didn't have much time for people who wouldn't shoulder their fair share of responsibility and expected other people to bail them out all the time, but he still wouldn't encourage their girlfriend to cheat on them. He'd never made a move.

Except, he remembered with a twinge of guilt, for the night Ashleigh had got engaged to Luke. He'd asked Claire to dance—solely for his sister's sake. But then Claire had looked up at him, her blue eyes huge and her mouth parted, and he'd reacted purely on instinct.

He'd kissed her.

A kiss that had shaken him to the core. It had shaken him even more when he analysed it. No way could he feel like *that* about Claire Stewart. She was his total opposite. It would never, ever work between them. They'd drive each other crazy.

He'd been too shocked to say a word, at first, but then she'd made some terrible joke or other and he'd somehow managed to get his common sense back. And he'd blanked out the memory.

Except now it was back.

And he had to acknowledge that the possibility of something happening between himself and Claire had always been there. Right now, the possibility hummed just a little harder. Probably because he hadn't dated anyone in the last three months—this was a physical itch, he told himself, and Claire definitely wasn't the right woman to scratch said itch. Their approach to life was way too different for it ever to work between them.

'Claire.' This time, he shook her a little harder, the

way he would've liked to shake himself and get his common sense back in place.

She woke with a jolt. She blinked, as if not quite sure where she was, and he saw her expression change the second that she realised what had happened. 'Sorry,' she said. 'I didn't intend to fall asleep. I hope I didn't snore too loudly.'

He could tell that this was her way of trying to make a joke and ease the tension between them. Good idea. He'd follow her lead on that one. 'Not quite pneumatic drill mode,' he said with a smile.

'Good.'

Like him, she thanked the pilot and the stewardess for getting them there safely. And then they were in the bright Italian sunshine, so bright that they both needed to use dark glasses. And Sean was secretly glad of the extra barrier. He didn't want Claire guessing that she'd shaken his composure, even briefly.

And no way was he going to let her struggle with three dress boxes. 'I'll take these for you.'

She rolled her eyes. 'They're not that heavy, Sean. They're just a bit bulky.'

'Even so.'

'I can manage.'

Did she think that he was being sexist? 'I'm taller than you and my arms are longer,' he pointed out. 'So it makes sense for me to carry the boxes.'

'Then I'll carry your suitcase and briefcase.'

He'd almost forgotten just how stubborn she could be. But, at the same time, he had a sneaking admiration for her independence. And he always travelled light in any case, so his luggage wouldn't be too heavy for her.

On the way from the plane to the airport terminal, Claire said to Sean, 'Perhaps you can let me have your friend's name and address, so I can send her some flowers.'

'Already done,' he said.

'From you, yes. I want to send her something from *me*.'

'Sure,' he said easily. 'I'll give you the details when we get to the hotel.'

'Thank you.' She paused. 'And I need to pick up my case and the bridesmaid's dress. I checked them in to the left luggage, this morning.'

'Wait a second.' He checked his phone. 'Good. Jen— my PA—has booked us a taxi from here to Sorrento and arranged the hydrofoil tickets.'

They went through passport control, then collected Claire's luggage. He waited while she checked with the airline whether Ashleigh's original dress had turned up yet. He knew from her expression that there was still no luck.

The taxi driver loaded their luggage into the car. Claire and Sean were sitting together in the back seat. She was very aware of his nearness, and it made her twitchy. She didn't want to be this aware of Sean. And how did you make small talk with someone who had nothing in common with you?

She looked out of the window. 'Oh, there's Vesuvius.' Looming over the skyline, a brooding hulk of a mountain with a hidden, dangerous core.

'You went there with Ashleigh, didn't you?' he asked.

'And Sammy. Three years ago. It was amazing— like nothing any of us had ever seen before. It was what I imagine a lunar landscape would look like, and we squeaked like schoolkids when we saw steam coming out of the vents.' She smiled at the memory. 'I think that's why Ash chose to get married in Capri, because she fell in love with the island when we came here and had a day trip there.'

They both knew the other reason why Ashleigh hadn't planned to get married in the church where she and Sean had been christened and their parents had got married—because their parents were buried in the churchyard and it had been too much for Ashleigh to bear, the idea of getting married inside the church while her parents were outside.

'It's a nice part of the world,' Sean said.

'Very,' Claire replied. She ran out of small talk at that point and spent the rest of the journey looking out of the window at the coastline, marvelling at the houses perched so precariously on the cliffsides and the incredible blueness of the sea. At the same time, all her senses seemed to be concentrating on Sean. Which was insane.

Finally the taxi dropped them at the marina in Sorrento. Claire waited with their luggage while Sean collected their tickets—and then at last they boarded the hydrofoil and were on their way to Capri.

There were large yachts moored at the marina. As they drew closer she could see the buildings lining the marina, painted in brilliant white or ice cream shades. There were more houses on the terraces banking up behind them, then the white stone peak of the island.

Once they'd docked, they took the funicular railway up to the Piazzetta, then caught a taxi from the square; she noticed that the cars were all open-topped with a stripy awning above them to shade the passengers. So much more exotic than the average convertible.

The taxi took them past more of the brilliant white buildings, in such sharp contrast to the sea and the sky.

There were bougainvillea and rhododendrons everywhere, and terracotta pots full of red geraniums. Claire
had always loved the richness and depth of the colours
on the south European coast.

At last, they reached the hotel.

'Thank you for arranging this,' she said as they collected their keys. 'And you said you'd give me your
friend's details?' She grabbed a pen and paper, ready
to take them down as Sean gave them to her. 'Thanks.
Last thing—milk, white or dark chocolate?'

'I have no idea. You're sending her chocolate?'

'You've already sent flowers.' She smiled. 'I guess
you can't really send anyone confectionery, with your
business being in that line.' Admittedly Farrell's specialised in toffee rather than chocolates, but it would
still be a bit of a *faux pas*. 'I'll play it safe and send a
mixture.'

'Good plan,' he said. 'See you later.'

He'd made it clear that he didn't plan to spend much
time with her. Which suited Claire just fine—the less
time they were in each other's company, the less like-
lihood there was of another fight.

She let the bellboy help her carry her luggage to her
room. She'd barely set the dress boxes on the bed in her
room when there was a knock on the door.

'Come in,' she called with a smile, having a very
good idea who it would be.

Ashleigh walked in—physically so like Sean, with
the same dark eyes and dark hair, but a million times
easier to be with and one of Claire's favourite people in
the whole world. Claire hugged her fiercely. 'Hey, you
beautiful bride-to-be. How are you?'

Ashleigh hugged her back. 'I'm so glad to see you!
I can't believe you've been flying back and forth be-

tween England and Italy all day. That's insane, Claire, even for you.'

Claire shrugged. 'You're worth it. Anyway, I'm here now.' She held her friend at arm's length. 'You look gorgeous. Radiant. Just as you should be.'

'And you look shattered,' Ashleigh said, eyeing her closely. 'You were up before dawn to get your first flight here.'

'I'm fine. I, um, had a bit of a nap on the plane,' Claire admitted.

'Good—and you must be in dire need of something to eat and a cold drink.'

'A cold drink would be nice—but, before we do anything else, I need you to try on these dresses so I can get the alterations started.' Claire hugged her again. 'I'm so sorry that it's all gone so wrong.'

'It wasn't your fault,' Ashleigh said loyally.

That wasn't how Sean saw it, but Claire kept that thought to herself.

Ashley tried on the dresses and looked critically at herself in the mirror. Finally, she made her decision. 'I think this one.'

'Good choice,' Claire said.

Thankfully, the dress didn't need much altering. Claire took the dressmaking kit from her luggage and pinned the dress so it was the perfect fit.

'You're not doing any more work on that tonight,' Ashleigh said firmly. 'It's another day and a half until the wedding, and you've been travelling all day, so right now I want you to chill out and relax.'

'I promise you, I plan to have an early night,' Claire said. 'But I still need to check the waistcoats on the men. And I would kill for a shower.' All the travelling had made her feel tired, as well as sticky; running

some cool water over her head might just help to keep
her awake a bit longer.

'Sort the men's fitting tomorrow after breakfast,'
Ashleigh said. 'Just have your shower, then come and
meet us on the terrace when you're done. I'll have a
long, cold drink waiting for you. With lots and lots of
ice.'

'That sounds like heaven,' Claire said gratefully.

When Ashleigh had gone, Claire hung up all the
dresses and waistcoats, and had a shower. Then she
joined her best friend, her husband-to-be and their best
man on the terrace. To her relief, Sean wasn't there.

'He had some phone calls to make,' Ashleigh explained. 'You know Sean. He always works crazy
hours.'

Probably, Claire thought, because he'd been thrown
in at the deep end when he'd had to take over the family business at the age of twenty-four after their parents
had been killed in a car crash. Working crazy hours had
got him through the first year, and it was a habit that
had clearly stuck. 'Well—cheers,' she said, and raised
her glass as the others echoed her toast.

Somehow Claire managed to avoid Sean for most of
the next day; their only contact was just after breakfast, when she did the final fitting of the waistcoats
and checked that they went perfectly with the suits and
shirts. She was busy for most of the day making the last-
minute alterations to Ashleigh's dress, and when she
was finished Sean was still busy making phone calls
and analysing reports.

Then again, the sheer romance of the island of Capri
would be wasted on a man like Sean, Claire thought.
He was too focused on his work to notice the gorgeous

flowers or the blueness of the sea. So much so that she'd half expected him not to join them for the surprise that she and Luke had organised for Ashleigh that evening; when he joined them in the taxi, she had to hide her amazement.

'So where are we going?' Ashleigh asked.

'You'll see. Patience, Miss Farrell,' Claire said with a grin. Actually, it was something that she was looking forward to and dreading in equal measure, but she knew that it was something her best friend would love, so she'd force herself to get over her fears. It was just a shame that Sammy wasn't there to join them as her flight from New York had been delayed. Which meant that, instead of being able to let Sammy defuse the awkwardness between herself and Sean, Claire was going to have to make small talk with him—because she could hardly talk only to the best man and the groom-to-be and ignore Sean completely.

Finally they arrived at the chairlift.

'Oh, fabulous!' Ashleigh hugged Claire and then her husband-to-be. 'I love this place. I didn't think we'd get time to do this.'

'It was Claire's idea,' Luke said with a smile. 'She said sunset at the top of Monte Solaro would be incredibly romantic.'

'Especially because it's outside the usual tourist hours and we'll have the place all to ourselves. I can't believe you arranged all this.' Ashleigh looked thrilled. 'Thank you so much, both of you.'

Twelve minutes, Claire reminded herself as she was helped onto the chair. It would only take twelve minutes to get from the bottom of the chairlift to the very top of the island. She wasn't going to fall off. It was perfectly safe. She'd done this before. Thousands and thousands of tourists had done this before. The chairs were on a continuous loop, so all she had to do was let them help her jump off at the top. It would be *fine*.

Even so, her palms felt slightly damp and she clung on to the green central pole of her chair for dear life. Thankfully, her bag had a cross-body strap, so she didn't have to worry about holding on to that, too. Her hands ached by the time she reached the top, but she managed to get off the chair without falling flat on her face.

Just as she and Luke had arranged, there was a table at the panoramic viewpoint overlooking the *faraglioni*, the three famous vertical columns of rock rising out of the sea. There was a beautiful arrangement of white flowers in the centre of the table, and white ribbons on the wicker chairs. When they sat down, the waiter brought over a bottle of chilled Prosecco and canapés.

'Cheers. To Ashleigh and Luke—just to say how much we love you,' Claire said, lifting her glass, and the others echoed the toast.

'I really can't believe you did this.' Ashleigh was beaming, and Claire's heart swelled. The night before the wedding, when Ashleigh should've been happily fussed over by her mum…Claire had wanted to take her best friend's mind off what she was missing, and she and Luke had talked over the options. The scary one had definitely been the best decision.

'It wasn't just me. It was Luke as well,' Claire said, wanting to be fair. 'It's just a shame Sammy couldn't make it.'

'She'll be here tomorrow,' Tom said confidently.

'You know, some brides actually get married up here,' Ashleigh said. 'Obviously they're not going to walk for an hour uphill in a wedding dress and high heels, so they ride on the chairlift. I've seen photographs where the bride carried her shoes in one hand and her bouquet in the other.'

'And I suppose Claire showed them to you,' Sean said.

Claire didn't rise to the bait, but she wished she hadn't already done the final fitting of his waistcoat, because otherwise she would've had great pleasure in being totally unprofessional and sticking pins into him.

'No,' Ashleigh said. 'Actually, she talked me out of it.'

'Because the design of your dress means you wouldn't fit in the seat properly and I didn't want your dress all creased in the photographs,' Claire said with a smile.

Ashleigh laughed. 'More like because you wouldn't be able to hang on to your shoes and your flowers and cling on to the central bar for dear life all at the same time.'

Claire laughed back. 'OK, so I'm a wuss about heights—but I would've done it if that's what you'd re-ally wanted, Ash. Because it's your day, and what *you* want is what's important.' Her words were directed at her best friend, but she looked straight into Sean's eyes, making it very clear that she meant every word.

He had the grace to flush.

It looked as if he'd got the message, then. Ashleigh came first and they'd put their differences aside for her sake.

Luke and Tom chatted easily, covering up the fact that Claire and Sean were barely speaking to each other. And gradually Claire relaxed, letting herself enjoy the incredibly romantic setting. They watched as the sun began to set over the sea; mist rose around the distant islands as the sky became striped with yellow and pink and purple, making them seem mysterious and other-worldly.

Claire took a few shots with her camera; she knew they wouldn't be anything near as good as Sammy's photographs, but it would at least be a nice memory. She glanced at Sean; he looked as if he was lost in thought, staring out at the sunset. Before she quite realised what she was doing, she took the snap.

Later that evening, back in her hotel room, she reviewed her photographs. There were some gorgeous shots of the sunset and the sea, of Ashleigh and Luke and Tom. But the picture she couldn't get out of her head was the impulsive one she'd taken of Sean. If they'd never met before, if there were no history of sniping and backbiting between them, she would've said he was the most attractive man she'd ever met and she would've been seriously tempted to get together with him.

But.

She'd known Sean for years, he was far from an easy man, and she really didn't need any complications in her life right now.

'Too much Prosecco addling your brain, Claire Stewart,' she told herself with a wry smile. 'Tomorrow, you're on sparkling water.'

Tomorrow.

Ashleigh's wedding day.

And please, please, let it be perfect.

CHAPTER THREE

'MISS STEWART?' THE woman from the airline introduced herself swiftly on the phone. 'I'm very pleased to say we've found the dress box that went missing.'

It took a moment for it to sink in. They'd actually found Ashleigh's original dress?

'That's fantastic,' Claire said. She glanced at her watch. Ashleigh's wedding wasn't until four o'clock. Which meant she had enough time to get the hydrofoil across to Sorrento and then a taxi to the airport to collect the dress, and she'd be back in time to get the dress ready while Ashleigh was having her hair and make-up done. Thankfully, she'd brought her portable steam presser with her in her luggage, so although the dress would be quite badly creased by now, she'd be able to fix it. 'Thank you very much. I'll be with you as soon as possible.'

'And if you could bring some identification with you, it would be helpful,' the airline assistant added.

'I'll bring my passport,' Claire said. Even before she'd said goodbye and ended the call, she was unlocking the safe in her wardrobe and taking her passport out.

When she went to tell Ashleigh the good news, Sean was there.

'It'd be quicker to get the dress couriered here,' he said.

'I've already lost the dress once. If you think I'm taking the risk of that happening again…' Claire shook her head. 'No chance.'

It also meant she had a bulletproof excuse to avoid Sean for the next few hours. Though that was slightly beside the point. She kissed Ashleigh's cheek. 'I'll text you when I've picked it up and I'm on my way back. But I'll be back well before it's time to have our hair and make-up done, I promise.'

Ashleigh hugged her back. 'I know. And thanks, Claire.'

'Hey. That's what best friends are for,' she said with a smile.

When Claire collected the dress, the box was in perfect condition, so she didn't have to worry that the contents had been damaged in any way. It didn't matter any more where the dress had been; the important thing was that she had it now, and Ashleigh would wear the dress of her dreams on her wedding day.

'Miss Stewart? Before you go,' the airline assistant said, 'I have a message for you. You have transport back to Capri. Would you mind coming this way?'

'Why?' Claire asked, mystified. She'd planned to get another taxi back to Sorrento, and then the hydrofoil across to Capri.

Before the airline assistant could answer, Claire's phone pinged with a message. 'Sorry, would you mind if I check this?' she asked, just in case it was Ashleigh.

To her surprise, the message was from Sean.

Transport arranged. Don't argue. Ashleigh worrying. Need to save time.

Sean had arranged transport for her? She swallowed hard. She knew Sean had done this for his sister's sake, not for hers, but it was still such a nice thing to do.

And the transport wasn't a taxi back to Sorrento. It was a helicopter. And the pilot told her that the flight from Naples to Capri took less time than the hydrofoil from Sorrento to Capri, so Sean had saved her the time of the taxi journey on top of that.

She texted back swiftly. Thank you. Tell her the dress is absolutely fine. Let me know how much I owe you for the transport. She knew Sean's opinion of her was already low and she was absolutely not going to let him think she was a freeloader, on top of whatever else he thought about her. She'd always paid her own way.

A text came back from him.

Will tell her. Transport on me.

Oh, no, it wasn't. Dress my responsibility, so *I* will pay. Not negotiable, she typed back pointedly. No way was she going to be in debt to Sean.

She'd half expected a taxi to meet her at the helipad, but Sean was in the reception area, waiting for her. He was wearing formal dark trousers and a white shirt—Claire didn't think he actually owned a pair of jeans—but for once he wasn't wearing a tie. His concession to casual dress, perhaps.

He looked gorgeous.

And he was totally off limits. She really needed to get a grip. Like *now*.

'What are you doing here?' she asked.

'Transport,' he said, gesturing to an open-topped sports car in the car park.

She didn't have much choice other than to accept. 'Thank you.' She looked at him. 'Is Ash OK?'

'She's fine,' he reassured her.

'Good.'

'And I owe you an apology.'

Claire frowned, surprised. Sean was apologising to her? 'For what?'

'Sniping at you last night—assuming that you'd given Ashleigh that crazy idea of getting married at the top of the mountain and going up by chairlift.'

'Given that I'm scared of heights,' she said dryly, 'I was quite happy to talk her out of that one on the grounds of dress practicalities.'

'But you went up on the chairlift last night.'

She shrugged. 'Luke and I wanted to distract her and we thought that would be a good way.'

'Yeah.'

She looked at him. He masked his feelings quickly, but she'd seen the flash of pain in his eyes. On impulse, she laid her hand on his arm. 'It must be hard for you, too.'

He nodded. 'It should be Dad walking down the aisle with her, not me.' His voice was husky with suppressed emotion. 'But things are as they are.'

'Your parents would be really proud of you,' she said.

'Excuse me?' His voice had turned icy.

She took her hand off his arm. 'OK. It's not my place to say anything and I wasn't trying to patronise you. But I thought a lot of your parents. Your mum in particular was brilliant when my mum died. And they would've been proud of the way you've always been there for Ash, always supported her—well, *almost* always,' she amended. To be fair, he'd been pretty annoyed about Ashleigh's change of planned career. He hadn't supported it at first.

'She's my little sister. What else would I do?'

It was a revelation to Claire. Sean clearly equated duty with love, or mixed them to the point where they couldn't be distinguished. And discussing this was way beyond her pay grade. She changed the subject again. 'So how much do I owe you for the flight?'

'You don't.'

'I've already told you, the dress is my responsibility, so I'll pay the costs. But thank you for organising it, especially as it means Ash isn't worrying any more.'

'We'll discuss it later,' he said. 'Ashleigh comes first.'

'Agreed—but that doesn't mean I'm happy to be in your debt,' she pointed out.

'I did this for Ashleigh, not for you.'

'Well, *duh*.' She caught herself before she said something really inflammatory. 'Sean, I know we don't usually get on too well.' That was the understatement of the year. 'But I think we're going to have to make the effort and play nice while we're on Capri.'

He slanted her a look that said very clearly that he didn't believe she could keep it up.

If she was honest, she wasn't sure she could keep it up, either. Or that Sean could, for that matter. But they were at least going to make the effort. Though they had a cast-iron excuse not to talk to each other for the next few minutes, because he needed to concentrate on driving.

She put the dress box safely in the back of the car, took her sunhat from her bag and jammed it on her head so it wouldn't be blown away, then sat in the front seat next to Sean. She still had her dark glasses on from the helicopter flight, so the glare of the sun didn't bother her.

Sean was a very capable driver, she noticed, even though he was driving on the right-hand side of the road instead of the left as he was used to doing in England. The road was incredibly narrow and winding, with no verges and high stone walls at the edges; it was busy with vans and scooters and minibuses, and every so often he had to pull over into the tiniest of passing places. If Claire had been driving, she would've been panicking that the car would end up being scraped on one of those stone walls; but she knew that she was very safe with Sean. It was an odd feeling, having to rely on someone she normally tried to avoid. And even odder that for once she didn't mind.

'Is there anything you need for the dress?' he asked as they pulled up outside the hotel.

'Only my portable steam presser, which I brought with me on my first trip.'

He looked confused. 'Why do you need a steam presser?'

'This dress has been in a box for three days. Even though I was careful when I packed it, there are still going to be creases in the material, and I don't have time to hang the dress in a steamy bathroom and wait for the creases to fall out naturally. And an ordinary iron isn't good enough to give a professional finish.'

'OK. Let me know if you need anything organised.'

He probably needed some reassurance that it wasn't going to go wrong, she thought. 'You can come and have a sneak peek at the dress, if you want,' she said.

'Isn't that meant to be bad luck?'

'Only if you're the bridegroom. Remember that the

dress needs pressing, so you won't be seeing it at its best,' she warned, 'but it will be perfect by the time Ash puts it on.'

Sean looked at Claire. Her sunhat was absolutely horrible, a khaki-coloured cap with a peak to shade her eyes; but he supposed it was more sensible than going out bareheaded in the strong mid-morning sun and risking sunstroke.

He wondered if she'd guessed that he wanted reassurance that nothing else was going to go wrong with the dress—just as she'd clearly noticed that moment when the might-have-beens had shaken his composure. She'd been a bit clumsy about it, but she hadn't pushed him to talk and share his feelings. She'd been kind, he realised now, and that wasn't something he associated with Claire Stewart. It made him feel weird.

But, if she could make the effort, then so could he. 'Thanks. I would appreciate that.'

'Let's go, then,' she said.

He followed her up to her room. Everywhere was neat and tidy. Funny, he'd expected the room to be as messy and chaotic as Claire's life seemed to be—even though her shop had been tidy. But then he supposed the shop would have to be tidy or it would put off potential clients.

She put the dress box on the bed. 'Right—how much do I owe you for that flight?'

'We've already discussed that,' he said, feeling awkward.

'No, we haven't, and I don't want to be beholden to you.'

'Ashleigh is my sister,' he reminded her.

'I know, and she's my best friend—but I still don't want to be beholden to you.'

He frowned. 'Now you're being stubborn.'

'Pots and kettles,' she said softly. 'Tell me how much I owe you.'

Actually, he liked the fact that she was so insistent on paying her fair share. It showed she had integrity. Maybe he'd been wrong to tar her with the same brush as her awful boyfriends. Just because she had a dreadful taste in men, it didn't necessarily mean that she was as selfish as they were—did it? 'OK.' He told her a sum that was roughly half, guessing that she'd have no idea how much helicopter transfers would cost.

'Fine. Obviously I don't have the cash on me right at this very second,' she said, 'but I can either do a bank transfer if you give me your account details, or give you the cash in person when we're back in England.'

'No rush. I'll give you my bank details, but making the transfer when you get back to England will be fine,' he said.

'Good. Thank you.' She opened the box, unpacked the dress, and put it on a hanger.

The organza skirt was creased but Sean could already see how stunning the ivory dress was. It had a strapless sweetheart neckline, the bodice was made of what he suspected might be handmade lace, and it looked as if hundreds of tiny pearls had been sewn into it. It was worthy of something produced by any of the big-name designers.

And Claire had designed this for his little sister. She'd made it all by hand.

Now he understood why she'd called her business that ridiculous name, because she was delivering exactly what her client wanted—a dream of a dress.

Clearly his lack of response rattled her, because she folded her arms. 'If you hate it, fine—but remember that this is what Ash wanted. And I'm giving you fair warning, if you tell Ash you hate it before she puts it on, so she feels like the ugliest bride in the world instead of like a princess, then you're so getting the rusty spoon treatment.'

'I don't hate it, actually. I'm just a bit stunned, because I wasn't expecting it to be that good,' he admitted.

She dropped into a sarcastic curtsey. 'Why, thank you, kind sir, for the backhanded compliment.'

'I didn't mean it quite like that,' he said. 'I don't know much about dresses, but that looks as if it involved a lot of work.'

'It did. But she's worth every second.'

'Yeah.' For a moment, he almost turned to her and hugged her.

But this was Claire 'Follow Your Heart' Stewart, the mistress of chaos. Their worlds didn't mix. A hug would be a bad, bad idea. 'Thanks for letting me see the dress,' he said. 'I'd better let you get on.'

'Tell Ash her dress is here safely, and I'll come and find her the second it's ready.'

He nodded. 'Will do.'

Once Claire was satisfied with the dress, she took it through to Ashleigh's room. Sammy opened the door. 'Claire-bear! About time, too,' she said with a grin. 'Losing the dress. Tsk. What kind of dressmaker does that?'

'Don't be mean, Sammy,' Ashleigh called. 'I'd cuff her for you, Claire, but I have to sit still and let Aliona take these rollers out of my hair.'

Claire hung up the dress, then enveloped Sammy with a hug. 'Hello to you, too. How was your flight?'

'Disgusting,' Sammy said cheerfully, 'but when I've finished taking photographs tonight then I'm going to drink Prosecco until I don't care any more.'

'Hangover on top of jet lag. Nice,' Claire teased. 'It's so good to see you, Sammy.'

'You, too. And oh, my God. How amazing is that dress? You've really surpassed yourself this time, Claire.'

Claire smiled in acknowledgement. 'I'm just glad we got it back.'

The hotel's hairdresser and make-up artist cooed over the dress, too, and then Claire submitted to being prettied up before putting on her own dress and then helping Ashleigh with hers.

Sammy posed them both for photographs on the balcony. 'Righty. I need to do the boys, now,' she said when she'd finished. 'See you at the town hall.'

'OK?' Claire asked when Sammy had gone.

Ashleigh gulped. 'Yes. Just thinking.'

'I know.' It would be similar for Claire, if she ever got married: she'd be missing her mum, though her dad would be there—*if* he approved of Claire's choice of man—and her mum's family would be there, with Ashleigh and Sammy to support her.

Not that Claire thought she'd ever get married. All the men she'd ever been involved with had turned out to be Mr Wrong. Men she'd thought would share her dreams, but who just couldn't commit. Men who'd been so casual with her emotions that she'd lost trust in her judgement.

'But I think they're here in spirit,' Claire said softly.

'They loved you so much, Ash. And Luke can't wait to make you his bride. You've got a good guy, there.'

'I know. I'm lucky.' Ashleigh swallowed hard.

'Hey. If you cry and your make-up runs, Sean will have my guts for garters,' Claire said. She went into a dramatic pose. 'Help! Help! Save me from your scary big brother!'

To her relief, it worked, and Ashleigh laughed; she was still smiling when Sean knocked on her door to say they needed to go.

CHAPTER FOUR

SEAN HAD ALREADY seen the dress—albeit not at its best—but seeing his little sister wearing it just blew him away. The ivory dress emphasised Ashleigh's perfect hour-glass shape by skimming in at the waist, then falling to the floor in soft folds. Her dark hair was drawn back from her face and pinned at the back as a base for her veil, and then flowed down in soft curls. She wore a discreet and very pretty tiara with sparkling stones and pearls to reflect the pearls in the bodice. And finally she was carrying a simple posy of dusky lavender roses, the same colour as Claire's dress; the stems were tightly bound with ivory ribbon.

'You look amazing, Ashleigh,' he said. 'Really amazing.'

Then he glanced at Claire. Again, he was shocked. He hadn't seen the bridesmaid's dress before, though he'd had a fair idea that it would be dusky lavender, the same colour as his waistcoat and the rose in his buttonhole. Although it, too, was strapless and had a sweetheart neckline, it was much plainer than Ashleigh's dress and ended at the knee. Claire's hair was dressed in a similar style to his sister's, though without a veil and with a discreet jewelled headband rather than a tiara. Her roses were ivory rather than lavender, as a counterpoint to the bride's bouquet, and her satin high heels were dyed to match her dress.

If he'd seen her across a crowded room as a complete stranger, he would've been drawn to her immediately. Approached her. Asked her out.

He pushed the thought away. This was Claire. He *did* know her. And, if they hadn't made a truce for Ashleigh's sake, they would've been sniping at each other within the next five minutes. She was absolutely not date material.

'Ready?' he asked.

'Ready,' they chorused.

The official civil ceremony was held at the town hall in Anacapri. Only the main people from the wedding party were there: Ashleigh and Luke, with Luke's best friend, Tom, as the best man, Claire as the bridesmaid and one of the witnesses, and himself as the other witness. Sammy was there, too, to take photographs.

After everything had been signed, the two open-topped cars took them to the private villa where the symbolic ceremony was being held and the rest of their family and friends were waiting to celebrate with them.

Luke and Tom went ahead to wait at the bridal arch, which was covered with gorgeous white flowers.

Then Ashleigh stood at the edge of the red carpet, her arm linked through Sean's. He could feel her trembling slightly. Nervous, excited and a little sad all at the same time, he guessed. 'Ashleigh, you're such a beautiful bride,' he said softly. 'Our parents would be so proud of you right now.'

Ashleigh nodded, clearly too overcome to speak, and squeezed his arm as if to say, 'You, too.'

'Come on. Let's get the party started,' he said, and

gave the signal to the traditional Neapolitan guitar and mandolin duo.

Their version of Pachelbel's 'Canon' was perfect. And Sean was smiling as he walked his little sister down the aisle to marry the man she loved.

Claire had seen the photographs and knew that the garden where Ashleigh and Luke were getting married was spectacular, but the photographs really hadn't done the place justice. The garden was breathtaking, overlooking the sea; lemon trees grew around the edge of the garden, their boughs heavy with fruit, and the deep borders were filled with rhododendrons and bougainvillea. There seemed to be butterflies everywhere. A symbol of good luck and eternal love, she thought.

She took the bouquet from Ashleigh and held it safely during the ceremony, and she had to blink back the tears as Ashleigh and Luke exchanged their vows, this time in front of everyone. She glanced at Sean, who was standing beside her, and was pleased to see that for once he was misty-eyed, too. And so he should be, on Ashleigh's wedding day, she thought, and she looked away before he caught her staring at him.

Everyone cheered when the celebrant said, 'You may now kiss the bride,' and Luke bent Ashleigh back over his arm to give her a show-stopping kiss.

'Let them have it, guys,' Sammy called as Ashleigh and Luke started to walk back down the aisle, and the confetti made from white dried flower petals flew everywhere.

Once the formal photographs had been taken, waiters came round carrying trays filled with glasses of Prosecco. Ashleigh and Luke headed the line-up to welcome their guests; and then, finally, it was time for the meal. Ashleigh had chosen a semi-traditional top table layout, so Claire as the chief bridesmaid was at one end, next to Luke's father. As Sean was standing in for the bride's father, he was at the other end, between Ashleigh and Luke's mother. And there were enough people between them, Claire thought, for them to be able to smile and hide their relief at not having to make small talk.

It was an amazing table, under a pergola draped with white wisteria. Woven in between the flowers were glass baubles, which caught the light from the tea-light candles set in similar glass globes on the table, and reflected again in the mirrored finish of the table. The sun was already beginning to set, and Claire had never seen anything so romantic in her life. And the whole thing was topped off by the traditional Neapolitan guitar and mandolin duo who played and sang softly during the meal.

If she ever got married, Claire thought, this was just the kind of wedding she'd want, full of love and happiness and so much warmth.

Finally, after the excellent coffee and tiny rich Italian desserts, it was time for the speeches. Luke's was sweet and heartfelt, Tom's made everyone laugh, but Sean's made her blink back the tears.

He really did love Ashleigh. And, for that, Claire could forgive the rest.

The cake—a spectacular four-tier confection, which Claire knew held four different flavours of sponge— was cut, and then it was time for the dancing.

Ashleigh and Luke had chosen a song for their bridal dance that always put a lump in her throat—'Make You Feel My Love'—and she watched them glide across the temporary dance floor. The evening band played it in waltz time, and Claire knew that Luke had been taking private lessons; he was step-perfect as he whirled Ashleigh round in the turns. The perfect couple.

Tradition said that the best man and the chief bridesmaid danced together next, and Claire liked Tom very much indeed; she was pleased to discover that he was an excellent dancer and her toes were perfectly safe with him.

'I love the dresses,' Tom said. 'If I wasn't gay, I'd *so* date you—a woman who can create such utter beauty. You're amazing, Claire.'

She laughed and kissed his cheek. 'Aww, you're such a sweetie, Tom. Thank you. But I wouldn't date you because I have terrible taste in men—and you're far too nice to be one of *my* men.'

He laughed. 'Thank *you*, sweetie. You'll find the right guy some day.'

'If I could find someone who'd make me as happy as Luke makes Ash,' she said softly, 'I'd consider myself blessed.'

'Me, too,' Tom said. 'And the other way round. They're perfect for each other.'

'They certainly are,' she said with a smile, though at the same time there was a nagging ache in her heart. Would she ever find someone who'd make her happy, or was she always destined to date Mr Wrong?

Sean knew it was his duty—as the man who'd given the bride away—to dance with the chief bridesmaid at some point. For a second, he stood watching Claire as she danced with Luke's father. She was chatting away, looking totally at ease. And then Sean registered what the band was playing: 'Can't Take My Eyes Off You'. He was shocked to realise that it was true: he couldn't take his eyes off Claire.

Which was absolutely not a good thing.

Claire Stewart was the last woman he wanted to get involved with.

And yet he had to acknowledge that he was drawn to her. There was something about her. He couldn't pin it down, which annoyed him even more—he couldn't put his feelings in a pigeonhole, the way he usually did. And that made her dangerous. He needed to stay well away from her.

Though, for tonight, he had to do the expected thing and make the best of it.

As the song came to an end, he walked over. 'I guess we need to play nice for Ashleigh.'

'I guess,' she said.

Even as the words came out of his mouth, he knew he was saying the wrong thing, but he couldn't stop himself asking, 'So is one of your awful boyfriends joining you later?'

'If that's your idea of nice,' Claire said, widening her eyes in what looked like annoyance, 'I'd hate to see how caustic your idea of snippy would be.'

He grimaced, knowing that he was in the wrong this time. 'Sorry. I shouldn't have put it quite like that.'

'Not if you were being nice. Though,' she said, 'I do admit that I have a terrible taste in men. I always seem to pick Mr Wrong.' She shrugged. 'And the answer's no, nobody's joining me. I'm happily single right now. And I'm way too busy at work right now to get involved with someone.'

Was that her way of telling him she wasn't interested? Or was she just giving him the facts?

Her perfume wasn't one he recognised; it was something mysterious and deep. Maybe that was what was scrambling his brain, rather than her nearness. Scrambling his brain enough to make him think that she was the perfect fit. The way she felt, in his arms...

'So isn't one of your sweet-but-temporary girlfriends joining you later?' Claire asked.

Ouch. Though Sean knew he deserved the question. He'd started it. 'No. Becca and I broke up three months ago. And I'm busy at work.' Which was his usual excuse for ending a relationship before things started to get too close.

'Two peas in a pod, then, us,' she said with a grin.

'I always thought we were chalk and cheese.'

She laughed. 'I was going to say oil and vinegar. Except they actually go together.'

'And we don't,' Sean said. 'So would you be the vinegar or the oil?'

'Difficult to say. A bit of both, really,' she said. 'I make things go smoothly for my clients. But I'm sharp with people who have an attitude problem. You?'

'Ditto,' he said.

This was *weird*.

They were actually laughing at themselves. Together. Not sniping at each other.

And this felt sparky. Fun. He was actually enjoying Claire's company—something that he'd never thought would happen in a million years.

This was the second song in a row they were dancing to. The music was slower. Softer. And, although he knew it was a seriously bad idea, he found himself drawing Claire closer. Swaying with her.

Oh, help, Claire thought. She'd been here before. Today, she'd paced herself and only drunk a couple of small glasses of Prosecco, well spaced out with sparkling water. But she could still remember the first night she'd kissed Sean Farrell. The way his mouth had felt against hers before he'd pulled away and given her a total dressing-down about being seventeen years old and in a state where an unscrupulous man could've taken advantage of her.

And again, at Ashleigh and Luke's engagement party, where they'd ended up dancing way too close and then Sean had kissed her, his mouth warm and sweet and so tempting that it terrified her.

Right now, it would be all too easy to let her hands drift up over his shoulders, curl round the nape of his neck, and draw his mouth down to hers. Particularly as they were no longer on the dance floor, in full view of the rest of the guests; at some point, while they'd been dancing together, they'd moved away from the temporary dance floor. Now they were in a secluded area of the garden. Just the two of them in the twilight.

'Claire.' His voice was a whisper.

And she knew he was going to kiss her again.

He dipped his head and brushed his mouth against hers, very lightly. It felt as if every nerve-end had been galvanised. He did it again. And again. This time, Claire gave in and slid her hands into his hair. His arms tightened round her and he continued teasing her mouth with those light, barely there kisses that made her want more. Maybe she made some needy little sound, because then he was really kissing her, and it felt as if fireworks were exploding all around them.

When he broke the kiss, she was shaking.

'Claire.' He sounded dazed.

That made two of them.

Part of her wanted to do this. To go with him—her room or his, it wouldn't matter. She knew they both needed a release from the tension of the last few days.

But the sensible part of her knew that doing that would make everything so much worse. How would they face each other in the morning? They certainly didn't have a future. Yes, Sean was reliable, unlike most of her past boyfriends—but he was also too regimented for her liking. Everything had to go within his twenty-year plan. Which was fine for a business, but it wasn't the way she wanted to live her personal life. She wanted to take time to smell the roses. Spontaneity. A chance to seize the day and enjoy whatever came her way. Live life to the full.

'We need to stop,' she said. While she could still be sensible. If he kissed her once more, she knew she'd say yes. So she'd say the word while she could still actually pronounce it. 'No.'

'No.' He looked at her, his eyes haunted. For a second, he looked so vulnerable. She was about to crack and place her palm against his cheek to comfort him, to tell him that she'd changed her mind, when she saw his expression change. His common sense had snapped back into place. 'You're absolutely right,' he said, and took a step back from her.

'I have bridesmaid stuff to do,' she said. It wasn't strictly true—the rest of the evening was all organised—but it was an excuse that she thought would save face for both of them.

'Of course,' he said, and let her go.

Even as she walked away, Claire regretted it. Her old attraction to Sean had never quite gone away, no matter how deeply she thought she'd buried it or how much she denied it to herself.

But she knew it had been the right thing to do. Because no way could things work out between her and Sean, and she'd had enough of broken relationships and being let down. Keeping things platonic was sensible, and the best way to avoid heartbreak.

Claire spent the rest of the evening socialising with the other guests, encouraging the younger ones to dance. All the time, she was very aware of exactly where Sean was in the garden, but she didn't trust herself not to make another stupid mistake. She'd got it wrong with him in the past. She couldn't afford to get it wrong in the future.

Finally, she went back to the hotel with the last few guests, kicked off her high heels, and curled up in one of the wrought iron chairs on the balcony of her room, looking out at the moon's sparkling path on the sea. She'd been sitting there for a while when there was a knock at her door.

She wasn't expecting anyone, especially this late at night—unless maybe someone had been taken ill and needed help?

She padded over to the door, still in bare feet, and blinked in surprise when she saw Sean in the doorway. 'Is something wrong?'

'Yes,' he said.

She went cold. 'Ash?'

'No.'

Then she saw that he'd removed his jacket and cravat. He looked very slightly dishevelled, and it made him much more approachable. And much, much harder to resist.

He was also carrying a bottle of Prosecco and two glasses.

'Sean?' she asked, completely confused.

'I think we need to talk,' he said.

Again, for a split second, she glimpsed that vulnerability in his eyes. How could she turn him away when she had a good idea of how he was feeling—the same way she was feeling herself? 'Come in,' she said, and closed the door behind him.

'I saw you sitting on your balcony,' he said.

She nodded. 'I was a bit too wired to sleep, so I thought I'd look out over the sea and just chill for a bit.'

'Good plan.' He gestured to her balcony. 'Shall we?'

Sean, the sea and moonlight. A dangerous combination. It would be much more sensible to say no.

'Yes,' she said.

He uncorked the bottle with a minimum of fuss and without spilling a drop of the sparkling wine, then poured them both a glass.

Claire held hers up in a toast. 'To Ashleigh and Luke,' she said, 'and may they have every happiness in their life together.'

'Absolutely,' he said, clinking his glass against hers. 'To Ashleigh and Luke.'

'So you're too wired to sleep, too?' she asked.

He nodded. 'I was walking in the hotel gardens. That's when I saw you sitting on the balcony.'

'So why do we need to talk, Sean?'

He blew out a breath. 'You and me.'

The idea sent a shiver of pure desire through her.

'I think it's been a long time coming,' he said softly.

'But we don't even like each other. You think I'm a flake, and I think you're...well...a bit *too* organised,' she said, choosing her words carefully.

'Maybe,' he said, 'because it's easier for us to think that of each other.'

She took a sip of Prosecco, knowing that he was right but not quite wanting to admit it. 'You turned me down.'

'Nearly ten years ago? You know why,' he said. 'I think we've both grown up and got past that.'

'I guess.' She turned her glass round. 'Though I'm not in a hurry to put myself back in that situation.'

'You won't be,' he said softly. 'Because you're not seventeen any more, you're not drunk, and I'm not responsible for you.'

The three barriers that had been in the way, back then. It had hurt and embarrassed her at the time, but later Claire had appreciated how decent he'd been. Not that they'd ever discussed it. It was way too awkward for both of them.

But, now he'd said it, she needed to know. 'Back then, if I hadn't been drunk, if I'd been eighteen, and if you hadn't been responsible for me—would you have...?'

'Let you seduce me?' he asked.

She nodded.

His breath shuddered through him. 'Yes.'

Heat curled in her belly. That night, she'd wanted him so desperately. And, if the circumstances had been different, he would have made love with her. Been her first lover.

All the words were knocked out of her head. Because all she could think about was the way he'd kissed her tonight in the garden, and the way he looked right now. Sexy as hell.

'Ashleigh's engagement,' he said softly. '*You* turned *me* down, that time.'

'Because I was being sensible.' She paused. 'This isn't sensible, either.'

'I know. But your perfume's haunted me all evening,' he said, his voice low and husky and drenched in desire. 'Your mouth. And you've been driving me crazy in that dress.'

She made a last-ditch attempt at keeping the status quo. 'This is a perfectly demure bridesmaid's dress,' she said. 'It's down to my knees.'

'And I can't stop thinking about what you might be wearing under it.'

Her breath hitched. 'Can't you, now?'

The same heat that curled in her belly was reflected in his eyes. 'Going to show me?' he invited.

'We're on my balcony. Anyone could see us. *You* saw me,' she pointed out.

'Then maybe,' he said, 'we should go inside. Draw the curtains.'

She knew without a shadow of a doubt what was going to happen if they did.

There would be repercussions. Huge ones.

But the old desire had lanced sharply through her, to the point where she didn't care about the repercussions any more. 'Yes.'

Without a word, he stood up and scooped her out of her chair. Carried her into the room and set her down on her feet. He turned away just long enough to close the curtains, then pulled her into his arms and kissed her

That first kiss in the garden had been tentative, sweet. This was like lighting touchpaper, setting her on fire. By the time he broke the kiss, they were both shaking.

'Show me,' he said softly.

She reached behind her back to the zip and slid it down; then she held the dress to her.

He raised an eyebrow. 'Shy?'

She shook her head. 'I'm waiting for you to get rid of your waistcoat and undo your shirt.'

He looked puzzled, and she explained, 'Because, if we're going to do this, it's going to be equal. Both of us. All the way.'

'All the way,' Sean repeated huskily. He removed his waistcoat, then undid his shirt and pulled it out of the waistband of his trousers. 'Better?'

'Much better. It makes you look touchable,' she said.

'Good—because I want you to touch me, Claire. And I want to touch you.' He gestured to her dress. 'Show me.'

She felt ridiculously shy and almost chickened out; but then took a deep breath and stepped out of the dress before hanging it on the back of a chair.

'Now that I wasn't expecting—underwear to match your dress.' He closed the gap between them and traced the outline of her strapless lacy bra with the tip of his finger.

'I had it dyed at the same time as my shoes,' she said.

'Attention to detail—I like that,' he said approvingly.

She slid her palms against his pectoral muscles. 'Very nice,' she said, and let her hands slide down to his abdomen. 'A perfect six pack. I wasn't expecting that.'

'I don't spend the whole day in a chair. The gym gives me time to think about things,' he said.

'Good plan.' She slipped the soft cotton from his shoulders.

'So now I'm naked to the waist, and you're not. You said we were in this together, Claire.'

'Then do something about it,' she invited.

Sean smiled, unclipped her bra and let the lacy garment fall to the floor. Then scooped her up, carried her to the bed, and Claire stopped thinking.

CHAPTER FIVE

CLAIRE'S MOBILE SHRILLED. Still with her eyes closed, she groped for the phone on the bedside table. 'Hello?'

'C'mon, sleepyhead! You went to bed before I did—you can't *still* be snoozing,' Sammy said cheerfully. 'There's a pile of warm pastries and a bowl of freshly picked, juicy Italian peaches down here with our name on them. And the best coffee ever.'

Breakfast.

Claire had arranged to meet Sammy for breakfast.

And right now she was still in bed. *With Sean.* Whose arms were still wrapped round her, keeping her close.

'Uh—I'll be down as soon as I can,' Claire said hastily. 'If you're hungry, start without me.'

'Don't blame me if the pastries are all gone by the time you get here. See you soon,' Sammy said, her voice full of laughter.

'Who was that?' Sean asked when Claire put the phone down.

'Sammy. We arranged to have breakfast together this morning.' Claire dragged in a breath. 'Except…Sean, I…' She frowned. 'And now I'm being incoherent and stupid, and that isn't me.'

'Lack of sleep,' he said, nuzzling her shoulder. 'Which is as much my fault as yours.'

Oh, help. When he was being sweet and warm like this, it made her want what she knew she couldn't have. And she really had to be sensible about this. 'Sean—we really can't do this,' she blurted out.

'Do what?'

'Be together. Or let anyone know about what happened last night.' She twisted round to face him. 'You and me—you know it would never work out between us in a month of Sundays. We're too different. You have a twenty-year plan for everything, and I hate being boxed in like that. We'd drive each other bananas.'

'So, what? We're going to pretend last night didn't happen?' he asked.

'That'd probably be the best thing,' she said. 'Because then it won't be awkward when Ash asks us both over to see the wedding photos and what have you.'

'Uh-huh.' His face was expressionless.

And now she felt horrible. Last night had been a revelation about just how much attention Sean paid to things and how good he'd made her feel. And it had been better between them than she'd ever dreamed it would be as a starry-eyed teenager. If only they weren't so different, she'd be tempted to start a proper relationship with him. Seriously tempted. But she knew it wasn't going to work out between them, and she didn't want her oldest friendship to become collateral damage of a fling that didn't last. She swallowed hard. 'Last night... You made it good for me. Really good.'

'Dear John—it's not you, it's me,' he intoned, raising an eyebrow.

'It's both of us, and you know it,' she said. 'You hate the fact that I follow my heart. I know what you call me, Sean.' Just as she was pretty sure that he knew what she called him.

He shrugged. 'I guess you're right.'

So why did it make her feel so bad—so *guilty*? 'I'm not dumping you, and you're not dumping me, because we were never really together in the first place,' she said. 'We'd be a disaster as a couple.'

'Probably,' he agreed.

'Sammy's waiting for me downstairs. I don't get to see her that much, with her job taking her away so much. I promised her I'd be there. I really have to go,' Claire said, feeling even more awkward. She wanted to stay. She wanted to pretend that she and Sean were two completely different people and that it would have a chance of working out between them.

But she had to face the facts. Tomorrow they'd both be back in London. And no way could things work between them there. Their lives were too opposite, and they just wouldn't fit.

'I know I'm being rude and bratty and everything else, but would you mind, um, please closing your eyes while I grab some clothes and have the quickest shower in the world?' she asked.

'It's a little late for shyness,' he said dryly, 'given that we saw every millimetre of each other last night.'

Not just saw, either. The memory made her face hot. They'd touched. Stroked. Kissed.

'Even so,' she said.

'As you wish.' He rolled over and closed his eyes. 'Let me know when it's safe to look.'

'I'm sorry. I really wish things could be different,' she said, meaning it. 'But this is the best way. A clean break.'

'Apart from the fact that my little sister is your best friend, and we'll still have to see each other in the future.'

'And we'll do exactly the same as we've done for years and years,' she said. 'We'll be polite to each other for her sake, and avoid each other as much as we can.'

'Uh-huh.'

'Like you said, last night—well, it's been a long time coming. And now we've done it and it's out of our systems.' Which was a big, fat lie, so it was just as well that he couldn't see her face. She had a nasty feeling that Sean Farrell would never be completely out of her system. Especially now she knew what it was like to kiss him properly. To touch him. To make love with him.

She shook herself and grabbed some clothes. 'It's OK to look,' she said as she closed the bathroom door.

She showered and dressed in record time. When she walked back into the bedroom, Sean was already dressed and sitting on the bed, waiting for her. Well, he would. He had impeccable manners. 'Thank you,' she said. 'Um—I guess I'll see you in London when Ash gets back. And I'll sort out the money I owe you for that helicopter flight.'

Downstairs, Sammy was pouring a cup of coffee from a cafetière when Claire walked over to her table. 'So who was he?' she asked.

'Who was what?' Claire asked.

'The guy who kept you awake last night and gave you that hickey on the left-hand side of your neck.'

Claire clapped a hand to her neck and stared at her friend in utter dismay. She hadn't noticed a hickey while she was in the bathroom—well, not that she'd paid much attention to the mirror, because she'd been too busy panicking about the fact that Sean Farrell was naked and in her bed, and she'd just messed things up again.

And he'd given her a hickey?

Oh, no. She hadn't had a hickey since she was thirteen, and her dad had been so mad at her that she'd never repeated that particular mistake. Until now.

When Claire continued to be silent, Sammy laughed. 'Gotcha. There's no hickey. But clearly I wasn't far wrong and there *was* a guy last night.'

'You don't want to know,' Claire said.

'I wouldn't be fishing if I didn't,' Sammy pointed out.

'It was a one off. And I feel suitably ashamed, OK? I said I wouldn't date any more Mr Wrongs.'

'Forgive me for saying, but you didn't have a date for Ash's wedding,' Sammy said. 'So I think he doesn't count as one of your Mr Wrongs.'

'Oh, he does. You couldn't get more wrong for me than him,' Claire said feelingly. More was the pity.

'Was the sex good?'

'Sammy!' Claire felt the colour hit her face like a tidal wave.

Her friend was totally unrepentant. 'Out of ten?'

Claire groaned. 'I need coffee.'

'Answer the question, Claire-bear.'

'Eleven,' Claire muttered, and helped herself to coffee, sugaring it liberally.

'Then maybe,' Sammy said, 'he might be worth working on. Sort out whatever makes him Mr Wrong.'

'That'd be several lifetimes' work,' Claire said wryly.

'Your call. Pastries or peaches?'

Claire couldn't help smiling. Only Sammy would ask something so outrageous followed by something so practical and mundane. 'I thought you'd already scoffed all the pastries? But if there are any left I'll have both,' she said.

'Attagirl.' Sammy winked at her. 'And I hope you

don't have a hangover. Because we're taking that boat out to the Blue Grotto this afternoon before we catch our flights—I've got a commission.'

'Do you ever stop working?' Claire asked.

'About as much as you do,' Sammy said with a grin. 'Anyway, mixing work and play means you get to fit twice as much into your day—and you enjoy it more.'

'True.'

'Pity about Mr Wrong.'

Yeah.

And Claire really wasn't looking forward to facing Sean, the next time they met. Somehow, before then she needed to get her emotions completely under control.

Claire enjoyed her trip to the Blue Grotto, and the colours and textures gave her several ideas for future dress designs; but on the plane home she found herself thinking about Sean. He'd been a very focused lover, very considerate. She still felt guilty about the way she'd called a halt to it, but she knew she'd done the right thing. Sean planned things out to the extreme, and she preferred to follow her heart, so they'd never be able to agree on anything.

Back at her flat, she unpacked and put the laundry on, checked her mail and her messages, and made notes for what she needed to do in the morning. Though she still couldn't get Sean out of her head. When she finally fell asleep, she had the most graphic dream about him—one that left her hot and very bothered when her alarm went off on the Monday morning.

'Don't be so ridiculous. Sean Farrell is completely off limits,' she told herself firmly, and went for her usual pre-breakfast run. Maybe that would get her common sense back in working order. But even then she couldn't stop thinking about Sean. How he'd made her feel. How she wanted to do what they'd done all over again.

After her shower, she opened her laptop and logged in to her bank account so she could transfer the money she owed Sean for the flight into his account. And, once that was done, she knew she wouldn't need any contact with him until Ashleigh and Luke were back from honeymoon. By which time, her common sense would be back.

She hoped.

She went down to open the shop, then headed for her workroom at the back to start work on the next dress she needed to make for the wedding show. She'd just finished cutting it out when the old-fashioned bell on her door jangled to signal that someone was coming through the front door.

She came out from the workroom to see a delivery man carrying an enormous bunch of flowers. 'Miss Stewart?' he asked.

'Um, yes.'

'For you.' He smiled and handed her the flowers. 'Enjoy.'

'Thank you.'

It wasn't her birthday and she wasn't expecting any flowers. Or maybe they were from Ashleigh and Luke to say thanks for her help with the wedding. She absolutely loved dusky pink roses; the bouquet was stuffed with them, teamed with sweet-smelling cream freesias and clouds of fluffy gypsophila. She'd never seen such a gorgeous bouquet.

She opened the envelope that came with it and felt her eyes widen with shock; she recognised the strong, precise handwriting immediately, because she'd seen it on cards and notes at Ashleigh's flat over the years.

Saw these and thought of you. Sean.

He'd sent her flowers.

Not just any old flowers—glorious flowers.

And he hadn't just asked his PA to do it, either. The handwriting was his, so he'd clearly gone to the florist in person, and maybe even chosen the flowers himself.

Sean Farrell had sent her flowers.

Claire couldn't quite get her head round that.

Why would he send her flowers?

She didn't quite dare ring him to ask him. So, once she'd put them in water, she took the coward's way out and texted him.

Thank you for the flowers. They're gorgeous.

He took his time replying, but eventually the text came through. Glad you like them.

Where was he going with this?

Before she could work out a way to ask without sounding offensive, her phone beeped again to signal the arrival of another text.

Thank you for the flight money. Bank just notified me. Do you have an appointment over lunch?

Why? No, that sounded grudging and suspicious. She deleted the message and started again. No worries, and no, she typed back.

You do now. See you at your shop at one.

What? Was he suggesting a lunch date? Dating her? But—but—they'd agreed that the thing between them would be a disaster if they let it go any further.

Sean, we can't.

But he didn't reply. And she was left in a flat spin.

By the time the bell on the front door jangled and she went through to the shop to see Sean standing there—and he'd turned her sign on the door to 'closed', she noticed—she was wound up to fever pitch.

'What's this about, Sean?' she asked.

'I thought we could have lunch together.'

'But...' Her voice faded. They'd already agreed that this was a bad idea—hadn't they?

'I know,' he said softly, and walked over towards her.

He was dressed in another of his formal well-cut suits, with his shoes perfectly shined and his silk tie perfectly knotted; he was a million miles away from the sensual, dishevelled man who'd spent the night in her bed in Capri. And yet he was every bit as delectable. Even though he wasn't even touching her, being this close to him made all her senses go on red alert.

'I can't get you out of my head,' he said.

Well, if he could be brave enough to admit it, so could she. She swallowed hard. 'Me, neither,' she said.

'So what do we do about this, Claire?' he asked. 'Because I have a feeling this isn't going away any time soon.'

'That night in Capri was supposed to—well—get it out of our systems,' she reminded him.

'And it didn't work,' he said. 'Not for me.'

His admission warmed her and terrified her at the same time.

'Claire?' he asked softly.

He deserved honesty. 'Me, neither.'

He leaned forward and brushed his lips against hers, ever so gently. And every nerve end on her mouth sizzled.

He tempted her. Oh, so much. But it all came back to collateral damage.

'We have to be sensible,' she said. 'And why am I the one saying this, not you? You're the one with—'

'—the twenty-year plan,' he finished. 'For the record, it's five years. Not twenty.'

'Even so. You have your whole life planned out.'

'There's nothing wrong with being responsible and organised,' he said.

'There's nothing wrong with being spontaneous, either,' she retorted.

He smiled. 'Not if it's like Saturday night, no.'

Oh, why had he had to bring that up again? Now her temperature was spiking. Seriously spiking. 'We're too different,' she said. 'You're my best friend's brother.'

'And?'

'There's a huge risk of collateral damage. I can't take that risk.' The risk of losing Ashleigh. Claire had already lost too much in her life. She wasn't prepared to risk losing her best friend as well. 'If it goes wrong between us. *When* it goes wrong between us,' she amended.

'Why are you so sure it will go wrong?'

That was an easy one. 'Because my relationships always go wrong.'

'Because you pick the kind of man who doesn't commit.'

She didn't have an answer to that. Mainly because she knew he was right.

'You pick men who say they're free spirits. And you

think that'll work because you're a free spirit, too. Except,' he said softly, 'they always let you down.'

Claire thought of her last ex. The one who'd let her down so much that she'd temporarily sworn off relationships. He definitely hadn't been able to commit. She'd found him in bed with someone else—and then she'd discovered that he was cheating on both of them with yet *another* woman. Messy and a half.

And the worst thing was that he'd assumed she'd be OK with it, because she was a free spirit, too… It had been a wake-up call. Claire had promised herself that never again would she date someone who could be so casual with her feelings. But it had shaken her faith in her judgement of men. In a room full of eligible men, she was pretty sure she'd pick all the rotten ones.

'I guess,' she said. 'And anyway, what about you? You never date anyone for longer than three weeks.'

'It's not quite that bad.'

'Even so, that's not what I want, Sean. Three weeks and you're out. That's just…' She grimaced. 'No.'

'I'm always very clear with my girlfriends. That it's for fun, that I'm committed to the factory and won't have time to…' His voice faded.

'Actually, that makes you the kind of man who won't commit,' she said softly. 'Like every other man I date.'

Sean had never thought of himself in that way before. He'd thought of the way he conducted his relationships as protecting his heart. Not letting himself get too involved meant not risking losing someone. He'd already lost too much in his life, and he didn't want to lose any more. So he'd concentrated on his career rather than on his relationships. Because the business was *safe*. Staying in control of his emotions kept his heart safe.

'What do you want, Sean?' she asked.

Such an easy answer—and such a difficult one. Though he owed her honesty. 'You. I can't think beyond that at the moment,' he admitted. And that was scary. Claire had accused him of having a twenty-year plan; although it wasn't anywhere near that long-range, he had to admit that he always planned things out, ever since his parents had died and he'd taken over the family business.

Planning had helped him cope with being thrown in at the deep end and being responsible for everything, without having the safety net of his father's experience to help him. And planning meant that everything was always under control. Just the way he liked it.

She bit her lip. 'I've got a wedding show in two months. My first collection. This could make all the difference to my career—this could be what really launches me into the big time. I'm hoping that one of the big wedding fashion houses might give me a chance to work with them on a collection. So I really don't have time for a relationship right now.'

'And I've just finished fighting off a takeover bid from an international conglomerate who wanted to add Farrell's to their portfolio,' he said. 'The vultures are still circling. I need to concentrate on the business and make absolutely sure they don't get another opening. If anything, I need to expand and maybe float the company on the stock market to finance the expansion. It's going to take all my time and then some.'

'So we're agreed: this is the wrong time for either of us to start any kind of relationship. By the time it *is* the right time, we'll both be back to our senses and we'll know it'd be the wrong thing to do anyway.'

That was something else she'd thrown at him—he

was the sensible one, the one who planned things out and was never spontaneous. So why wasn't he the one making this argument instead of her? Why had he sent her flowers and moved an appointment so he could see her for lunch?

It was totally crazy. Illogical.

And he couldn't do a thing to stop it.

Which exhilarated him and terrified him at the same time. With Claire, there was a real risk of losing control. And if he wasn't in control…what then? The possibilities made his head spin.

The only thing he could do now was to state the facts. 'I want you,' he said softly. 'And I think you want me.'

'So, what? We have a stupid, crazy, insane affair?'

He grimaced. 'Put like that, it sounds pretty sleazy.'

'But that's what you're offering.'

Was it? 'No.'

She frowned. 'So what *are* you suggesting, Sean?'

'I don't know,' he said. And it was a position he'd never actually been in before. He'd always been the one to call the shots. The one who initiated a relationship and the one who ended it. He shook his head, trying to clear it. But nothing changed. It was still that same spinning, out-of-control feeling. Like being on the highest, fastest, scariest fairground ride. 'All I know is that I want you,' he said.

'There's too much at stake. No.'

'Unless,' he said, 'we have an agreement.'

Her eyes narrowed. 'What kind of agreement?'

'We see each other. Explore where this thing goes. And then, whatever happens between us, we're polite to each other in front of Ashleigh. Nobody gets hurt. Especially her.'

'Can you guarantee that?' she asked softly.

'I can guarantee that I'll always be polite to you in front of Ashleigh.' He paused. 'The rest of it—I don't think anyone could guarantee that. But maybe it's worth the risk of finding out.' Risk. Something he didn't usually do unless it was precisely calculated. This wasn't calculated. At all. He needed his head examined.

'Maybe,' she said.

He curled his fingers round hers. His skin tingled where it touched her. 'Come and have lunch with me.'

She smiled then. Funny how it made the whole room light up. That wasn't something he was used to, either.

'OK,' she said. 'I just need to get my bag.'

'Sure.' He waited for her; then, when she'd locked the shop door behind them, he took her hand and walked down the street with her.

CHAPTER SIX

CLAIRE WAS WALKING hand in hand with Sean Farrell. Down the high street in Camden. On an ordinary Monday lunchtime.

This was surreal, she thought.

And she couldn't quite get her head round it.

But his fingers were wrapped round hers, his skin was warm against hers, and it was definitely happening rather than being some kind of super-realistic dream—because when she surreptitiously pinched herself it hurt.

'So what do you normally do for lunch?' Claire asked.

'I grab a sandwich at my desk,' he said. 'In the office, we put an order in to a local sandwich shop first thing in the morning, and they deliver to us. You?'

'Pretty much the same, except obviously I eat it well away from my work area so I don't risk getting crumbs or grease on the material and ruining it,' she said.

'So we both work through lunch. Well, that's another thing we have in common.'

There was a gleam in his eye that reminded her of the first thing they had in common. That night in Capri. She went hot at the memory.

'So how long do you have to spare?' he asked.

'An hour, maybe,' she said.

'So that's enough time to walk down to Camden Lock, grab a sandwich, and sit by the canal while we eat,' he said.

'Sounds good to me.' The lock was one of her favourite places; even though the area got incredibly busy in the summer months, she loved watching the way the narrow boats floated calmly down the canal underneath the willow trees. 'But this is a bit strange,' she said.

'How?'

'I've been thinking—we've known each other for years, and I know hardly anything about you. Well, other than that you run Farrell's.' His family's confectionery business, which specialised in toffee.

'What do you want to know?' he asked.

'Everything. Except I don't know where to start,' she admitted. 'Maybe we should pretend we're speed-dating.'

He blinked. 'You've been speed-dating?'

'No. Sammy has, though. I helped her do a list of questions.'

'What, all the stuff about what you do, where you come from, that sort of thing?' At her nod, he said, 'But you already know all that.'

'There's other stuff as well. I think the list might still be on my phone,' she said.

'Let's grab some lunch, sit down and go through your list, then,' he said. 'And if we both answer the questions, that might be a good idea—now I think about it, I don't really know that much about you, either.'

She smiled wryly. 'I can't believe we're doing this. We don't even like each other.'

He glanced down at their joined hands. 'Though we're attracted to each other. And maybe we haven't given each other a proper chance.'

From Claire's point of view, Sean was the one who hadn't given her a chance; but she wasn't going to pick a fight with him over it. He was making an effort, and she'd agreed to see where this thing took them. It was exhilarating and scary, all at the same time. Exhilarating, because this was a step into the unknown; and scary, because it meant trusting her judgement again. Her track record where men were concerned was so terrible that…

No. She wasn't going to analyse this. Not now. She was going to see where this took them. Seize the day.

They walked down to Camden Lock, bought bagels and freshly squeezed orange juice from one of the stalls, and sat down on the edge of the canal, looking out at the narrow boats and the crowd.

Claire found the list on her phone. 'Ready?' she asked.

'Yup. And remember you're doing this, too,' he said.

'OK. Your favourite kind of book, movie and music?' she asked.

He thought about it. 'In order—crime, classic film noir and anything I can run to. You?'

'Jane Austen, rom-coms and anything I can sing to,' she said promptly.

'So we're not really compatible there,' he said.

She wrinkled her nose. 'We're not that far apart. I like reading crime novels, too, but I like historical ones rather than the super-gory contemporary stuff. And classic noir—well, if Jimmy Stewart's in it, I'll watch it. I love *Rear Window*.'

'I really can't stand Jane Austen. I had to do *Mansfield Park* for A level, and that was more than enough for me,' he said with a grimace. 'But if the rom-com's witty and shot well, I can sit through it.'

She grinned. 'So you're a bit of a film snob, are you, Mr Farrell?'

He thought about it for a moment and grinned back. 'I guess I am.'

'OK. What do you do for fun?'

'You mean you actually think I might have fun?' he asked.

She smiled. 'You can be a little bit too organised, but I think there's more to you than meets the eye—so answer the question, Sean.'

'Abseiling,' he said, his face totally deadpan.

She stared at him, trying to imagine it—if he'd said squash or maybe even rugby, she might've believed him, but abseiling? 'In London?' she queried.

'There are lots of tall buildings in London.'

She thought about it a bit more, and shook her head. 'No, that's not you. I think you're teasing me.' Especially because he knew she was scared of heights.

'Good call,' he said. And his eyes actually *twinkled*.

Sean Farrell, teasing her. She would never have believed that he had a sense of humour. 'So what's the real answer?' she asked.

'Something very regimented,' he said. 'Sudoku.'

'There's nothing wrong with doing puzzles,' she said. Though trust Sean to pick something logical.

'What about you? What do you do for fun?' he asked.

Given how he'd teased her, he really deserved this. She schooled her face into a serious expression. 'Shopping. Preferably for shoes.' Given what she did for a living, that would be totally plausible. 'Actually, I have three special shoe wardrobes. Walk-in ones.'

'Seriously?' He looked totally horrified.

'About as much as you go abseiling.' She laughed. 'I like shoes, but I'm not that extreme. No, for me it's cooking for friends and watching a good film and talking about it afterwards.'

'OK. We're even now,' he said with a smile. 'So what do you cook? Anything in particular?'

'Whatever catches my eye. I love magazines that have recipes in them, and it's probably one of my worst vices because I can never resist a news stand,' she said. 'What about you?'

'I can cook if I have to,' he said. 'Though I admit I'm more likely to take someone out to dinner than to cook for them.'

She shrugged. 'That's not a big deal. It means you'll be doing the washing up, though.'

'Was that an offer?' he asked.

'Do you want it to be?' she fenced.

He held her gaze. 'Yes. Tell me when, and I'll bring the wine.'

There was a little flare of excitement in her stomach. They were actually doing this. Arranging a date. Seeing each other. She could maybe play a little hard to get and make him wait until Friday; but her mouth clearly had other ideas, because she found herself suggesting, 'Tonight?'

'I'd like that. I've got meetings until half past five, and some paperwork that needs doing after that—but I can be with you for seven, if that's OK?' he asked.

'It's a date,' she said softly.

He took her hand and brought it up to his mouth. Keeping eye contact all the way, he kissed the back of her hand, just briefly, before releasing it again; it made Claire feel warm and squidgy inside. Who would've thought that Sean Farrell was Prince Charming in disguise? Not that she was a weak little princess who needed rescuing—she could look after herself perfectly well, thank you very much—but she liked the charm. A lot.

'Next question,' he said.

'OK. What are you most proud of?' she asked.

'That's an easy one—my sister and Farrell's,' he said.

His family, and his family business, she thought. So it looked as if Sean Farrell had a seriously soft centre, just like the caramel chocolates his factory made along with the toffee.

'How about you?' he asked.

'The letters I get from brides telling me how much they loved their dress and how it really helped make their special day feel extra-special,' she said.

'So you're actually as much of a workaholic as you think I am?'

'Don't sound so surprised,' she said dryly. 'I know you see extreme things on a fashion catwalk and the pages of magazines, but it doesn't mean that designers are all totally flaky. I want my brides to feel really special and that they look like a million dollars, in a dress I've made just for them. And that means listening to what their dream is, and coming up with something that makes them feel their dream's come true.'

'Having seen the dress you made for Ashleigh, I can understand exactly why they commission you,' he said. 'Next question?'

'What are you scared of?'

'Easy one. Anything happening to Ashleigh or the business.'

But he didn't meet her eye. There was clearly something else. Something he didn't want to discuss.

'You?' he asked.

'Heights. I'm OK in a plane, but chairlifts like that

one in Capri make my palms go sweaty. Put it this way, I'm never, ever going skiing. Or abseiling.'

'Fair enough. Next?'

She glanced down at her phone to check. 'Your most treasured possession.'

'I can show you that.' He took his wallet out of his pocket, removed two photographs and handed them to her. One was of himself with Ashleigh, and the other was himself on graduation day with his parents on either side of him. Claire had a lump in her throat and couldn't say a word when she handed them back.

'You?' he asked.

'The same,' she whispered, and took her own wallet from her bag. She showed him a photograph of herself and her parents on her seventeenth birthday, and one of her with Ashleigh and Sammy and the Coliseum in the background.

He took her hand in silence and squeezed it briefly. Not that he needed any words; she knew he shared her feelings.

She put the photographs away. 'Next question—is the glass half full or half empty?'

'Half full. You?'

'Same,' she said, and glanced at her watch. 'We might have to cut this a bit short. Last one for now. Your perfect holiday?'

'Not a beach holiday,' he said feelingly. 'That just bores me silly.'

'You mean, you get a fit of the guilts at lying on a beach doing nothing, and you end up working.'

'Actually, I'm just not very good at just sitting still and doing nothing,' he admitted.

'So you'd rather have an active holiday?'

'Exploring somewhere, you mean?' He nodded. 'That'd work for me.'

'Culture or geography?'

'Either,' he said. 'I guess my perfect holiday would be Iceland. I'd love to walk up a volcano, and to see the hot springs and learn about the place. You?'

'I like city breaks. I have a bit of an art gallery habit, thanks to Sammy,' she explained. 'Plus I love museums where they have a big costume section. I should warn you that I really, really love Regency dresses. And I can spend hours in the costume section, looking at all the fine details.'

'So you see yourself as Lizzie Bennett?'

'No,' she said, 'and I'm not looking for a Darcy—anyway, seeing as you hate Austen, how come you know more than just the book you did for A level?'

'Ex-girlfriends who insisted on seeing certain films more than once, and became ex very shortly afterwards,' he said dryly.

'Hint duly noted,' she said. 'I won't ever ask you to watch *Pride and Prejudice* with me. Even though it's one of my favourite films.'

'Nicely skated past,' he said, 'but let's backtrack—you said you like holidays where you go and look at vintage clothes. And you said you look at details, so I bet you take notes and as many photos as you can get away with. Isn't that partly work?'

'Busted.' She clicked her fingers and grinned. 'I have to admit, I don't really like beach holidays, either. It's nice to have a day or two to unwind and read, but I'd rather see a bit of culture with friends. I really loved my trips in Italy with Ash and Sammy.'

'So what's your perfect holiday?' he asked.

'Anywhere with museums, galleries and lots of nice

little places to eat. Philadelphia and Boston are next on my wish list.'

'This is scary,' he said. 'A week ago I would've said we were total opposites.'

She thought about it. 'We still are. We have a few things in common—probably more than either of us realised—but you like things really pinned down and I like to go with the flow.' She smiled. 'And I bet you have an itinerary on holiday. Down to the minute.'

'If you don't know the opening times and days for a museum or what have you, then you might go to see it when it's closed and not get a chance to go back,' he pointed out. 'So yes, I do have an itinerary.'

'But if you go with the flow, you discover things you wouldn't have known about otherwise,' she pointed out.

'Let's agree to disagree on that one.' He glanced at his watch. 'We'd better head back.'

'You don't have to walk me back, Sean. Go, if you have a meeting.'

'I was brought up properly. I'll walk you back,' he said.

'I'm planning a slight detour,' she warned.

He looked a little wary, but nodded. 'We'll do this your way, then.'

Her detour was to an ice cream shop where the ice cream was cooled with liquid nitrogen rather than by being put in a freezer. 'I love this place. The way they make the ice cream is so cool,' she said, and laughed. 'Literally.'

'It's a little gimmicky,' he said.

'Just wait until you taste it.'

To her surprise, he chose the rich, dark chocolate. 'I would've pegged you as a vanilla man,' she said.

'Plain and boring?'

'Not necessarily. Seriously good vanilla ice cream is one of the best pleasures in the world—which is why I just ordered it.'

'True. But remember what I do for a living. And my favourite bit of my job is when I work with the R and D team. Am I really going to pass up chocolate?'

This was a side of Sean she'd never really seen. Teasing, bantering—*fun*. And she really, really liked that.

She watched him as he took a spoonful of ice cream. He rolled his eyes at her to signal that he thought she was overselling it. And then she saw his pupils widen.

'Well?' she asked.

'This is something else,' he admitted. 'I can forgive the gimmicky stuff. Good choice.'

'And if you hadn't gone with the flow, you wouldn't have known the place was there.' She grinned. 'Admit it. I was right.'

'You were right about the ice cream being great. That's as far as I go.' He held her gaze. 'For now.'

It should've been cheesy and made her laugh at him. But his voice was low and sexy as hell, and there was the hint of a promise in his words that made her feel hot all over, despite the ice cream. It was enough to silence her, and she concentrated on eating her ice cream on the walk back to her shop.

'Well, Ms Stewart,' he said on her doorstep. 'I'll see you later. Though there is something you need to attend to.'

She frowned. 'What's that?'

'You have ice cream on the corner of your mouth.' Just as she was about to reach up and scrub it away, he stopped her. 'Let me deal with this.'

And then he kissed the smear of sweet confection away. Slowly. Sensually. By the time he'd finished, Claire was close to hyperventilating and her knees felt weak. Sean was kissing her *in the street*. This was totally un-Sean-like behaviour and it put her in a flat spin.

'Later,' he whispered, and left.

Although Claire spent the rest of the day alternately talking to customers and working on the dress, in the back of her head she was panicking about what to cook for him. She had no idea what he liked. She could play safe and cook chicken—she was fairly sure that he wasn't a vegetarian. Wryly, she realised that this was when Sean's 'plan everything down to the last microsecond' approach would come in useful.

She could text him to check what he did and didn't like. But that meant doing it his way and planning instead of being spontaneous—and she didn't want to give him the opportunity to say 'I told you so'. Then again, she didn't want to cook a meal he'd hate, or something he was allergic to, so it would be better to swallow her pride.

She texted him swiftly.

Any food allergies I need to know about? Ditto total food hates.

The reply came back.

No and no. What's for dinner?

She felt safe enough to tease him.

Whatever I feel like cooking. Carpe diem.

When he didn't reply she wondered if she'd gone too far. Then again, he'd said that he was going to be in meetings all afternoon. She shrugged it off and concentrated on making the dress she'd cut out that morning.

Though by the end of the afternoon she still hadn't decided what to cook. She ended up having a mad dash round the supermarket and picked up chicken, parma ham, asparagus and soft cheese so she could make chicken stuffed with asparagus, served with tiny new potatoes, baby carrots and tenderstem broccoli.

Given that Sean was a self-confessed chocolate fiend, she bought the pudding rather than making it from scratch—tiny pots of chocolate ganache, which she planned to serve with raspberries, as their tartness would be a good foil to the richness of the chocolate.

Once she'd prepared dinner, she fussed around the flat, making sure everywhere was tidy and all the important surfaces were gleaming. Then she changed her outfit three times, and was cross with herself for doing so. Why was she making such a big deal out of this? She'd known Sean for years. He'd seen her when she had teenage spotty skin and chubby cheeks. And this was her flat. It shouldn't matter what she wore. Jeans and a strappy vest top would be fine.

Except they didn't feel fine. Sean was always so pristine that she'd feel scruffy.

In the end, she compromised with a little black dress but minimal make-up and with her hair tied back. So he'd know that she'd made a little more effort than just dragging on a pair of jeans and doing nothing with her hair, but not so much effort that she was making a big deal out of it.

The doorbell rang at seven precisely—exactly

what she'd expected from Sean, because of course he wouldn't be a minute late or a minute early—and anticipation sparkled through her.

Dinner.

And who knew what else the evening would bring?

CHAPTER SEVEN

HE WAS ACTUALLY *NERVOUS*, Sean realised.

Which was crazy.

This was Claire. He'd known her for years. There was nothing to be nervous about. Except for the fact that this was a date, and in the past they'd never really got on. And the fact that, now he was getting to know her, he was beginning to realise that maybe she wasn't the person he'd thought she was.

Would it be the same for her? He had no idea.

He took a deep breath and rang the doorbell.

When she opened the door, she was barefoot and wearing a little black dress, and her hair was tied back at the nape with a hot pink chiffon scarf. He wanted to kiss her hello, but was afraid he wouldn't be able to stop himself—it had been tough enough to walk away at lunchtime. So instead he smiled awkwardly at her. 'Hi. I wasn't sure what to bring, so I brought red and white.'

'You really didn't need to, but thank you very much.' She accepted the bottles with a smile. 'Come up.'

She looked so cool, unflustered and sophisticated. Sean was pretty sure that she wasn't in the slightest bit nervous, and in turn that made him relax. This was just dinner, the getting-to-know-you stuff. And he really should stop thinking about how easy it would be to untie that scarf and let her glorious hair fall over her shoulders, then kiss her until they were both dizzy.

He followed her up the stairs and she ushered him in to the kitchen.

'We're eating in here, if that's OK,' she said. 'Can I get you a drink? Dinner will be ten minutes.'

'A glass of cold water would be fabulous, thanks.' At her raised eyebrows, he explained, 'It's been a boiling hot day and I could really do with something cold and non-alcoholic.'

'Sure.' She busied herself getting a glass and filled it from the filter jug in the fridge, adding ice and a frozen slice of lime. When she handed the glass to him, her fingers brushed against his; it sent a delicious shiver all the way down his spine.

Her kitchen was a place of extremes. The work surfaces had all been used, and it looked as if most of her kitchen equipment had been piled up next to the sink. The fridge was covered with magnets and photos, and a cork board on one wall had various cards and notes pinned to it, along with what looked like a note of a library fine. Chaos. And yet the bistro table was neatly set for two, and there was a compact electric steamer on the worktop next to the cooker, containing the vegetables. So there was a little order among the chaos.

Much like Claire herself.

'Something smells nice,' he said.

'Dinner, I hope,' she said, putting the white wine into the fridge.

He handed her a box. 'I thought these might be nice with coffee after dinner.'

'Thank you.' She smiled. 'Toffee, I assume?'

'Samples,' he said, smiling back. 'There have to be some perks when you're dating a confectioner.'

'Perks. Hmm. I like the sound of that, though if we're talking about a lot of calories here then I might have to start doubling the length of my morning run.' She did a cute wrinkly thing with her nose that made his knees go weak, then looked in the box. 'Oh, you brought those lovely soft caramel hearts! Fabulous. Thank you.'

Clearly she liked those; he made a mental note, and hoped she wouldn't be disappointed with what these actually were. 'Not *quite*,' he said.

'What are they, then?'

'Wait until coffee. Is there anything I can do to help?'

'No, you're fine—have a seat.' She gestured to the bistro table, and he sat down on one of the ladder-back chairs.

Small talk wasn't something Sean was used to doing with Claire, and he really wasn't sure what to say. It didn't help that he was itching to kiss her; but she was bustling round the kitchen, and he didn't want to distract her and ruin the effort she'd put into making dinner. 'It's a nice flat,' he said.

She nodded. 'I like it here. The neighbours are lovely, the road's quiet, and yet I'm five minutes away from all the shops and market stalls.'

Work. An excellent subject, he thought. They could talk about that. 'So how did the dressmaking go today? Are you on schedule for your big show?'

'Fine, thanks, and I think I am. How about your meetings?'

'Fine, thanks.' Then it finally clicked that she wasn't as cool and calm as she seemed. She was being superpolite. So did that mean that she felt as nervous about this as he did? 'Claire, relax,' he said softly.

'Uh-huh.' But she still looked fidgety, and he noticed that she didn't sit down with him. Was she just feeling a little shy and awkward because of the newness of their situation, or was she having second thoughts?

'Have you changed your mind about this?' he asked, as gently as he could.

'No-o,' she hedged. 'It's not that.'

'What is it, then?'

'I'm usually a reasonable cook.' She bit her lip. 'What if it all goes wrong tonight?'

Nervous, then, rather than second thoughts. And suddenly his own nerves vanished. He stood up, walked over to her and put his arms round her. 'I'm pretty sure it'll be just fine. If it's not, then it doesn't matter. I'll carry you to your bed and take your mind off it—and then I'll order us a pizza instead.' He kissed the corner of her mouth, knowing he was dangerously close to distracting her, but wanting to make her feel better. 'Claire, why are you worrying that the food's going to be bad tonight?'

'Because it's *you*,' she said.

Because she thought he'd judge her? He had to acknowledge that he'd judged her in the past—and not always fairly. 'You already know I'd rather wash up or take someone out to dinner than cook for them, so I'm in no position to complain if someone cooks me something that isn't Michelin-star standard.'

'I guess.' She blew out a breath. 'It's just… Well, this is you and me, and it feels…'

He waited. What was she going to say? That it felt like a mistake?

'Scary,' she finished.

He could understand that. Claire fascinated him; yet, at the same time, this whole thing scared him witless. Her outlook was so different from his. She didn't have a totally ordered world. She followed her heart. If he let her close—what then? Would he end up with his heart broken? 'Me, too,' he said.

The only thing he could do then was to kiss her, to stop the fear spreading through him, too. So he covered her mouth with his, relaxing as she wrapped her arms round him, too, and kissed him back. Holding her close, feeling the warmth of her body against his and the sweetness of her mouth against his, made his world feel as if the axis was in the right place again.

A sharp ding made them both break apart. 'That was the steamer. It means the vegetables are done,' Claire said, looking flustered and adorably pink.

'Is there anything I can do to help?' he asked again.

This time, to his relief, she stopped treating him like a guest who had to be waited on. 'Could you open the wine? The corkscrew's in the middle drawer.'

'Sure. Would you prefer red or white?'

'We're having chicken, so it's entirely up to you.'

He looked at her. 'You'd serve red wine with chicken?'

'Well, hey—if you can cook chicken in red wine, then you can serve it with red wine.'

He wrinkled his nose at her. 'Am I being regimented again?'

'No. Just a teensy bit of a wine snob,' she said with a grin. 'You need to learn to go with the flow, Sean. *Carpe diem.* Seize the day. It's a good motto to live by.'

'Maybe.' By the time he'd taken the wine from her fridge, found the corkscrew in the jumble of her kitchen drawer, uncorked the bottle and poured them both a glass, she'd served up.

He sat down opposite her and raised his glass. 'To us, and whatever the future might bring.'

'To us,' she echoed softly, looking worried and uncertain—vulnerable, even—and again he felt that weird surge of protectiveness towards her. It unsettled him, because he didn't generally feel like that about his girl-friends.

'This is really lovely,' he said after his first mouthful. Chicken, stuffed with soft cheese and asparagus, then wrapped in parma ham. Claire Stewart was definitely capable in the kitchen, and he could tell that this had been cooked from scratch. He'd assumed that she'd be the sort to buy ready-made meals from the supermarket; clearly that wasn't the case.

'Thank you.' She acknowledged his compliment with a smile.

'But you're not reasonable.'

She frowned. 'Excuse me?'

'You called yourself a reasonable cook,' he said. 'You're not. You're more than that.'

'Thank you. Though I wasn't fishing for compliments.' She shrugged. 'I used to like cooking with my mum. Not that she ever followed a recipe. She'd pick something at random, and then she'd tweak it.'

'So I'm guessing that you didn't follow a recipe for this, did you?' he asked.

'I cooked us dinner. It's not exactly rocket science,' she drawled.

Why had he never noticed how deliciously sarcastic she could be?

'What?' she asked

He blinked. 'Sorry. I'm not following you.'

'You were smiling. What did I say that was so funny?'

'It was the way you said it.' He paused. 'Do you have any idea how delectable you are when you're being sarcastic?'

It was her turn to blink. 'Sarcasm is sexy?'

'It is on you.'

She grinned. 'Well, now. I think tonight has just got a whole lot more interesting. Are you on a sugar rush, Sean?'

'Excuse me?'

'Working where you do, you have toffee practically on tap. Eat enough of the stuff and you'll be on a permanent sugar rush. Which, I think, must be the main reason why you're complimenting me like this tonight.'

No. It was because it was as if he'd just met her for the first time. She wasn't the girl who'd irritated him for years; she was a woman who intrigued him. But he didn't want to sound soppy. 'Honey,' he drawled, 'the only sugar I want right now is you.'

She laughed at him. 'Now you've switched to cheese.'

'No. You're the one who's served cheese.' He indicated the stuffing for the chicken. 'And very nice it is, too.'

Her mouth quirked. 'Keep complimenting me like this, and...'

'Yeah?' he asked, his voice suddenly lower. What was she going to do? Kiss him? That idea definitely worked for him.

'Oh, shut up and eat your dinner,' she said, looking flustered.

'Chicken,' he said, knowing that she'd pick up on the double use of the word—and he was seriously enjoying fencing with her. Why had he never noticed before that she was bright and funny, and sexy as hell?

Probably because he'd had this fixed idea of her as a difficult girl who attracted trouble. That was definitely true in the past, but now...Now, she wasn't who he'd always thought she was. She'd grown up. Changed.

And he really liked the woman he was beginning to get to know.

She served pudding next—a seriously rich chocolate ganache teamed with tart raspberries. 'Come and work for my R and D department,' he said, 'because I think you'd have seriously good ideas about flavouring.'

She smiled. 'I know practically nothing about making toffee, and if I make banoffee pie I always buy a jar of *dulce de leche* rather than making my own.'

'That's a perfectly sensible use of your time,' he said.

She grinned. 'It's not so much that you have to boil a can of condensed milk for a couple of hours and keep an eye on it.'

'What, then?'

'I had a friend who tried doing it,' she explained. 'The can exploded and totally wrecked her kitchen.'

'Ouch.' He grimaced in sympathy, and took another spoonful of pudding. 'This is a really gorgeous meal, Claire.'

'I didn't make the ganache myself—it's a shop-bought pudding.'

'I don't care. It's still gorgeous. And I appreciate the effort. Though, for future reference, you could've ordered in pizza and I would've been perfectly happy,' he said. 'I just wanted to spend time with you.'

'Me, too,' she said softly. 'But I wanted to—well…'

Prove to him that she wasn't the flake he'd always thought she was? 'I know. And you did.'

And how weird it was that he could follow the way she thought. Scary, even. She was the last woman in the world he'd expected to be so in tune with.

Once he'd helped her clear away, she said, 'I thought we could have coffee in the living room.'

'Sounds good to me.'

'OK. You can go through and put on some music, if you like,' she suggested.

Claire's living room had clearly been hastily tidied, judging by the edges of the magazines peeking from the side of her sofa—he remembered her telling him that she was addicted to magazines; but the flowers he'd sent her that morning were in a vase on the coffee table, perfectly arranged. Clearly she liked them and hadn't just been polite when she'd thanked him for them earlier. And, given the pink tones in the room, he'd managed to pick her favourite colours.

Her MP3 player was in a speaker dock. He took it out and skimmed through the tracks. Given what she'd said at lunchtime, he'd expected most of the music to be pop, but he was surprised to see how much of it was from the nineteen-sixties. In the end, he picked a general compilation and switched on the music.

She smiled when she came in. 'Good choice. I love the Ronettes.' She sang a snatch of the next line.

'Aren't you a bit young to like this stuff?' he asked.

'Nope. It's the sort of stuff my gran listens to, so I grew up with it—singing into hairbrushes, the lot,' she said with a smile. 'Best Friday nights ever. Totally girly. Me, Mum, Gran, Aunt Lou and my cousins. Popcorn, waffles, milkshake and music.'

It was the first time she'd talked about her family. 'So you're close to your family?' he asked.

'Yes. I still clash quite a bit with my dad,' she said, 'but that's hardly tactful to talk about that to you.'

'Because I'm male?'

'Because,' she said softly, 'I'd guess that, like Ash, you'd give anything to be able to talk to your dad. And here am I grumbling about my remaining parent.

Though, to be fair, my dad is nothing like yours was. Yours actually *listened*.'

Fair point. He did miss his parents. And, when the whole takeover bid had kicked off, Sean would've given anything to be able to talk about it to his dad. But at the same time he knew that relationships were complicated. And it was none of his business. Unless Claire wanted to talk about it, he had to leave the subject alone.

She'd brought in a tray with a cafetière, two mugs, a small jug of milk and the box he'd given her earlier. 'Milk and sugar?' she asked.

'Neither, thanks. I like my caffeine unadulterated,' he said with a smile.

Claire, he noticed, took hers with two sugars and a lot of milk. Revolting. And it also made him worry that she wouldn't like the samples he'd brought; she probably preferred white chocolate to dark. Then again, he'd been wrong about a lot of things where Claire was concerned.

'Right. This box of utter yumminess. Whatever else I might have said about you in the past,' she said, 'I've always said that you make seriously good toffee.'

Honesty compelled him to say, 'No, my staff do. I'm not really hands-on in the manufacturing department.'

'Now that surprises me,' she said. 'I would've pegged you as the kind of manager who did every single job in the factory so you knew exactly what all the issues are.'

'I have done, over the years,' he said. 'Everything from the manufacturing to packing the goods, to carrying the boxes out for delivery. And every single admin role. And, yes, I worked with the cleaning team as well. Nowadays, I have regular meetings with each department and my staff know that I want to know about any problems they have and can't smooth out on their own.'

'Attention to detail.'

Her voice sounded almost like a purr. And there was a suspicious glow of colour across her cheeks.

'Claire?'

'Um,' she said. 'Just thinking. About Capri. About...'

And now he was feeling the same rush of blood to the head. 'Close your eyes,' he said.

Her breathing went shallow. 'Why?'

'Humour me?'

'OK.' She closed her eyes.

He took one of the dark salted caramel chocolates from the box and brushed it against her lips. Her mouth parted—and so did the lashes on her left eye.

'No peeking,' he said.

In return, she gave him an insolent smile and opened both eyes properly. 'So we're playing, are we, Mr Farrell?'

'We are indeed, Ms Stewart. Now close your eyes.' He teased her mouth with the chocolate and made her reach for it before finally letting her take a bite.

'You,' she said when she'd eaten it, 'have just upped your game considerably. I love the caramel-filled hearts, but these are spectacular.'

'You liked them?' Funny how that made him feel so good.

'Actually, I think I need another one, to check.'

He laughed. 'Oh, really?'

'Yes, really.' She struck a pose.

No way was he tcasing her with chocolate when she looked like that, all pouting and dimpled and sexy as hell. Instead, he leaned over and kissed her.

The next thing he knew, they were both lying full length on the sofa and she was on top of him, his arms were wrapped tightly round her, and one of his hands was resting on the curve of her bottom.

'You're telling me that was chocolate?' she dead-panned.

'Maybe. Maybe not.' He moved his hand, liking the softness of her curves. 'Claire. You're…'

'What?'

'Unexpectedly luscious,' he said. 'None of this was supposed to happen.'

'Says the man who made me close my eyes and lean forward to take a bite of chocolate. Giving him a view straight down the front of my dress, if I'm not mistaken.'

'It was a very nice view,' he said, and shifted slightly so she was left in no doubt of his arousal.

'This is what chocolate does to you?' she asked.

'No. This is what *you* do to me.'

She leaned forward and caught his lower lip between hers, teasing him. 'Indeed, Mr Farrell.'

'Yeah.' He was aware that his voice sounded husky. She'd know from that exactly how much she affected him.

'So did you come prepared?' she asked.

He couldn't speak for a moment. And then he looked into her eyes. 'Are you suggesting…?'

'Capri, redux?' She held his gaze and nodded.

He blew out a breath. 'I didn't come prepared.'

'Tsk. Not what I expected from Mr Plan-Everything-Twenty-Years-in-Advance,' she teased.

'How do you manage to do that?' he asked plain-tively.

'Do what?'

'Make me feel incredibly frustrated and make me want to laugh, all at the same time?'

'Go with the flow, sweetie,' she drawled.

He kissed her again. 'OK. Tonight wasn't about ex-pectations. It wasn't about sending you flowers this morning so you'd sleep with me tonight. It was about getting to know you better.'

'Platonic, you mean?'

'I'd like to be friends.'

'Uh-huh.' She sounded unaffected, but he'd seen that little vulnerable flicker in her expression and he didn't let her move. He pulled her closer.

'I didn't say *just* friends. I want to be your lover as well.'

Her pupils went gratifyingly large.

'But I didn't come prepared because I'm not taking you for granted.'

To his surprise, he saw a sheen of tears in her eyes. 'Claire? What's wrong?'

She shook her head. 'I'm being wet.'

'Tell me anyway.'

'That's not how it usually is, for me,' she admitted.

Not being taken for granted? He brushed his mouth very gently against hers. 'That's because you've been dating the wrong men, thinking they're Mr Right.'

'I always thought you'd be Mr Wrong,' she admitted.

'And I always thought you'd be Ms Wrong,' he said. 'But maybe we should give each other a little more of a chance.'

'Maybe,' she said softly. 'But next time—I think I'm going to be prepared.'

'You and me, both.' He nuzzled the curve of her neck. 'Careful, Claire. You might turn into a bit of an *über*-planner if you keep this up.'

As he'd hoped, she laughed. 'And you might start going with the flow without having to be reminded.'

He laughed back. 'I think we need to move. While we still both have some self-control.'

'Good plan.' But when she climbed off him, he didn't

let her move away and sit in a different chair. He kept hold of her hand and drew her down beside him.

'This works for me,' he said. 'Just simply holding hands with you.'

For a moment, she went all dreamy-eyed. 'Like teenagers.'

'What?'

She shook her head. 'Ah, no. I'm not confessing that right now.'

Confessing what? He was intrigued. 'I could,' he suggested sweetly, '*make* you confess. Remember, I'm armed with seriously good chocolate.'

She drew his hand up to her mouth and kissed each knuckle in turn. 'But I also happen to know you're a gentleman. So you won't push me right now.'

So even when she hadn't liked him, she'd recognised that he had integrity and standards and knew that she was safe with him? That warmed him from the inside out. 'I won't push you right now,' he agreed. He handed her the box. 'Help yourself.'

'Salted caramel in dark chocolate. Fabulous. Are they all like that?'

'No. There's a Seville orange version and an espresso.'

'Nice choices. And you said earlier they were samples.' She looked thoughtful. 'So are you experimenting with new lines?'

'Possibly.'

She rolled her eyes. 'Sean, I'm hardly going to rush straight off to one of your competitors and sell them the information.'

'Of course you're not.' He frowned. 'Do you think I'm that suspicious?'

'You sounded it,' she pointed out.

'It's an experiment, moving into a slightly different form of toffee,' he said, 'but I need to put them through some focus groups first and see what my market thinks.'

'Ah, research. Looking at growing your market share.' She smiled. 'So either you sell the same product to more people, or you sell more products to the same people.'

At his raised eyebrow, she sighed. 'I'm not a total dimwit, you know. I've had my own business for three years.'

'I know, and it's not just that. Ashleigh told me you turned down an unconditional offer from Cambridge for medicine, and I know you wouldn't get that sort of offer if you weren't really bright.' He looked at her. 'I always wondered why you became a wedding dress designer instead of a doctor.'

She looked sad. 'It's a long story, and I don't really want to tell it tonight.'

Because she didn't trust him not to judge her? 'Fair enough,' he said coolly.

'I wasn't pushing you away, Sean,' she said. 'I just don't want to talk about it right now.'

'So what do you want, Claire?' He couldn't resist the question.

'Right now? I want you to kiss me again. But we've both agreed that's, um, possibly not a good idea.'

'Because I'm not prepared, and neither are you. So we'll take a rain check,' he said.

'How long?' She slapped a hand to her forehead. 'No. I didn't ask that and you didn't hear me.'

'Right. And I wasn't thinking it, either,' he retorted. 'When?'

'Wednesday?'

Giving them two days to come to their common sense. 'Wednesday,' he agreed. 'I would offer to cook for you, except you'd get a sandwich at best.'

She laughed. 'I can live with sandwiches.'

'No, I mean a proper date.'

'Planned to the nth degree, Sean-style?' she asked.

Why did planning things rattle her so much? In answer, he kissed her. Hard. And she was breathless by the time she'd finished.

'That was cheating,' she protested.

'Yeah, yeah.' He rubbed the pad of his thumb along her lower lip. 'And?'

'Go home, Sean, before we do something stupid.'

'Rain check,' he said. 'Wednesday night. I'll pick you up at seven.' He leaned forward and whispered in her ear, 'And, by the time I've finished with you, you won't remember what your name is or where you are.'

Her voice was gratifyingly husky when she said, 'That had better be a promise.'

'It is.' He stole one last kiss. 'And I always keep my promises. Which reminds me—I have washing-up duties.'

'I'll let you off,' she said.

'The deal was, you'd cook and I'd wash up.'

'Do you really think it's a good idea for us to be that close to each other, in the presence of water, and while neither of us is, um, prepared?'

He didn't quite get the reference to water, but he agreed with the rest of it. 'Good point. Rain check on the washing up, then, too?'

She laughed. 'No need. I have a dishwasher. It's horribly indulgent, given that I live on my own, but it's nice when I have friends over for dinner.' She paused, and added in a softer, sexier, deeper tone, 'Or my lover.'

Which sounded as if she was going to invite him back.

And that set his pulse thrumming.

'Right.' He couldn't resist one last kiss, one that sent his head spinning and left her looking equally dazed. 'Enjoy the chocolate,' he said. And then he left, while he was still capable of being sensible.

CHAPTER EIGHT

SEAN SENT CLAIRE a text later that evening.

Sweet dreams.

Yes, she thought, because they'd be of him. She typed back, You, too x.

He'd turned out to be unexpectedly sweet, so different from how he'd always been in the past. He was still a little regimented, but there was huge potential for him to be...

She stopped herself. No. This time she wasn't going to make the same old mistake. She wasn't going into this relationship thinking that Sean might be The One, that there would definitely be a happy-ever-after. OK, so he wasn't like the men she usually dated; but that didn't guarantee a different outcome for this relationship, either.

And this was early days. Sean had a reputation for not dating women for very long; the chances were, this would all be over in another month. Claire knew that she needed to minimise the potential damage to her heart and make sure that her best friend didn't get caught in any crossfire. Which meant keeping just a little bit of distance between them.

Even though Claire tried to tell herself to be sensible, she still found herself anticipating Wednesday. Wondering if he'd kiss her again. Wondering if they'd end up at his place or hers. Wondering if this whole thing blew his mind as much as it did hers.

Wednesday turned out to be madly busy, and Claire spent a long time on the phone with one of her suppliers, sorting out a mistake they'd made in delivering the wrong fabric—and it was going to cost her time she didn't have. A last-minute panic from one of her brides took up another hour; and, before she realised it, the time was half past six.

Oh, no. She still needed to shower, wash her hair, change and do her make-up before Sean arrived. She called him, hoping to beg an extra half an hour, but his line was busy. Swiftly, she tapped in a text as she went up the stairs to her flat.

Sorry, running a bit late. See you at half-seven?

She pressed 'send' and dropped the phone on her bed before rummaging through her wardrobe to find her navy linen dress.

She'd just stepped out of the shower and wrapped a towel round her hair when her doorbell rang.

No. It couldn't be Sean. It couldn't be seven-thirty already.

Well, whoever it was would just have to call back another time.

The bell rang again.

Arrgh. Clearly whoever it was had no intention of being put off. If it was a cold-caller, she'd explain firmly and politely that she didn't buy on the doorstep.

She blinked in surprise when she opened the door

to Sean. 'You're early!' And Sean was never early and never late; he was always precisely on time.

'No. We said seven.'

She frowned. 'But I texted you to say I was running late and asked if we could make it half past.'

'I didn't get any text from you,' he said.

'Oh, no. I'm so sorry.' She blew out a breath. 'Um, come up. I'll be twenty minutes, tops—make yourself a coffee or something.'

'Do you want me to make you a drink?'

She shook her head. 'I'm so sorry.'

He stole a kiss. 'Stop apologising.'

'I'll be as quick as I can,' she said, feeling horribly guilty. Why hadn't she kept a better eye on the time? Or called him rather than relying on a text getting through?

She had to dry her hair roughly and tie it back rather than spending time on a sophisticated updo, but she was ready by twenty-five past seven.

'You look lovely,' he said.

'Thank you.' Though she noticed that he'd glanced at his watch again. If only he'd lighten up a bit. It would drive her crazy if he ran this evening to schedule, as if it were a business meeting. 'Where are we going?' she asked brightly.

'South Bank.'

'Great. We can play in the fountains,' she said with a smile. 'It's been so hot today that it'd be nice to have a chance to cool down.'

He simply glanced at his suit.

And she supposed he had a point. Getting soaked wouldn't do the fabric any favours. Or her dress, for that matter. But the art installations on the South Bank were *fun*.

'I called the restaurant to say we'd be late,' he said.

Sean and his schedules. Though if they didn't turn up when they were expected, the restaurant would be perfectly justified in giving their table to someone else, so she guessed it was reasonable of him. 'Sorry,' she said again.

This was the side of Sean she found harder to handle. Mr Organised. It was fine for business; but, in his personal life, surely he could be more relaxed?

They caught the tube to the South Bank—to her relief, the line was running without any delays—and the restaurant turned out to be fabulous. Their table had a great view of the river, and the food was as excellent as the view. Claire loved the fresh tuna with mango chilli salsa. 'And the pudding menu's to die for,' she said gleefully. 'It's going to take me ages to choose.'

'Actually, we don't have time,' Sean said, looking at his watch,

'No time for pudding? But that's the best bit of dinner out,' she protested.

'We have to be somewhere. Maybe we can fit pudding in afterwards,' he said.

Just as she'd feared, Sean had scheduled this evening down to the last second. If she hadn't been running late in the first place, it might not have been so much of a problem. But right now she was having huge second thoughts about dating Sean. OK, so he managed to fit a lot in to his life; but all this regimentation drove her crazy. They were too different for this to work.

'So why exactly do we have to rush off?' she asked.

'For the next bit of this evening,' he said.

'Which is?'

'A surprise.'

Half past eight was too late for a theatre performance to start, and if they'd been going to the cinema she thought he would probably have picked a restaurant nearer to Leicester Square. She didn't work out what he'd planned until they started walking towards the London Eye. 'Oh. An evening flight.'

'It's the last one they run on a weeknight,' he confirmed. 'And we have to pick up the tickets fifteen minutes beforehand. Sorry I rushed you through dinner.'

At least he'd acknowledged that he'd rushed her. And she needed to acknowledge her part in the fiasco. 'If I hadn't been running late, you wouldn't have had to rush me.' She bit her lip. 'I'm beginning to think you might be right about me being chaotic. I should've checked that the text had gone or left you a voicemail as well.'

'It's OK. Obviously you had a busy day.'

She nodded. 'There were a couple of glitches that took time to sort out,' she said. 'And I'm up to my eyes in the wedding show stuff.'

'It'll be worth it in the end,' he said.

'I hope so. And I had a new bride in to see me this morning. That's my favourite bit of my job,' Claire said. 'Turning a bride-to-be's dreams into a dress that will suit her and make her feel special.'

'That's why you called your business "Dream of a Dress", then?' he asked.

'Half of the reason, yes.'

'And the other half?' he asked softly.

'Because it's my dream job,' she said.

He looked surprised, as if he'd never thought of it that way before. 'OK. But what if a bride wants a dress that you know wouldn't suit her?'

'You mean, like a fishtail dress when she's short and curvy?' At his nod, she said, 'You find out what it is she loves about that particular dress, and see how you can adapt it to something that will work. And then you need tact by the bucketload.'

'Tactful.' He tipped his head on one side and looked at her. 'But you always say what you think.'

'I do. But you can do that in a nice way, without stomping on people.'

The corners of his mouth twitched. 'I'll remember that, the next time you don't mince your words with me.'

She laughed back. 'You're getting a bit more bearable, so I might be nicer to you.'

He bowed his head slightly. 'For the compliment.' Then he took her hand and lifted it to his mouth, pressed a kiss into her palm, and folded her fingers round it.

It made her knees go weak. To cover the fact that he flustered her, she asked, 'How was your day?'

'Full of meetings.'

No wonder he found it hard to relax and go with the flow. He was used to a ridiculously tight schedule.

But at least he seemed to relax more once they were in the capsule and rising to see a late summer evening view of London. Claire was happy just to enjoy the view, with Sean's arm wrapped round her.

'I was thinking,' he said softly. 'I owe you pudding and coffee. I have good coffee back at my place.'

'Would there be caramel hearts to go with it?' she asked hopefully.

'There might be,' he said, the teasing light back in his eyes.

This sounded like a spontaneous offer rather than being planned, she thought. So maybe it could make up for the earlier part of the evening. 'That sounds good,' she said. 'Coffee and good chocolate. Count me in.'

And, to her pleasure, he held her hand all the way

back to his place. Now they weren't on a schedule any more, he was less driven—and she liked this side of him a lot more.

The last time Claire had been to Sean's house, she'd waited on the path outside while he picked up his luggage. This time, he invited her in. She discovered that his kitchen was very neat and tidy—as she'd expected— but it clearly wasn't a cook's kitchen. There were no herbs growing in pots, no ancient and well-used implements. She'd guess that the room wasn't used much beyond making drinks.

His living room was decorated in neutral tones. Claire was pleased to see that there were lots of family photographs on the mantelpiece, but she noticed that the art on the walls was all quite moody.

'It's Whistler,' he said, clearly realising what she was looking at. 'His nocturnes—I like them.'

'I would've pegged you as more of a Gainsborough man than a fan of tonalism,' she said.

He looked surprised. 'You know art movements?'

'I did History of Art for GCSE,' she said. 'Then again, I guess those paintings are a lot like you. They're understated and you really have to look to see what's there.'

'I'm not sure,' he said, 'if that was meant to be a compliment.'

'It certainly wasn't meant to be an insult,' she said. 'More a statement of fact.'

He poured them both a coffee, added sugar and a lot of milk to hers, and gestured to the little dish he'd brought on the tray. 'Caramel hearts, as you said you liked them.'

'I do.' She smiled at him, appreciating the fact that he'd remembered and made the effort.

'You can put on some music, if you like,' he suggested, indicating his MP3 player.

She skimmed through it quickly and frowned. 'Sean, I don't mean to be horrible, but all your playlists are a bit—well...'

'What?' he asked, sounding puzzled.

'They're named for different types of workouts, so I'm guessing all the tracks in each list have the same number of beats per minute.'

'Yes, but that's sensible. It means everything's arranged the way I want it for whatever exercise I'm doing.'

'I get that,' she said, 'but don't you enjoy music?'

He frowned. 'Of course I do.'

'I can't see what you listen to for pleasure. To me this looks as if you only play set music at set times.' Regimented again. And this time she couldn't just let it go. 'That works for business but, Sean, you can't live your personal life as if it's a business.'

'Right,' he said tightly.

So much for reaching an understanding. She sighed. 'I'm not having a go at you. I'm just saying you're missing out on so much and maybe there's another way of doing things.'

'Let's agree to disagree, shall we?'

Sean had closed off on her again, Claire thought with an inward sigh—and now she could guess exactly why his girlfriends didn't last for much longer than three weeks. He'd drive them crazy by stonewalling them as soon as they tried to get close to him, and then either he'd gently suggest that they should be just friends, or they'd give up trying to be close to him.

She also knew that telling him that would be the quickest way of ending things between them; and from the few glimpses she'd had she was pretty sure that, behind his walls, the real Sean Farrell was someone really worth getting to know.

'OK, I'll back off,' she said. 'But you have absolutely nothing slushy and relaxing on here.'

He coughed. 'In case you hadn't noticed, I'm male.'

She'd noticed, all right.

'I don't do slushy,' he continued. 'But...' He took the MP3 player gently from her and flicked rapidly through the tracks.

When the music began playing, she recognised 'Can't Take My Eyes Off You', but it was a rock version of the song.

'The band played this at Ashleigh's wedding,' he said, 'and I found myself looking straight at you—that's why I asked you to dance.'

'And there was I thinking it was because it was traditional,' she deadpanned.

'No. I just wanted to dance with you.'

His honesty disarmed her. Just when he'd driven her crazy and she was thinking of calling the whole thing off, he did something like this that made her melt inside.

He drew her into his arms, and Claire was surprised to discover that, even though the song was fast, they could actually dance slowly to it.

'And then, when I was dancing with you,' he continued, 'I wanted to kiss you.'

She found herself moistening her lower lip with her tongue. 'Do you want to kiss me now, Sean?'

'Yes.' He held her gaze. 'And I want to do an awful lot more than just kiss you.'

Excitement thrummed through her, but she tried to play it cool. 'Could you be more specific?'

'I want to take that dress off,' he said, 'lovely as it is. And I want to kiss every inch of skin I uncover.'

'That sounds like a good plan,' she said. 'So what do I do?'

He smiled. 'I'm surprised you don't already know that one. Isn't it what you're always saying? Be spontaneous. Follow your heart. Go with the flow.'

'So that means,' she said, 'I get to take that prissy suit off you?'

'Prissy?' he queried. 'My suit's *prissy*?'

'It's beautifully cut, but it's so neat and tidy. I'd like to see you dishevelled,' she said, 'like you were that morning in Capri.'

'Would that be the morning you threw me out of your bed?'

'Yes, and don't make me feel guilty about it. That was mainly circumstances,' she said.

'Hmm.'

'Besides, I can't throw you out of your own bed,' she pointed out.

'Now that's impeccable logic.' He frowned. 'Though, actually, if you said no at any point I hope you realised I'd stop.'

She stroked his face. 'Sean, of course I know that. You're...'

'Dull?'

She shook her head. 'I was going to say honourable.'

He brushed the pad of his thumb across her lower lip, making her skin tingle. 'You normally call me regimented.'

'You can be. You were tonight, and I nearly left you to it and went home.' She smiled. 'But there's a huge difference between regimented and dull.'

'Is there?'

'Let me show you,' she said. 'Take me to bed.'

'I thought you'd never ask.'

To her surprise, he scooped her up and actually carried her up the stairs. She half wanted to make a snippy comment about him being muscle-bound, to tease him and push him, but at the same time she didn't want to spoil the moment. She was shocked to discover that she actually quite liked the way he was taking charge and being all troglodyte.

Once they were in his room, he set her down on her feet.

His bedroom was painted in shades of smoky blue—very masculine, with a polished wooden floor, a rug in a darker shade that toned with the walls and matched the curtains, and limed oak furniture. But what really caught Claire's eye was his bed. A sleigh bed, also in limed oak, and she loved it. She'd always wanted a bed like that, but there really wasn't the room for that kind of furniture in her flat. Sean's Victorian terraced house was much more spacious and the bed was absolutely perfect.

'The last time you took your dress off for me,' he said, 'your underwear matched. Does it match today?'

'That's for me to know,' she said, 'and for you to find out.'

'Is that a challenge?'

'In part. It's also an offer.' She paused. 'Um, before this goes any further, do we have Monday's problem?'

'We absolutely do not,' he confirmed.

'Good.' Because she was going to implode if she had to wait much longer.

He drew the curtains and turned on the bedside light; it was a touch lamp, so he was able to dim the glow. Then he sat on the edge of the bed. 'Show me,' he invited.

She unzipped her dress and stepped out of it, then hung it over the back of a chair.

'What?' she asked, seeing the amusement in his face.

'You're a closet neat freak,' he said.

'No. Just practical. This is linen. It creases very, very badly. And I'm not walking out of here looking as if I've just been tumbled in a haystack.'

He gave her a slow, sexy smile. 'I like that image. Very much. You, tumbled in a haystack.'

She shook her head. 'It's not at all romantic, you know. Straw's prickly and itchy and totally unsexy.'

'And I assume you know that because you've, um, gone with the flow?'

'Listen, I haven't slept with everyone I've dated, and I certainly haven't slept with anyone else as fast as I fell into bed with *you*,' she said, folding her arms and giving him a level stare.

He stood up, walked over to her and brushed his mouth against hers. 'I'm not calling you a tart, Claire. We both have pasts. It's the twenty-first century, not the nineteen-fifties. I'm thirty and you're twenty-seven. I'd be more surprised if we were both still virgins.' He traced the lacy edge of her bra with one fingertip. 'Mmm. Cream lace. I like this. You have excellent taste in clothing, Ms Stewart.'

'It's oyster, not cream,' she corrected.

He grinned. 'And you have the cheek to call me prissy.'

'Details,' she said. 'You need to get them right.'

'We're in agreement there.'

She coughed.

'What?' he asked.

'I'm in my underwear. You can see that it matches,

so I've done my half of the bargain. And right now, Mr Farrell, I have to say that you're very much overdressed.'

'So strip me, Claire,' he said, opening his arms to give her full access to his clothes.

It was an offer she wasn't going to refuse.

Afterwards, curled in Sean's arms, Claire turned her face so she could kiss his shoulder. 'I'd better go.'

'Not yet. This is comfortable.' He held her closer. 'Stay for a bit longer. I'll drive you home.'

So Sean the super-efficient businessman was a cuddler? Ah, bless, Claire thought. And, actually, she rather liked it. It made him that much more human. 'OK,' she said, and settled back against him.

Funny how they didn't really need to talk. Just being together was enough. It was *peaceful*. Something else she would never have believed about herself and Sean; but she liked just being with him. When he wasn't being super-organised down to the last microsecond. And it seemed that he felt the same.

So maybe, just maybe, this wasn't all going to end in tears.

When she finally got dressed and he drove her home, he parked outside her flat. 'So. When are you free next?' he asked.

'Sunday?' she suggested. 'I have the shop on Saturday.'

'Sunday works for me.'

'You organised tonight, so I'll organise Sunday,' she said. 'And that means doing things my way.'

'Going with the flow.' He looked slightly pained.

'It means being spontaneous and having fun,' she said. 'I'll pick you up at nine. And I won't be late.'

'No?' he asked wryly.

'No.' She kissed him. 'The first bit of tonight was, um, a bit much for me. But I loved dinner. I loved the London Eye and just being with you. Those kind of things works for me. It's just...' She shook her head. 'Schedules are for work. And I keep my work and my personal life separate.'

'Hmm,' he said, and she knew he wasn't convinced. But then he made the effort and said, 'I enjoyed being with you.'

But the fact she'd been late had really grated on him. He didn't have to tell her that.

He kissed her lightly. 'I'll walk you to your door.'

'Sean, it's half a dozen paces. I think I'm old enough to manage.'

He spread his hands. 'As you wish.'

'I'm not pushing you away,' she said softly. 'But I don't need protecting—the same as you don't.' She already had one overprotective male in her life, and that was more than enough for her. And it was half the reason why she'd always chosen free-spirited boyfriends who wouldn't make a fuss over everything or smother her.

Though maybe she'd gone too far the other way, because they'd all been disastrous.

But could Sean compromise? Could they find some kind of middle ground between them? If not, then this was going to be just as much a disaster as her previous relationships.

'Thank you for caring,' she said, knowing that his heart was in the right place—he just went a bit too far, that was all. 'I'll see you Sunday.'

'Spontaneous. Go with the flow.'

'You're learning. *Carpe diem*,' she said with a smile, and kissed him. 'Goodnight.'

CHAPTER NINE

WHEN CLAIRE WENT to pick Sean up on Sunday morning he was wearing formal trousers, a formal shirt and a tie. At least this time it wasn't a complete suit, but it still didn't work for what she wanted to do. And they looked totally mismatched, given that Claire was wearing denim shorts, a strappy vest and matching canvas shoes. Sean looked way too formal.

'Do you actually own a pair of jeans?' she asked.

'No.'

It was just as well she'd second-guessed. 'Right, then.' She delved into her tote bag and brought out a plastic carrier bag bearing the name of a department store.

'What's this?' he asked.

'Pressie. For you.' When he still looked blank, she added, 'The idea is that you wear it. As in right now.'

He looked in the bag. 'You bought me a pair of jeans?'

'Give the monkey a peanut,' she drawled.

'How do you know my size?'

She rolled her eyes. 'I measured you for a wedding suit, remember?'

He sighed. 'Claire, you didn't need to buy me a pair of jeans.'

'You don't own any. So actually, yes, I did.'

He looked at her, and she sighed. 'Sean, don't be difficult about this. I bought you a present, that's all. It's what people do when they date.'

He still didn't look convinced.

'Look, you bought me those gorgeous flowers, and I don't think you'd enjoy it if I bought you flowers—well, not that I think you *can't* buy a man flowers,' she clarified, 'but I don't think you're the kind of man who'd really appreciate them.'

'Probably not,' he admitted.

'Most people would buy their man some chocolate, but I can hardly give chocolate to someone who owns a confectionery company, can I? Which leaves me pretty stuck for buying you a gift. It's just an ordinary pair of jeans, Sean. Nothing ridiculously overpriced. So come on. Do something you haven't done since you were a teenager,' she coaxed, 'and wear the jeans. And swap those shoes for your running shoes.'

'My running shoes?' he queried.

She nodded. 'Because I bet you don't have a pair of scruffy, "go for a walk and it doesn't matter if they're not perfectly polished" shoes.'

'There's nothing wrong with looking smart at work,' he protested.

'I know, but you're not at work today, Sean. You're playing. You can keep the shirt, but lose the tie.'

'Bossy,' he grumbled, but he did as she asked. By the time he'd changed into the jeans and his running shoes, he looked fantastic—much more approachable. *Touchable*. Claire was glad she'd picked a light-coloured denim that looked slightly worn. It really, really suited him.

She folded her arms and looked at him.

'What now?' he asked. 'I'm not wearing the tie.'

'But your top button is still done up. Fix it, and roll your sleeves up.'

'Claire…'

'We did your date your way,' she said. 'And you agreed that we'd do this one my way.'

'This is the giddy limit,' he said, and for a moment she thought he was going to refuse; but finally he indulged her.

'That's almost perfect,' she said, then sashayed over to him, reached up to kiss him, and then messed up his hair.

'Why did you do that?' he asked, pulling back.

'It's the "just got out of bed" look. Which makes you look seriously hot,' she added. 'Like you did in Capri.'

He gave her a predatory smile. 'So if you think I look hot…'

'Rain check,' she said. 'Because we're going out and having fun, first.'

There was a bossy side to Claire, Sean thought, that he'd never seen before. The whole idea of giving up control—that just wasn't how he did things.

Claire Stewart was dangerous with a capital D where his peace of mind was concerned.

'This is your car?' He looked at the bright pink convertible Mini stencilled with daisies that was parked on the road outside his house. 'Oh, you are kidding me.'

'What's wrong with my car?' She put her finger into the keyring and spun her keys round.

What was wrong with the car? Where did he start?

He closed his eyes. 'OK. I know, I know, go with the flow.' He groaned and opened his eyes again. 'But, Claire. *Pink*. With daisies. Really?'

Finally she took pity on him. 'I borrowed it from a friend. I don't have a car of my own at the moment.'

'Then we could go wherever it is in mine,' he suggested hopefully.

'Nope—we're doing this my way.' She gave him another of those insolent grins. 'Actually, my friend wants to sell this. I was thinking about buying it from her.'

He pulled a face, but said nothing.

'Very wise, Sean, very wise,' she teased.

She tied her hair back with a scarf, added some dark glasses that made her look incredibly sexy, and then added the disgusting khaki cap he remembered from Capri and which cancelled out the effect of the glasses. Once they were sitting in the car, she put the roof down, connected her MP3 player, and started blasting out sugary nineteen-sixties pop songs. Worse still, she made him sing along; and Sean was surprised to discover that he actually knew most of the songs.

By the time they got to Brighton, he'd stopped being embarrassed by the sheer loudness of the car and was word-perfect on the choruses of all her favourite songs.

'Brighton,' he said.

'Absolutely. Today is "Sean and Claire do the seaside",' she said brightly.

'And this isn't planned out?'

She rolled her eyes. 'Don't be daft—you don't plan things like going to the seaside. You go with the flow and you have *fun*.' She parked the car, then took his hand and they strolled across to the seafront.

This was so far removed from what he'd normally do on a Sunday. He might sit in his garden—perfectly manicured by the man he paid to mow the lawn, weed the flower beds, and generally make the area look tidy—but nine times out of ten he'd be in his study, working.

He couldn't even remember the last time he went to the seaside. With one of his girlfriends, probably, but he hadn't paid much attention.

But with Claire, he was definitely paying attention.

He hung back slightly. 'Those are very *short* shorts.' And it made him want to touch her.

She just laughed. 'I have great legs—I might as well show them off before they go all wrinkly and saggy when I'm old.'

'You're…' He stopped and shook his head.

'I'm what, Sean?'

'A lot of things,' he said, 'half of which I wouldn't dare utter right now.'

'Chicken,' she teased.

'Discretion's the better part of valour,' he protested.

She laughed and took him onto the pier. They queued up to go on the fairground rides.

'You couldn't get fast-track tickets?' he asked.

She rolled her eyes. 'Queuing is part of the fun.'

'How?' he asked. In his view, queuing was a waste of time. If something was worth visiting, you bought fast-track tickets; otherwise, you didn't bother and you used your time more wisely.

'Anticipation,' she said. 'It'll be worth the wait.'

He wasn't so sure, but he'd agreed to do this her way. 'OK.'

But then they queued for the roller coaster.

'I thought you hated heights?'

'I do, but it'll be worth it if it loosens you up a little,' she said. 'It's OK to stop and smell the roses, Sean. If anything it'll enrich the time you spend on your business, because you'll look at things with a wider perspective.'

'Playing the business guru now, are you?'

'I don't play when it comes to business,' she said, 'but I do remember to play in my free time.'

'Hmm.'

He wasn't that fussed about the thrill rides, but for her sake he pretended to enjoy himself.

They grabbed something quick to eat, then went over to the stony, steeply sloping beach next. The sea was such an intense shade of turquoise, they could have been standing on the shore of the Mediterranean rather than the English Channel. He'd never seen the sea in England look so blue. And this, he thought, was much more his style than waiting in a queue for a short thrill ride that did nothing to raise his pulse.

Claire, on the other hand, could seriously raise his pulse...

'Shoes off,' she said, removing her own canvas shoes, 'and roll up your jeans.'

'You're so bossy,' he grumbled.

She grinned. 'The reward will be worth it.'

'What reward?'

She fluttered her eyelashes at him. 'Wait and see.'

He had to admit that it was nice walking on the edge of the sea with her, his shoes in one hand and her hand in his other. The sound of the waves rushing onto the pebbles and the seagulls squawking, the scent of the sea air and the warmth of the sunlight on his skin. Right at that moment, he'd never felt more alive.

It must have shown in his face, because she said softly, 'Told you it was rewarding.'

'Uh-huh.' He smiled at her. 'Talking of rewards...' He leaned forward and kissed her. But what started out as a sweet, soft brush of her lips against his soon turned hot.

He pulled back, remembering that they were in a

public place and with families around them. 'Claire. We need to…'

'I know.' Her fingers tightened round his. 'And this was what I wanted today. For you to let go, just a little bit, and have some fun with me.'

'I *am* having fun,' he said, half surprised by the admission.

'Good.' Her face had gone all soft and dreamy and it made him want to kiss her again—later, he promised himself.

When they'd finished paddling, they had to walk on the pebbles to dry off—Claire clearly hadn't thought to bring a towel with her—and then she said, 'Time for afternoon tea. And I have somewhere really special in mind.'

'OK.' He didn't mind going with the flow for a while, especially as it meant holding her hand. There was something to be said about just wandering along together.

As they walked into the town, he could see the exotic domes and spires of Brighton Pavilion.

Another queue, he thought with a sigh. It was one of the biggest tourist attractions in the area. Again, if she'd planned it they could've bought tickets online rather than having to queue up. He hated wasting time like this.

But, when they got closer, he realised there was something odd. No queues.

A notice outside the Pavilion informed them that the building was closed for urgent maintenance. Just for this weekend.

Sean just about stopped himself pointing out that if Claire had planned their trip in advance, then she would've known about this and she wouldn't have been disappointed.

'Oh, well,' she said brightly. 'I'm sure we can find a nice tea shop somewhere and have a traditional cream tea.'

Except all the tea shops nearby were full of tourists who'd had exactly the same idea. There were queues.

'Sorry. This is, um, a bit of a disaster,' she said.

Yes. But he wasn't going to make her feel any worse about it by agreeing with her. *'Carpe diem,'* he said. 'Maybe there's an ice cream shop we can go to instead.'

'Maybe,' she said, though he could tell that she was really disappointed. He guessed that she'd wanted to share the gorgeous furnishings of the Pavilion with him—and there had probably been some kind of costume display, too.

They wandered through the historic part of the town, peeking in the windows of the antiques shops and little craft shops, and eventually found a tea shop that had room at one of the tables. Though as it was late afternoon, the tea shop had run out of scones and cream.

'Just the tea is fine, thanks,' Sean said with a smile.

They had a last walk along the beach, then Claire drove them home. 'Shall I drop you back at your house, or would you like to come back to my place and we can maybe order in some Chinese food?' she asked.

Given what she'd said to him by the sea, Sean knew what she wanted to hear. 'I think,' he said, 'we'll go with the flow.'

Her smile was a real reward—full of warmth and pleasure rather than smugness. 'We won't go home on the motorway, then,' she said. 'We'll find a nice little country pub where we can have dinner.'

Except it turned out that every pub they stopped at didn't do food on Sunday evenings.

'I can't believe this,' she said. 'I mean—it's the summer. Prime tourist season. Why on earth wouldn't any of them serve food on Sunday evenings?'

Sean didn't have the heart to ask why she hadn't planned it better. 'Go back on to the motorway,' he said. 'We'll get a takeaway back in London.'

'I'm so sorry. Still, at least we can keep the roof down and enjoy the sun on the way home,' Claire said.

Which was clearly all she needed to say to jinx it, because they were caught in a sudden downpour. By the time she'd found somewhere safe to stop and put the car's soft top back up, they were both drenched. 'I'm so sorry. That wasn't supposed to happen,' Claire said, biting her lip.

'So we were literally going with the flow. Of water,' Sean said, and kissed her.

'What was that for?' she asked.

'For admitting that you're not always right.' He stole another kiss. 'And also because that T-shirt looks amazing on you right now.'

'Because it's wet, you mean?' She rolled her eyes at him. 'Men.'

He smiled. 'Actually, I wanted to cheer you up a bit.'

'Because today's been a total disaster.'

'No, it hasn't. I enjoyed the sea.'

'But we didn't get to the Pavilion, we missed out on a cream tea, I couldn't find anywhere for dinner and we just got drenched.' She sighed. 'If I'd done things your way, it would've been different.'

'But when I planned our date, we ended up rushing and that was a disaster, too,' he said softly. 'I think we might both have learned something from this.'

'That sometimes you need to plan your personal life?' she asked.

'And sometimes you need to go with the flow,' he said. 'It's a matter of compromise.'

'That works for me, too. Compromise.' And her smile warmed him all the way through.

On the way back to London, he asked, 'So are you seriously going to buy this car?'

'What's wrong with it?'

'Apart from the colour? I was thinking, it's not very practical for transporting wedding dresses.'

'I don't need a car for that. I'm hiring a van for the wedding show,' she said.

'So why don't you have a car?' he asked.

'I live and work in London, so I don't really need one—public transport's fine.'

'You needed a car today to take us to the seaside,' he pointed out.

'Not necessarily. We could have gone by train,' she said.

'But then you wouldn't have been able to sing your head off all the way to Brighton.'

'And we wouldn't have got wet on the way home,' she agreed ruefully.

'We really need to get you out of those wet clothes,' he said, 'and my place is nearer than yours.'

'Good point,' she said, and drove back to his.

Sean had the great pleasure of peeling off her wet clothes outside the shower, then soaping her down under the hot water. When they'd finished, he put her clothes in the washer-dryer while she dried off. And then he had the even greater pleasure of sweeping her off her feet again, carrying her to his bed, and making love with her until they were both dizzy.

Afterwards, she was all warm and sweet in his arms. He stroked her hair back from her face. 'You were going to tell me how come you're not a doctor.'

'It just wasn't what I wanted to do,' she said.

'But you applied to study medicine at university.'

She shifted onto her side and propped herself on one elbow so she could look into his face. 'It was Dad's dream, not mine. It's a bit hard to resist pressure from your parents when you're sixteen. Especially when your father's a bit on the overprotective side.' She wrinkled her nose. 'Luckily I realised in time that you can't live someone else's dream for them. So I turned down the places I was offered and reapplied to design school.'

He frowned. 'But you were doing science A levels.'

'And Art,' she said. 'And the teacher who taught my textiles class at GCSE wrote me a special reference, explaining that even though I hadn't done the subject at A level I was more than capable of doing a degree. At my interview, I wore a dress I'd made and I also took a suit I'd made with me. I talked the interviewers through all the stitching and the cut and the material, so they knew I understood what I was doing. And they offered me an unconditional place.'

He could see the pain in her eyes, and drew her closer. 'So what made you realise you didn't want to be a doctor?'

'My mum.' Claire dragged in a breath. 'She was only thirty-seven when she died, Sean.' Tears filmed her eyes. 'She barely made it past half the proverbial three score years and ten. In the last week of her life, when we were talking she held my hand and told me to follow my dream and do what my heart told me was the right thing.'

Which clearly hadn't been medicine.

Not knowing what to say, he just stroked her hair.

'Even when I was tiny, I used to draw dresses. Those paper dolls—mine were always the best dressed in class. I used to sketch all the time. I wanted to design dresses. Specifically, wedding dresses.'

He had a feeling he knew why she tended to fight with her father, now.

Her next words confirmed it. 'Dad said designers were ten a penny, whereas being a doctor meant I'd have a proper job for life.' She sighed. 'I know he had my best interests at heart. He had a tough upbringing, and he didn't want me ever to struggle with money, the way he did when he was young. But being a doctor was *his* dream, not mine. He said I could still do dressmaking and what have you on the side—but no way would I have had the time, not with the crazy hours that newly qualified doctors work. It was an all or nothing thing.' She grimaced. 'We had a huge fight over it. He said I'd just be wasting a degree if I studied textile design instead, and he gave me an ultimatum. Study medicine, and he'd support me through uni; study textiles, and he was kicking me out until I came to my senses.'

That sounded like the words of a scared man, Sean thought. One who wanted the best for his daughter and didn't know how to get that through to her. And he'd said totally the wrong thing to a teenage girl who'd just lost the person she loved most in the world and wasn't dealing with it very well. Probably because he was in exactly the same boat.

'That's quite an ultimatum,' Sean said, trying to find words that wouldn't make Claire think he was judging her.

'It was pretty bad at the time.' She paused. 'I talked to your mum about it.'

He was surprised. 'My mum?'

Claire nodded. 'She was lovely—she knew I was going off the rails a bit and I'd started drinking to blot out the pain of losing Mum, so she took me under her wing.'

Exactly what Sean would've expected from his mother. And now he knew why she'd been so insistent that he should look after Claire, the night of Ashleigh's eighteenth birthday party. She'd known the full story. And she'd known that she could trust Sean to do the right thing. To look after Claire when she needed it.

Claire smiled grimly. 'The drinking was also the worst thing I could have done in Dad's eyes, because his dad used to drink and gamble. I think that was half the reason why I did it, because I wanted to make him as angry as he made me. But your mum sat me down and told me that my mum would hate to see what I was doing to myself, and she made me see that the way I was behaving really wasn't helping the situation. I told her what Mum said about following my dream, and she asked me what I really wanted to do with my life. I showed her my sketchbooks and she said that my passion for needlework showed, and it'd be a shame to ignore my talents.' She smiled. 'And then she talked to Dad. He still didn't think that designing dresses was a stable career—he wanted me to have what he thought of as a "proper" job.'

'Does he still think that?' Sean asked.

'Oh, yes. And he tells me it, too, every so often,' Claire said, sounding both hurt and exasperated. 'When I left the fashion house where I worked after I graduated, he panicked that I wouldn't be able to make a go of my own business. Especially because there was a recession on. He wanted me to go back to uni instead.'

'And train to be a doctor?'

'Because then I'd definitely have a job for life.' She wrinkled her nose. 'But it's not just about the academic side of things. Sure, I could've done the degree and the post-grad training. But my heart wouldn't have been in it, and that wouldn't be fair to my patients.' She sighed. 'And I had a bit of a cash flow problem last year. I took a hit from a couple of clients whose cheques bounced. I still had to pay my suppliers for the materials and, um…' She wrinkled her nose. 'I could've asked Dad to lend me the money to tide me over, but then he would've given me this huge lecture about taking a bigger deposit from my brides and insisting on cash or a direct transfer to my account. Yet again he would've made me feel that he didn't believe in me and I'm not good enough to make it on my own. So I, um, sold my car. It kept me afloat.'

'And have you changed the way you take money?'

She nodded. 'I admit, I learned that one the hard way. Nowadays I ask for stage payments. But there's no real harm done. And Dad doesn't know about it so I avoided the lecture.' Again, Sean could see the flash of pain in her eyes. 'I just wish Dad believed in me a bit more. Gran and Aunty Lou believe in me. So does Ash.'

'So do I,' Sean said.

At her look of utter surprise, he said softly, 'Ashleigh's wedding dress convinced me. I admit, I had my doubts about you. Especially when you lost her dress. But you came up with a workable solution—and, when the original dress turned up, I could see just how talented you are. Mum was right about you, Claire. Yes, you could've been a perfectly competent doctor, but you would've ignored your talents—and that would've been a waste.'

Her eyes sparkled with tears. 'From you, that's one hell of a compliment. And not one I ever thought I'd hear. Thank you.'

'It's sincerely meant,' he said. 'You did the right thing, following your dreams.'

'I know I did. And I'm happy doing what I do. I'm never going to be rich, but I make enough for what I need—and that's important.' She paused. 'But what about you, Sean? What about your dreams?'

'I'm living them,' he said automatically.

'But supposing Farrell's didn't exist,' she persisted. 'What would you do then?'

'Start up another Farrell's, I guess,' he said.

'So toffee really is your dream?' She didn't sound as if she believed him.

'Of course toffee's my dream. What's wrong with that?' he asked.

'You're the fourth generation to run the business, Sean,' she said softly. 'You have a huge sense of family and heritage and integrity and duty. Even if you didn't really want to do it, you wouldn't walk away from your family business. Ever.'

It shocked him that she could read him so accurately. Nobody else ever had. She wasn't judging him; she was just stating facts. 'I like my job,' he protested. He *did*.

'I'm not saying you don't,' she said softly. 'I'm just asking you, what's your dream?'

'I'm living it,' he said again. Though now she'd made him question that.

It was true that he would never have walked away from the business, even if his parents hadn't been killed. He'd always wanted to be part of Farrell's. It was his heritage.

But, if he was really honest about it, he'd felt such

pressure to keep the business going the same way that his father had always run things. After his parents had died in the crash, he'd needed to keep things stable for everyone who worked in the business, and keeping to the way things had always been done seemed the best way to keep everything on a stable footing.

He'd been so busy keeping the business going. And then, once he'd proved to his staff and his competitors that he was more than capable of running the business well, he'd been so busy making sure that things stayed that way that he just simply hadn't had the time to think about what he wanted.

Just before his parents' accident, he'd been working on some new product ideas. Something that would've been his contribution to the way the family business developed. He'd loved doing the research and development work. But he'd had to shelve it all after the accident, and he'd never had time to go back to his ideas.

Though it was pointless dwelling on might-have-beens. Things were as they were. And the sudden feeling of uncertainty made him antsy.

Sean had intended to ask Claire to stay, that night; but right at that moment he needed some distance between them, to get his equilibrium back. 'I'd better check to see if your clothes are dry.'

They were. So it was easy to suggest making a cold drink while she got dressed. Easier still to hint that it was time for her to go home—particularly as Claire took the hint. He let her walk out of the door without kissing her goodbye.

And he spent the rest of the evening wide awake, miserable and regretting it. She'd pushed him and he'd done what he always did and closed off, not wanting her to get too close.

But her words went round and round in his head. *What's your dream?*

The problem was, you couldn't always follow your dreams. Not if you had responsibilities and other people depended on you.

Everybody has a dream, Sean.

What did he really want?

He sat at his desk, staring out of the window at a garden it was too dark to see. Then he gritted his teeth, turned back to his computer and opened a file.

Dreams were a luxury. And he had a business to run—one that had just managed to survive a takeover bid. Dreams would have to wait.

CHAPTER TEN

SEAN SPENT THE next day totally unable to concentrate.

Which was ridiculous because he never, but never, let any of his girlfriends distract him from work.

But Claire Stewart was different, and she got under his skin in a way that nobody ever had before. He definitely wasn't letting her do it, but it was happening all the same—and he really didn't know what to do about it.

Part of him wanted to call her because he wanted to see her; and part of him was running scared because she made him look at things in his life that he'd rather ignore.

And he still couldn't get her words out of his head. *Everybody has a dream, Sean.* Just what was his?

He still hadn't worked out what to say to her by the evening, so he buried himself in work instead. And he noticed that she hadn't called him, either. So did that mean she, too, thought this was turning out to be a seriously bad idea and they ought to end it?

And then, on Tuesday morning, his PA brought him a plain white box.

'What's this?' he asked.

Jen shrugged. 'I have no idea. I was just asked to give it to you.'

There was no note with the box. He frowned. 'Who brought it?'

'A blonde woman. She wouldn't give her name. She said you'd know who it was from,' Jen said.

His heart skipped a beat.

Claire.

But if Claire had actually come to the factory and dropped this off personally, why hadn't she come to see him?

Or maybe she thought he'd refuse to see her. They hadn't exactly had a fight on Sunday evening, but he had to acknowledge that things had been a little bit strained when she'd left. Maybe this was her idea of a parley, the beginning of some kind of truce.

And hadn't she said about not sending him flowers and how you couldn't give chocolates to a confectioner?

'Thank you. I have a pretty good idea who it's from,' he said to Jen, and waited until she'd closed the door behind her before opening the box.

Claire had brought him cake.

Not just cake—the most delectable lemon cake he'd ever eaten in his life.

He gave in and called her business line.

She answered within three rings. 'Dream of a Dress, Claire speaking.'

'Thank you for the cake,' he said.

'Pleasure.'

Her voice was completely neutral, so he couldn't tell her mood. Well, he'd do things her way for once and ask her straight out. 'Why didn't you come in and say hello?'

'Your PA said you were in a meeting, and I didn't really have time to wait until you were done.'

'Fair enough.' He paused. He knew what he needed to say, and he was enough of a man not to shirk it. 'Claire, I owe you an apology.'

'What for?'

'Pushing you away on Sunday night.'

'Uh-huh.'

He sighed, guessing what she wanted him to say. 'I still can't answer your question.'

'Can't or won't?'

'A bit of both, if I'm honest,' he said.

'OK. Are you busy tonight?'

'Why?' he asked.

'I thought we could go and smell some roses.'

Claire-speak for having some fun, he guessed.

'Can you meet me at my place?'

'Sure. Would seven work for you?'

'Fine. Don't eat,' she said, 'because we can probably grab something on the way. Some of the food stalls at Camden Lock will still be open at that time.'

Clearly she intended to take him for a walk somewhere. 'And is this a jeans and running shoes thing?' he checked.

'You can wear your prissiest suit and your smartest shoes—whatever you like, as long as you can walk for half an hour or so and still be comfortable.'

When Sean turned up at her shop at exactly seven o'clock, Claire was wearing a navy summer dress patterned with daisies and flat court shoes. Her hair was tied back with another chiffon scarf—clearly that was Claire's favoured style—but he was pleased that she didn't add her awful khaki cap, this time. Instead, she just donned a pair of dark glasses.

They walked down to Camden Lock, grabbed a burger and shared some polenta fries, then headed along the canalside towards Regent's Park. He'd never really explored the area before, and it was a surprisingly pretty walk; some of the houses were truly gorgeous, and all the while there were birds singing in the trees and the calm presence of the canal.

'I love the walk along here. It's only ten minutes or so between the lock and the park,' she said.

And then Sean discovered that Claire had meant it literally about coming to smell the roses when she took him across Regent's Park to Queen Mary's Garden.

'This place is amazing—it's the biggest collection of roses in London,' she told him.

There were pretty bowers, huge beds filled with all different types of roses, and walking through them was like breathing pure scent; it totally filled his senses.

'This is incredible,' he said. 'I didn't think you meant it literally about smelling the roses.'

'I meant it metaphorically as well—you must know that WH Davies poem, "What is this life if full of care, We have no time to stand and stare,",' she said. 'You have to make time for things like this, Sean, or you miss out on so much.'

He knew she had a point. 'Yeah,' he said softly, and tightened his fingers round hers.

He could just about remember coming to see the roses in Regent's Park as a child, but everything since his parents' death was a blur of work, work and more work.

Six years of blurriness.

Being with Claire had brought everything into sharp focus again. Though Sean wasn't entirely sure he liked what he saw when he looked at his life—and it made him antsy. Claire was definitely dangerous to his peace of mind.

She drew him over to look at the borders of delphiniums, every shade of white and cream and blue through to almost black.

'Now these I *really* love,' she said. 'The colour, the shape, the texture—everything.'

He looked at her. 'So you're a secret gardener?'

'Except doing it properly would take time I don't really have to spare,' she said. 'Though, yes, if had a decent-sized garden I'd plant it as a cottage garden with loads of these and hollyhocks and foxgloves, and tiny little lily-of-the-valley and violets.'

'These ones here are exactly the same colour as your eyes.'

She grinned. 'Careful, Sean. You're waxing a bit poetic.'

Just to make the point, he kissed her.

'Tsk,' she teased. 'Is that the only way you have to shut me up?'

'It worked for Benedick,' he said.

'*Much Ado* is a rom-com—and I thought you said you didn't like rom-coms?'

'I said I didn't mind ones with great dialogue—and dialogue doesn't get any better than Beatrice.' He could see Claire playing Beatrice; he'd noticed that she often had that deliciously acerbic bite to her words.

'And it's a good plot,' she said, 'except Hero ends up with a man who isn't good enough for her. I hate the bit where Claudio shames her on their wedding day, and it always makes me want to yell to her, "Don't do it!" at the end when she marries him.'

'They were different times and different mores, though I do know what you mean,' he said. 'I wouldn't want Ashleigh to marry a weak, selfish man.'

She winced. 'Like Rob Riverton. And I introduced her to him.'

'Not one of your better calls,' Sean said.

'I know.' She looked guilty. 'I did tell her to dump

him because he wasn't good enough for her and he didn't treat her properly.'

A month ago, Sean wouldn't have believed that. Now, he did, because he'd seen for himself that Claire had integrity. 'Claire,' he said, yanked her into his arms and kissed her.

'Was that to shut me up again?' she asked when he broke the kiss.

'No—it was because you're irresistible.'

She clearly didn't know what to say to that, because it silenced her.

They walked back along the canalside to Camden, hand in hand; then he bought them both a glass of wine and they sat outside, enjoying the late evening sunshine before walking back to her flat.

'Do you want to come in?' she asked.

'Is that wise?'

'Probably not, but I'm asking anyway.'

'Probably not,' he agreed, 'but I'm saying yes.'

They sat with the windows open, the curtains open and music playing; there was a jug of iced water on the coffee table, and she'd put frozen slices of lime in the jug. Sean was surprised by how at home he felt here; the room was decorated in very girly colours, compared to his own neutral colour scheme, but he felt as if he belonged.

'It's getting late. I ought to go,' he said softly. 'I have meetings, first thing.'

'You don't have to go,' Claire said. 'You could stay.' She paused. 'If you want to.'

'Are you sure?'

'I'm sure.'

In answer, he closed her curtains and carried her to her bed.

* * *

The next morning, Claire woke before her alarm went off to find herself alone in bed, and Sean's side of the bed was stone cold. She was a bit disappointed that he hadn't even woken her before he left, or put a note on the pillow. Then again, he'd said that he had early meetings. He'd probably left at some unearthly hour and hadn't wanted to disturb her sleep.

At that precise moment he walked in, carrying a tray with two paper cups of coffee and a plate of pastries. 'Breakfast is served, my lady.'

'You went out to buy us breakfast? That's—that's so *lovely*,' she said, sitting up, 'but you really didn't have to. I have fruit and yoghurt in the fridge, plus bread and granola in the cupboard.'

'I noticed a bakery round the corner from yours. I thought croissants might be nice, and I'm running a bit short on time so I bought the coffee rather than making it.'

'That sounds to me like an excuse for having decadent tendencies,' she teased.

He laughed back. 'Maybe.'

He sat on the bed and shared the almond-filled croissants with her. 'You thought I'd gone without saying goodbye, didn't you?'

'Um—well, yes,' she admitted.

'I wouldn't do that to you. I would at least have left you a note.' He finished his coffee and kissed her lightly. 'Sorry. I really *do* have to go now. Can I call you later?'

'I'd like that.' Claire wrapped herself in her robe so she could pad barefoot to the kitchen with him and kiss him goodbye at her front door.

She still couldn't quite get over the fact he'd gone out to buy them a decadent breakfast. And he'd stayed last night. This thing between them was moving so incredibly fast; it scared and exhilarated her at the same time. She guessed it would be the same for Sean. But would it scare him enough to make him push her away again, the way he had the other night? Or would he finally let her in?

They were both busy during the week, but Sean texted her on Friday.

Do you have any appointments over lunch?

Sorry, yes.

And, regretfully, she wasn't playing hard to get. She really did have appointments that she couldn't move.

OK. Are you busy after work?

Yes, but that was something she could move.

Why?

Am trying to be like you and plan a spontaneous date.

She couldn't help laughing. Planning and spontaneity didn't go together.

OK.

Cinema? he suggested.

Depends. Is popcorn on offer?

Could be... he texted back.

Deal. Time and place?

Can pick you up.

She wanted to keep at least some of her independence.

Saves time if I meet you there.

OK. Will check out films and text you where and when.

Claire had expected him to choose some kind of noir movie, but when she got to the cinema and met him with a kiss she discovered that he'd picked a rom-com.

'Is this to indulge me?' she asked.

'I've seen this one before. The structure's good and the acting's good,' he said.

'You're such a film snob,' she teased, but it warmed her that he'd thought of what she'd enjoy rather than imposing his choices on her regardless.

They sat in the back row, holding hands, and Claire enjoyed the film thoroughly. Back at his place afterwards, they were curled in bed together, when Sean said, 'I had a focus group meeting today.'

She remembered the samples he'd given her. 'Did it go how you wanted?'

'Not really,' he said. 'We need a rethink.'

'For what it's worth, I've always thought that your caramel hearts would be great as bridal favours. That's the sort of thing my brides always ask me if I know about, because not everyone likes the traditional sugared almonds.'

'Bridal favours?' he queried.

'Uh-huh—the hearts could be wrapped in silver or

gold foil, and you can offer a choice of organza bags with them in say white, silver or gold, so brides can buy the whole package. They could be ordered direct from your website, or you could offer the special bridal package through selected shops.'

He nodded. 'That's brilliant, Claire. Thank you. I never even considered that sort of thing.'

'Why would you, unless you were connected to a wedding business?' she pointed out.

'I guess not.'

'So why didn't the focus group like the salted caramels? I thought they were fabulous.'

'It's a move too far from the core business. Farrell's has produced hard toffee for generations. We're not really associated with chocolates, apart from the caramel hearts—which were my mum's idea.'

'Are you looking to move away from making toffee, then?'

'Yes and no,' he said. 'What I want to do is look at other sorts of toffee.'

She frowned. 'Am I being dense? Because toffee's—well—toffee.'

'Unless it's in something,' he said. 'Toffee popcorn, like the one you chose tonight at the cinema. Or toffee ice cream.'

'You weren't concentrating on the film, were you?' she asked. 'You were thinking about work.'

'I was thinking about you, actually,' he said. 'But the toffee popcorn did set off a lightbulb in the back of my head.' He wrinkled his nose. 'If I took the business in that direction, it'd mean buying a whole different set of machinery and arranging a whole different set of staff training. I'd need to be sure that the investment would be worth the cost and Farrell's would see a good return on the money.'

'Unless,' she said, 'you collaborated with other manufacturers—ones who already have the factory set-up and the staff. Maybe you could license them to use your toffee.'

'That's a great idea. And I could draw up a shortlist of other family-run businesses whose ideas and ethos are the same as Farrell's. People who'd make good business partners.'

'That's your dream, isn't it?' she asked softly. 'To keep your heritage—but to put your own stamp on it.'

'I guess. Research and development was always my favourite thing,' he admitted. 'I wanted to look at developing different flavours of toffee. Something different from mint, treacle, orange or nut. I was thinking cinnamon or ginger for Christmas, or maybe special seasonal editions of the chocolate hearts—say a strawberries and cream version for summer.'

'That's a great idea,' she said. 'Maybe white chocolate.'

'And different packaging,' he said. 'Something to position Farrell's hearts as the kind of thing you buy as special treats.'

'You could sell them in little boxes as well as big ones,' she said. 'For people who want a treat but don't want a big box.'

He kissed her. 'I'm beginning to think that I should employ you on my R and D team.'

'Now that,' she said, 'really wouldn't work. I'm used to doing things my way and I'd hate to have to go by someone else's rules all the while. Besides, I don't want you bossing me about and I think we'd end up fighting.'

He wrinkled his nose. 'I don't want to fight with you, Claire—I like how things are now.'

'Me, too,' she admitted.

'Make love, not war—that's a great slogan, you know.'

She grinned. 'Just as long as it's not all talk and no action, Mr Farrell.'

He laughed. 'I can take a hint.' And he kissed her until she was dizzy.

CHAPTER ELEVEN

OVER THE NEXT couple of weeks, Claire and Sean grew closer. Claire didn't get to see Sean every evening, but she talked to him every day and found herself really looking forward to the times they did see each other. And even on days when things were frustrating and refused to go right, or she had a client who changed her mind about what she wanted at least twice a day, it wasn't so bad because Claire knew she would be seeing Sean or talking to him later.

And he indulged her by taking her to one of her favourite places—the Victoria and Albert Museum. She took him to see her favourite pieces of clothing, showing him the fabrics, the shapes and the stitching that had inspired some of her own designs. When they stopped for a cold drink in the café, she looked at him.

'Sorry. I rather went into nerd mode. You should have told me to shut up.'

He smiled. 'Actually, I really enjoyed it.'

'But I was lecturing you, making you look at fiddly bits and pieces that probably bored you stupid.'

'You were lit up, Claire. Clothing design is your passion. And it was a privilege to see it,' he said softly. He reached across the table, took her hand and drew it to his lips. 'Don't ever lose that passion.'

He'd accepted her for who she was, Claire thought with sudden shock. The first man she'd ever dated who'd seen who she was, accepted it, and encouraged her to do what she loved.

In turn, Sean gave her a personal guided tour of the toffee factory. 'I'm afraid the white coat and the hair covering are non-negotiable,' he said.

'Health and safety. This is a working factory. And the clothes are about function, not form—just as they should be,' she said.

'I guess.' He took her through the factory, explaining what the various stages were and letting her taste the different products.

'I love the fact you're still using your great-grandparents' recipe for the toffee,' she said. 'And the photographs.' She'd noticed the blown-up photographs from years before lining the walls in the reception area. 'It's lovely to see that connection over the years.'

'A bit like you,' he said, 'and the way you hand-decorate a dress exactly the same as they would've done it two hundred years ago.'

'I guess.'

They were halfway through when Sean's sales manager came over.

'Sean, I'm really sorry to interrupt,' he said, smiling acknowledgement at Claire. 'I'm afraid we've got a bit of a situation.'

'Hey—don't mind me,' Claire said. 'The business comes first. I can do a tour at any time.'

'Thanks,' Sean said. 'What's the problem, Will?'

'I had the press on the phone earlier, talking about the takeover bid,' Will said. 'I explained that it's not happening and Farrell's is carrying on exactly as before, but someone's clearly been spreading doubts among our biggest customers, because I've been fielding phone calls ever since. And one of our customers in particular says he wants to talk to the organ grinder, not the monkey.'

'You're my sales manager,' Sean said. 'Which makes you as much of an organ grinder as I am.'

Will looked awkward. 'Not in Mel Archer's eyes.'

'Ah. *Him.*' Sean grimaced. 'Claire, would you mind if I let Will finish the tour with you?'

'Sure,' she said.

'I'll talk to Archer and explain the situation to him,' Sean said. 'And I'll make it very clear to him that I trust my senior team to do their jobs well and use their initiative.'

'Sorry.'

'It's not your fault,' Sean said. 'I'll see you later, Claire.'

She smiled at him. 'No worries. I'll wait for you in reception.'

'Sorry. It's the monkey rather than the organ grinder for you, too,' Will said.

She smiled. 'Sean says you're an organ grinder. That's good enough for me.'

Will finished taking her round and answered all her questions. Including ones she knew she probably shouldn't ask but couldn't help herself; this was a chance to see another side of Sean.

'So have you worked for Sean for long?' she asked Will.

'Three years,' Will said. 'And he's probably the best manager I've ever worked with. He doesn't micromanage—he trusts you to get on and do your job, though he's always there if things get sticky.'

'Which I guess they would be, in a toffee factory,' Claire said with a smile.

Will laughed. 'Yeah. Pun not actually intended. What I mean is he knows the business inside out. He's there if you need support, and if there's a problem you can't solve he'll have an answer—though what he does is ask you questions to make you think a bit more about it and work it out for yourself.'

So her super-efficient businessman liked to teach people and develop his staff, too. And it was something she knew he wouldn't have told her himself.

From the half of the tour Sean had given her and the insights Will added, Claire realised that maybe Sean really was living his dream; he really did love the factory and his job, and not just because it was his heritage and he felt duty-bound to preserve it for the next generation. Though she rather thought that if he'd had a choice in the matter, he would've worked in the research and development side of the business.

'He's a good man,' she said, meaning it.

When Ashleigh and Luke returned from their honeymoon, they invited Claire over to see the wedding photographs. She arrived bearing champagne and brownies. Sean was there already, and she gave him a cool nod of acknowledgement before cooing over the photographs and choosing the ones she wanted copies of.

A little later, he offered to help her make coffee. 'Have I done something to upset you?' he asked softly when they were alone in Ashleigh's kitchen.

'No.' Clare frowned. 'What makes you think that?'

'Just you seemed a little cool with me tonight.'

'In front of Ash, yes—she expects me to be just on the verge of civil with you. If I'm nice to you, she's going to guess something's going on, and I don't want her to know about this.' Claire took a deep breath. 'She's already asked me a couple of questions, and I told her we came to a kind of truce in Capri—once you realised it wasn't my fault her wedding dress disappeared—and you were one step away from grovelling.'

'You told her I was *grovelling*?'

Claire grinned. 'She just laughed and said grovelling isn't in your vocabulary, and she'd give it a week before we started sniping at each other again.'

He moved closer. 'I'm definitely not grovelling, but I'm not sniping either.' He paused. 'In fact, I'd rather just kiss you.'

'I'd rather that, too,' she said softly, 'but I'm not ready for Ash to know about this yet.'

'So I'm your dirty little secret?'

'For now—and I'm yours,' she said.

At the end of the evening, Sean said, 'Claire, it's raining—I'll give you a lift home to save you getting drenched.'

'This is quite some truce,' Ashleigh said, giving them both a piercing look. 'Though you probably won't make it back to Claire's before the ceasefire ends.'

'I won't fight if she doesn't,' Sean said. 'Claire?'

'No fighting, and thank you very much for the offer of the lift.'

Ashleigh narrowed her eyes at both of them, but didn't say any more.

'Do you have any idea how close you were to breaking our cover?' Claire asked crossly on the way home. 'I'm sure Ash has guessed.'

'What's your problem with anyone knowing about you and me?' Sean asked.

'Because it's still early days. And, actually, unless my calendar's wrong, you'll be dumping me in the next few days anyway.'

'How do you work that out?'

'Because, Sean Farrell, you never date anyone for more than three weeks in a row.'

'I don't dump my girlfriends exactly three weeks in to a relationship,' he said. 'That's a little old and a little unfair.'

'But you dump them,' Claire persisted.

'No, I break up with them nicely and I make them feel it's their decision,' he corrected.

'When it's actually yours.'

He shrugged. 'If it makes them feel better about the situation, what's the problem?'

'You're impossible.'

He laughed. 'Ashleigh said we wouldn't make it back to your place before we started fighting. She was right.'

'I'm not fighting, I'm just making a statement of facts—and don't you dare kiss me to shut me up,' she warned.

'I can't kiss you when I'm driving,' Sean pointed out, 'so that's a rain check.'

'You really are the most exasperating…' Unable to think of a suitable retort, she lapsed into silence.

'Besides,' he said softly, 'you'd be bored to tears with a yes-man or a lapdog.'

'Lapdog?' she asked, not following.

'"When husbands or when lapdogs breathe their last." Alexander Pope,' he explained helpfully.

She rolled her eyes. 'I forgot you did English A level.'

'And dated a couple of English teachers.'

'Would one of those have been the one who made you see a certain rom-com more than once?'

'Yes. At least you haven't done that.'

'You're still impossible,' she grumbled.

'Yup,' he said cheerfully.

'And, excuse me, you just missed the turning to my place.'

'Because we're not going to your place. We're going to mine.'

'But I have a bride coming in first thing tomorrow morning for a final fitting,' she protested.

'I have a washer-dryer, an alarm clock, a spare un-used toothbrush, and I'll run you home after breakfast.'

She sighed. 'You've got an answer for everything.'

'Most things,' he corrected, and she groaned.

'I give up.'

'Good,' he said.

He stripped her very slowly once he'd locked his front door behind them, put her clothes in the laundry, then took her to bed. And he was as good as his word, finding her a spare toothbrush, making her coffee in the morning, making sure her clothes were dried, and taking her home.

She kissed him lingeringly in the car. 'See you later. And thanks for the lift.'

Ashleigh dropped by at lunchtime.

'Well, hello, stranger—long time, no see,' Claire teased. 'What is it, a little over twelve hours?'

'We're having lunch,' Ashleigh said. 'Now.'

'Why does this feel as if you're about to tell me off?' Claire asked.

'Because I am. When did this all happen?'

Claire tried to look innocent. 'When did all what happen?'

'You know perfectly well what I mean. You and my brother. And don't deny it. You're both acting totally out of character round each other.'

'He just gave me a lift home last night,' Claire said,

crossing her fingers under the table. It had been a lot more than that.

'Hmm.' Ashleigh folded her arms and gave Claire a level stare.

Claire gave in. 'Ash, it's early days. And you know Sean; it's probably not going to last.'

'Why didn't you tell me?'

'Because when it all goes wrong I don't want our friendship to be collateral damage.'

Ashleigh hugged her. 'Idiot. Nothing would stop me being friends with you.'

'Sean doesn't want you to be collateral damage, either,' Claire pointed out.

Ashleigh rolled her eyes. 'I won't be, and don't you go overprotective on me like my big brother is—remember I'm older than you.'

'OK,' Claire said meekly.

'I thought something was up when he helped you make coffee, and then when he offered you a lift home...I knew it for sure,' Ashleigh said.

'It's still really, really early days,' Claire warned.

'But it's working,'

'At the moment. We still fight, but it's different now.' Claire smiled. 'Sean's not quite as regimented as I thought he was.'

Ashleigh laughed. 'Not with you around, he won't be.'

'And he's stopped calling me the Mistress of Chaos.'

'Good, because you're not.' Ashleigh hugged her again. 'I can't think of anyone I'd like more as my sister-in-law. I've always thought of you as like my sister anyway.'

'We haven't been together long,' Claire warned, 'so I'm not promising anything.'

'I think,' Ashleigh said, 'that you'll be good for each other.'

'Promise me you won't say anything? Even to Luke?'

'It's a bit too late for Luke,' Ashleigh said, 'but I won't say anything to Sean.'

'Thank you. And you'll be the first to know if things move forward. Or,' Claire said, 'when we break up.'

In the two weeks before the wedding show Claire was crazily busy and had almost no free time for dates. Sean took over and brought in takeaways to make sure she ate in the evenings; he also made her take breaks before her eyes started hurting, and gave her massages when her shoulders ached.

Even though part of Claire thought he was being just a little bit overprotective, she was grateful for the TLC. 'I really appreciate this, Sean.'

'I know, and you'd do the same for me if I had an exhibition,' he pointed out. 'By the way, I'm in talks with a couple of manufacturers about joint projects and licensing. Talking to you and brainstorming stuff like that,' he said, 'really helped me see the way I want the company to go in the future.'

'Following your dreams?'

'Maybe,' he said with a smile, and kissed her.

The week before the wedding show, Claire took Sean to meet her family—her father, her grandmother, Aunt Lou and her cousins. Clearly she'd talked to them about him, Sean thought, because they already seemed to know who he was and lots about him. Then he realised that they knew Ashleigh and his background was the same as hers.

Even though they were warm and welcoming and

treated him as if he were one of them, chatting and laughing and teasing him, he still felt strange. His grandparents would've been older than Claire's and had died when he was in his teens. This was the first time for years that Sean had been in a family situation where he wasn't being the protective big brother and the head of the family, and it made him feel lost, not knowing quite where he was supposed to fit in.

It didn't help that Claire's father grilled him mercilessly about his intentions towards Claire. Sean could understand it—he shared Jacob's opinion of Claire's previous boyfriends, at least the ones that he'd met—but it still grated that he'd be judged alongside them.

And he could also see what Claire meant about her dad not believing in her. Jacob didn't see the point of spending time and money making six sets of wedding clothes that hadn't actually been ordered by clients, and he'd said a couple of times during the evening that he couldn't see how Claire would possibly get a return on her investment. Claire had smiled sweetly and glossed over it, but Sean had seen that little pleat between her brows that only appeared when she was really unhappy about something. Clearly she was hurt by the way her father still didn't believe in her.

Well, maybe he could give Jacob Stewart something to think about. 'I always do trade shows,' he said. 'They're really good for awareness—and it makes new customers consider stocking you when they see the quality of your product.'

'Maybe,' Jacob said.

'I don't know if you saw the dress Claire made for my sister, but it was absolutely amazing. She's really good at what she does. And what gives her the extra edge is that she loves what she does, too. That gives her clients confidence. And it's why they tell all their friends about her. Her referral rate is stunning.'

Jacob said nothing, but raised an eyebrow.

Sean decided not to push it any further—the last thing he wanted was for Jacob to upset Claire any further on the subject and knock her confidence at this late stage—but he had to hide a smile when he saw the fervent thumbs-up that Claire's grandmother and aunt did out of Jacob's viewpoint.

Though he was quiet when he drove Claire home.

'I'm sorry, Sean. I shouldn't have asked you to meet them—it's too early,' she said, guessing why he was quiet and getting it totally wrong. 'It's just, well, they'll all be coming to the wedding show and I thought it'd be better if you met them before rather than spring it on you then.'

'No, it was nice to meet them,' he said. 'I liked them.' He wanted to shake her father, but judged it not the most tactful thing to say.

'They liked you—and Dad approved of you, which has to be a first.'

He couldn't hide his surprise. 'Even though I argued with him?'

'You batted my corner,' she said. 'And I appreciate that. I think he did, too. Dad's just…a bit difficult.'

'He'll come round in the end,' Sean said. 'When he sees your collection on the catwalk, he'll understand.'

'Hardly. He's a guy. So he's not the slightest bit interested in dresses,' Claire said, though to Sean's relief this time she was smiling rather than looking upset. 'I just have to remember not to let it get to me.'

'You're going to be brilliant,' Sean said. 'Come on. Let's go to bed.'

She smiled. 'I thought you'd never ask…'

* * *

Over the next week, Claire worked later and later on last-minute changes to the wedding show outfits, and the only way Sean could get her out of her workroom for dinner was to haul her manually over his shoulder and carry her out of the room.

'You need to eat to keep your strength up, and you can't live off sandwiches for the next week,' he told her, 'or you'll make yourself ill.'

'I guess.' She blinked as she took in the fact that her kitchen was actually being used and something smelled gorgeous. 'Hang on, dinner isn't a takeaway.'

'It's nothing fancy, either,' Sean said dryly, 'but it's home-cooked from scratch and there are proper vegetables.' He gave her a rueful smile. 'And at least you have gadgets that help.'

'My electric steamer. Best gadget ever.' She smiled back and stroked his face. 'Sean, thank you. It's really good of you to do this for me.'

'Any time, and you know you'd do the same if I was the one up to my eyes in preparation for a big event, so it's not a big deal.' He kissed her lightly. 'Sit down, milady, because dinner will be served in about thirty seconds.'

But when he'd dished up and they were eating, he noticed that she was pushing her food around her plate. 'Is my cooking that terrible? You don't have to be polite with me—leave it if you hate it.'

'It's wonderful. I'm just tired.' She made an effort to eat.

He tried to distract her a little. 'So do you have a dream of a dress?'

'Not really,' she said.

'So all these years when you've sketched wedding

dresses, you never once drew the one you wanted for yourself?'

'I guess it would depend when and where I got married—if it was on a beach in the Seychelles I wouldn't pick the same dress, veil or shoes as I'd pick for a tiny country church in the middle of winter in, say, the far north of Scotland.'

'I guess,' he said. 'So which kind of wedding would you prefer?'

'It's all academic,' she said.

He could guess why she wasn't answering him—she was obviously worried he'd think she was hinting and had expectations where he was concerned.

'Is that why the outfits in your wedding collection are so diverse?'

'Yes—four seasonal weddings, one vintage-inspired outfit, and one that's more tailored towards a civil wedding,' she explained.

'That's a good range,' he said. 'It will show people what you can do.'

'I hope so.' For a second she looked really worried and vulnerable.

'Claire, you know your stuff, you're good at what you do and your work is really going to shine at the show.' He reached over to squeeze her hand. 'I believe in you.'

'Thank you, though I wasn't fishing for compliments.'

'I know you weren't, and I was being sincere.'

'Sorry.' She wrinkled her nose. 'Ignore me. It's just a bit of stage fright, or whatever the catwalk equivalent is.'

'Which is totally understandable, given that it's your first show.' He cleared their plates away. 'Let me get you some coffee.'

She gave him a tired smile. 'Sorry, I'm really not pulling my weight in this relationship right now.'

'Claire, you're so busy you barely have time to breathe. I'm not going to give you a hard time about that; I just want to take some of the weight off your shoulders,' he said.

'Then thank you. Coffee would be lovely.'

He made two mugs of coffee and set them on the table. 'This is decaf,' he said, 'because I think you're already going to have enough trouble getting to sleep and the last thing you need is caffeine.'

'I guess.'

And he hoped that what he was about to do would distract her enough to let her fall asleep in his arms tonight and stop worrying quite so much about the wedding show.

He rescued the box he'd stowed in her fridge earlier—a box containing a very important message. He checked behind the door that he hadn't accidentally disturbed the contents of the box and mixed up the order of the lettered chocolates, then brought out and placed the box on the table in front of her.

She gave him a tired smile. 'Would these be some of your awesome salted caramels? Or are you trying out new stuff on me as your personal focus group?'

'Open the box and see,' he invited.

She did so, and her eyes widened as she read the message. When she looked back at him, he could see the sheen of tears in her eyes. *'Sean.'*

'Hey. They say you should say it with flowers, but I know you like to be different, so I thought I'd say it in chocolate.' He'd iced the letters himself. *I love you Claire.* He paused. 'Or maybe I just need to say it.' He swallowed hard. Funny how his throat felt as if it were filled with sand. 'I've never said this to anyone before. I love you, Claire. I think I probably have for years, but the idea of letting anyone close scared me spitless. You know you asked me what scared me? *That.* Deep down guess I was worried that I'd end up losing my partner like I lost my parents, so it was easier to keep you at a distance.'

'So what changed?' she asked.

'Capri,' he said. 'Seeing the way you just got on with things and sorted out the problems when Ashleigh's dress went missing. And then dancing with you. I really couldn't take my eyes off you—it wasn't just the song. I tried to tell myself that it was just physical attraction, but it's more than that. So very much more.'

'Oh, Sean.' She blinked back the tears.

And now he just couldn't shut up. 'And in these last few weeks, getting to know you, I've seen you for who you really are. You're funny and you're brave and you're bossy, and you think outside the box, and—you know your speed dating question thing, about what you're looking for in a partner? I can answer that, now. I'm looking for *you*, Claire. You're everything I want.' He gave her a wry smile. 'Though my timing's a bit rubbish, given that you're up to your eyes right now.'

'Your timing's perfect,' she said softly. 'You know, I had a huge crush on you when I was fourteen, but you were my best friend's older brother, which made you off limits. And you always made me feel as if I was a nuisance.'

'You probably were, when you were a teenager.'

She laughed. 'Tell it to me straight, why don't you?'

He laughed back. 'You wouldn't have it any other way, and you know it—I love you, Claire.'

'I love you, too, Sean.' She pushed her chair back, came round to his side of the table, wrapped her arms round him and kissed him. 'Over the last few weeks

I've got to know you and you're not quite who I thought you were, either. You're this human dynamo but you also think on your feet. You're not regimented and rule-bound.'

'No?'

'Well, maybe just a little bit—and you do look good in a suit.' She smiled at him. 'Though how I really like you dressed is in faded jeans, and a white shirt with the sleeves rolled up. It makes you much more touchable.'

'Noted,' he said.

He could see that she was so tired, she didn't even have the energy to drink her coffee. So he carried her to bed, cherished her, and let her fall asleep in his arms. He wasn't ready to sleep yet; it was good just to lie in the dark with her in his arms, thinking. How amazing it was that she felt the same way about him. So maybe, just maybe, this was going to work out.

CHAPTER TWELVE

ON THE MORNING of the wedding show, Claire was up before six, bustling around and double-checking things on her list.

Then her mobile phone rang. Sean couldn't tell much from Claire's end of the conversation, but her face had turned white and there was a tiny pleat above her nose that told him something was definitely wrong.

When she ended the call, she blew out a breath. 'Sorry, I'm going to have to neglect you and make a ton of phone calls now.'

'What's happened?'

'That was the modelling agency.' She closed her eyes for a moment. 'It seems that the six male models that I booked through the agency are all really good friends. They went out together for a meal last night, and they've all gone down with food poisoning so they can't do the show.'

'So the agency's going to send you someone else?'

She shook her head. 'All their models are either already booked out or away. So they're very sorry to let me down, but it's due to circumstances beyond their control and they're sure I'll understand, and of course they'll return my fee.'

The sing-song, patronising tone in which she replayed the conversation told Sean just how angry Claire was—and he wasn't surprised. She'd been very badly let down.

'I'll just have to go through my diary and beg a few favours, and hope that I can find six men willing to stand in for the models.' She raked a hand through her hair. 'And I need to look at my list and see where I can cut a few corners, because I'll have to alter their clothes to fit the stand-ins, and…' She shook her head, looking utterly miserable.

He put his arms round her and hugged her. 'You need five. I'll do it.'

She stared at him as if the words hadn't quite sunk in. '*You'll* do it?'

'Well, obviously I don't know the first thing about a catwalk,' he said, 'so someone's going to have to teach me how to do the model walk thing. But everyone's going to be looking at the clothes and not the model in any case, so I guess that probably doesn't matter too much.'

'You'll do it,' she repeated, sounding disbelieving.

'Is it that much of a stretch to see me as a model?' he asked wryly.

'No, it's not that at all. You'd be *fabulous*. It's just that—it's a pretty public thing, standing on a catwalk at a wedding show with everyone staring at you, and it's so far from what you normally do that I thought you'd find it too embarrassing or awkward or…' She tailed off. 'Oh, my God, Sean. You'd really do that for me?'

'Yes,' he said firmly.

'Thank you.' She hugged him fiercely. 'That means I only have to find five.'

'You've already got enough to do. I'll find them for you,' he said. 'I reckon we can count on Luke and Tom, and I have a few others in mind. Just tell me the rough heights and sizes you need, and I'll ring round and sort it out.'

'Your height and build would be perfect, but I can adjust things if I need to—the men's outfits are easier to adjust than the women's, so I guess I'm lucky that it was the male models and not the female ones or the children who had to bail out on me. Sean, are you really sure about this?'

'Really,' he confirmed. 'I'm on Team Claire, remember? Now go hit that shower, I'll have coffee ready by the time you're out, and I'll start ringing round.'

She hugged him. 'Have I told you how wonderful you are? Five minutes ago it felt as if the world had ended, and now...'

'Hey—you'd do the same for me,' he pointed out.

Half an hour later, Sean had it all arranged. Luke and Tom agreed immediately to stand in, plus Tom's partner. Sean called in his best friend and his sales manager from the factory, and they all agreed to meet him and Claire at the wedding show two hours before it started, so Claire could do any last-minute necessary alterations to their outfits. Then he made Claire sit down and eat breakfast, before helping her to load everything into the van she'd hired for the day.

'Sure we've got all the wedding dresses?' he asked before he closed the van doors. 'Though I guess we're going to Earl's Court rather than Capri, so we should be OK.'

'Not funny, Sean.' She narrowed her eyes at him.

He kissed her lightly. 'That was misplaced humour and I apologise. It's all going to be fine, Claire. Just breathe and check your list.'

'Sorry, I'm being unfair and overly grouchy. Ignore

me.' She looked over her list. 'Everything's ticked off and loaded, so we're ready to roll.'

'At least we've got the bumps out of the way this side of the catwalk. It's all going to be fine now.' He kissed her again. 'By the way, I meant to tell you, I've got some extra giveaways for you. Will from the office is bringing them to the show.'

'Giveaways?' Her eyes went wide. 'Oh, no. I completely forgot about giveaways. I meant to order some pens. I've been so focused on the outfits that it totally slipped my mind.'

'You have business cards?'

'Yes.'

'Grab them,' he said, 'and we'll get a production line stuffing them at the show.'

'Stuffing what?' She looked at him blankly.

'My genius girlfriend talked about wedding favours. I had some samples run up, with white organza bags and gold foil on the caramel hearts. The bag is just the right size to put your business card in as well—and don't worry about the pens. Everyone will remember the chocolate.'

'Sean, that's above and beyond.'

'No, it's supporting you,' he corrected, 'and it also works as a test run for me, so we both win. Let's get this show on the road.'

At the wedding show, people were busy setting up exhibition stands and the place was bustling. Claire was busy measuring her new male models and doing alterations; then, when the female models arrived, she filled them in on the situation and got them to teach the men how to walk. Her stand was set up with showbooks of her designs, and her part-time shop assistant Iona was there to field enquiries and take contact details of people

who were interested in having a consultation about a
wedding dress. Will had brought the organza bags and
chocolates with him, so Sean had a production line of
people stuffing bags with the chocolates and Claire's
business card. He knew how much was riding on this.

And it also worried him. Claire had already had to
deal with extra problems that weren't of her making
today. If this didn't go to plan, all her hard work would
have been for nothing.

What he wanted to do was to make sure that the
people she wanted to see her collection actually saw
it. She'd already mentioned the names of some of the
fashion houses who were going to be there. A little networking might just give them the push they needed to
make sure they saw Claire's work.

While Claire was making last-minute fixes to the
dresses, Sean slipped away quietly to find the movers
and shakers of her world. Claire had just about finished
by the time he returned.

'Everything OK?' he asked.

'Yes.' She smiled at him. 'You're amazing and I love
you. Now go strut your stuff.'

The dresses all looked breathtaking. He knew how
much work had gone into them, along with Claire's heart
and soul. Please let the reviewers be kind rather than
snarky, he begged silently. Please let her get the kudos
she deserved. Please let the fashion houses keep their
word and come to see her. Please let them give her a
chance.

Claire's hands were shaking visibly. Ashleigh was sitting next to her; she took Claire's hands and held them
tightly. 'Breathe. It's going to be just fine.'

'They all look amazing,' Claire's grandmother added.

'You're going to wow the lot of them,' Aunt Lou said, reaching over to pat her shoulder.

Only Jacob was silent, but Claire hadn't really expected anything from her dad; she knew that fashion shows weren't his thing. The fact that he'd actually turned up meant that he was on her side for once—didn't it?

But finally the catwalk segment of the show began. Her collection was on first. The models came down the catwalk, one group at a time: the bride, groom and bridesmaids. Autumn. Winter. Spring. Summer. Sean, looking incredibly gorgeous in morning dress and a top hat with his vintage-inspired bride beside him; her heart skipped a beat when he caught her eye and smiled at her. The contemporary civil wedding.

And then finally, the whole collection of six stood on the stage in a tableau. Claire became aware of music, lights—and was that applause?

'You did it, love,' her grandmother said and hugged her. 'Listen to everyone clapping. They think you're as fantastic as we do.'

'We did it.' Claire was shaking with a mixture of relief and adrenaline. She swallowed hard. 'I need to get back to my stand.'

'Iona can cope for another five minutes,' Aunt Lou said with a smile. 'Just enjoy this bit.'

A woman came over to join them. 'Claire Stewart?' she asked.

Claire looked up. 'Yes.'

'Pia Verdi,' the woman introduced herself, and handed over her business card.

Claire's eyes widened as she took in the name of one of the biggest wedding dress manufacturers in the country.

'I like what I've just seen up there, and I'd like to

talk to you about designing a collection for us,' Pia said. 'Obviously you won't have your diary on you now, but call my PA on Monday morning and we'll set up a meeting.'

'Thank you—I'd really like that,' Claire said.

The one thing she'd been secretly hoping for—her chance in the big league. To design a collection that would be sold internationally and would have her name on it.

She just about managed to keep it together until Sean—who'd clearly changed out of his wedding outfit at top speed—came out. He picked her up and spun her round, and she laughed.

'We did it, Sean.'

'Not me. You're the one who designed those amazing outfits.'

'But you supported me when I needed it. Thank you so, so much.' She handed him the business card and grinned her head off. 'Look who wants to talk to me next week!'

'They're offering you a job?' he asked.

'Better than that—they're asking me to talk to them about designing a collection. So I'll get my name out there, but I still get to do my brides and design one-offs as well. It's the icing on the cake. Everything I wanted. I'm so happy.'

'That's brilliant news.' He hugged her. 'I'm so proud of you, Claire. You deserve this.'

'Thanks.' She beamed at him. 'Though I'd better come down off cloud nine and get back to the stand. It's not fair to leave Iona on her own.'

'I'm so glad Pia Verdi came to see you,' he said.

She frowned as his words sank in. 'Hang on. Are you telling me you know her?'

'Um, not exactly.'

Her eyes narrowed as she looked at him. 'Sean?'

He blew out a breath. 'I just networked a bit while you were sorting stuff out, that's all.'

Claire went cold. 'You *networked*?'

'I just told her that your collection was brilliant and she needed to see it.'

Bile rose in Claire's throat as she realised what had actually happened. So much for thinking that she'd got this on her own merit. That her designs had been good enough to attract the attention of one of the biggest fashion houses.

Because Sean had intervened.

Without him talking to her, Pia Verdi probably wouldn't even have bothered coming to see Claire's collection.

And, although part of Claire knew that he'd done something really nice for her, part of her was horrified. Because what this really meant was that Sean was as overprotective as her father. Whatever Sean had said, he didn't really believe in her: he didn't think that she could make it on her own, and he thought she'd always need a bit of a helping hand. To be looked after.

Stifled.

So what she'd thought was her triumph had turned out to be nothing of the kind.

'You spoke to Pia Verdi,' she repeated. 'You told her to come and see my collection.'

He waved a dismissive hand. 'Claire, it was just a little bit of networking, that's all. You would've done the same for me.'

'No.' She shook her head. 'No, I wouldn't have thought that I needed to interfere. Because I *know* you can do things on your own. I *know* that you'll succeed without having someone to push you and support you. And you...' She blew out a breath. 'You just have to be in control. All the time. That's not what I want.'

'Claire, I—'

'No,' she cut in. 'No. I think you've just clarified something for me. Something important. I can't do this, Sean. I can't be with someone who doesn't consult me and who always plays things by the book—*his* book.' She shook her head. 'I'm sorry. I know you meant well, but...this isn't what I want.' She took a deep breath. There was no going back now. 'It's over.'

'Claire—'

She took a backward step, avoiding his outstretched hand. 'No. Goodbye, Sean.'

She walked away with her head held high. And all the time she was thinking, just how could today have turned from so spectacularly wonderful to so spectacularly terrible? How could it all have gone so wrong?

Even though her heart was breaking, she smiled and smiled at everyone who came to her exhibition stand. She talked about dresses and took notes. She refused help from everyone to pack things away at the end of the show and did it all herself; by then, her anger had burned out to leave nothing but sadness. Sean had taken her at her word and left, which was probably for the best; but her stupid heart still wished that he were there with her.

Well, too late. It was over—and they were too different for it to have worked out long term. So this summer had just been a fling. One day she'd be able to look back on it and remember the good times, but all she could think of now was the bitterness of her disappointment and how she wished he'd been the man she thought he was.

* * *

Stupid, stupid, *stupid*.

Sean hated himself for the way the light had gone from Claire's eyes. Because he'd been the one to cause it. He'd burst her bubble big-time—ruined the exuberance she'd felt at her well-deserved success. He'd meant well—he'd talked to Pia Verdi and the others with the best possible intentions—but now he could see that he'd done completely the wrong thing. He'd taken it all away from Claire, and he'd made her feel as if the bottom had dropped out of her world.

It felt as if the bottom had fallen out of his world, too. He'd lost something so precious. He knew it was all his own fault; and he really wasn't sure he was ever going to be able to fix this.

He definitely couldn't fix it today; he knew he needed to give her time to cool down. But tomorrow he'd call her. Apologise. Really lay his heart on the line—and hope that she'd forgive him and give him a second chance.

CHAPTER THIRTEEN

IT SHOULD HAVE been a night of celebration.

Not wanting to jinx things before the wedding show, Claire hadn't booked a table at a restaurant in advance; though she'd planned to take her family, Sean, Ashleigh and Luke out to dinner that evening, to thank them for all the support they'd given her in the run-up to the show.

But now the food would just taste like ashes; and she didn't want her misery to infect anyone else. So she smiled and smiled and lied her face off to her family and her best friend, pretending that her heart wasn't breaking at all. 'I'm fine. Anyway, I need to get the van back to the hire company, and start sorting out all these enquiries...'

Finally she persuaded them all to stop worrying about her, and left in the van on her own. But, by the time she'd dropped all the outfits back at her shop, delivered the van back to the hirer and caught the tube back to her flat, she felt drained and empty. Dinner was a glass of milk—which was just about all she could face—and she lay alone in her bed, dry-eyed and too miserable to sleep and wishing that things were different.

Had she been unfair to Sean?

Or were her fears—that he'd be overprotective and stifling in the future, and they'd be utterly miserable together—justified?

Claire still hadn't worked it out by the time she got up at six, the next morning. It was ridiculously early for a Sunday, but there was no point in just lying there and brooding. Though she felt like death warmed up after yet another night of not sleeping properly, and it took three cups of coffee with extra sugar before she could function enough to take a shower and wash her hair.

Work seemed to be about the best answer. If she concentrated on sketching a new design, she wouldn't have room in the front of her head to think about what had happened with Sean. And maybe the back of her head would come up with some answers.

She hoped.

She was sketching in her living room when her doorbell rang.

Odd. She wasn't expecting anyone to call. And she hadn't replied to any of the messages on her phone yet, so as far as everyone else was concerned she was probably still asleep, exhausted after the wedding show.

And who would ring her doorbell before half past eight on a Sunday morning, anyway?

She walked downstairs and blinked in surprise when she opened the door.

Sean was standing there—dressed in jeans and a white shirt rather than his normal formal attire—and he was carrying literally an armful of flowers. She could barely see him behind all the blooms and the foliage of delphiniums, stocks, gerberas and roses.

She blinked at him. 'Sean?'

'Can I come in?' he asked.

'I…' Help. What did she say now?

'I'll say what I've got to say on your doorstep, if I have to,' he said. 'But I'd rather talk to you in private.'

She wasn't too sure that she wanted an audience, either. 'Come up,' she said, and stood aside so he could go past and she could close the door behind them.

'Firstly,' he said, 'I wanted to say sorry. And these are just…' He stopped, glanced down at the flowers and then at her. 'I've gone over the top, haven't I?'

'They're gorgeous—though I'm not sure if I have enough vases, glasses and mugs to fit them all in,' she said.

'I just wanted to say sorry. And I kind of thought I needed to make a big gesture, because the words aren't quite enough. And I know you love flowers. And…' His voice trailed off.

'You're carrying an entire English cottage garden there.' She was still hurt that he didn't truly believe in her, but she could see how hard he was trying to start making things right. And as he stood there in the middle of all the flowers, looking completely like a fish out of water…how could she stay angry with him?

'Let's get these gorgeous flowers in water before they start wilting.' She went into the kitchen and found every receptacle she had, and started filling them with water. 'They're lovely. Thank you. Where did you get them?' she asked. 'Covent Garden flower market isn't open on Sundays.'

'Columbia Road market,' he said. 'I looked up where I could get really good fresh flowers first thing on a Sunday morning.'

She thought about it. 'So you carried all these on the tube?'

'Uh-huh.' He gave her a rueful smile. 'I had to get someone to help me at the ticket barrier.'

He'd gone to a real effort for her. And he'd done something that would've made people stare at him—something she knew would've made him feel uncomfortable.

So this apology was sincerely meant. But she still needed to hear the words.

When they'd finished putting the flowers in water—including using the bowl of her kitchen sink—she said, 'Do you want a coffee?'

'No, thanks. I just need to talk to you,' he said. He took a deep breath. 'Claire, I honestly didn't mean to hurt you. I just wanted to help. But I realise now that I handled it totally the wrong way. I interfered instead of supporting you properly and asking you what you needed me to do. I made you feel as if you were hopeless and couldn't do anything on your own—but, Claire, I *do* believe in you. I knew your designs would make any of the fashion houses sit up and take notice. But the wedding show was so busy, I didn't want to take the risk that they wouldn't get time to see your collection and you wouldn't get your chance. That's the only reason I went to talk to Pia Verdi.'

His expression was serious and completely sincere. She knew he meant what he said.

And she also knew that she owed him an apology, too. They were *both* in the wrong.

'I overreacted a bit as well,' she said. 'I'd been working flat out for weeks and, after the way everything had gone wrong from the first…well, I think it just caught me at the wrong time. Now I've had time to think about it, I know your heart was in the right place. You meant well. But yesterday I felt that you were being overprotective and stifling, the way Dad is, because you don't think I can do it on my own. You think that I need looking after all the time.'

'Claire, I'm not your father. I know you can do it on your own,' he said softly. 'And, for the record, I don't think you need looking after. Actually, I think it would drive you bananas.'

'It would.' She took a deep breath. 'I want an equal partnership with someone who'll back me and who'll let me back them.'

'That's what I want, too,' Sean said.

Hope bloomed in her heart. 'Before yesterday—before things went wrong—that's what I thought we had,' she said.

'We did,' he said. 'We *do*.'

She bit her lip. 'I've hurt you as much as you hurt me. I was angry and unfair and ungrateful, I pushed you away, and I'm sorry. And, if I try to think first instead of reacting first in future, do you think we could start again?'

'So Ms Follow-Your-Heart turns into a rulebook devotee?' Sean said. 'No deal. Because I want a partner who thinks outside the box and stops me being regimented.'

'You're not regimented—well, not *all* the time,' she amended.

'Thank you. I think.' He looked at her. 'I can't promise perfection and I can't promise we won't ever fight again, Claire.'

'It wouldn't be normal if we didn't ever fight again,' she pointed out.

'True. I guess we just need to learn to compromise. Do things the middle way instead of both thinking that our way's the only way.' He opened his arms. 'So. You and me. How about it?'

She stepped into his arms. 'Yes.'

'Good.' He kissed her lingeringly. 'And we'll talk more in future. I promise I won't think I know best.'

'And I promise I won't go super-stubborn.'

He laughed. 'Maybe we ought to qualify that and say we'll *try*.'

'Good plan.'

He arched an eyebrow. 'Are you going to admit that planning's good, outside business?'

She laughed. 'That would be a no. Most of the time. Are you going to admit that being spontaneous means you have more fun?'

He grinned. 'Not if I'm hungry and I've just been drenched in a downpour.'

'Compromise,' she said. 'That works for me.'

'Me, too.' He kissed her again. 'And we'll make this work. Together.'

EPILOGUE

Two months later

CLAIRE WAS WORKING on the preliminary sketches for her first collection for Pia Verdi when her phone beeped.

She glanced at the screen. Sean. Probably telling her that he was going to be late home tonight, she thought with a smile. Although they hadn't officially moved in with each other, they'd fallen into a routine of spending weeknights at her place and weekends at his.

V and A. Thirty minutes. Be there.

Was he kidding?

Three tube changes! Takes thirty minutes PLUS walk to station, she typed back.

And of course he'd know she knew this. The Victoria and Albert Museum was her favourite place in London. She'd taken him there several times and always lingered in front of her favourite dress, a red grosgrain and chiffon dress by Chanel. She never, ever tired of seeing that dress.

Forty minutes, then.

Half a minute later, there was another text.

Make it fifty and change into your blue dress. The one with the daisies.

Why?

Tell you when you get here.

She grinned. Sean was clearly in playful mode, so this could be fun. But why did he want to meet her at the museum? And why that dress in particular?

She still didn't have a clue when she actually got to Kensington. She texted him from the museum entrance: Where are you?

Right next to your favourite exhibit.

Easy enough, she thought, and went to find him.

He was standing next to the display case, dressed up to the nines: a beautifully cut dark suit and a white shirt, but for once he wasn't wearing a tie. That little detail was enough to soften the whole package. Just how she liked it.

'OK. I'm here.' She gestured to her outfit. 'Blue dress. Daisies. As requested, Mr Farrell.'

'You look beautiful,' he said.

'Thank you. But I'm still trying to work out why you wanted to meet me here.'

'Because I'm just about to add to your workload.'

She frowned. 'I don't understand.'

He dropped to one knee. 'Claire Stewart, I love you with all my heart. Will you marry me?'

'I…' She stared at him. 'Sean. I can't quite take this in. You're really asking me to marry you?'

'I'm down on one knee and I used the proper form,' he pointed out.

This was the last thing she'd expected on a Thursday afternoon in her favourite museum. 'Sean.'

'I've been thinking about it for the last month. Where else could you ask a wedding dress designer to marry you, except in her favourite place in London? And next to her favourite exhibit, too?'

Now she knew why he'd asked her to wear his favourite dress: to make this just as special for him. And why he'd said he was adding to her workload—because now she'd have a very special wedding dress to design. Her own.

She smiled. 'Sean Farrell, I love you with all my heart, too. And I'd be thrilled to marry you.'

He stood up, swung her round, and kissed her thoroughly. Then he took something from his pocket. 'We need to formalise this.'

She blinked. 'You bought me a ring?'

'Without consulting you? No chance. This is temporary. Go with the flow. *Carpe diem*,' he said, and slid something onto the ring finger of her left hand.

When she looked at it, she burst out laughing. He'd made her a ring out of unused toffee wrappers.

'We'll choose the proper one together,' he said. 'Just as we'll make all our important decisions together.'

'An equal partnership,' she said, and kissed him. 'Perfect.'

* * * * *

"Who?"

Sydney blinked up at her father. "What?"

"Who are you dating?"

Her gaze slid to the stranger, and she thought maybe white knights *did* ride to the rescue. It was worth a shot. What could happen? Even if this backfired, maybe her dad would get the message that she was serious about convincing him to back off.

"Him." She angled her head. "I'm going out with him."

Before her father could turn and look, she was on her way over to the man. Stopping in front of him, she looked up and said in a low voice, "I will forever be in your debt if you go with me on what's about to happen. It's a family thing." She put a fair amount of pleading into her tone and her expression. "I'm begging you. And I'll make it up to you. I swear."

The Bachelors of Blackwater Lake:
They won't be single for long!

A DECENT PROPOSAL

BY
TERESA SOUTHWICK

Published in Great Britain 2015
by Mills & Boon, an imprint of Harlequin (UK) Limited,
Eton House, 18-24 Paradise Road, Richmond, Surrey, TW9 1SR

© 2015 Teresa Southwick

ISBN: 978-0-263-25127-2

23-0415

Harlequin (UK) Limited's policy is to use papers that are natural, renewable and recyclable products and made from wood grown in sustainable forests. The logging and manufacturing processes conform to the legal environmental regulations of the country of origin.

Printed and bound in Spain
by CPI, Barcelona

Teresa Southwick lives with her husband in Las Vegas, the city that reinvents itself every day. An avid fan of romance novels, she is delighted to be living out her dream of writing for Mills & Boon.

To my nephew, C.J. Boyle.
Your courage and determination inspire me every day.
There's no question that you have a hero's heart.

Chapter One

Sydney McKnight knew there was no way a white knight would ride in on his stalwart steed and save her, but a girl could hope.

Needing a good save is what happens when first thing in the morning your father, who was also your boss, hits you with the "are you seeing anyone?" question. It was a sure bet this conversation wasn't headed anywhere she wanted to go.

Standing outside the office of McKnight Automotive, she glanced around for an escape, but short of making a run for it, there was no way out. Time to get the attention off herself and back where it belonged. On her father, who she and her brothers just found out had been seeing someone in secret. For months. And now Tom McKnight was looking to find out if his daughter would be in a committed relationship anytime soon so that he could take the next step in his own.

"Dad, you didn't have to sneak around and date. The boys are fine with it."

"It wasn't Alex and Ben that concerned me, Syd. It's you." He met her gaze and there was no looking away or mistaking his meaning. "I will always have a special place in my heart for your mother."

Complications from childbirth had caused her mother's death. Syd knew she wasn't to blame for it but that didn't stop a small stab of guilt. "For years everyone has been telling you to get on with your life, Dad. Now we know you did, a while ago. With Mayor Goodson. It's about darn time and I'm completely fine with it. Fly. Be free. Be happy."

Her father's expression tightened into a mask of stubborn resolve. "How can I be happy until I know your personal life is in order?"

That was code for having a man. What her father didn't get was that first you had to *want* a man messing up your personal life and Syd didn't. This wasn't the first time they'd had this conversation, but she was going to do her best to make it the last.

"Dad—" She stopped and took a deep breath, tapping into her well of patience, which at this point was hitting rock-bottom. "I know you want to protect me, make sure I'm okay. And it's really sweet, but I'm a big girl now."

"I know you are, honey, but I can't help worrying about you. Sue me. I want you to be settled, safe and happy." He ran his fingers through his thick silver hair. "Maybe it's about me being emotionally unavailable to you after your mom died."

Emotionally unavailable? "You've been watching TV talk shows again, haven't you?" she teased.

"Maybe." His grin was fleeting.

"There's nothing to make up for, Dad. I understand. Losing your wife was a shock. You're a terrific father.

The best. You did a great job. Alex, Ben and I turned out pretty awesome."

"You'll get no argument from me about that." His blue eyes twinkled with paternal pride. "The thing is, honey, your brothers are both married and have started their families."

And she was still very single, which translated to all alone. He didn't say it, but the implication hung in the silence between them.

Over her father's shoulder, Sydney saw an expensive, low-slung sports car growl to a crawl on Main Street in order to make the turn into McKnight Automotive. The beautiful, red, high-performance vehicle said something about the person driving it. For one thing, whoever it was didn't mind being noticed. A machine like that was an attention magnet. Her fingers itched to get a look at what was under the hood—of the car.

Focus, Sydney, she thought. "Alex and Ben were lucky to find their wives, Dad. You wouldn't want me to marry in haste then find out it was a mistake, would you?"

The sports car pulled into the driveway then roared past them and stopped under the covering that connected the business office and service bays of the garage. A dark tint on the windows prevented her from seeing who was behind the wheel, but she realized anticipation was swelling inside her to get a look at this person.

"Of course I don't want you to rush into marriage," her father said. "But I know how it feels to be alone. At least if I knew you were dating someone…"

"I date." Sort of.

"Anyone steady?"

If steady dating was the formula for a lasting relationship, she'd be married now. She'd had a boyfriend for years and the whole thing had blown up in her face. "Dad, don't worry about me. Just move on with your life. You deserve to be happy and I won't stand in your way."

"So, you're not dating," he said.

"Sure I am."

The sports-car driver got out and her heart actually skipped a beat, which had never happened to her before. The driver was a man. Aviator sunglasses hid his eyes, adding to his mystique, but she could see enough to know he wasn't a troll. He was thirtysomething and had dark hair. An expensive suit perfectly fit his tall frame, broad shoulders and narrow hips.

"Who?"

She blinked up at her father. "What?"

"Who are you dating?"

Her gaze slid to the stranger and she thought maybe white knights *did* ride to the rescue. It was worth a shot. What could happen? Even if this backfired, maybe her dad would get the message that she was serious about convincing him to back off.

"Him." She angled her head. "I'm going out with him."

Before her father could turn and look, she was on her way over to the man. Stopping in front of him she looked up and said in a low voice, "I will forever be in your debt if you go with me on what's about to happen. It's a family thing." She put a fair amount of pleading into her tone and her expression. "I'm begging you. And I'll make it up to you. I swear."

One corner of his mouth rose but with the sunglasses she couldn't see his expression. Her father joined them and there wasn't time for the stranger to respond.

"Sydney Marie McKnight, what in the world is going on? You've got some explaining to do."

"This is my dad, Tom McKnight." She slid her hand into the man's large palm and smiled up at him. "Dad, this is… This is the man I've been going out with." Dear God, she didn't know his name! She was holding his hand and didn't feel a wedding ring, so that was something.

The man she'd "been going out with" pushed the sunglasses to the top of his head. Amusement sparkled in his eyes. They were blue—a shade just on the other side of piercing and guaranteed to make a woman weak in the knees.

"Nice to meet you, sir." He held out his right hand. "Burke Holden."

Okay, then. The sports-car-driving, expensive-suit-wearing stranger didn't plan to rat her out just yet.

Her father shook the man's hand, but suspicion was written all over his face. "So you're going out with my daughter."

"That's what she tells me."

Very smooth, she thought. Quick, too. Fate would no doubt charge an exorbitant fee for putting a man with exactly the right skill set directly in her path. But that was a problem for another time.

"I haven't seen you around Blackwater Lake." Tom folded his arms over his chest.

"My company owns that property up on the mountain." It wasn't a direct response, just the insinuation that he'd been spending a lot of time here.

"Where the new resort is going to be."

"Yes, sir."

Syd liked the feel of her hand in the stranger's since the contact made it much easier to play this part. "You know better than anyone, Dad, that Mayor Goodson has worked hard to promote expansion in Blackwater Lake. She's determined to do it in a responsible, balanced way—not duplicating established businesses but attract new ones. And that will create the need for more services, jobs, build the tax base in a slow, steady, stable way. More people move to town and their cars need maintenance and repair."

"Part of the resort deal includes building a small regional airport," Burke explained. "There's no point in expanding anything without giving folks transportation choices to get here more easily."

"Makes sense." Tom nodded. "So you're not looking to put Blackwater Lake Lodge out of business? Because my daughter-in-law owns it."

Her family did actually, but Syd decided to keep that thought to herself. Camille Halliday McKnight had married her doctor brother, Ben. In the beginning, she'd had her doubts about the heiress but Cam was the sweetest, most down-to-earth filthy rich person Syd had ever met. And her brother was happy, which was the most important thing.

"No, sir. My company is interested in building condominiums with retail space below. A mixed-use development. The project is big enough to bring in revenue to existing local businesses. Workers will need lodging and food. It's a win for everyone."

"Maybe." Eyes narrowed, Tom looked down at her but directed the next question to Burke. "How long have you known my daughter?"

Oh, boy. Time to jump in and help. "Dad, have you ever met someone and right from the beginning you felt as if you'd known them your whole life?"

"No. And in case you're wondering, I noticed you didn't answer the question."

"Look, Dad—" The sound of the office phone ringing interrupted.

"I'll get it. But we're not finished with this, Sydney." Her father gave her a *dad* look then headed inside to answer the call.

When they were alone, Syd blew out a long breath. "Thanks for going along, Mr. Holden—"

"Burke, please. After all, we're going out. I'm the guy

you met and felt as if you'd known all your life." His voice was teasing, his smile incredibly attractive. "So, do you want to tell me what that was all about?"

"Not really, but I owe you an explanation." She gathered her thoughts. "Here goes. Twenty-five words or less. You're obviously a busy man."

"Yes, but this is the most intriguing thing that's ever happened to me."

"I doubt that, but okay. If you say so." A man who looked like him probably had intriguing encounters with women every day. "My dad has been a widower for a long time, actually since the day I was born."

"Your mother died in childbirth?" He looked shocked.

"Yes. And for years everyone has been telling him to get a life, but he wouldn't. Recently my older brother dropped by the house unexpectedly and found Dad in a compromising situation with the mayor. I can't say more or the idea of him with a woman—doing stuff in bed— will be burned in my brain and require years of therapy. Long story short, for close to a year they've been secretly dating."

"Way to go, Tom." There was an admiring expression on Burke's face when he glanced at the office doorway.

She laughed, then grew serious. "He's found love again."

"Good for him. But what does that have to do with you?"

"He wants to ask the mayor to marry him but won't get on with it because of me. Both of my brothers have gone all white-picket-fence and settled down. Marriage, babies, the whole deal. Dad wants the same for me. Or at least to know I'm dating and moving somewhere in the vicinity of settling down."

"I see."

"You probably think I'm crazy, and who could blame

you? You just had the bad luck to arrive as I was being grilled like raw hamburger. I'd just told him a big fat lie about going out with someone. He wanted to know who and there you were. I'm terribly sorry to have dragged you into the madcap McKnight family like this. But I really do appreciate what you did."

"Like I said, very intriguing." He slid his hands into his pockets. "What are you going to do now?"

"Nothing. He's met you. That gives him a visual and he'll propose to Loretta and they'll get married."

"Won't you need a date for the wedding?"

"You'll be conveniently out of town." She smiled at him. "After all, you're a very busy man. And at just the right time I'll share the news that you and I have broken up."

"Hmm." The corner of his mouth quirked up. "Will I have dumped you?"

She laughed. "Not after you were so understanding. The least I can do is take the blame. Or it will just be one of those things that didn't work out. No one's fault."

"But I'll be heartbroken," he protested.

"Something tells me you'll find someone to make it better."

"I've heard of speed dating," he said, shaking his head, "but this is the fastest relationship I've ever had."

"Aren't you glad you were in the right place at the right time?" Wow, he really was smooth. Looks, charm and wit made him a triple threat. The single ladies of Blackwater Lake would be forming a line, but Syd wouldn't be in it. She wasn't interested in complicating her life. "And that reminds me—what brings you to McKnight Automotive?"

"Oil change."

"Okay. It's on the house." When he opened his mouth to protest, she said, "I insist. I told you I'd make it worth your while."

"All right. Thanks."

"You helped me out of a jam so it's the least I can do. Want to wait for it? We have a comfortable lounge with coffee, soft drinks and snacks."

"No, someone is picking me up." At that moment, a big, black SUV pulled into the driveway and parked behind the sports car. "As a matter of fact, there's my ride."

"Give me a number where I can reach you when it's ready," she said.

Burke pulled a business card out of his wallet and handed it over. "Thanks, Sydney Marie McKnight."

"No—thank you."

Burke smiled, then walked to the passenger side of the car and got in. The vehicle drove out of the lot and she watched until the taillights disappeared down the street.

Tom came out of the office. "Someone needs a tow out on Lakeview Drive. I'll take care of it."

"Okay."

"Burke seems like a nice young man."

"He is." It wasn't every guy who would get sucked into a scenario like that and just go with it. Points to the handsome stranger.

"I want the four of us to go out to dinner."

"Four?" Her stomach dropped.

"Loretta and me. You and Burke."

"I don't know, Dad. He's…busy," she said lamely.

"Everyone is but he's managed to find the time to date you." Her father's voice had an edge of suspicion. "And everyone has to eat. So we'll double-date. Unless you're lying to your old man."

It was hard not to flinch. There probably wasn't a place in hell low enough for her. Still, she was doing the wrong thing for the right reason and that had to count for something.

"Really, Dad. You raised me better than that." This bad was all on her.

She cared about her father's happiness. He'd spent so many years being sad and alone and he wasn't getting any younger. He deserved happiness and she wouldn't be the one who stood in his way. If she had to scheme to make sure it happened, by God she would.

The guy had seemed really easygoing and she was giving him a free oil change. What could it hurt to ask?

"I'll check with Burke and see what I can set up."

"I'll call again tomorrow, son." Burke held the cell phone to his ear, not sure why he was prolonging this.

"Okay." His child's familiar, formal tone was the polar opposite of enthusiastic.

"If you need anything, you know how to get in touch."

"Yeah." There was a long silence, then Liam said, "I have homework."

"Right." He probably wasn't the only father on the planet whose kid would rather do homework than talk to him, but it sure felt that way. "I love you. 'Bye, son."

"'Bye."

Feeling guilty and inadequate, Burke hit the end-call button on his cell phone. He never knew what to say to his son and heard in the kid's voice how much he was let down whenever they talked. Not calling would save them both the ordeal of an awkward conversation, but unlike his own father he wouldn't take the easy way out. So he would be in touch every day while he was away from home.

His ex-wife was no better. During divorce negotiations she'd put up zero fight when he wanted physical custody. Now she lived in Paris and he had the best housekeeper in Chicago. Most of the time that made it okay for him not to be there. At least that's what he told himself. Today he didn't quite buy it. Meeting Sydney McKnight and her father, Tom, might account for that.

He found himself envying their obviously close relationship. She had gone above and beyond to convince her dad to move on with his life. That was loyalty, a happy by-product of a father who'd been a positive influence on his daughter. Burke couldn't help wondering if twenty years from now Liam would go to that much trouble for him.

Normally he didn't feel lonely on a business trip but today was different. In a lot of ways. He was sitting on a stool in the Blackwater Lake Lodge bar. There were a couple of businessmen, two women who'd stopped in for a drink after work and several couples having a predinner cocktail. He was nursing a beer while he waited for Sydney to personally deliver his car.

She'd contacted him and offered; now he found himself looking forward to seeing her again. Stereotyping probably described his attitude, but he'd never expected to see a woman so beautiful, sexy and smart working in a garage.

And speaking of beautiful women, there was one who'd just come around the corner from the lobby and waved when she saw him. Her last name was McKnight, too, but Camille was married to Sydney's brother, Ben. Burke considered her a friend and she knew about his bad-relationship karma. That's probably why she'd never told him about her husband's sister.

She stopped beside him and they hugged. "Hi."

"Hello, Mrs. McKnight. Marriage looks good on you." In spite of his dark mood it was impossible not to smile in the presence of a woman glowing the way this one was. "You're positively radiant."

"Thank you, kind sir." She put her hand on his arm. "Love does that to a person. You should try it sometime."

"Been there, done that. It didn't work out."

She wrinkled her nose. "That wasn't love. Brenda was selfish and self-absorbed. Probably still is."

"Almost certainly," he agreed.

The Holden and Halliday families had been friends for

years and partners in various business ventures, including a small stake in the project he was here to work on.

"How's Liam?" she asked. "He's how old now?"

"Eight. Getting big."

"You must miss him when you have to be away on business," Cam said.

Burke nodded ruefully. "It's not easy."

"The time goes by so quickly." She sighed. "My little girl is growing so fast."

"That's right. You're a mom now." He grinned. "Motherhood agrees with you. How old is…" He didn't know the child's name and shrugged apologetically.

"Amanda—Ben and I call her Mandy. She's fifteen months. You have to meet her while you're here."

"I'd like that—"

A flash of red coming around the corner caught his eye and he did a double take. The blazer belonged to Sydney McKnight and she wore it over a white silk blouse tucked into jeans that fit her like a second skin. High heels made her legs look a lot longer than he knew they were. She was pretty in her work clothes and stunning in the sophisticated outfit.

Camille followed his gaze. "Ah, my sister-in-law. Wow, she really cleans up well. But then she always dresses like a fashion model when she's not at the garage. She looks fabulous."

Burke had noticed. Earlier her hair had been pulled into a sassy ponytail but now it fell like dark silk past her shoulders. Layers framed her small face and highlighted her big, brown eyes. She could be in *Car and Driver* magazine or grace the cover of *Glamour* or *Cosmopolitan*.

Sydney saw the two of them and looked surprised for a moment before heading in their direction. She stopped in front of them.

"Cam, it's nice to see you." She leaned in for a quick

hug. Then she looked at him. "So, you've met my sister-in-law?"

"Actually we've known each other for years," he explained. "As a matter of fact, the Hallidays have invested in my resort."

Sydney blinked. "You own the development company?"

"With my cousin, yes." Her surprised expression was genuine. "Why?"

"You just said your company owned the land."

"We do," he said.

"I just thought you were on the payroll, not the guy who signed the paychecks for everyone." Syd glanced at Cam, who nodded a confirmation. "Be sure to share with my father that you know this guy. He had your back today."

"Oh?" Cam said.

"That's right," Burke agreed. "I brought my car into the garage for an oil change and he gave me the third degree about the new project followed by a subtle warning that it better not put the lodge out of business."

"I'll be sure and tell Tom not to worry. He's so thoughtful. I'm so happy he finally found someone, and the mayor is a good woman." Cam looked first at Burke, then her gaze rested on Sydney. "Is this a coincidence you two meeting here?"

Sydney dangled a ring of keys on the end of her finger. "Like Burke said, he brought his car in for an oil change and I'm delivering it now."

"And I appreciate the service."

"Happy to oblige."

"So everyone is happy." Cam grinned at both of them then released a regretful sigh as she checked the watch on her wrist. "I'd love to stay and chat but I really need to get home to Ben and the baby."

"Give them both a hug for me," Sydney said.

"I will." She looked at Burke. "We'll put a date on the

calendar soon for dinner so you can meet my husband and Mandy."

"I look forward to it," he said.

Cam smiled, then turned and walked out of the bar, leaving him alone with Sydney. Their gazes locked and he felt something squeeze tight inside him. He wasn't sure what it meant but knew she'd completed her errand and would leave if he didn't come up with a reason for her to stay. And he really wanted her to stay.

"Can I buy you a drink?" he asked. "It's the least I can do. What with you going out of your way to bring my car back here to the lodge."

"I'd like that." She gracefully slid onto the bar stool beside his. Without hesitation she said, "Chardonnay, please."

Burke signaled the bartender and asked her to open the best white she had. He toyed with the empty beer bottle in front of him. "I can't decide if this delivery system of yours is good customer service or you just wanted to drive my car."

"Both. And for the record it's a really nice car," she said, grinning. Then the amusement faded and she couldn't quite meet his gaze, which was different from the uniquely direct woman he'd met this morning.

"You look very chic."

She glanced down. "Thanks. Are you surprised?"

"Because you make your living working on cars?" He thought for a moment and decided to be completely honest. "You're a beautiful woman, Sydney. I was surprised from the very first moment I saw you this morning."

"What a lovely thing to say. And I appreciate it." Her smile was a little shy, but also…nervous? "Because there's something I'd like to ask. A really big favor—"

"Your drinks." The twentysomething blonde waitress put down a small, square napkin, a wineglass and another beer in front of him. She picked up the empty bottle and said, "Let me know if you need anything else."

"Will do. Thanks," Burke said. He held up his beer. "To new friends."

Sydney touched her glass to his bottle. "Friends."

She was definitely nervous about something. Then her words sank in. Favor. Something to ask. "What's up?"

"This is harder than I thought."

"Just spit it out," he advised. "That's usually best."

She took a long drink of Chardonnay, then set the glass down and looked him straight in the eye. "Nothing ventured…"

"Now I'm really curious." His impression of her from their first meeting was of a confident, forthright woman so this hesitation struck him as out of character. "The worst that can happen is I'll say no."

"Actually that's not the worst. And saying yes would not be the smartest answer."

"Come on, Syd." Shortening her name came easily and naturally, but he didn't have time to wonder why that was. "Just tell me what's on your mind."

"Okay." She took a deep breath. "I really need you to go out with me on a date."

Chapter Two

"You probably think I'm a gold-digging stalker."

"Why would I?" Burke was more curious and intrigued than anything else.

"Today at the garage you said your company owns the property on the hill that's going to be developed. As in the way people say my company is doing a hostile take-over but I just work for them and do what I'm told. As in a highly placed executive or something. It didn't cross my mind that you *owned* the company. I had no idea you were in the same league with Camille's family. The one where billionaires come to play."

"Surprise."

Sitting on the bar stool, she angled her body toward him. "And I hit on you!"

"It happens."

"I just bet it does." There was humor in her dark eyes. Usually getting hit on turned him off. Sydney McKnight had the opposite effect. Color him shocked by this unexpected reaction to a small-town girl.

"Seriously, Burke, I wasn't hitting on you. Not exactly. Not you…you. Any single man who was in the right age group and happened to drive up at that moment would have done just as well."

"Way to let the air out of my ego balloon." He took a sip of his beer.

"I'm not being mean. Just honest."

"I like that about you, the honesty part." And so many other things. Like the graceful arch of her dark eyebrows. The way her full lips curved up as if she found something secretly amusing. And the intelligence sparkling in her eyes.

"The thing is, Burke—and I don't mean this in an offensive way—but what you think of me isn't my biggest problem."

He rested his elbow on the edge of the bar and half turned toward her. "That would imply that you might be in a bit of a predicament."

"That would be accurate."

"I see."

When he moved his leg, her knee bumped his thigh and it felt oddly intimate for a bar setting. More people had wandered in for drinks but it seemed as if he and Sydney were alone. He found himself wishing they were.

"Did I hurt your feelings, when I insinuated that your opinion of me isn't important? That certainly wasn't my intention."

"Not at all. Do I look like my feelings are hurt?"

She sipped her white wine and studied him. "I don't know you well enough to make that determination. There was just an odd expression on your face."

Hmm, she was very perceptive. He'd have to watch

himself around her. "I assure you my feelings are just fine. So tell me about your problem."

"Well it's like this. My father is a little skeptical about our relationship."

Burke laughed. "Can you blame him? It does feel suspiciously like a scenario from a TV sitcom."

"I don't know what came over me." She sighed and shook her head. "You have no reason to believe this but I swear I've never done anything like that in my life. Accosting a strange man and pulling him into my situation."

"*Accost* is sort of a strong word."

She grinned. "I mean this in the nicest possible way, but you're very good at going with the flow. Lying without really telling an untruth."

"Thank you, I think."

"Seriously, it was very generous of you not to rat me out on the spot."

"I'm a generous guy."

"Why didn't you, by the way? Tell my dad I was crazy, I mean."

That was a very good question and one he didn't really have an answer for. "Chalk it up to curiosity about what you were up to."

She nodded, then looked down and toyed with her cocktail napkin. "The thing is…" Her gaze lifted, meeting his. "Dad wants proof that we're actually dating."

"You mean like photographs with a time and date stamp? Movie-ticket stubs? Eyewitness accounts?"

"If only." She sighed. "He wants to go out to dinner. A double date. You and me. Dad and Loretta—Mayor Goodson." She held up a hand to stop any protest and went on quickly. "Just think about it. I swear this isn't a scheme to snag a wealthy husband, but I can see where you might think that."

Normally that's exactly what he would think, followed

quickly by the thought that it was a wasted effort. He would never get married again. Once was enough, and he'd learned he wasn't a very good husband. The best thing to come out of the relationship was his son, but he wasn't a very good father, either.

"I appreciate you hearing me out, Burke." She finished the wine in her glass. "I love my father very much and would do anything to see that he's happy."

"He's lucky to have a daughter like you."

Frustration tightened her delicate features. "If he was really lucky, he'd have a daughter who was settled and he wouldn't have to worry about her. I think I'm a big disappointment to him."

"I sincerely doubt that. And take it from me—settling down with the wrong person is a bigger problem than being alone."

"Sounds like the voice of experience talking." She studied him for a moment, then said, "But you don't have to tell me about it. That's personal, and on a need-to-know basis. I don't need to know."

"There's not much to tell and if you really wanted the information it would be easy to do an online search." He tapped his fingers on the bar. "Most people go into marriage believing it's the right thing and I'm no exception. It wasn't right. Things didn't work and we got a divorce. Completely amicable and civilized. Including dealing with the custody of our son."

"You have a child." It wasn't a question.

"Yes." His fingers tightened on his beer bottle.

When he didn't say more, she nodded. "You know, I have this ridiculous urge to say I'm sorry. But it sounds like you're okay with everything."

"I am." Except for the fact that his son would always carry the scar of coming from a broken home and a mother who showed no interest in him.

"Anyway, think it over. My cell number is on the card I gave you." She picked up her small purse from the bar and slid the strap onto her shoulder. "Give me a call and let me know if you're in for round two of this covert operation."

"You're leaving?"

"Yes. I've taken up enough of your time."

No, she hadn't taken up nearly enough, he thought. "But you dropped off my car. How are you going to get home?"

"I'll call Dad. Thanks for listening, Burke." She slid to the edge of the bar chair, getting ready to go.

"Wait." He put his hand over hers to stop her. "I have a question."

"Okay. Shoot." Her gaze lowered to where he was touching her, but she didn't pull away.

"I can't help thinking that every unattached guy in town would want to go out with you. Wouldn't you be better off with one of them?"

"I had one of them." Her eyes darkened for a moment before she smiled, an expression with just the barest hint of bitterness. "It didn't work out. Ancient history." She slid off the stool. "The fact is, you're the guy who had the bad luck to pull into McKnight Auto Repair at just that moment. I shot my mouth off and you went along with it. Now you're either in or you're not."

"And what if I'm not?"

"My father will not propose to the woman he loves and live happily ever after. If you're okay with ruining his life…" A teasing smile turned up the corners of her full mouth. "No guilt."

"Right. Guilt doesn't motivate me." Unless Liam was the one using it. "But count me in."

"Really?" A bright smile lit up her whole face. "You're sure?"

"Yes. I would love to have dinner with your father and the mayor. And you, of course."

"Oh, Burke. I could kiss you."

"Feel free," he said generously.

"Right. You don't really mean that."

Yes, he really did. "I'm happy to help."

"I don't know why you're willing to go along with this but I'm grateful. Seriously, thanks."

"You're welcome."

Oddly enough it had been an easy decision. The simple answer was that he'd agreed because she asked and he wanted to see her again. Granted, he could have asked her out, but he'd already have had a black mark against him because of turning down her request. Now she owed him.

She leaned against the bar, a thoughtful look on her face. "I've never done anything like this before, but I know my father. He'll ask questions. In fact he already did. We're going to need a cover story. How we met. How long we've been dating. That sort of thing."

"It makes sense to be prepared."

"So we should get together soon and discuss it."

"What about right now?" he suggested.

Her eyes widened. "You don't waste time, do you?"

"No time like the present. Have you already had dinner?"

She shook her head. "Why?"

"Do you have a date?" If not, there was a very real possibility that she'd changed into the red blazer, skinny jeans and heels just for him. Probably wanted to look her best while making her case. Still, he really hoped she wasn't meeting another guy.

She gave him an ironic look. "Seriously? If I was going out with someone, I wouldn't have asked you to participate in this crazy scheme."

"Crazy? I don't know, it's a decent proposal." He shrugged. "So you're free. Have dinner with me. What about the restaurant here at the lodge? It's pretty good."

"The best in town." But she shook her head. "Too intimate."

So she didn't want to be alone with him. "Oh?"

"Something more public. People should see us together." She snapped her fingers. "The Grizzly Bear Diner would be perfect."

"I know the place. Both charming. And romantic."

"You're either being a smart-ass or a snob."

"Heaven forbid."

"You haven't been there yet?" she asked.

"No, I have."

He signaled the bartender and when she handed the bill to him, he took care of it. Then he settled his hand at the small of her back and said, "Let the adventure begin."

Sydney sat in the passenger seat beside Burke as he expertly drove the expensive sports car from Blackwater Lake Lodge to the Grizzly Bear Diner on Main Street. She wasn't sure what she itched to get her hands on more—the steering wheel of the hot car, again, or the man holding it. She'd said she would have hit on any single man who happened to drive into McKnight's Automotive just then, but, wow, she couldn't imagine anyone more perfect.

She would be lying if she said him having money wasn't cool. But after talking in the bar, she was much more intrigued by his wit and sense of humor. There was a glint in his blue eyes that could be about mischief or something more sizzling and she didn't particularly care which.

"Here we are." He pulled the car to a stop right in front of the diner.

"That's unusual."

"What?"

She met his gaze. "Getting a spot out front. I guess since this is a weeknight and school just started up after the summer, it must be a slow night."

"Are you disappointed?"

"Not really," she said. "But more people would help spread the word to my dad that we're an item."

He exited the driver's side and came around to open her door. Offering his hand to help her out, he said, "It doesn't look very crowded but we'll work with what we've got. Maximize resources."

"Okay."

When he locked the car and took her hand in his she was instantly stricken with a bad case of the tingles—from head to toe. Every nerve was on high alert and threatening to light up all her feminine hormones.

The buzz died when they walked inside and Syd recognized the new hostess, who just happened to be an old friend. Well, former friend. More of a frenemy. Violet Walker—actually it was Stewart now. The woman looked up from behind the wooden stand with the sign that said Please Wait To Be Seated. The automatic "welcome to the diner" smile froze on her face.

Still holding Syd's hand, Burke must have felt a reaction because he asked, "Something wrong?"

Other than the fact that she'd come face-to-face for the first time in years with her former bestie who'd stolen and married the man Syd had expected would propose to her?

"No," she answered in a tight voice. "Everything's just peachy."

They walked closer to the other woman and Syd said, "Hello, Violet."

"Sydney. Hi." The familiar blue eyes were filled with guilt.

"I didn't know you—and Charlie—were back."

"Surprise."

Syd was pretty much at her tolerance limit for surprises tonight. That didn't stop her from noticing that Violet's thick brunette hair was shorter, cut in an edgy bob that was very flattering.

"You look great, Syd."

"So do you."

That was no automatic response. Violet was curvier and it looked good on her. She'd always been too thin. If anything she was even prettier now than when she'd begged forgiveness for falling in love with Sydney's boyfriend.

Violet looked at the man still holding Syd's hand. "Nice to see you again, Mr. Holden."

"It's Burke, remember?" His tone hinted that he'd said it more than once. But he'd said he knew the place, which probably meant he'd been here a few times.

"Right. You've been in here enough to know everyone's name." The other woman's smile was strained. "Two for dinner?"

"Yes. A booth in the back if you have it."

"Right this way."

There weren't many people in the place, but all of them were long-time residents of Blackwater Lake who knew what had happened between the former best friends. As they walked clear to the back of the diner, Syd felt all of them looking, wondering, and decided a slow night had been a blessing in disguise. Not that news of her and Burke wouldn't spread, but it was easier to see Violet again in front of a smaller crowd.

Violet stopped at an empty booth. "How's this?"

"Perfect," Burke responded.

"Enjoy your dinner." The words were professional and matched the smile on her face.

When she was gone and they were seated across the table from each other, Burke asked, "So, want to tell me what that was all about?"

"Not really, no."

He opened his mouth to ask more, but the diner owner

walked over. Michelle Crawford, a brunette whose hair was streaked with silver, was somewhere in her fifties. Her brown eyes were filled with concern.

"Hi, Syd. Burke, it's good to see you again." She settled a look on Syd. "You didn't know Violet and Charlie moved back, did you? And this is the first time you've seen her since…" She lowered her voice. "You know. I could tell by the expression on your face."

Any hope that no one had noticed her reaction went right out the window. "No," she said, "I didn't know they were back."

"Oh, honey—" Michelle touched her shoulder. "Your dad should have warned you."

"He knows?" The words were automatic, but obviously he did. "Probably a heads-up slipped his mind. But it's fine, Michelle. Been a long time. Don't give it another thought."

"All right, honey. Glad you're okay." She smiled, then pointed to the menus stacked behind the napkin holder. "I'll let you look over the choices and be back in a few minutes to take your orders."

When she was gone, Burke's eyebrows drew together. "Whether you want to or not, it's probably best that you bring me up to speed on your ancient history."

"Are you going to tell me about yours?" He was divorced and had a son. She was curious about that.

"As it pertains to our agreement, yes. Like you said— need-to-know basis. But Blackwater Lake is your turf. And what happened to you is probably something you would tell a boyfriend."

Before Syd could respond, an older couple walked over to the table. Tillie Newman and her husband, Pete, were friends of her father and brought their Ford F-150 truck in for an oil change every six months, like clockwork.

"Hi, you two." Syd looked at them, trying to figure

out how to deflect what she knew was coming. "Mr. and Mrs. Newman, have you met Burke Holden? His company is building the resort we've heard so much about." She glanced at him. "Burke, this is Tillie and Pete Newman."

"Nice to meet you." He stood and shook hands with them.

"Same here. Welcome to Blackwater Lake." Tillie's brown eyes brimmed with sympathy when she looked at Syd. "Sorry to interrupt, but we saw you and Violet. You could just cut the awkwardness with a knife. I just had to make sure you're all right, sweetheart."

"I am. That's all water under the bridge. Or over the dam. Whatever the saying is. No need to be concerned about me."

Tillie looked relieved. "I'm glad. We always liked Violet and Charlie. Real nice to see them move back where they both grew up. It had to be hard, what happened between you."

It had been incredibly hard at the time, Syd recalled. "Time heals all."

"There's my girl." Tillie smiled and said, "We'll leave you two alone now. Come along, Pete."

"Take care, Syd. Truck's due for that oil change soon," the older man said.

"See you then." She lifted her hand in farewell and watched their backs for as long as she could. When procrastinating was no longer possible, she met Burke's curious gaze. "So you're probably jumping to all kinds of conclusions."

"It doesn't take a world-class detective to connect the dots."

Syd nodded. "The Charlie they mentioned is a guy I dated in high school and college. I thought he was moving toward a marriage proposal. It turned out that he was— just not to me."

"Violet?" he ventured.

"Yes. She was my best friend since first grade."

"That must have been tough." He reached over and covered her hand with his own. "He's the one you mentioned. The one who didn't work out."

"Yup." She glanced away for a moment. "This is the first time I've seen her since all that went down."

"And?"

She knew he was asking how she was feeling about it all. "I was shocked to see her since my father failed to share the news of her return. But…"

"What?" he asked.

"I was so hurt and angry back then." She shrugged. "It's all gone. It really is okay that they're back. Their parents are here and I'm sure happy to have them close by again."

"So you're sure you don't want to postpone our planning session for another time and place yet to be determined?"

"I'm sure," she said adamantly. "And even if I wasn't, no way I would leave. McKnights are made of sterner stuff than that."

"Okay, then." He grabbed the menus and handed her one. "What do you recommend?"

"You tell me. Seems you've been here enough that you're on a first-name basis with people."

"It's a small town." His look was ironic. "And there aren't many dining choices. I've been here a little over a month and have made the rounds. More than once."

"Is this where you pitch the new resort as a solution to our cuisine choice issues?"

"No. This is where I remind you that even if I'd only been here once, I'd stick out like a fly in milk. I'm… memorable."

"True." It was hard to believe she hadn't met him before today. Not only because he was right about it being a small town. But she also felt as if they'd known each other much longer. She grinned. "As far as this menu—I like the She Bear burger."

He looked down and read the description and raised an eyebrow. "Jalapeño? Mushrooms, bacon and Swiss cheese?"

"I hear disapproval in your tone. Don't knock it until you've tried it."

He was studying the choices and a sort of tender look came over him. "Liam—my son—would like this place."

"You're looking at the Baby Bear combo." When he nodded she said, "You miss him, don't you?"

"Yeah." There was an expression in his eyes that said he didn't want to elaborate. "I think I'll have the Papa Bear combo."

When they closed their menus it was a sign to Michelle and she was back to take their orders. "I'll have these out in a few minutes."

After the diner owner was gone, Burke rested his forearms on the edge of the table and met her gaze. "So what questions do you think your father will ask?"

"For starters he'll want to know where and how we met. Just so you know, he won't go for an online dating service."

"Oh?"

Syd settled the paper napkin over her knees then straightened the knife, fork and spoon that had been wrapped up inside it. "He's an old-fashioned guy and doesn't believe 'the machines,' as he calls them, should be a part of meeting your soul mate."

"Okay. So it has to be a plausible face-to-face encounter." He linked his fingers. "Where do you hang out that our paths could have crossed?"

"Bar None, the bar where locals go. Potter's Ice Cream Parlor and The Harvest Café. Here at the diner. But word would have gotten out if we even talked for five minutes under the watchful eye of Michelle Crawford."

She looked around the diner, with its pictures of grizzly bears on the walls. At the front of the place there was a counter lined with swivel stools. The back half had scattered tables in the center of the room and booths lining the perimeter.

"Okay. Any ideas?" he asked.

"There's a multiscreen movie theater at the mall about forty-five minutes away."

"I've been there," he said.

"Do you like movies?"

"Yes. Besides that it's something a person can do alone and not get pity stares."

"Oh?"

He nodded. "I've noticed that when you eat by yourself people give you weird looks."

She realized that he was lonely and it took considerable effort to keep pity out of the look she gave him. It was her sense that he wouldn't appreciate the sentiment.

"So, Mr. Gazillionaire Real-Estate Developer, is the crown too tight? Are the jewels too heavy?"

One corner of his mouth curved up. "I'm not sure what that means."

"Just that you have buckets of money, expensive clothes, a car that most people drool over and you're concerned about the way people look at you?"

He shifted on the seat. "When you put it like that…the correct response would be no."

"That's what I thought." The glint was back in his eyes and she much preferred that. "So we could have met at the movies."

"Is that plausible for you?"

"I go alone all the time. It's relaxing after a marathon

shopping spree. For the record no one pities a solo shopper."

"Good to know." He nodded. "I'm guessing we'll need to explore explanations for why no one has seen us around town together."

"That one is easy." She leaned forward. "People in this town talk and we just wanted to keep it quiet. Just for us."

"Very romantic," he commented. "That works."

"Sure does. It's the explanation I got from my dad about why he kept his romance with Mayor Goodson under wraps. A lot longer than what you and I are talking about." She was still irked about his secrecy. This small charade with Burke might be a little bit about payback. And her comment that she was made of sterner stuff wasn't just hot air. She could have handled the news about his new relationship. "I'm too old for him to give me the 'do as I say, not as I do' line."

They discussed things and tossed questions back and forth until he held up his hands in surrender. "I feel as if I should be taking notes."

"You're right." She nodded. "Kiss rule."

"Excuse me?" One eyebrow rose questioningly. The look in his blue eyes turned a little sharper, a little sexier and a lot interested.

"*K-I-S-S*. Keep it simple, stupid."

"Ah." His gaze never left hers and the intensity level escalated.

"You were thinking something else?"

"Yes. And before you judge, remember this is logical."

"Enlighten me," she said drily.

"We may be forced into kissing. After all this—you and me as a couple—needs to be convincing."

Their burgers were delivered, breaking the sensuous spell. But all through dinner she had a hard time not staring at his mouth and wondering what his lips would feel like against her own. Was he a good kisser? She would put money on it.

Sydney found she was looking forward to "dating" Burke Holden and was intrigued at the prospect of kissing him.

Chapter Three

Two days after his strategy session with Sydney at the diner, Burke was sitting in the five-star restaurant at Blackwater Lake Lodge nursing a Scotch while waiting for her to join him with her father and the mayor. He was watching when Tom McKnight and Mayor Loretta Goodson walked in with a stunning, dark-haired woman wearing a little black dress. He recognized Sydney, but...holy shoot, it felt as if all the blood drained from his head and proceeded to points south of his belt. Fortunately muscle memory and manners took over so he was able to not embarrass himself and politely stand up as the trio approached.

Burke held out his hand to the older man and said, "It's good to see you again, sir."

"Likewise." Tom McKnight looked at the older woman beside him. "I think you already know Loretta?"

"We've had a number of meetings about the resort."

Burke shook her hand. "Madam Mayor, it's always a pleasure."

"I couldn't agree more, Burke." Loretta Goodson was a very attractive brunette and probably looked a whole lot younger than she actually was. All those meetings had proved that she was a tough negotiator who cared deeply about her town.

Syd smiled up at him. "Hi."

"Hi, yourself." He slid his arm loosely around her waist and bent to kiss her cheek. It wasn't the way he really wanted to kiss her for the first time, but appropriate for the situation. "Why don't we all sit."

"Good idea," Syd agreed.

The Fireside Restaurant service was impeccable and tonight was no exception. When the newcomers were seated, their waiter appeared to take drink orders, then promised to give them time before bringing over dinner menus.

"So, where did you two meet?" Tom didn't waste any time and had come right to the point.

Since the man was looking directly at him Burke fielded the question. "I'm something of a movie buff and when you're alone in a new town it's an entertaining place to kill a couple of hours."

"Syd likes movies, too." Fortunately her dad jumped to the implied conclusion. "But how is it you managed to keep secret the fact that you're seeing my daughter?"

"Come on, Dad," Syd admonished. "Isn't that a little like the pot calling the kettle black?"

"She has a point, Tom." Loretta's voice was quiet but firm. "We've been seeing each other for months. I know some of that was about protecting your children, but part of it was about keeping it just for us."

Burke looked at Syd who had an "I told you so" expression in her eyes. She'd definitely called that one.

The waiter brought their drinks, then came back with

menus when Burke gave him the signal. It was quiet at the table as everyone scrutinized the choices. He'd eaten here enough in the last few weeks to know what he wanted and would much rather have looked Sydney over. Tonight she'd pulled her hair off her face and back into a messy side bun, leaving her neck bare.

The urge to taste her skin just below her ear was very powerful and if the two of them were alone at a quiet table in the shadows, that's exactly what he would have done. The strong attraction he felt certainly helped to pull off the pretense of having an interest in her because it really wasn't a pretense.

He *was* interested.

When everyone was ready the waiter took their orders. As it happened, he and Sydney chose almost the same things. Fireside chopped salad, although she asked for it without blue cheese crumbles. Filet mignon, medium rare. Baked potato with sour cream, butter and chives on the side.

Syd gave him a look that was half saucy, half surprised. "You have good taste."

Tom's expression was still just this side of skeptical. "He hasn't brought you here before?"

"If he had, you would have known about it," his daughter reminded him. "Camille owns the place and is normally the soul of discretion when it comes to lodge guests. But family is a different matter entirely. She couldn't keep something like that from you."

"It's a good quality in a daughter-in-law." Tom leveled his gaze at Burke as if to say he'd better have equally good qualities.

"Toast." Loretta raised her glass of white wine. "To new beginnings and happy endings."

They all touched glasses then took a sip of their respective drinks. When he glanced at Syd, he noticed a guilty look on her face and questioned whether or not he would have recognized the expression if he wasn't in on this scheme of hers. It made him wonder about her growing up and who better to ask than her father.

"What was Sydney like when she was a little girl?"

The older man looked fondly at his daughter. "Stubborn. Determined to get her way. She didn't like dolls the way other little girls did, but that could be from having two older brothers." He grinned. "Of course, she had me wrapped around her little finger."

"You did a wonderful job raising her," Burke said and sincerely meant it.

"She raised herself."

Loretta shook her head and put her hand on his arm. "You don't give yourself nearly enough credit, Tom. I know how difficult that time was for you, suddenly losing your wife. Then you were thrown into the deep end of the pool with two young boys and an infant daughter to bring up by yourself, while running your own business. The McKnight kids didn't get to be successful adults without your guidance and being a steady role model for them."

"You're making me blush." He took Loretta's hand in his own and smiled tenderly at her.

"I could go on torturing you," she teased. "I know how you hate to have anyone singing your praises."

Burke watched the older couple banter and laugh, comfortable with each other and clearly in love. From what Syd had said and Loretta had just corroborated, he knew Tom McKnight had had a rough go of it and had been alone for a long time. Burke realized how much his daughter loved him. She wanted him to be happy and was going above and beyond so that he would take the next step in his relationship.

A small deception. Wrong thing; right reason. Theirs was a close and loving relationship forged by his being there day after day. It made Burke feel even more guilty than usual about the long stretches of time he spent away from his own son.

Dinner was really pleasant and surprisingly interrogation-free, right up until the dessert menus arrived.

Syd looked hers over. "I'd love some coffee and just a few bites of something sweet."

"Order it and just eat what you want," Burke suggested.

"That's so wasteful," she protested. "And, unlike my leftover steak, dessert can be pretty unappetizing the next day."

"We could split something."

"I'm not sure we could agree and I don't want you to compromise for me."

"I'd be happy to compromise for you," he said. "But what if we do agree?"

"Okay. Tell me what your favorite is." She tilted her head to the side, making her neck look longer and even more tempting.

Quite possibly a nibble right at the juncture of her neck and shoulder could be his favorite, but that wasn't what she'd meant. So he answered honestly. "The mile-high chocolate cake. I've been all over the world and it's the best I've ever tasted. Anywhere."

"What do you know?" She smiled as if he'd given her the moon. "That just happens to be my all-time favorite, too."

"Then the deal is sealed."

When the waiter returned they ordered coffee all-around, one piece of cake and four forks. It was definitely enough for the whole table to share.

"Speaking of deals…are you two getting serious?" Tom glanced at Burke, then at Sydney.

"Dad!" She looked mortified. "Inappropriate."

"Not for a father," he insisted.

"Are you asking me what my intentions are?" Burke questioned.

"Sounds old-fashioned when you put it like that, but I guess that is what I'm asking."

This potential line of inquiry hadn't come up in their planning session. He looked at Sydney, wondering if she wanted to tackle that one, but she still looked shocked and speechless.

"Well, sir, for now we're taking things slow. Just getting to know each other. We both agree that's the best idea. Then we'll see what happens."

Tom mulled it over, then nodded. "Seems wise to do that."

Burke had to conclude that they'd passed the first hurdle. He'd done his best to answer everything honestly and still keep his word to Syd. But he realized that he liked her a lot and that was another topic they hadn't talked about. What if he actually wanted to date her?

In fact, tonight was their first official date and he was seriously considering taking things to the next level.

Sydney watched Burke charge the dinner-for-four to his room at the lodge and she was incredibly appreciative of the gesture. He and her father had done the masculine tug-of-war over the check that men always do, but Burke, as they said, was younger and faster. Although thanks had been expressed, she made a mental note to thank him again for his generosity the next time she saw him. And offer to split the bill with him.

The four of them stood and walked toward the restaurant exit, her father and Loretta in the lead. Burke leaned over and whispered close to her ear, "How do you think we did?"

It was difficult to form a reply, what with her unexpected breathlessness at his nearness. But she managed to recover. "We did pretty well," she admitted. "Loretta jumping in for backup was unexpected, but certainly strengthened the narrative we were promoting."

"Good. Apparently I played my part adequately, then."

"*Adequate* sets a very low bar for what you did. Your act was perfect."

Before she could say more, the couple in front of them stopped and waited. They were standing by the rustic stone fireplace in the lodge lobby with the registration desk nearby. Leather sofa and chairs formed a comfortable conversation area.

Tom extended his hand. "Burke, thanks again for dinner. I look forward to getting to know you better."

"Same here, sir." He looked at the mayor. "I believe we have a meeting this week."

She nodded. "We need to discuss local concerns about the resort."

"I'll be there to answer any and all questions." He didn't look the least bit concerned and his superior confidence was incredibly attractive.

"Are you ready to go, Syd?" her dad asked.

"You're leaving?" Burke put his hand at the small of her back.

"I rode into town with Dad and Loretta. So…" She shrugged.

"Stay for a nightcap." His eyes had just the right amount of intensity for a smitten man who didn't want to say goodnight yet. "I'll drive you home."

She wanted to protest that this wasn't part of the plan, but that would blow their cover for sure. "You must be tired after a long day. I don't want you to go out of your way."

"If I can spend more time with you, driving you home is not going out of my way." Now a definite challenge joined the intensity in his eyes.

Syd wasn't sure what game he was playing and was

wary of jumping in with her "come and get me" high heels. She'd picked this particular dress on purpose, knowing it was a little dangerous. The point had been to prove that she'd been dressing for a man's approval. This was an inconvenient time to realize it had done the job maybe a bit too well. When push came to shove she really had no choice.

She gave him her most brilliant smile and said, "I would love to stay. You don't mind, do you, Dad?"

"Of course not. As long as you make it to work on time in the morning."

She kissed his cheek while her own was flushed with the implication that she'd spend the night with Burke. "I won't be late tonight."

"But don't wait up," Burke said. "When Syd and I start talking, we lose track of time."

"Take good care of my girl." Her dad had that protective expression on his face.

"I will, sir. Good night."

When the older couple was gone, Burke took her hand and tucked it into the bend of his elbow before turning toward the lodge bar, where she'd first met him to propose this unlikely collaboration. Somehow the situation had slipped from her control and having a drink could further fuzzy her faculties on top of what her attraction to him did. Instinct was telling her she should stay sharp.

She looked up at Burke. "What about a walk instead?"

"In those shoes?" He took one step back and the corners of his mouth curved into a smile as he leisurely studied the four-inch pumps and her legs, all the way to where the hem of the dress stopped above her knees.

She shivered at the male approval clearly etched on his face. "I'm tough. Have you ever heard that Ginger Rogers did everything Fred Astaire did, only backwards and in heels?"

"I have actually. But I'm not quite sure what your point is since we're not dancing."

Says who? she thought.

"I'm not quite sure I had one," she admitted. "But as you probably know, there's a lighted walking path on the lodge grounds with benches here and there. If my feet can't take it, we can stop."

"A walk sounds good. It's a beautiful evening."

Burke put his fingers over hers, trapping her hand on his arm as they walked out the rear exit. To anyone observing them, they were a couple. Body language to support the story.

The evening air was cool, but not cold. As they strolled slowly down the cement path she noticed the moon peeking through the pine trees scattered over the grassy area.

"Did you know there was a full moon tonight?" she asked.

"No." He looked up. "But now that you mention it, this one is more beautiful than it is in Chicago."

"It occurs to me that the stage is perfectly set for romance. It's just a darn shame this is all going to waste on us."

"How do you mean?"

"We're just playing at it."

"That's the rumor," he answered mysteriously.

"And speaking of starting rumors..." She'd intended to express her gratitude for dinner the next time she saw him but hadn't realized she'd be alone with him quite so soon. But now was as good a time as any. "I just wanted to tell you how much I appreciate what you're doing for my dad. I didn't expect you to buy dinner tonight and I appreciate that so much. If you'd like I can reimburse you—"

"Of course not. Why would you think that?"

"I didn't mean to offend you. And I don't want to take

advantage of you. You're doing me a favor so I feel as if I should take the financial responsibility."

"No." He shook his head. "For so many reasons. But I sincerely meant what I said about it being my pleasure. I like your father. And he's a lucky man. Loretta is a wonderful woman. So I'm happy to give their happy ending a nudge."

How sweet was that?

She leaned into him just a little. "And I mean it when I say how appreciative I am for your participation." She thought about his moves from the moment he stared at her when she walked in, the kiss on the cheek, meaningful glances through dinner. Meeting his gaze, she said, "You're very good at this. The pretending, I mean. Should I be worried?"

"I'm getting whiplash. You went from appreciative to worried in a nanosecond."

"Don't get me wrong. I'm thankful for your talent but it makes me think you have practice."

"No." He laughed. "Just chalk it up to negotiating skills put to another purpose. I pay attention to details. I'm results-oriented and logistics are my strong suit."

"Well, you're playing your part to the hilt. That's really unexpected."

"Call me an overachiever." He stopped suddenly and looked down at her, something dark and exciting drifting into his eyes. "But consider this—did it ever occur to you that I'm not playing?"

She wasn't able to completely absorb the meaning of his words before he lowered his mouth to hers. The touch was soft and sweet. Seeking and seductive. His hand moved over her back, fingers brushing the bare skin. Shivers slid up and down her spine and her nerve endings started to dance. Heat balled in her belly when he put his arm around her waist and settled her more firmly against him.

It wasn't supposed to happen, but she kissed him back. She couldn't stop herself, didn't want to. Had she unknowingly given off vibes? Somehow let him know how attractive she found him? Whatever the reason, she was enjoying the heck out of this.

When he pulled back and looked at her, she could hear and see that his breathing was unsteady. She would have taken a great deal of satisfaction from that fact except hers was ragged, too. That wasn't good.

They stared at each other for several moments and she knew she had to say something. *Keep it light,* she thought. "That was a nice touch. Like I said, acting is your strong suit. But I'm surprised that you kissed me."

"The fact that you're a beautiful woman doesn't explain my motivation?"

Oh, how she wanted to be flattered, but it wasn't wise to go there. "It would, except that you've been seen with some of the world's most beautiful women."

"But none of them can keep the engine in my car purring like a kitten. And I don't mean that as a double entendre. You are a rare, unusual and special woman."

"Thank you." With every fiber of her being she wanted to believe that. "But remember we have to keep our eye on the ball. There are lofty goals at stake."

"It's never far from my mind."

"Good. Then you understand when I say that you can't be kissing me for no reason."

"Maybe I had one." He indicated the light just beside them that made their every move visible to the people milling around the lodge patio not far away. A member of the staff was straightening the outdoor furniture.

"So we could be seen. It's what a man dating a woman would do."

How silly was she to be even the tiniest bit disappointed

to learn that he didn't mean it? Later she would give herself a stern talking-to about how ridiculous her reaction was.

"Yes. And speaking of dating, we have to plan our next move. Your father's remark about looking forward to getting to know me better was his way of letting us know he's watching."

"I got that, too."

And she got something else from tonight. A warning that her control regarding Burke Holden was nothing but an illusion. He was a strong man, a powerful man accustomed to getting his own way. She'd dated guys and broken up with them and never looked back, but she had a sneaking suspicion that this could be different.

That didn't make her happy, but unfortunately she was stuck.

Chapter Four

On his way to the county buildings on the other side of Blackwater Lake, Burke drove past McKnight Auto and glanced over. Several cars were lined up waiting for service orders to be written up, but there was no sign of Sydney. He hadn't realized how much he'd hoped for a glimpse of her until he didn't get one. If she hadn't approached him with her unorthodox proposal, would he have asked her out?

On his part the attraction had been instantaneous so there was a better-than-even chance he would have. But after dinner with her father and the mayor the other night, it was crystal clear that if he'd followed his usual pattern of avoiding a woman he would have missed something… exciting? Special? Life-changing?

Maybe all of the above. But whatever happened, this *thing* could never be permanent. When it came to his personal life, *permanent* and *forever* weren't part of the vocabulary.

He turned left onto Mountain Street and drove a couple of blocks. The city and county government offices were on the right. He knew where the mayor's office was, having been there several times, and the construction-permits office was somewhere under the same roof.

He parked in the rear lot and walked through the heavy glass doors into the lobby. There was a directory on the wall and Burke saw that the building inspector's office number was located on the second floor. There was an elevator, but he found the stairs and headed up. Too many hours behind a desk could add weight to his midsection. He worked out daily at the lodge fitness center but never missed an opportunity to move more.

When he was home, Liam frequently asked him to play ball, any kind. Baseball, football, soccer. Too often Burke had to say no because of work commitments. He wished he could delegate a lot of details and be home more, but he'd tried that a few times and there was no one he trusted enough. Things got missed, delays resulted and when that happened it cost the company millions. Burke was building an already successful business with his cousin Sloan and someday it would be Liam's. He felt an obligation to leave it more profitable than he'd found it.

Burke located the office and went inside. There was a waiting area with a couch, chairs and a coffee table. A high desk was situated on the left and he walked over. A blonde woman somewhere in her late thirties or early forties was standing there.

"Hi. I'm Burke Holden."

"Sally Gardiner," she said, introducing herself. "I've heard about you."

"Really?" He in no way meant to flirt, but what was a guy supposed to say to that? Just be friendly. "I hope it was positive."

"You're the fella who's building that new resort up on

the mountain. You've got a flashy red sports car. And you had dinner with Sydney McKnight and her dad and the mayor at the Fireside the other night."

"News travels fast. And it's all true," he said.

"Generally stories being passed around town are factual and details aren't made up or exaggerated." She grinned. "Folks here in Blackwater Lake take pride in the integrity of our rumor mill."

"Good to know," he said.

"If anything, whoever's doing the telling plays down personal opinion. But you're even more handsome than I heard."

"Thank you. I'd hate to disappoint."

"So," she said, "are you and Sydney an item?"

In a way, he thought, but not how she meant. "Well…"

"Sorry. I'm nosy. But the thing is, folks are going to ask me. It'll be all over town that you were in here today." She shrugged.

"An item?" Burke thought for a moment. "Not unless you define an item as a man and woman who are getting to know each other."

"Hmm." It seemed as if she was the tiniest bit disappointed in the answer. "Okay, then. What is it I can do for you today, Mr. Holden?"

"Burke, please. You'll probably be seeing a lot of me around here." He smiled pleasantly, but there was no response from the clerk. "I'm here to look into building permits for the resort."

"You'll need to speak with the building department supervisor."

"That would be great. Is he free?"

"I'll check for you. Have a seat."

"Thanks."

Burke did as asked but had hoped to be shown in without having to wait. There was a lot to do back at the office and he had a scheduled call with his cousin soon. After ten minutes he began to look at his watch. Probably he should have called ahead to make an appointment. He didn't want to be perceived as presumptuous. That little detail would spread like a wind-driven wildfire and not make his work life in this small town easier.

Just when he was wondering whether or not to leave a message that he would call and schedule a time, Sally walked back behind the counter.

"Sorry I took so long, Burke. Had to update John on some things. He'll see you now."

Burke had seen John Donnelly, Building Supervisor, stenciled on the door to this office. "Thank you."

"Follow me. Through there." She pointed to the door separating the waiting area from the back offices.

Sally led him down the hall to the last office, which was probably the biggest. The door was open and she poked her head in. "John, this is the fella I was telling you about."

"Thanks, Sally." The man was in his late fifties, with gray hair and brown eyes. He was a little over six feet tall because they were eye-to-eye when he stood and held out his hand. "John Donnelly. Nice to meet you, Mr. Holden."

"Burke."

"Okay." He indicated the two chairs in front of a desk where construction plans were unrolled for further scrutiny. In the corners of the room, similar rolls were standing up in stacks, probably blueprints waiting for approval. "Have a seat, Burke."

"Thanks."

"What can I do for you?"

"I wanted to introduce myself. As you probably know, I'm in charge of building the resort up on the mountain. It's my job to facilitate construction, cross the *t*'s and dot the *i*'s. In my experience, the process of doing that is much smoother after I get to know who I'll be working with."

John, cool and assessing, leaned back in his desk chair. "I can see that."

"It would also be helpful to know what paperwork the county requires. Every one is a little different."

"Sure." The other man nodded.

"I've researched codes and zoning restrictions for Blackwater Lake but wanted to find out from the guy in charge if I have the latest information."

"I can help you with that."

"It would speed things along to know how many copies of the building plans and site plans you require. How much detail we need to add. Make sure you don't have to ask for more documentation." Burke looked at the man, who was nodding his agreement.

"That would sure help us out at this end," he admitted.

"Mayor Goodson assured me that the length of time required and the permit application process is shorter and less intense than a city like Chicago, Los Angeles or New York. Simply because here there's not the large volume of requests."

"True enough. But we keep busy."

"I have no doubt. The thing is, delays can be costly and time-consuming." Stuff that needlessly kept him away from home. And Liam. "I'd like to avoid that if possible."

"I can sure understand that." John leaned forward and rested his elbows on the desk. "And here's where I'm coming from, Burke. It's come to my attention that you're seeing Sydney McKnight."

"We've met," Burke said cautiously. The man's pleasant tone didn't change, but there was something uncompromising in his dark eyes. "Sir, I don't mean to be critical here. And I'm aware that things are different in a small town. But I'm a little confused about how that information is relevant to my getting construction and electrical permits issued in a timely fashion."

John pointed to a picture on his desk, one of several and nearly obscured by the unrolled paperwork. It was a photo of this man with his arm affectionately thrown across Syd's shoulders. Both were smiling. "Sydney is my niece."

Burke did his best not to show surprise. If the last name had been the same, he'd have been better prepared. This guy must be her deceased mother's brother. "I see."

"Maybe you do. Maybe not. It's not clear from what I hear whether or not you're dating my niece, but you should know that I've been extraprotective of her since the day she was born. So I'd prefer that she's a happy camper. That girl and my brother-in-law have been through a lot. I'd sure hate to see anyone do anything to hurt her." He hesitated a moment, letting the words sink in. "And whatever the mayor told you about a short waiting period for plan approval could be a little off. If you get my drift."

Burke definitely got it. The drift was clear. Don't do Sydney wrong or the permits could be delayed, costing him time and money.

He stood and met the other man's gaze. "I assure you that Sydney is safe with me."

"Sure hope so, son."

Burke shook the man's hand, left the office, nodded to Sally behind the desk, then walked into the hall and back down the stairs the way he'd come. This was an aspect of small-town life that he hadn't taken into account. Since his philosophy was not to get deeply involved with a woman, it hadn't occurred to him there was a potential conflict of interest if he did.

Still, he was pretty sure he'd told Syd's uncle the truth about her being safe with him. She wasn't looking to get serious and had volunteered to handle the details about them breaking up. Considering that, she should be able to pull off convincing everyone that she wasn't hurt by their relationship.

But any ideas Burke had of taking things to the next level with her would be best ignored. Personal risks weren't his style and factoring in the business complications made taking any chances too costly.

Still, he was committed to helping convince Syd's father they were a couple. That would make her happy and now he had business reasons for keeping her that way.

After rotating the tires, Syd looked at the underside of the 2012 Chevrolet sport utility vehicle up on the hydraulic lift. Always a good idea to make sure the frame was solid. The customer had said the ride wasn't as smooth as it could be. Part of the reason could be that Blackwater Lake was surrounded by rural area. Critters large and small crossed the roads whenever they felt the need and mostly at inconvenient times.

She didn't like thinking about that, but stuff turned up and finding it here at the shop was in her job description, so she looked and fortunately didn't see anything wrong. She would change the oil, then check the fuel injection system.

There were footsteps on the cement floor behind her. A man's footsteps in dress shoes, not boots or sneakers. Burke Holden.

Could be someone else, but she had a feeling it wasn't. Just thinking his name made her heart beat a little faster. She took a deep breath then turned to face him. "Hi."

"Hi, yourself."

"I'm guessing you didn't see the sign."

One corner of his mouth quirked up. "You mean the one about customers not being allowed in the service area?"

"That would be the one."

"It's a liability issue and I don't plan on having an accident, let alone filing a lawsuit against your business."

"Good to know."

He moved closer and pulled her into his arms, then lowered his mouth to hers. The sudden and unexpected intimacy sucked the air from her lungs and started her pulse racing. His lips were soft, so soft, and she felt herself sinking into the kiss in spite of the warning her brain was trying to send that she shouldn't respond.

He cupped the side of her face in his palm and brushed his thumb over her cheek, caressing, mesmerizing, tempting. The sound of a tricked-out truck roaring by on the street brought her to her senses, reminding her where she was.

She pulled back, hoping he wouldn't see that his kiss had affected her, made her tremble from head to toe. Brushing her dirty hands over her equally dirty work shirt and pants, she said, "I'm greasy. It's going to get all over those expensive clothes you're wearing."

He glanced down at his slacks and sports shirt and shrugged. "A devoted boyfriend doesn't care about things like that."

Speaking in the third person was a dead giveaway that he wasn't talking about himself. And for some reason that kiss had felt a lot like a giant "take that," as if he was trying to make a point to someone. "Why did you kiss me?"

"Your father's watching."

"How do you know?"

"I stopped in the office. He told me where to find you and warned me about customers in the service bay."

Syd peeked past him and saw that it was true. Tom McKnight was looking at them through the window of his office. It was so tempting to wave, but she held back. Make it look real and natural, she reminded herself. The man's future happiness was at stake.

She looked up at Burke. "I have to say again that you're very good at role-playing."

"It's a gift." His face had faux humility all over it.

"I didn't expect to see you here." But she was happy he'd stopped by, a thought that was something to rationalize later.

"I just met your uncle."

"Oh?"

He nodded. "I went to the county building services office about permits for the resort. Turns out he handles that sort of thing."

In the brief time she'd known Burke Holden, Syd had grown accustomed to his easygoing manner. It was missing in action at the moment.

"And?" she asked.

"Several things, actually." He smiled but there was no amusement in his eyes. "Sally Gardiner wanted to know if we're an item."

So the rumor mill was already grinding out information. It was good when a plan came together. "Don't keep me in suspense. What did you tell her?"

"That you and I are in the process of getting acquainted. She would have to make the determination about whether or not we're item-worthy."

"Good answer."

"Thank you."

"What else happened?" she asked. He'd said there were several things.

"Your uncle John warned me that if I hurt you the process for obtaining building permits would be significantly longer than I'd been led to believe."

"Did he actually say that in so many words?"

"Not exactly. It was more of a general implication."

So he had more skin in the game now. That's why he'd kissed her as if there was something at stake. "I'm sorry, Burke—"

"It would have been helpful if I'd known you were related to the man in charge of signing off on building permits."

She heard the annoyance in his voice and chalked it up to him not liking surprises. Couldn't blame the man for that. They weren't her favorite thing, either.

"I'm sorry, but I didn't know you were going to see him."

"I need permits before breaking ground on this project. That's a given."

Now she was starting to get annoyed. Syd put a hand on her hip and met his gaze. "I'm a mechanic, not a builder. It's not my job to know how that process works and I can't read your mind. If you'd mentioned it, I'd have passed on the information of a family connection." She took a deep breath. "I asked you to do me a favor and I'm grateful for your help. But if this is going to impact your business in a negative way feel free to back out. I will explain to Uncle John that this is my fault."

He stared at her for a moment, then smiled, chasing away most of the tension. "I think we just had our first fight."

Syd wanted to stay irritated but couldn't manage to maintain it. She laughed. "Who won?"

"I think it was a draw."

"Seriously though, how macho and protective was my uncle?"

"On a scale of one to ten?" He thought for a moment. "About a twelve. Firm but friendly."

"Uncle John isn't a mean, vindictive man. And he's extraordinarily professional. His integrity is impeccable. I'm sure he would never use his position of authority to settle a score. And I would never let it go that far."

"I believe you, Syd." He dragged his fingers through his hair. "But I need to hedge my bets. We've put a lot of time and money into materials, delivery, manpower and schedules. There's built-in flexibility for unexpected delays, but too many could be a big problem."

"I'll talk to him. Don't worry," she said. "He's really a sweetheart."

"Maybe, but the boundaries he set for his niece's boyfriend were quite clear." One corner of his mouth lifted. "And I'd rather wait before you talk with him and possibly jeopardize the plan."

"So you still want to go through with it?" She wouldn't blame him in the least if he backed out of the whole thing.

"Not only do I want to see it through, it's quite possible the number of official dates we agreed on won't be enough to convince him that I didn't have nefarious intentions such as leading you on."

"Are you talking about my dad or Uncle John?"

"Both."

"That's really generous of you, Burke." She shook her head. "But I really feel awful about this and it's not what you signed on for. I had no idea this could end up being a professional problem for you. I was only thinking about helping my dad."

"As far as potential business problems are concerned, let's cross that bridge if and when it becomes necessary. For now we act as if spending time together isn't a hardship."

It wasn't a hardship and she wasn't acting. "If it's a problem for you, hanging out with me, I mean—"

"Not at all." He took her hand and linked their fingers. "In fact it's interesting. Going through the 'getting to know you' stage on the way to 'being an item' phase of our relationship with everyone watching is…different."

"Really?" She was pretty sure the words were sincere, but figured the doubts creeping in were normal under the circumstances.

"Really. The thing is, what you asked me to do is way beyond what most daughters would do. I have to conclude that you'd do anything for someone you love. Any man would be lucky to be that someone. And it makes you quite a unique and intriguing woman."

"That's nice of you to say."

"It's not just words, Syd. I truly mean it." He grinned.

"Well…thank you." She didn't know what to make of that comment or the intensity of the gaze he settled on her. Somehow, the line was starting to blur between what constituted acting like a man who was interested and what was real. And the probability was that his motivation for doing this was to avoid business problems.

"And now, just in case your father is still watching…"

He leaned down and kissed her again. Just a quick brush of lips. The gesture a smitten man would make when he was saying goodbye to the woman with whom he was smitten. After pulling back, he moved in again for one more brief touch of his mouth to hers, as if he was reluctant to say goodbye.

"I have to go. I'll call you later."

"Okay."

She watched him walk away and was more confused than calmed by this visit.

The feel of her hand in his had felt warm and wonderful. She liked kissing him, too, which was fortunate because it was an aspect of playing the part she'd asked him to play.

The downside was that it felt too real. Falling for the man she'd pulled into her scheme wasn't part of the plan. She'd gotten him into this mess and now he was playing his part to the hilt so his resort project wouldn't be delayed.

Something about the way this was all changing made *her* want to back out. But she was doing this for her father and Tom McKnight hadn't raised a quitter.

Chapter Five

"Are you sure you want to go to this park dedication?" Sydney asked.

"Yes." It had been Burke's idea and they were on their way there now.

He looked at her sitting in the passenger seat of his car and had the absurd thought that she looked really good there. Her dark hair was long and loose, sexy and silky. A yellow, thin-strapped tank top left her shoulders bare and denim shorts hugged her hips in the nicest way possible. "It's a beautiful day. The sun is out. Sky is blue. And I've been told that this perfect weather won't last much longer."

"Who told you that?"

Actually her old friend Violet had mentioned it when he'd gone to the Grizzly Bear for lunch one day.

"People in the diner who have lived here." He glanced over and saw her mouth curve up, an indication that a sassy remark was coming his way.

"Do you believe everything strangers tell you?"

"As a matter of fact, I've grown quite close to some of the regulars at the Grizzly Bear Diner. That tends to happen when a guy is away from home and eating all his meals in restaurants."

"I'm guessing that's supposed to make me take pity and invite you over for a home-cooked meal?"

Burke was looking at the road ahead and couldn't see her expression, but heard the teasing in her voice. "Is it working?"

"We could make it one of our mutually agreed upon designated dates."

"Yeah."

He should be glad the terms of her proposal were clearly spelled out. The added pressure of a delay in building permits should have made him grateful that this didn't start out complicated.

But it was going in that direction. Ever since the day he'd stopped by the garage and told her about the conversation with her uncle, he'd gotten the distinct impression that Syd was putting him off. He'd asked her to dinner one night and got a vague response about having other plans. She declined an invitation to a movie with the excuse of an emergency job that required overtime at the garage.

There were notices all over town about the grand opening of the new park and all the planned activities to celebrate it. This morning he'd called at the last minute and before he could ask her out, she'd said she was going. He'd informed her that he was, too, and said he would come by her house in an hour to get her. Before she could wiggle out of it, he hung up. Now here they were, almost to the park that was located two blocks south of the square in the center of town.

He pulled into the newly paved parking lot and found a space between freshly painted white lines. A large banner was strung between two pine trees and proclaimed the grand opening of Blackwater Lake Park. Newly seeded grass was roped off, but cement paths led to a children's play area with multiple configurations of climbing apparatus, slides and swings. It was set on a hard foam foundation to make unanticipated landings a little more forgiving.

Burke felt a pang when he thought how much Liam would enjoy this, but he wasn't here. His son was following his usual routine at home and Burke hated that they were separated even though he believed stability was the most favorable option. Being a single dad, he always felt conflicted about what was in his son's best interest.

"It's awfully quiet over there," Syd said. "Either you hate this date with me, or the park has triggered some unhappy suppressed childhood memories."

He looked at her and his smile was forced. "I was just thinking how much my son would like this park."

"So he's got a thing for the outdoors?"

"He's a boy." Burke shrugged.

"Right. Enough said." She was studying him closely. "You really miss him, don't you?"

"Yeah, I do." She'd noticed his mood when he'd taken her to the diner for dinner. And the longer he and his son were apart, the more he could feel the emotional distance between them growing. Daily phone calls were unsatisfying. Infrequent trips home weren't enough to build a strong bond.

"You'll be here awhile, right? Why don't you have him with you? Unless his mother objects."

Burke hadn't told her much about his ex-wife and didn't really want to now so he ignored her comment. "When I got here in August I thought about having him here with me, at least for a few weeks until school started. But he doesn't know anyone and I'm working long hours."

"There are ways to deal—"

"What do you say we put the serious stuff on hold and go have some fun?" he suggested.

"That's code and it means you really don't want to talk about this." She stared at him for several moments, then nodded and opened her door. "Okay. Sounds like a plan. Dad's already here. He had to show up early to help organize. When I texted and told him we were coming, he answered that he'd grabbed a table and there was room for us."

They exited the car and headed up the walkway to the area designated for activities. Near a mature expanse of grass there were picnic tables already occupied by families. There were blankets and chairs arranged nearby for folks who got there too late.

Park barbecues were smoking as town officials and volunteer chamber-of-commerce members were cooking hamburgers and hot dogs paid for out of community funds. He saw Tom McKnight and Mayor Goodson working together and brushing up against each other intimately, the way couples do.

Speaking of couples…

Burke took Syd's hand into his own. He sensed more than felt her want to pull away, but she didn't and he liked the feel of her fingers in his palm. Taking their relationship public was working for him in a big way.

"Lights, camera, action," he said.

They made their way along the path and greeted people. Burke was surprised how many he knew and Syd said hello to everyone. She stopped to chat with an older couple about their aging truck and he glanced up ahead. Violet Stewart, hostess at the diner and Syd's former friend, was there with two kids and a nice-looking man who was probably her husband…and the guy who had dumped Syd years ago. Burke knew when she spotted them because he felt her tense.

66 A DECENT PROPOSAL

He leaned down to whisper in her ear. "We can take a detour."

"Not my style."

So they kept going and stopped by the young family. Burke nodded. "Hi, Vi."

"Burke." There was forced cheerfulness in the woman's voice. Her gaze drifted to Syd. "Hi."

"Hey." She looked at the man and it wasn't hard to tell this was the first time she'd seen him since all the bad stuff went down. "Charlie."

"How are you, Syd?"

"Good." She squeezed Burke's hand, then let it go. "Charlie Stewart, this is Burke Holden."

The two men shook hands and said all the right things while tension flowed like a swollen river between the two women.

"Well…we have to go meet my dad." Syd angled her head in the general direction of the barbecues.

"Yeah." There was a lot of regret in Violet's voice. "It was good to see you. Have fun, you two."

"Right. You guys, too. Later." Syd lifted a hand, then headed for the table near where her father was cooking.

Side by side they sat on the bench. Their shoulders brushed and heat that had nothing to do with the Montana sun shining above shot through him. Burke did his best to ignore the sensation because of the tricky situation.

Still, he was curious about something and they were far enough away from everyone not to be overheard. "How was it seeing Charlie again?" he asked.

"Weird," she said, glancing around at the people nearby watching her and the couple who had hurt her in the past.

"Weird bad or good?"

"Not bad," she admitted. "It's been a long time. I don't feel anything for him. But Violet—"

"She seems nice," he said.

"And how do you know?"

"I've seen her a lot in the diner. It's what happens when a guy—"

"Has to eat out in restaurants," she finished for him with a grin. It faded quickly. And there was wistfulness in her voice when she said, "She is nice. And they look good together. Two beautiful kids. A boy and girl. The perfect family."

"There's no such thing as perfect."

"I know. And that wasn't a bitter comment. Far from it." She met his gaze. "I envy her. I'm envious of them."

"So you want a family?"

She shrugged. "It's what my dad wants for me."

"What are you after?" he asked, really curious.

"It's easier to tell you what I *don't* want." She glanced around and people looked away. "This is the downside of small-town life. Call me stubborn, but I'm not going to give them anything to talk about. I intend to talk to Violet, but not when it would be a public spectacle."

"Good for you." He slung his arm across her shoulders and pulled her into a side hug, aware that she'd veered away from a thumb up or down on the topic of children and family. "Gossip may be a negative aspect of small-town life, but it works for our purposes. We're all about making a public spectacle of ourselves."

At that moment Tom McKnight turned to smile and wave at his daughter. She leaned in to Burke and put her hand on his jeans-covered thigh. Yeah, this arrangement was working for him in unexpectedly awesome ways.

When the coast was clear, she put some distance between them and removed her hand, curling her fingers into her palm as if it was scorched. Count him in on that.

"So," she said, clearing her throat. "You certainly have lots of acquaintances in town."

"There's a good reason for that."

"What might it be?" she asked sweetly.

"I'm dating the sweetheart of Blackwater Lake and everyone has gone out of their way to make my acquaintance. They're watching over you. The only hitch in the plan is that when we break up, they'll want to cut my heart out with a spoon."

"Only if you elope with my best friend."

"And who would that be?"

"I don't have one anymore." Her gaze was wistful when it shifted to the young family not far away. "But in the plus column we can consider this date number two."

"How do you figure? By my count this is our first."

"Don't forget dinner with Dad and Loretta."

"Ah." He didn't want to count that one because it was a double date and they hadn't been alone. Mostly it annoyed him to be counting down the times he would see her.

The depth of his reluctance to put a finite number of meetings on their arrangement was surprising. More and more he was realizing that she was the most intriguing woman he'd met in a very long time.

"How pathetic did you have to look to get Cam to invite you to dinner?" Syd asked Burke.

"No more than usual." He glanced over at her and grinned.

The day after the park dedication she was in the car beside him again. This was getting to be a habit and it was unclear as yet if that was a good thing or not. On the good side, he looked awfully sexy behind the wheel of this expensive, sporty car. She debated whether or not to tell him when winter arrived, which could be a matter of weeks because Montana weather could be unpredictable, he was going to want a four-wheel-drive vehicle. Knowing how he loved this car, she decided to keep the comment to herself.

She was more curious about something else than what car he would choose to drive on icy roads. "How do you feel about having Sunday dinner with my family?"

"I'm looking forward to it," he said.

"So how did the invitation come about?"

"After I dropped you off at home yesterday and came back to the lodge, I ran into Cam. She invited me then."

"Her idea?" Syd asked, teasing. She'd been with him in the bar when her sister-in-law talked to him about setting a date to meet her husband and daughter. "You didn't plead for a home-cooked meal?"

"I would have if I'd thought of it. But the word on the street is spreading about us and it was high time I met the rest of the McKnights."

"Okay, then."

Syd listened for even a tiny trace of nerves in his voice but heard nothing. Ice water in his veins, she thought. Probably for the best since she was nervous enough for both of them.

"You do know my brothers will be there, right? With their wives? And children. Small ones. Babies, really. Just adorably toddling around."

"You left out your dad and Loretta."

"They're not the ones I'm concerned about since we already had dinner with them. It's Alex and Ben. My brothers are no one's fools."

"You think they'll suspect we're trying to pull a fast one?"

"Dad is wary and he's probably said something to them."

"Then we'll have to lay it on thick." Something in his voice said he wouldn't mind that a bit.

Syd couldn't help the small ripple of pleasure at the thought. If she was being honest, getting cozy with him was a very appealing option.

Burke confidently and competently drove the car around the lake. From here it wasn't far to her brother's house. "This is a really beautiful area."

"I love it." The words were simple but incredibly heart-felt. "I can't imagine living anywhere else."

She looked at the water, where late-afternoon sun turned it a brilliant blue. Closer to the shoreline, shadows from the mountains and trees crept slowly toward the mid-dle of the lake. "My brother Alex builds custom homes around here. He built Ben and Cam's and his own. Ellie, his wife, is an architect and drew up the plans."

"I'll have to talk to him about that."

"What? Are you thinking of moving here?" That sur-prised her for a lot of reasons.

"When the resort is booming, this area is going to be exclusive. Location, location. A second home would be a good investment."

For a moment she'd thought it might be personal, but not so much. He was a businessman, after all, and they had an agreement. There was nothing personal about that. Right now all she could worry about was getting through this family dinner unscathed.

Burke made a right turn into the driveway of Ben and Cam's home. He pulled to a stop beside her father's truck. Alex's car was there, too, which meant they were the last to arrive. Syd looked at the house and the bright lights coming from inside. There was a three-car garage and the front yard had an expanse of velvety green grass encircled by manicured bushes and flowers. They got out of the car and walked to the imposing double-door entry, where she pushed the doorbell.

"Here goes nothing," she muttered before the door was opened.

Camille Halliday McKnight stood there with her warm

welcoming smile. "Hi, you two. Glad you could join us, Burke. Come in."

"I'm grateful for the invitation. For a nomad like me restaurant food can get old."

"Syd…" Her sister-in-law's voice had a chiding note in it. "Shame on you for not having him over to dinner at your house."

They hadn't even been here a minute and she was busted already. If they were really dating she would have cooked for him. Cam's remark caught her completely off guard and she couldn't think of anything to say.

"She's mentioned it." Burke to the rescue with a loose interpretation of their understanding. "But I've been busy and we've been taking things slow. Didn't want to go public with this too soon."

"Like father, like daughter," Cam said, closing the door behind them. "I was completely surprised to find out your dad and the mayor had been secretly dating for a while."

"Go figure," Syd said. "We McKnights are an unconventional bunch."

"Come and meet everyone," Cam invited.

She led them through the large, two-story entry with an overhead chandelier, then into the spacious family room with connecting kitchen. Loretta was setting the table and Alex's wife was stirring something on the stove.

She waved and said, "I'm Ellie. Nice to meet you, Burke."

"Likewise," he said.

Her eighteen-month-old daughter, Leah, was sitting on the family room floor with her nearly two-year-old cousin, Amanda. The two little girls were surrounded by toys.

Alex and Ben stood with their father by the river-rock fireplace and all three turned to look at Sydney and Burke. She knew it wasn't possible but felt as if *fraud* was tattooed across her forehead. *Never let them see you sweat,* she thought, then slid her hand into Burke's and plastered a big smile on her face as they joined the group.

"Alex, Ben, this is Burke Holden." She watched as her brothers shook his hand, polite but suspicious.

"So you're going out with my baby sister," Alex said. He hadn't lost the oldest-brother protective streak he'd honed as the oldest boy looking out for his younger siblings.

"Yes." This time Burke didn't say "that's the rumor" because they really had gone out.

Syd knew her brother badly wanted to ask what his intentions were, but to his credit he held back.

Ben held out his hand. "I hear you're building a big resort."

"It's going to be a very successful endeavor for my company, but for Blackwater Lake, too. I was just saying to Syd that property values are going to go through the roof." He looked at Alex. "Your development here on the lake is going to be the place to live."

"We just hope it doesn't grow so fast that ancillary services can't keep up," Ben said. "Medical care for example."

"I've talked to the mayor about that and a hospital is going to be in the short-term plans. A small regional airport is going in simultaneously with the building near the ski resort."

"You've thought of everything," her dad said.

"Probably not, but the team and I are doing our best on this project. We don't want to mess it up."

"And we'd prefer that you don't," Alex said. "This is our home."

Syd listened and could read between the lines of what was being said. Watching their faces, she tried to see them objectively. Her brothers were about the same height as their father, a little over six feet, and both had brown eyes. Alex's hair was dark, almost black, while Ben's had highlights from the sun making it lighter. That was ironic since he was a doctor—an orthopedic specialist—and spent most of his time indoors. As a building contractor, Alex was outside most of the time.

"How do you like Blackwater Lake?" he asked.

"It's what I would call idyllic," Burke answered. "My cousin and partner, Sloan, is the one who brought the area to my attention a few years ago and we both agree on the potential."

Just then Syd felt a small hand on her leg and looked down to see blonde, blue-eyed Amanda smiling up at her. She babbled something that sounded a lot like "auntie."

"Hi, baby girl." Syd bent and picked up the toddler. "You're getting so big and even more beautiful than last week when I saw you."

Cam, sporting oven mitts, was looking on from the kitchen.

"You're just prejudiced, Auntie Syd."

"Definitely. And proud of it." She looked down when another little hand patted her leg. With dark hair and eyes, Leah favored her daddy, Alex. "Hi, munchkin. You're so big, too. And even more beautiful than when I saw you last week." She looked at Ellie, the child's mother, and said, "Gotta keep it even."

"Good for you, Auntie Syd." Ellie smiled fondly.

It was obvious the toddler wanted to be held, too, but Syd had her hands full. "I can't pick you up, sweetie."

As if Leah understood, she turned and slapped the closest leg, which happened to be Burke's. When your world perspective came from such a low center of gravity, probably all males in jeans looked like your daddy.

This could go one of two ways. Either the little one would get loud in her demands, or lose interest and move on. Neither of those things happened. It never occurred to Syd that Burke would voluntarily pick up Leah, but pick her up he did.

"Hey, little bit. How's life treating you?"

The little girl's smile showed off the fact that she was intrigued by the handsome stranger as so many women often were.

"I'll take her," Alex offered.

"That's okay." Burke studied the child in his strong arms. "She's a cutie. In about fifteen years both of your dads are going to have their hands full."

"Don't remind us." The look on Ben's face said he was rejecting that idea with every fiber of his being. "Dad's been doing a good job of rubbing that in since Amanda and Leah were born."

"I've been offering to pay for my granddaughters' room and board until age thirty-five at that convent in the Himalayas." Tom grinned at his sons. "God knows I wish I'd done that for your sister."

"You know I'm standing here, right?" Syd said.

"I do. And this isn't anything I haven't said to your face," her father replied.

"Okay, then." She snuggled the little girl in her arms more securely and kissed the chubby cheek. "Men can be so annoying."

"You know we're all standing here, right?" Burke said, one eyebrow lifted.

"Yes, but in case anyone missed it, I'd be happy to say it louder," she offered.

"We got the message." Alex seemed unfazed. "And just so you know, there's not a zinger you can come up with that would keep me from protecting my little girl as long as I live. Or any other important woman in my life for that matter." He slid an unmistakably protective look at her and Burke seemed to get the message.

"Well said." Burke nodded slightly, letting the other man know he understood.

The little girl he was holding patted his cheek to get

his attention, then pointed to the pile of toys in the center of the room. At the same time, Amanda was squirming to get down, so Syd complied and set her on the rug, where she looked up then at the playthings and grunted.

"Offhand I'd say we're being drafted for duty," Burke commented.

"I wasn't sure you were picking up the signals." She shrugged. "You don't have to. I can handle this."

When he put Leah down, she grabbed his hand and leaned her tiny body in the direction she wanted to go. His smile was full of boyish charm guaranteed to melt female hearts from coast to coast and Syd was no exception.

"This little girl is not going to take no for an answer," he said. "Let's do this."

"Okay," Syd said to Cam, Ellie and Loretta, who were busy with dinner prep. "We would help you guys in the kitchen but these girls are determined to play."

"Trust me," Ben said behind her. "If you play with them, that is helping in the kitchen."

"Good. Works for me."

She and Burke sat on the beige rug near the toys and let the toddlers hand them dolls, plastic cell phones and a scaled-down pink play stroller. Her nieces were chattering in a language no one could understand with the possible exception of their moms. She watched Burke, trying to decide if he was really this good-natured or just a gifted actor who would really rather take a sharp stick in the eye than play with girl toys.

The thing was, she didn't think he was that talented a performer and got the feeling he really liked kids. This high-powered, focused, *über*successful CEO was a sucker for children.

Color her surprised.

About fifteen minutes later Cam and Ellie directed their husbands to take the babies upstairs for a diaper change, adding that dinner would be ready in about thirty minutes. The dads grabbed up their daughters and disappeared as ordered. Syd enjoyed seeing her big strong brothers tamed. It was a sign that they were happy to be settled down with two exceptional women who loved them.

Still in troop-commander mode, Cam told Syd that she should give Burke a tour of the backyard. A look in her sister-in-law's eyes said she was being given a break and should take advantage.

Syd nodded then said to Burke, "Want to see the backyard?"

"Sure."

Her dad grinned at Loretta. "Since diaper duty has already been assigned, I'll help you with whatever you're doing."

The mayor smiled back. "That means looking over my shoulder and critiquing."

"Maybe." The twinkle in Tom McKnight's eyes was good to see.

Syd wondered why she hadn't noticed that before her father's secret relationship had been outed. For better or worse, now that she had noticed, she would do everything in her power to keep that happy look right where it was.

Burke stood and held out his hand to help her up. When she was on her feet, he didn't let go. Between the warm, cozy feeling of her fingers in his and the adorable image of him playing with the girls, Sydney wasn't so sure it was a good idea to be alone with him. But it wasn't about her or what she wanted, so she led him to the French doors that would take them outside.

Strategically placed lights illuminated the brick patio and outside furniture. There was a pool and spa in the center of the yard and a gazebo in the far corner that overlooked the lake below in the distance. Like the front, there was an abundance of grass and shrubs. This place was like something out of a fairy tale, Syd thought.

"This is Ben's backyard," she announced.

"I would never have guessed." Burke looked around. "It's beautifully done."

"I couldn't agree more." She removed her hand from his and folded her arms over her chest. "So, we got over that hurdle. First meeting of the whole family."

"They all seem very nice."

"Even though my brother Alex subtly threatened you?" she asked.

"I respect his instinct to look after the people he cares about."

"You know he really won't beat you up when our quote-unquote romance goes south, right?"

"If he decided to, I think I could hold my own. I actually envy him," Burke said. "Both of your brothers."

"Why?"

"They've got it all. The things money can't buy, I mean."

In the lengthening shadows of dusk it was difficult to read the emotion on his face, but she got the distinct impression that there was regret in his voice. It occurred to her that she didn't know a lot about him. She hadn't asked too many questions, feeling that it wasn't right to pry, what with him doing her such a huge favor. But now she was curious.

He hadn't responded when she'd wondered out loud if his son's mother would object to Liam spending time here in Blackwater Lake. So all she really knew was that he was amicably divorced and the custody agreement had been harmonious as well. He'd asked about her past and she'd said you show me yours and I'll show you mine. But he'd only agreed that she would need to know as it pertained to their agreement.

Now, for some reason, she needed to know. "So, I have some questions."

Chapter Six

"You mentioned your cousin. Are you an only child?" Syd asked.

"Yes. Sloan is like the brother I never had. We're pretty close."

"And you have a son." Syd felt like an attorney interrogating a witness, but the questions kept popping into her mind.

"He's the best thing I ever did." But again there was regret in his voice.

"Tell me about his mother," she said.

"What do you want to know?"

"Good question." She shrugged. "Do you get along? Is she a good mom?"

"No."

There wasn't a shred of doubt in his tone. "But you said the divorce and custody negotiations were amicable."

"Because when I asked for sole custody she didn't argue. She didn't want him. She'd lost both of her parents

a while ago and the echo of divorce and custody negotiations had barely died away when she moved to Paris."

"But she's been back to see her son."

"No."

Sydney was shocked speechless. You heard about this
sort of thing in news stories, movies and books, but she'd
never known of anyone in real life experiencing it.

When she could speak, she asked, "Who looks out for
him?"

"The housekeeper. She's been with me since before he
was born. I tease about getting custody of her in the divorce." He smiled. "She loves Liam like her own."

"So there was no one to object if you'd brought Liam
to Blackwater Lake for the summer."

"No. But all his friends are there in Chicago. His activities. His schedule and routine. I finally decided that
stability for him was the most important thing."

"More than having his dad?" She frowned, puzzled.
"The details could be worked out and it would be an adjustment for him, but I would think that having him close
by would be good for you both. You could take an afternoon off. Have lunch together. Work at home when he's
asleep. Where there's a will…"

Frowning, he looked down at her. "You feel strongly
about this."

She nodded. "My dad was a single father and ran a business. He raised my brothers and me. Granted, Blackwater
Lake is a place where folks pitch in to help their own, but
Dad was there at night. To read me bedtime stories and
tuck me in. He checked out my homework and my boyfriends. He was *there*."

"You don't hold back, do you?"

"There's very little point in that." She shrugged. "I call
'em as I see 'em."

"I can't decide if you're being supportive or trying to make me feel guilty."

"I get the feeling that you don't need any help with a guilt complex, Burke."

"You're right. I decided a long time ago that feeling responsible for the bad stuff is a natural by-product of being a divorced father. That's how I make peace with it."

"I can't believe his mother didn't want him."

He shook his head. "To her he was a mistake and she always treated him that way. It's a sad reality that as bad a father as I am, I'm better than his mother."

"I just can't wrap my mind around doing something like that," she said.

"Because you obviously like children. You're good with them."

"I just give them whatever they want." She laughed. "It's what an aunt does."

"Clearly those little girls adore you."

"Because I never say no unless it's something that will hurt them."

"I remember those days with Liam." His voice was filled with wistfulness and regret. "It was simpler then."

There was such sadness and self-reproach in the words that she felt an overwhelming urge to put her arms around him, comfort him. The next best thing was to change the mood. "Tell me about him," she suggested.

"He's bright and funny. Athletic. Just a great kid. I really hate the feeling that I'm screwing him up. You only get one shot with a kid."

Something about that statement sounded final, as if he'd already blown any chance to get it right. Intellectually she understood that everyone's approach to parenting each child was unique, but she had a feeling that's not what he meant.

He'd said he envied her brothers, their families. He'd commented that Sloan was like a brother to him, implying that he'd wanted siblings. Because of that Syd would have thought he wouldn't want his son to be an only child.

"It won't always be just the two of you, Burke. Surely when you meet the right person you'll want to add to your family."

He shook his head. "No."

"But why?"

"I found out I'm not good at marriage, for one thing. And more important, I wouldn't want another child to have me for a father."

At that moment the French door behind them opened and Cam's voice drifted out. "Dinner's ready."

"We'll be right there," Syd answered automatically. When the door closed again, she said, "Burke, I think you're being too hard on yourself—"

"You're wrong. Let's go inside and eat." Clearly he didn't want to talk about this anymore.

Syd had suddenly lost her appetite. He was so good with kids and really seemed to enjoy them. It was hard to believe he was as bad at parenting as he so obviously believed.

But why should she care what he believed? Why should it matter so much?

What they had was a relationship of convenience. They both had their reasons for putting on this act. It had all made sense until she'd seen him holding that little girl in his arms and the gentle way he'd played with both of her nieces.

There would never be anything serious between her and Burke Holden. But that didn't stop her from feeling as if his revelation had cost her something really important.

Something that mattered very much.

* * *

A week later, first thing Monday morning Sydney grabbed a cup of coffee and a donut from the customer waiting area at McKnight Auto, then headed for the exit that went outside to the service bay. Her father's office was on the way and she stopped in the doorway. From this position she could see out the window in case someone drove up. From out of nowhere Burke's image popped into her mind.

He'd come by twice and both were memorable. The first time she'd asked him to participate in a crazy scheme to convince her father she had a boyfriend. The second time he'd kissed her, the kind of kiss that made her want to put up a commemorative plaque that said, Burke Holden Kissed Me Beside the Hydraulic Lift.

Earth to Syd, she thought. Focus.

"Morning, Dad."

He looked up from his computer. "Hi, Syd."

She took a bite of donut and the white powdered sugar sprinkled the front of her work shirt. It was probably the most benign substance that would muck up her clothes today, but getting dirty didn't bother her. From the time she was a little girl, she'd always liked it. Oil and transmission fluid were the lifeblood of a car and part of the tools of her trade. The purr of a repaired engine was music to her ears.

And the man sitting behind the desk was the one who'd taught her everything she knew. She liked to touch base with him in the morning before they both got busy. They lived under the same roof, but somehow this quiet time before the day started was when important things were shared. And the man had spent most of his time at Loretta's house lately so there wasn't much time to chat. In the days since the family dinner at Cam and Ben's she hadn't seen much of her dad except at work.

"You and Burke do anything over the weekend?" he asked.

"No." Syd had no intention of asking him what he and the mayor had been doing.

"What's wrong with him?" her father demanded.

"I'm not sure what you mean."

"Your brothers tell me they liked him. He seems an upstanding sort."

That's the way she pegged Burke, too. "Alex and Ben are pretty smart."

For once, fate had dropped a good man in her lap. He was handsome, funny and seemed to get along well with the adult males in her family as well as being great with kids. Dinner had been really fun. He fit in and for once she hadn't been the odd one out. She'd had a date, albeit a fake one. It was nice not being alone. Which made her sad when she thought about what he'd told her in the backyard.

"I say again—what's wrong with him? Letting a pretty girl like you be alone on Friday and Saturday. If he doesn't step up, some other fella is going to come along and squeeze him out."

She felt a stab of guilt for the deception and was *this* close to coming clean. But her dad looked so happy and lighthearted. In her whole life she'd never seen his eyes twinkle like this and the spring in his step made him seem ten years younger. She didn't want anything to change that. Still, she could use this opportunity to nudge him where she thought he should go.

"You should listen to yourself and take your own advice." She finished her donut.

Tom stood and walked around the desk. "What does that mean?"

"If you don't seal the deal and marry Loretta pretty soon, some other fella will steal her right out from under your nose. She won't wait forever."

"Maybe I'll seal the deal." His eyebrows drew together. "Or maybe not."

She was about to call him out on that but a minivan pulled up outside. "Got a customer."

Her father turned to look as a woman exited the vehicle. "Uh-oh. That's Violet Walker—"

"It's Stewart now," Syd reminded him.

"I can write up the work order. I understand if you don't want to."

He told her that he hadn't mentioned Violet being back in town because of not wanting to remind her of that painful time. He'd hoped she and Violet wouldn't run into each other. And that had worked out so well, she'd wanted to say. No, she had to deal with this. It was an opportunity and she realized she'd been waiting for one.

"It's okay." She met her father's gaze. "Took a lot of guts for her to come here. I want to talk to her."

"That's my girl. I'll be right here if you need me." He dropped a kiss on the top of her head and went back to his computer work.

Syd dropped her disposable coffee cup in the trash by the door then grabbed a clipboard with service form already attached. She walked outside and met her former BFF face-to-face beneath the overhang connecting the office to the service bay.

"Hi, Violet."

"Sydney." She looked tense but determined. "The van needs an oil change. I would take it somewhere else, but this is the only place in town. I hope it's okay, but if not—"

"Of course it's okay."

"Charlie offered to bring it in, but I said it would be better this way."

"That would have been fine. But, the fact is, I've been wanting to talk to you ever since that day at the park."

"Really?" There was eagerness in the single word before a wary expression tightened her features. "Why?"

"To clear the air." She smiled. "It's a small town."

"Yeah. That's one of the reasons Charlie and I moved back. For our parents, but also because this is a great place to raise kids."

"And we're going to run into each other."

Vi nodded. "I could feel everyone at the park watching to see what would happen between us."

"Me, too. I'd have said something to you then, but it was more fun to give the people of Blackwater Lake *nothing* to talk about."

"I know what you mean." A small smile eased some of the tension. "It always bugged you when people gossiped."

"Because we couldn't get away with anything." A series of long-ago memories scrolled through Syd's mind like a video. "If I spit on the sidewalk, someone would tell my dad."

"I know." Violet grinned. "Remember that time we decided to run away and join the circus?"

"Oh, gosh—" Syd laughed and nodded. "I haven't thought about that for years. We cut school and went to the grocery store to buy snacks with our allowances. Thinking ahead for the road trip."

"Not far enough ahead." Vi chuckled at the memory. "I'm not quite sure what we were going to be in the circus or why we thought they would hire us even if we happened to run across one."

"Fortunately it didn't get that far because someone called my dad."

"And my parents," she added. "To this day I have no idea who ratted us out."

"I have my suspicion although it was never confirmed. It's my theory that there's some kind of parental code of silence," Syd said. "And you're one of them. Look at you.

A mom now and Charlie's a dad. Two beautiful kids—a boy and girl."

"Right? Todd and Bailey are the best things Charlie and I ever did."

Syd knew for a fact that she didn't begrudge this woman her life or have any animosity about the past. But envy was something else. Violet was once her best friend and now she had a husband, children. She had everything Syd wanted. It was everything Syd's dad wanted for her so that he could move forward with his own life.

But the everything she wanted had always been vague until recently, Syd realized. Somehow Burke had made it come into focus.

"You and Charlie have a beautiful family, Vi," she said softly.

"Syd, I'm sorry. We never meant for it to happen and you have to know that neither of us would deliberately hurt you. You're our friend. At least you were," Violet added.

"I know." Clearly Violet had heard the wistfulness in Syd's voice but it had nothing to do with what happened all those years ago. She reached out and touched the other woman's arm, squeezing reassuringly. "It's obvious that he didn't love me or he wouldn't have fallen so hard for you."

"You have to know I didn't do anything. I never came on to him and he didn't to me, either. It's just that we all hung out together. Charlie and I felt the attraction. We both tried to fight the feelings but couldn't. We should have talked to you but eloping seemed like a good idea at the time. I just feel awful about what happened and the way we handled it. And so does Charlie."

"What do you say we put it behind us?"

"Are you sure?" There was hope in the other woman's eyes. "I think that would be wonderful, but can you forgive and forget?"

"No doubt about it. I already have."

"That's really a load off my mind." Violet's smile was genuine and relaxed now. "I'm so glad."

"Me, too." She studied her friend—maybe not best friends forever, but definitely friends again. "And I have to say that you look fantastic. You were always beautiful, but the whole maternal, wifely thing is working for you. What's your secret? You're positively glowing."

"Funny you should phrase it like that." She paused dramatically. "I'm going to have another baby."

"Oh, my. Congratulations." Syd honestly meant it, even though that pesky envy poked her again. "That's wonderful. Is Charlie happy about it?"

"Ecstatic."

Lucky Violet, she thought.

Every life was filled with peaks and valleys, but this news seemed to make her own valley even deeper. It was off the map of reason, but when Burke had said unequivocally that his future did not have a place in it for more children, Syd had been disappointed on a level that made no sense.

Now the news of her friend's pregnancy made her disappointment even more acute.

There was an explanation for this reaction, but she didn't even want to think about it. She took his revelation as a warning to avoid trouble ahead. If the incident with Violet and Charlie had taught her anything it was that knowing the bad was better than getting blindsided.

After work Sydney walked into Bar None, Blackwater Lake's local drinking establishment. It was rugged and rustic, with dark beams overhead and a wood plank floor. Illumination came from lantern-shaped lights scattered throughout the place in booths and on tables. In the center of the room was the big, rectangular oak bar with brass foot rail. This was a weeknight so not many of the swivel stools were occupied, but a quick glance at the men and women told her none of them were the friend she was meeting.

She scanned the booths lining the exterior then spotted a woman waving. Maggie Potter was sitting at a bistro table in the far corner and Syd headed that way.

She hoisted herself up onto the chair across from her friend. "Hi."

"Hey, yourself." The pretty, dark-eyed brunette smiled.

"Sorry I'm late. Have you been here long?"

"Just a few minutes. Long enough to order our usual."

White wine. This was a standing date for them and nine times out of ten a glass of Chardonnay was involved along with something to eat. The food was different from the diner, which was a more family-oriented place. Bar None had a happy-hour menu that suited Syd and Maggie, two single ladies on the town.

"So, where's that adorable little girl of yours tonight?"

A tender expression settled on Maggie's face. "She's staying with Uncle Brady and her soon-to-be-official Aunt Olivia. Just between you and me, I think they want to start a family soon and are practicing on Danielle."

"Have they set a date?"

"No. All we get are a lot of maybe Christmas. Or Valentine's Day. I think it will be spur-of-the-moment. And small."

"Sounds nice."

Maggie nodded. "In the meantime I'm happy to let them dote on my little girl. I love Danielle more than anything, but I do so enjoy a break from her."

Syd figured that was because her friend was both mother and father to the child. Maggie's husband had been a soldier and died in Afghanistan before his daughter was born.

She thought about Burke, a single father who thought

he was doing a bad job of parenting. She didn't believe that. The reality was that sometimes kids got dealt a lousy hand but that didn't mean they couldn't thrive in spite of it.

Just then the owner of the establishment carried over two glasses of wine. Delanie Carlson was somewhere in her twenties, a curvy, blue-eyed redhead. She'd inherited Bar None when her father passed away last year. Syd knew that she'd gone through some rough times financially and was one of the Blackwater Lake business owners who would benefit from the resort being built. To make ends meet, she'd rented out rooms over the bar, but there was bound to be a spike in revenue during construction as well as when the visitor count jumped after opening.

"Here you go, ladies." Delanie put a wineglass in front of each of them. "Are you ready to order or do you need another minute?"

Syd glanced at her unopened menu. "I haven't had a chance to look over the choices."

Dee grinned. "It hasn't changed since last week. Or the week before that. Or—"

"Are you implying I should know it by heart?"

"*Implying* would be more diplomatic than saying straight out that surely you have it memorized by now. So I guess you could say I'm just implying."

Syd laughed. "It's a good thing we're friends or I could take that the wrong way."

"Okay. Enjoy the wine. I'll be back."

Maggie watched the bar owner walk away, then said, "Speaking of friends…I heard you and Violet ran into each other at the park dedication. How did that go?"

"If it hadn't been civilized, you wouldn't have to ask." She took a sip of her wine and savored the crisp, cold liquid. "Coincidentally, I saw her today at the shop. She brought her car in for service."

Maggie's dark eyes widened. "Wow. Is there anything I should know?"

"We talked. She apologized, which wasn't necessary since she already did a long time ago. I just wasn't ready to listen then." She shrugged. "They're happy and have a beautiful family."

"And you're envious," her friend commented.

"Not that she's with Charlie. Just that she has a husband and children." Syd remembered the news. "And she's pregnant again. I'm happy for her. And I'm so over what happened."

"So you're friends again?"

"I'd say so. Not like we were but—" Syd was distracted when the front door opened and Burke walked in. He glanced around as if looking for someone, then his gaze settled on her and he headed over.

"What a pleasant surprise. You didn't mention you'd be here tonight." He leaned in and gave her a quick kiss.

"I didn't?"

She knew she hadn't because the information was on a need-to-know basis and he didn't need to know. He was playing the part of boyfriend to perfection and she couldn't help wondering why he was so good at deception. She needed to act like his girlfriend and found it far too easy to do that. And, gosh darn it, she wanted a much longer kiss than that paltry peck on the mouth. She felt as if her head was going to explode.

"I don't think we've met. Burke Holden," he said to Maggie.

She shook his hand. "Maggie Potter. I own the ice cream parlor and the adjacent lunch counter with my business partner. I've heard you've been in and I'm sorry I missed you. I'm always in the office upstairs."

Syd resisted the urge to shake her head to clear it.

"Maggie and I get together here at Bar None about once a week for a girls' night."

"I didn't mean to interrupt."

"That's okay," Maggie said. "It's nice to finally put a name and face together."

And what a face he had, Syd wanted to say. If only he was shallow the way so many handsome men were, their understanding would be much less complicated.

"It's nice to meet you, Maggie." He looked at the door when it opened and a man walked in. "Speaking of meeting…I'm here on business and he just walked in."

"Don't let us keep you." Syd made the mistake of looking into his deep blue eyes and felt as if she'd been sucked into a vortex. The problem was that she didn't know whether or not she wanted out.

"I wish you *could* keep me," he said with feeling. "It would be a lot more fun. Even if I did crash a girls' night." There was genuine regret in the look he gave Maggie. "I hope I'll see you again soon."

"Me, too."

"I'll call you, Syd." And then he walked over and shook hands with the newcomer before settling in a booth on the other side of the bar.

She might not be able to see him, but Syd knew he was in the room. All his intensity just seemed to alter the molecular composition of air.

"So," Maggie said. "Is he the reason you're over Violet stealing your boyfriend?"

"I was over it long before Burke came to town."

"Okay," her friend said. "Looked to me as if you like him a lot."

"Really?" Syd met her friend's gaze. "What did I do?"

"Hard to put into words. Just a feeling." Maggie looked thoughtful. "The best way to describe it is that you looked at Burke the way Olivia does my brother, Brady. And she's in love with him."

Oh, dear God. It didn't mean anything. Really, it was all about reacting to a good-looking man and had nothing to do with deeper feelings, she told herself.

She just hoped herself wasn't telling a lie.

"We're just good friends," she explained.

"I hope so." There was concern swirling in Maggie's eyes. "Because I've heard he's here to get the resort project going."

"I'm not sure why that bothers you but I can see that it does."

"I'm worried because his home is in Chicago. Or so I've been told."

"That's true," Sydney confirmed.

"Have you thought about what happens to you when he leaves Blackwater Lake to go back to his home base? I don't think it's a stretch to say that you're not open to relocating."

True, Syd thought. Her family was here and so was her job. But it was more than that. Someday she would take over the business her father had built.

"We've talked a little." That wasn't a complete lie. They did talk when together. Just not about where they were going from here because there was no *here*. "We just figure that things will work out when the time comes."

That also wasn't a lie. In the beginning they'd talked about what would happen at the end. So, she was beginning to get the hang of telling half truths. Her father would be so proud.

"Please don't think I'm prying. I just don't want to see you hurt again," Maggie said.

"I understand." And she did. But enough about her. "So how's the business expansion working for you?"

"Good." Maggie sipped her wine. "I'm planning to run

an ad in the paper to rent out my two upstairs bedrooms to pay for it."

Syd picked up her wineglass and took a sip, then asked, "Why?"

"I have a business loan and need to put away all the money I can. Just in case."

"But your brother owns a very successful technology company. Call it a wild guess, but wouldn't he help you out if necessary?"

"Yes. But I wouldn't ask or take anything from him." Her friend's dark eyes grew darker, a sign she was thinking about the husband she'd lost far too soon. "It's something I need to do on my own. For Danny. When we got married it was clear that my brother was on his way and would be incredibly successful. Danny was always trying to prove himself. He wouldn't have wanted me to take Brady's help."

"And renting the rooms?"

"Everyone knows when construction starts on the resort there will be a shortage of places to live. I already have someone lined up, an older woman I know who lost her husband, too. And anyone else who expresses interest in the other room for rent can be checked out. I've already talked to Sheriff Fletcher about that." She shrugged. "There's an outside entrance, which makes the upstairs more separate. I'll provide breakfast and dinner. It's all worked out. It's very trendy and can be really lucrative."

Syd recalled what Burke had said about the scarcity of places to stay here in Blackwater Lake. There was a lot of potential for profit. And when it came to the husband Maggie had lost, Syd had learned that there was no changing Maggie's mind once it was made up.

"I'm sure it will work out great," she said.

Just then Delanie came over and it was time to put in

their orders. While her friend chatted with the bar owner, Syd heard Burke's laugh from the other side of the room.

At some point she wouldn't have the opportunity to run in to him anywhere in Blackwater Lake because he would be gone. His leaving eventually was what made him perfect for this assignment. The fact that he lived somewhere else would be a convenient excuse for an amicable breakup. Before that happened, hopefully her father would feel comfortable enough about his daughter's future to marry Loretta. And when the time was right, Syd would end her charade with Burke.

The sooner the better—because far too often she looked at him and started thinking, what if they really had something? The problem was that *something* opened the door to everything and that was the foundation for pain and disappointment.

Wondering what might have been came with no risk and she was good with that.

Chapter Seven

Burke wasn't a spontaneous guy. So, by definition, buying a bouquet of flowers and heading to a woman's house without calling first to ask her to dinner was something he didn't do.

Except he was doing it.

He was almost to Sydney's house with flowers and planned to ask her to dinner. A fancy dinner at Fireside. It wasn't clear whether the high altitude and lack of oxygen here in the Montana mountains was causing this uncharacteristic behavior, or if there was something else going on. Whatever was responsible didn't matter. When the idea had popped into his mind, he couldn't shake it loose no matter how hard he tried. And he'd definitely tried.

He turned the car into her driveway and parked in front of the house. It was a modest-sized beige craftsman-style with a porch, two dormers and chocolate-brown shutters framing the windows. The two vehicles there belonged to Syd and her dad, which meant they were both home. So far, so good.

He grabbed the cellophane-wrapped bouquet resting on the passenger seat, hoping she hadn't started dinner yet. If so, he planned to charm her into putting it away for tomorrow. After exiting the car, he walked to the front door and rang the bell.

Almost immediately Tom McKnight answered, car keys in hand. Apparently he was on his way out. Looking at the flowers he said, "For me? You shouldn't have."

"If I'd known you were a bouquet kind of guy, I'd have brought two. But these are for Sydney."

"Nice move." Tom nodded approvingly. "I'm on my way to Loretta's and I think I'm going to take a play from your book. Where'd you get these?"

"The grocery store on Main Street. Although I'm told there won't be any soon. In the fall and winter it's a challenge to stock them."

"Thanks for the tip." Her father met his gaze. "Syd didn't say anything. Did she know you were coming?"

"No. I wanted to surprise her. Take her to dinner."

Again the man nodded his approval. "As the ladies would say, you're not just another pretty face, Holden. You've got style. But don't keep her out too late."

"Yes, sir."

"'Bye, Syd. Don't expect me back tonight. And Burke is here," he called over his shoulder before walking to his truck.

Moments later Syd stood in the doorway and was staring at the flowers as if they were an especially big, hairy spider. "What are you doing here?"

"I came to see you."

"With flowers?" Her tone said that was a breach of contract.

"Yes." He noted her skeptical expression. "Unless it's illegal in Montana for a guy to surprise a girl with flowers."

"It's definitely a surprise."

For him, too. This wasn't going quite the way he'd thought it would. "In case it's not clear, these are for you."

"Thanks." She took the bouquet he offered but held it as if she expected something to jump out and bite her.

"What's wrong?"

"That's what I'd like to know."

"Does there have to be a crisis for me to bring flowers and ask you to put on that little black dress so I can take you to dinner?"

"Yeah. Kind of. Our agreement isn't about bouquets and surprises—" She stopped and her eyes widened as if a light went on. "Oh, I get it. Nice move."

That's the second time a McKnight had said those words to him but he had a sneaking suspicion each of them meant something different.

"Can I come in?" he asked.

"Oh. Sure." She stepped back as he entered, then closed the door behind him.

"So," he said, "what is it you think I'm doing?"

"This 'surprise' is all about convincing Dad that we're a couple."

"Actually, I—"

"It's a great idea, Burke. And it worked better than you probably even expected."

"How so?" He certainly hadn't expected this but he wouldn't call it better.

"You surprise me with flowers and dinner in front of Dad. Color him impressed. But he's on his way to Loretta's and won't be back tonight." She beamed as if that's all there was to it.

"And?" he prompted.

"Dad bought the act completely. He thinks you walk on water and you don't even have to take me out."

Burke didn't know whether to shake her or kiss her. But since it appeared that she was trying to get out of spending time with him, he figured the best move was to do none of the above.

"What if I want to take you out?"

She blinked up at him as if that question came from out of nowhere. "Then I would have to say that comes under the heading of changing the rules. Seriously, I really appreciate your help. But I think we can consider this date number two." Apparently she noticed his frown because she added, "I'm just trying to make this as easy as possible for you."

That attitude in a woman was refreshing. His ex had always seemed to make things as hard as possible. Except with their son. She'd wanted no part of the responsibility of raising a child. In its own way, that was hard, too. Not for him, but for Liam.

"I'm not sure we should be counting dates," he finally said. "Things should unfold organically."

"That word. *Organic.* What does it mean? Why can't people just say natural?" The wary look was back. "We agreed to a certain number of times going out. Why shouldn't we count?"

"Because I really want to take you to dinner."

"Again I have to ask—why?"

That was the big question and he didn't have a really good answer. The truth was that ever since running in to her at Bar None last night, he couldn't stop thinking about her. He'd wanted to kiss her. Technically he had done that, but it wasn't the way he really wanted to kiss her. Since he couldn't get her off his mind, it followed that he wanted to see her tonight. If he had to put a finer point on this he'd chalk it up to loneliness, to living in a hotel without the comforts of home or family. That was as complicated as he was willing to get.

"I don't like eating alone." He slid his fingers into the pockets of his suit pants. "Look at it as doing me a favor."

"And I can't go like this?" She was weakening.

He inspected her yellow T-shirt, thin and worn in the most interesting places just like her jeans, and bare feet with hot-pink painted toenails. A need that had nothing to do with food tightened inside him. He would give almost anything to get her out of those clothes until all she had on was the sexy polish on her toes.

He cleared his throat. "As fetching as you look, your outfit is more appropriate for the diner than Fireside."

"Really? You want to spring for a nice dinner?"

"Yes." When she opened her mouth to protest, he put a finger to her lips to stop the words. "Don't ask me why."

"I wasn't going to."

"Yes, you were." He turned her toward the stairs. "Now go change. I'm starving."

"And I'm getting the most expensive meal on the menu," she said over her shoulder as she hurried up the stairs.

And worth every penny, he thought.

While waiting for her to change, he stared out the front window and savored his triumph. He was looking forward to spending the evening with a beautiful woman. There was something to be said for overcoming a challenge, but the truth was he wouldn't have taken no for an answer.

He hadn't had to work this hard for a date since he was a teenager, and probably not even then. For some reason he felt more satisfaction from wearing down Syd than he'd ever felt with any other woman.

Syd looked across the candlelit table at Burke. She was having a wonderful time since agreeing to come here. But flowers? A surprise dinner invitation from her pretend boyfriend? Who could blame her for being skittish? This…thing…between her and Burke Holden was feeling less like an agreement and more like *dating*.

At the moment she couldn't find the will to care what it was called. She'd made good on her vow to order the most expensive item on the menu. Actually Burke had asked if she liked steak and lobster. When she'd said yes, he told the waiter she would have that. It was too much food so she'd scarfed down the lobster and the steak was going to be tomorrow's lunch. Now she was rocking a lovely wine glow and sharing a piece of the best chocolate cake in Montana with the handsome man who'd brought her here.

And how cute was he?

A question she had no desire to answer because it opened the door to stuff she would rather not think about. Preferably ever.

"I'll be sure to let Uncle John know how nice you're being to me," she teased. "We could take a selfie and text it to him."

"No, we can't."

"Has anyone ever told you that you're a stick-in-the-mud?"

"I've been called worse," he said.

"Tell me."

He shook his head. "It's not something I'm comfortable repeating in polite company."

"Who said I was polite?" she responded.

"Maybe not, but you're a woman."

The way his voice dropped and got all husky on that word put a hitch in her breathing. His eyes took on an expression that was focused and intense, making her wonder what he would do if they were alone. And speaking of alone, she had a question.

"So you don't like eating by yourself?"

"I prefer company." The corner of his mouth curved up.

She dragged her fork through the thick chocolate icing, then looked at him. "Realistically you could have talked almost anyone in Blackwater Lake into going to dinner with you. But you brought me flowers and showed up without warning to surprise me. Why?"

"I'm particular about dinner companions. How would it look if I brought another woman here?" He met her gaze. "We haven't accomplished our mission yet."

"I guess, based on our original agreement, I just don't understand why you would go to so much trouble," she said.

"Okay, let me explain." He set down his fork and met her gaze. "I like you, Sydney. Sooner or later I would have asked you out if you hadn't hit on me first."

"I didn't hit on you," she protested. "You were just in the wrong place at the wrong time. If Phil the plumber had driven up at that moment I'd have hit on—" She stopped and cleared her throat. "I mean, I would have asked for his help with my problem."

"Maybe." His tone said he didn't believe that for a minute. "The fact is we did meet. And I agreed to your proposal. Although I don't think the ruse is necessary."

Aha, he had a purpose. The flowers and surprise were about sweetening the deal. "So you think I should tell my dad the truth? You want out of the agreement because you don't want to see me?"

"Not at all. I agreed to help move your father along in the courting process. Although I don't think the ruse is necessary to accomplish that objective."

"Why not?"

"Because your father will get where he needs to be when it feels right to him. And not because you are or are not in a committed relationship of your own."

"Then why are you helping me?" she asked.

"I very much want to see you. That's what the flowers and surprise were all about."

"You want to date me?"

"Yes."

On a scale of one to ten this was a fifteen on the surprise scale. "Why?"

His expression was ironic, as if to say "you really don't know?"

"Because I want to get to know you better. You're a beautiful and interesting woman."

"Wow." This was a first for her and she didn't know what to say to that.

"I like you. I'm attracted to you."

Translation: he wanted to sleep with her. She let that idea kick around for a few seconds and realized she had no opposition to that scenario.

"Okay."

"But I feel the necessity to be completely honest. I'm not the kind of guy your father wants for you."

"And you know this…how?"

"I meant what I said that night in your brother's backyard. I've been married and don't plan to do it again. There won't be more children. The only commitment I can make is to be Liam's father and do what's best for him."

"That's as it should be," she agreed.

"So, what do you say?"

"I don't remember the question," she lied.

"Are you okay with us going out? Having fun. No strings, no promises?"

She was much more comfortable with pretending to have fun with him, but had to admit she always had fun with him and that had nothing to do with their deal. That reaction was unexpected although maybe she should have expected something considering how strong her attraction had been to him from the beginning.

"Syd?"

She looked up. "Can I think about it?"

"Of course." He reached across the table and rested his hand over hers. "And whatever your answer is, I will keep my word in regard to our agreement."

"That's very decent of you."

"I'm a decent guy."

His sudden grin would melt the heart of any woman who was still breathing and Syd was no exception. How was she supposed to resist that?

The intensity was starting to close in on her. "You call yourself decent? In spite of the worst unrepeatable things people have said about you?"

"They were just frustrated."

He lifted a hand to signal the waiter for the check. When it was taken care of, they left the restaurant and walked outside to his car.

"It's a beautiful night." Syd took a deep breath, pulling the cool, clean mountain air into her lungs. "I love this time of year. Soaking up the good weather for as long as possible."

"Does the cold get to you? Chicago winters are pretty intense, too."

"No." She thought about the question. "I guess I'm used to subzero temperatures from time to time."

"You basically work outside," he pointed out.

"I'm used to that, too." She shrugged. "There are portable heaters for the service bay and ways to block out the most bitter cold. It helps that I love what I do."

"And you're good at it." He unlocked the car, opened the passenger door and guided her inside.

From the time she'd first expressed an interest in boys, her father had said she shouldn't go out with a guy who didn't open doors for a woman. He'd raised her brothers to do that and it seemed Burke had learned the lesson from someone. If she was doing a pro-and-con list to decide whether or not to take him up on his dating offer, being a gentleman would definitely go in the pro column. In fact everything about him was leading her to say yes. Before Burke, fun had been in very short supply.

He started the car and Syd paid attention to the sound of the engine, listening for a hesitation, miss or any sign of trouble. She heard none. That was disappointing because she would love an excuse to get her hands on the motor. It didn't take long to drive to her house and Burke stopped in the driveway behind her fuel-efficient compact car.

After turning off the ignition, he looked at her. "I think you should invite me in."

"For a nightcap?"

"For anything you want. An invitation would be much appreciated."

The innuendo raised tingles all over her body. "Would it now?"

I'm attracted to you.

The memory of his words kicked up her heart rate and made her pulse dance in the most exciting possible way.

"Yes, it would. Your father's not coming home."

If her dad hadn't announced his plans to the world she could have used his imminent return as an excuse. If she wanted one. But suddenly it was crystal clear that she wasn't ready for the evening to end.

"Would you like to come inside? For something?" Where in the world did that seductive tone come from?

"I thought you'd never ask."

He opened his door then came around to hers. She put her palm in the hand he held out and he steadied her as she slid out of the passenger seat. Then he walked her to the front door and took her key to unlock it.

Inside, she flipped the switch on the wall to illuminate the room before putting her evening bag and to-go box on the small table just inside the door. After that she stepped out of her four-inch heels. She'd barely turned toward him when Burke had her in his arms. He tilted his head to the side and lowered his mouth to hers.

Sydney sighed at the softness of his lips. Relief poured through her that he was doing exactly what she wanted. She nestled closer to his tall, lean body and slid her hands beneath his suit coat, working up his back. His shirt was soft to the touch and his muscles bunched and contracted under her hands.

He traced her lips with his tongue and she opened to him, savoring the heat that exploded in her belly when he dipped inside. The sound of their escalated breathing filled the room and fueled her need.

Burke lifted his head and met her gaze, his eyes searching. "Are you ready to give me an answer to my question now?"

He'd said he wanted to get to know her better and this definitely qualified, so count her in. It also answered her question about what he would do if they were alone, and she couldn't deny her willingness to participate. She wasn't sure why she'd stalled because he'd had her at flowers and dinner.

"Yes," she whispered.

"Yes, you have an answer? Or yes, you want to spend time with me?"

"Both."

She slid her hands up his chest to his shoulders and lifted his suit coat, dragging it down his arms before dropping it on the floor. Then she reached up and unknotted his tie, pulling one end hand over hand until it was free of his collar. With a twist of his fingers he undid the button at his throat and Syd helped with the rest marching down the front of his shirt.

When she tried to repeat the maneuver used in taking

off his coat, he captured her hands and kissed the knuckles of each before guiding them around his waist.

"My turn." He reached behind her and slowly dragged down the zipper on her dress.

Cool air rushed in, caressing her skin. She wasn't wearing a bra and if this dress came off she would have on nothing but black lace panties. Anticipation was building inside and her blood rushed through her veins. Roared in her ears.

There was a distant sound and it took several moments to realize it was Burke's cell. He pulled her close and said, "Ignore that. It can wait."

"Are you sure?" She looked up to see his expression. "It's just late enough not to be a good time for the phone to ring."

He hesitated a moment longer, then yanked the device from his pocket. The frown turned angry when he looked at the caller ID and hit talk. "What is it, Dad?"

He listened for several moments, his expression growing darker by the second. Finally he said, "I'll be there tomorrow."

Without another word he clicked off.

Syd struggled to clear her head and pull up the zipper on her dress. Something told her that whatever she'd agreed to by saying yes would have to wait. "What's wrong?"

"I have to go to Chicago." He took another step away and dragged his fingers through his hair.

"Is your father all right?"

"Fine." He practically snapped out the word. "It's Mary—the housekeeper. She's in the hospital. They're doing tests."

Mary was the woman who'd been with him since his son was a baby and obviously the news worried him. But it wasn't just that. "Where is Liam? Who's taking care of him?"

"My father." He didn't look happy about that. "I have to go."

"Of course. This will be scary for him."

He nodded grimly. "And staying with his grandfather isn't the best option. The old man isn't someone you can count on."

Syd was surprised at the hostility in his tone but didn't ask. Mostly it was none of her business and this wasn't the time for probing questions. "What are you going to do?"

It was obvious that his mind was racing, clicking through possible scenarios to problem-solve the situation. "Work is crazy now. The time frame for the resort is tight. I can't afford to be gone."

She remembered what he'd said about the boy's friends and activities being in Chicago. And that was why he'd opted not to bring him to Blackwater Lake, even for the end of summer. "Is there anyone else to take care of Liam?"

"No one I can think of. I would have to personally interview a replacement for Mary. But there's no time for that." He met her gaze. "Unless there's something I haven't thought of, Liam will have to come back here with me."

She could tell by the harried expression on his face that this wasn't the time to say that might not be such a bad thing.

Instead, she put her arms around his waist and rested her cheek against his chest. "I'm sorry this is happening."

"Me, too." He kissed the top of her head. "I apologize, but I have to go. Arrangements to make—"

"I understand." She gave him a reassuring smile. "Go do what you have to."

"I'll call you." He kissed her cheek, then let himself out the door.

Syd stared at it for a long time after he'd left and a number of things came to mind. Burke could have had his father put the boy on a plane to Montana. He hadn't and was personally going to get him. He could have had someone else interview a substitute housekeeper, but he wouldn't do that, either. To her way of thinking he'd handled this situation as a caring parent should.

And yet he didn't consider himself a good father. She was no shrink, but it was a good bet that core belief was rooted in his relationship with his own father. How she would love to hear that story and tell him he was very wrong about his parenting skills.

Chapter Eight

Burke was tired.

The last couple of days had been hectic and his surly eight-year-old didn't help. There'd been no choice but to bring Liam back to Blackwater Lake. He couldn't leave the boy with his grandfather. It was bad enough that the man had already screwed him up. If anyone was going to screw up Liam, Burke would do it.

He glanced over at the boy, sitting on the leather sofa in his office. It was in the five-story building Brady O'Keefe had built to house his company. O'Keefe Technology had four floors and rented out number five to Burke. When his cousin Sloan arrived he would need work space and as the resort project kicked into full gear, they'd need a place to put a lot of employees. So while this floor was pretty empty now, very soon it would be activity central.

He looked over at Liam again and the fierce frown on the kid's face made him feel as if he'd been smacked with the guilty stick. Obviously the boy was unhappy, but Burke hadn't done this on purpose. How could he make his child understand the situation?

Before he went crazy trying to answer that question his intercom buzzed. He hit the talk button and said, "Yes, Lydia?"

"There's someone here to see you."

"Thanks." Without saying anything else, he clicked off.

Normally he would have asked who was there or had them sent in. The fact that he didn't told Burke two things. Number one: he was grateful for the interruption. Number two: he needed a break. The electricity in this room was so thick you could charge a car battery with it.

He stood and walked around his desk. "There's someone here to see me, Liam."

"Yeah. I heard."

"I'll be right back."

The only response was a grunt; the kid didn't even look up from his handheld video game. Burke would have preferred he pick up the book sitting beside him but that was a battle for another day.

When he came out of his office, Lydia wasn't sitting at her desk.

"Sydney." He could truthfully say he'd never been so glad to see anyone in his life. It felt like years since he'd nearly taken her to bed. God, he'd regretted having to leave her that night.

"Lydia said to tell you she'll be right back. She went to the ladies' room," she said. "How are you?"

"Okay."

She was so beautiful, even dressed for work as she was now, although his favorite was the little black dress that he'd almost taken off her. But there was something about just looking at her that made him feel refreshed.

He walked over and kissed her. They were alone if you didn't count his son in the other room. But he didn't care who was or wasn't watching. He kissed her like a starving man and felt as if he couldn't get enough. A little moan escaped her lips and the sound of it set him on fire. But this was a place of business.

Forcing himself to pull away, he smiled down at her. "What are you doing here?"

"I heard you were back."

Her tone wasn't peeved or accusing, but he felt another slap with the guilty stick. "I'm sorry I didn't call. I know I promised, but it's been crazy—"

"I can imagine," she interrupted. "It's okay. I was just passing by and thought I'd stop in and say hi. Unless you're too busy."

"I am, but this is a good time for a break."

Her gaze was assessing. "You look tired. What happened with Liam?"

"He's in my office." He glanced past his executive assistant's desk to the partially opened door. "Mary is still in the hospital. She needs surgery."

"I hope it's not serious."

"When you're in your sixties any surgery is serious. The doctors say she'll be fine, but there will be recovery time." He rubbed a hand across the back of his neck, recalling the conversation that pulled the rug out from under him. "Bottom line is she's retiring. Effective immediately."

"Can she afford to?"

"I'll make sure of it. I owe her more than I can ever repay."

There was concern in her dark eyes. "What are you going to do?"

"Long-term I'm not sure. Short-term, I have to enroll him in school. I've filled out all the forms for Blackwater Lake Elementary, but they need his records from Chicago before he can start. It will be a couple of days so he's with me until that gets squared away."

"It must be nice to have him here."

"Yes. And no."

"How so?" she asked.

"He's been…difficult." Mouthy. Disrespectful. Stubborn. Rebellious. Those adjectives would work, too.

"Change is never easy." Her voice was soft, comforting. Consoling.

"I wish he didn't have to go through this. Liam is very close to Mary."

"It's tough. Unfortunately this is the stuff that builds character. But you already understand that, don't you?"

"I know how it feels to be on the receiving end of being told that everything is going to change."

"What happened?" Her eyes filled with sympathy.

"My mother got sick. Cancer. She died when I was a little older than Liam. It's hard for a kid to process something like this." He met her gaze. "On top of worrying about Mary, he didn't want to leave his friends and activities. Especially sports."

"There are organized sports for kids here in Blackwater Lake."

"As he pointed out school has started and teams have already been formed. He's right about that, but the timing of this makes him even more resentful."

"Give him time, Burke."

She put her hand on his forearm, the part where his rolled-up shirt sleeve left the skin bare. The touch, slight though it was, reassuring as it was meant to be, still sent the blood rushing to points south of his belt. He wanted her naked in his arms. And this wasn't the time or place to be thinking things like that. But it seemed he had little control over her effect on him.

"I don't have much choice," he said. "And in the meantime, I'm the only one he has to take his anger out on."

"Just talk to him. He's pretty young and won't understand, but he'll always remember that you were there for him when he was going through a rough patch."

The advice touched a nerve because that was his chief complaint about his own father. When his mom died, his dad seemed never to be home. Work was always more important than what was going on with Burke.

"Would you like to meet him? Unless you don't have time…"

"I'd love to."

He thought her reaction was sincere and said, "Okay, then. Follow me."

They walked over to the door and he pushed it open. "Hey, Liam, I'd like to introduce you to a friend of mine."

The boy glanced up, but the sullen expression didn't budge. There was only a small amount of satisfaction to be had from the fact that he wasn't the only target of his son's hostility.

"Liam, this is Sydney McKnight. Syd, my son, Liam."

She walked over and sat down beside him. "It's nice to meet you, Liam. Your dad has told me a lot about you."

"Yeah. Whatever."

Burke felt the simmering anger tighten inside him. "That's rude, son. I know Mary didn't teach you that kind of behavior."

"It's okay, Burke." Syd stared at the boy until he looked straight at her. "How do you like Blackwater Lake?"

"It's small and there's nothing to do here." He took a quick look around the office as if to say this was ground zero of boredom.

"It will be better when you start school," she told him.

"School here is probably small and boring, too." The childish tone was full to overflowing with contempt. "It doesn't matter anyway. I don't care."

Burke figured he could take whatever the boy dished out, but Sydney didn't need this. "Liam—"

The child stood and headed for the door. "I have to go to the bathroom."

When he was gone Burke blew out a long breath. "What a charmer."

"He takes after you," she teased.

"Wow, feel the love." He slid her a wry glance. "Seriously, Syd, I'm sorry about that. He has issues with me but normally he's polite to strangers."

"Don't worry about it. I'd be willing to bet that giant chip on his shoulder is all about being a scared kid whose whole world just turned upside down."

"I'd be glad if you're right because I pretty much decided it had more to do with him hating me."

"I'm sure that's not true," she said.

Burke figured she was wrong about that. He'd gone through a phase of not liking his own father very much. After Burke let go of any expectations for the old man, he and Walker Holden had reached a state of benign coexistence. They tolerated each other when necessary. His expectations of the relationship with his own son were higher than that, but it looked as if that was doomed to failure.

"Fingers crossed that you're right and going to school will help. By the way, I had to put down an emergency contact number and I gave them yours. I hope you don't mind."

"Not a problem. They probably won't need it but I'm happy to help if necessary. It's the way folks roll here in Blackwater Lake." She actually looked as if she meant what she'd said.

"Thanks." He glanced out to his assistant's desk. "Lydia's back. She's not going to like what I'm going to ask her to do."

"What's that?"

"I have a meeting this afternoon. It has to be canceled and rescheduled."

"Because of Liam. You can't take him with you?" she asked.

He shook his head. "A difficult eight-year-old would be a distraction. And I can't really blame him. If I had to listen to a bunch of grown-ups talking for hours, I'd be difficult, too."

"See? You get where he's coming from." She smiled at him, then stood and walked closer. "Your instincts are spot-on. You, sir, are your own worst critic."

"No. I think Liam takes first place on that."

She sighed. "My father always said it's in the rules and part of the job description that kids are going to give their parents a hard time." She tapped her lip. "And speaking of Dad, I just had an idea."

"About what?"

"How to not annoy your executive assistant." She met his gaze. "Liam doesn't want to be cooped up here. How about if I take him to the garage with me?"

"But you have to work. I couldn't ask you to do that."

"You didn't. I volunteered. And my dad won't mind. He always brought me there when I was a little girl. He managed to work with a child around."

"I don't know."

"We can find stuff to keep him busy, although, fair warning, he might get dirty."

"I don't care about that," he said.

"Then it's settled." During the short silence her eyes narrowed. "Unless you don't trust me."

"Of course I do. It just seems like an imposition."

"I would tell you if it was. Or I'd have kept my mouth shut and not offered in the first place."

Burke couldn't fault that reasoning and finally said, "Okay. Thanks. I don't know how I can repay you for this, but I really owe you."

"I'll think of something."

The saucy, suggestive look in her eyes heated his blood and threatened to fry his brain. He had some ideas that brought to mind twisted sheets and tangled legs, and fervently hoped what she thought of as payback would be along those lines.

"And who do we have here? Is this your young apprentice?"

Syd recognized her father's voice and the veiled reference to *Star Wars,* but was surprised that he'd managed to approach without her hearing. Looking down at Liam, who moved a little closer beside her, she figured that it was because she had a thing or two on her mind.

"Dad, this is Liam Holden, Burke's son. Liam, this is my father, Tom McKnight."

The little boy held out his hand and solemnly said, "How do you do, Mr. McKnight. It's nice to meet you."

"I didn't know Burke had a son." Her dad leaned over and shook hands then gave her a look that said this level of good manners and courtesy wasn't normal for a kid his age. "You're very polite, son."

"My dad told me I have to be."

"He's right." Her father nodded approvingly. "It sure helps smooth the way with people you meet."

"I guess." Liam lifted a thin shoulder.

"Welcome to Blackwater Lake, Liam. How do you like it so far?"

"Thank you, sir. And so far it's boring."

"I guess your dad told you to be honest, too," Tom said drily.

"Yes, sir." Liam glanced up at her. "But it's a little better since Sydney came to see my dad."

Tom looked at her, then the boy. "Ah."

"I stopped by Burke's office and offered to bring Liam over here. He's been very helpful. Watching and hand-ing me tools." If the dirt stains on the front of his shirt and pants were anything to go by, the kid was having the time of his life.

Her father's eyebrows lifted. "You know only employees are allowed in the service bay."

"That's why we're not in the service bay." The car was just outside with her rolling toolbox beside it. "It's a beautiful day so I pulled it out here to do the tune-up."

"I see."

She met his gaze and felt a compulsion to defend her actions, not unlike when she'd been a teenager. "The housekeeper who cares for Liam has suddenly taken ill and Burke brought him back to Blackwater Lake. He was cooped up in his father's office and bored to tears."

"I wasn't crying," Liam explained. "I'm not a crybaby."

"Of course you're not and I didn't mean to imply that. It's just an expression to explain how bored you actually were."

"Really bored," he said vehemently.

"Burke had a meeting this afternoon and he was going to cancel it. I figured helping out would be…helpful. Isn't that what folks here in Blackwater Lake do?"

"You're working, too," her father pointed out, ignoring the question.

"But my job is different. It's more flexible. And fun."

"This is an awesome place, Mr. McKnight."

"Call me Tom."

"Yes, sir. I mean Tom," Liam said.

Syd knew her father and knew by the expression on his face that he was struggling with something. Part of it could be that she hadn't told him Burke had a child.

Finally he said to the boy, "Would you like a soda, Liam?"

"Dad," she interjected, "I don't know if soda is the best drink—" The warning look in his eyes made her stop talk-

ing. Funny how he could still do that even though she was
all grown up.

"It won't hurt him. You used to have one almost every
day after school."

"Sydney got to come here when she was a kid?" Liam's
tone said that had to be on a par with going to an amusement park. When her father nodded, he said, "Cool."

"So, Liam, would you like something to drink?"

"That would be awesome."

"Okay. Let's go to my office."

After they left, she started a visual inspection beneath
the hood of the car. She checked the drive and serpentine
belts. They looked loose and would need adjustment so
she turned her attention to the tension pulleys.

She could do this in her sleep and her mind wandered
while she worked. Something about the little boy tugged
at her heart. He was the spitting image of Burke—brown
hair, blue eyes and a smile that would melt a woman's
heart. In about ten years he was going to be pretty hard
for girls to resist.

The fact that he favored his father gave her a sense of
poetic justice on Burke's behalf. It would have been so
wrong for this boy to take after the woman who'd walked
out and didn't fight for custody.

The same woman who had made Burke anti-marriage
and children. That was just a darn shame because the man
had a lot to offer a woman.

In hindsight, she realized it probably wasn't the smartest move to go see him, but her car kind of steered its way
over. When it was time for the next service on her vehicle,
she'd be sure to check that out. Curiosity was annoying
and inconvenient, but also a powerful motivator. After
not hearing from him, she just had to find out how things
were going and it was a good thing she had. They'd barely
walked out of Burke's office and the kid's hostile attitude

disappeared. Maybe the two Holden men being stuck with each other for a while was a blessing in disguise, forcing them to work through their issues.

Behind her she heard footsteps and voices. As the older man and young boy walked toward her, she smiled. Her dad had a way with kids and Liam looked completely comfortable, chatting away as if he'd known Tom McKnight for years instead of minutes. He had a soda in one hand and two small cars in the other.

"Where'd you get those?" she asked, nodding at the toys.

"One was Alex's and the other Ben's. The boys used to play with them here when your mother needed the afternoon for errands or just some time off to recharge her battery." He smiled at the pun.

"I'm surprised you still have them," she said, a lump in her throat.

Her dad shrugged. "I just found them in a drawer."

Right, and she was the princess of an exotic foreign country. The man didn't like clutter and cleaned out on a regular basis. He'd kept these two toy cars for sentimental reasons and she loved him for it.

"You're a big softie."

Liam looked up at her. "Your dad said you didn't like toy cars. You wanted to play with the real thing."

"That's true," she confirmed. "Do you like cars, Liam?"

"Yeah." He glanced up at her father, the beginnings of hero worship in his eyes. "Tom said he would let me look at an engine. And touch it."

"That old one out back that you used to practice on when you were a kid," her dad clarified. "A little hands-on experience."

There was no reason to keep that old hunk of metal except as another sentimental gesture. With a heart that soft, no wonder he'd grieved the loss of his wife for so long.

She crouched down in front of Liam. "Is that what you want to do?"

"Yeah." Blue eyes so like his father's were bright with excitement.

"Okay." She should have thought of that. Rookie mistake. Pulling the rag from her back pocket, she started to wipe her hands. "I'll take you back there—"

"No need. Finish what you're doing. I'll take him." His eyes twinkled. "I miss having a young apprentice."

She said it again. "You're just a big softie."

"If that information gets around, I'll know who spread the rumor," he teased. "And I'll deny everything."

"I've got a news flash for you, big guy." Syd stood on tiptoe and kissed his cheek. "It's not a secret."

"Remind me to have a word with your brothers about that." He dropped a big hand on the small shoulder. "Come along, Liam."

"Do we need tools or anything?" Liam's expression was full of awe, with a dash of excitement mixed in for good measure. "Sydney has a whole bunch of them in that big red box with the wheels on it."

"No tools yet," her dad explained. "At first you just have to look and learn the names of everything."

"Will you teach me?"

"Sure."

The two walked around the service bay building and disappeared. The sight of her father taking the young boy under his wing brought back so many memories of hanging out here when she was little. Either school had been out and there was no child care. Or the babysitter got sick. Whatever the reason, when she had no place to go and no one to keep an eye on her she'd come to McKnight Automotive. Her father was her hero and she'd wanted to do what he did.

Until now it had never occurred to her how complicated

raising a little girl without a mother could be. When her brothers were little, her mother had been around. Losing her when his daughter was born had to have been so hard on her dad. Harder than Syd could even imagine. Bringing a new baby into the world should have been a happy event, but when you lost the love of your life that would leave a mark on the soul.

The realization made her more determined than ever to make sure her dad got his second chance at happiness. If that required a little subterfuge then so be it.

Whatever the circumstances, being a single parent was a lot harder than she'd ever thought and Burke was struggling with it. She'd been lucky to live in Blackwater Lake, where neighbors stepped in to lend a hand.

He wasn't staying, but he was here now. And she would help him.

Chapter Nine

A few days after meeting Liam and bringing him to work, Sydney got a call from Burke. The good news was the kid was finally in school. The bad news: there was an emergency. Burke was tied up in a permit meeting, an emergency of his own. He asked if there was any way she could pick up the boy, and promised to get away as soon as possible. Although she would have done it anyway, the worry and stress in his voice made her feel sorry for him and convinced her to help out.

She let her dad know what was going on and headed over to Blackwater Lake Elementary, which was about ten minutes beyond the garage on the north side of town. After parking in the lot, she headed up the sidewalk, past the flagpole and into the office at the front of the school.

It hadn't changed much since she'd been a student there. Blue industrial-strength carpet, pale yellow walls and the tall information desk that didn't seem quite as tall as it had when she'd been a student here.

Liam was sitting on the orange plastic seat of a chair against the wall. Another boy was there, too, with a chair between them. He was about the same age and looked familiar.

"May I help you?" There was a middle-aged woman standing behind the desk.

"Yes. I'm Sydney McKnight. I'm the emergency contact for Liam Holden."

"I talked to his father." The woman nodded. "There's been an incident—"

The office door opened behind her and Syd turned to see who it was. Violet walked in, looked at the boys, then noticed Syd standing there. She came over to the desk.

"Hi, Cheryl. I got a call about Todd."

"Yes. I was just about to explain the situation to Sydney."

"Why?"

"She's the emergency contact for the other boy involved. Burke Holden is his father."

"The multibazillionaire who's building the resort?"

"That's the one," Cheryl confirmed. "Anyway, Todd and Liam were fighting at recess. Blackwater Lake Elementary has a zero-tolerance policy about that sort of thing."

"Did Todd start it?" Violet asked.

Before the woman could answer Sydney said, "Doesn't matter. They both get sent home."

"That's right," the woman confirmed.

Violet looked surprised. "How did you know?"

"Because I'm sure things haven't changed and I have brothers. I bet your sisters never got sent home for fighting on the playground."

"You'd win that bet." She turned to glance at her son. "This is a new experience for me."

"The boys can come back tomorrow," Cheryl said. "And

hopefully with the time to think about this, their attitudes will have improved."

"So we're finished here?" Syd asked.

"Yes."

"Okay." She turned to Liam, who didn't appear especially combative. He looked small, a little scared and a lot sorry. "Let's go, kiddo."

Violet walked over to her blond, blue-eyed son. "Come on, Todd."

The boys picked up their backpacks and the four of them walked outside.

When they got to the sidewalk beside the flagpole, Syd put her hand on Liam's shoulder and stopped. "Do you want to tell me what happened?"

"No."

Violet coughed and Syd didn't dare look at her because she knew that was an attempt to cover a laugh. Syd had walked right into that one. Of course he didn't *want* to tell her what went on.

"It's almost lunchtime." Violet was checking her watch. "What do you say we sort this out over burgers and fries at the diner? I have to tell my boss why I'll be a little late for my shift anyway."

"Why?" Syd asked.

The other woman looked at her son. "I didn't plan on needing child care this early in the day. When I'm working, a high school girl comes over and is there to meet the kids when they get home from school. She gets them snacks and supervises homework until Charlie gets off work."

"I see."

She thought over the idea of lunch and remembered once asking her dad why he always took her brothers out to eat when they were in trouble. His answer: he had them for at least an hour and they had to talk. Usually he got useful information. The wisdom of it had never been clear to her until now.

"Okay," she said to Violet. "The diner it is."

They separated and took their respective vehicles into town and parked in the rear lot behind the Grizzly Bear Diner. After going inside Violet arranged for a table then talked to Michelle Crawford about her predicament. Syd texted Burke that she had Liam and let him know where they were. In a few minutes Violet joined them at a booth in the back and took the vacant seat beside her son.

"I have the best boss in the world."

"She has three grown sons," Syd pointed out wryly. "I guess it's all sorted out?"

"Yeah. I can keep Todd here with me for the lunch shift, then run him home when the sitter's there."

"I'm not a baby." Todd's tone was defensive and resentful.

"You're right," his mom said. "And your dad and I have raised you to use words. Hitting someone is never okay."

"Dad said I should defend myself if someone is picking on me."

Syd stared at Liam. She didn't know him well but he seemed like a sweet kid going through a difficult time, not a bully. "Were you picking on Todd?"

"No." The single word was defensive and resentful. The two boys were obstinate and hostile.

"Hi, Vi." The waitress—her name tag said Carla—came over to the table to take their orders. "What can I get you?"

When asked what they wanted the boys both lifted their shoulders in a shrug. Syd and Violet exchanged a glance then agreed on two Mama Bear combos and two Bear Cub combos that consisted of chicken nuggets, fries and a soft drink.

When they were alone again Violet said, "Liam is new

in town, Todd. In Blackwater Lake we make people feel welcome."

"I wasn't mean," he protested.

Syd had a feeling any blame for the altercation could be shared equally and in the spirit of peace negotiations it might be best not to single either of them out.

"You know," she said, "sometimes stuff just happens and gets out of hand. I think the school sends everyone involved home to think about it and figure out how to handle things differently in the future." She glanced at Violet, who nodded slightly.

"Sydney's right. This was a learning experience that you didn't have to get sitting at a desk in the classroom. A teachable moment."

"Does that mean we have homework?" Todd's expression was supposed to be innocent, but smacked of nine-year-old sarcasm.

Liam snickered. "That was a good one."

And the tension was broken. Todd pulled a couple of superhero action figures from his backpack, which seemed to surprise his mother—the toys probably shouldn't have been taken to school. A talk for another time. The boys each took a figure and started fake fighting with them, reaching across the table.

"I see the potential spilling hazards of this," Violet said. "But I don't have the heart to break this up. They're getting along. Talking."

"Like us." Syd smiled.

"Yeah. Who'd have thought?"

"You know I realized something after you brought your car into the shop." Syd unrolled silverware from her paper napkin and checked out the boys who were paying no attention to the adults. Still, she lowered her voice. "I was never in love with Charlie. We became a habit, not a couple."

"How do you know?" Violet looked surprised at the admission. "It's been ten years. Maybe you're just over it?"

She shook her head. "Memories came back when we talked. And a little while ago outside school I knew you were trying not to laugh when I asked if Liam *wanted* to tell me what happened. It hit me. After you guys left, I missed you. I was mourning the loss of my best friend."

There were tears in Violet's eyes when she reached across the table to grab Syd's hand. "I missed you, too."

"I'm glad you're here. I'm glad you moved back. I look forward to having my best friend around again."

"I look forward to that, too."

The food came then and they all dug in. With the air cleared all around, it seemed everyone was ravenous. A weight lifted from Syd's shoulders that might not have if she hadn't been Burke's emergency contact. This lunch was a good move, for her and Violet and the boys, too. Not unexpectedly, they finished first.

"Mom, I have to go to the bathroom."

"Me, too," Liam said.

Syd and Violet slid from the booth, letting the boys out. One of them said, "Race you," and the two took off.

"I was going to tell them no water fights," Syd said, "but I didn't want to give them any ideas."

"You have good mom instincts." Violet dragged a French fry through ketchup.

"I consider that a compliment. It has to be said that you handled this thing at school really well. No freaking out or overreacting. So calm and common sense."

"Thanks." Vi got a look on her face, a tell that personal questions were coming. "So, you're the emergency contact for Burke Holden's son."

"Yeah."

"C'mon, Syd. Give. Details. What's the story?"

"We're friends." She shrugged. "He asked, and like you

told Todd, folks in Blackwater Lake try to make newcomers feel welcome."

"I know you, Syd." Violet's eyes narrowed. "There's something you're not saying."

There were a lot of things she wasn't saying and didn't plan to. It was tempting to talk to her friend and share everything like she used to. But in this situation she couldn't. Not that Violet would spill the beans, but it could get awkward for her. Syd didn't want to put their newly repaired friendship in jeopardy.

Before she could answer, she saw Burke enter the diner, look around and head in her direction. He stopped at the end of their booth and she thought her heart would jump right out of her chest. This was unexpected and she was really happy to see him. Too happy for her peace of mind.

"I got here as soon as I could. What happened? Where's Liam?"

"In the restroom," Syd said. Then she proceeded to explain about the fight and the fact that the boys had worked out their differences. There was nothing to worry about.

"I'm really sorry to involve you, Syd," he said. "And Violet, I apologize if my son caused you any trouble. It won't happen again."

She laughed. "I appreciate that, but I won't hold you to it. Kids are unpredictable. On the upside, stuff blows over pretty quickly. Don't worry about this."

"That's very generous of you." He looked at Syd. "When I made you my emergency contact, I never dreamed that I'd really have to take you up on it. Liam will have consequences for this behavior, I assure you. I'm thinking in terms of grounding him for the rest of his life."

"I think a father-son talk might do more good," she suggested. "He's been yanked out of his comfort zone and is probably reacting to that. Besides, he and Todd seem to have made peace."

"And dare I say it?" Violet asked. "Maybe a friend-ship is budding?"

"That would be great." He looked at each of them. "As a gesture of goodwill, I took care of the lunch check."

"Very generous of *you*. Have you eaten yet?" Violet's tone was full of questions that had nothing to do with his lunch and everything to do with Syd and any relationship she might have with the handsome hotshot businessman. When he shook his head, she said, "Please join us. But before you do, it has to be said that the boys have been in the bathroom longer than seems necessary. We need a man to go in there and make sure there are no water fights going on."

"I can do that." He smiled at each of them. "Back in a minute."

"He's cute," Violet commented when he was out of ear-shot. "How did you meet him?"

"He brought his car in to the shop for an oil change." That was absolutely true. "And then things took off from there."

And how.

Burke had said he liked her and would have gotten around to dating her on his own. Maybe that was the truth. Maybe it wasn't. But they were after different things from a relationship. He didn't want more children and that was a deal breaker for her. As far as she could see, there was no way to negotiate a compromise.

As far as she was concerned it would be better if he stuck to her proposal. That would be the decent thing to do.

On the drive back to work Syd had some time to think. Violet deeply regretted the way she'd handled falling in love with Charlie—she really was sorry about not being honest with Syd right from the start. Making peace with

Violet was a relief and that realization made the burden of deceiving her father even more troublesome.

She pulled in to the automotive lot and parked her car, then went straight to the main office, where her dad was behind his flat-topped metal desk doing computer work. Before she could say anything, he glanced up and something about his expression reminded her of being sixteen years old and waiting for a boy to pick her up. He was troubled about something.

"How did things work out with Liam?" Tom's voice was soft and even, as if he was trying too hard to appear unconcerned.

"He's suspended from school for the rest of the day. Fighting." She slid her hands into the pockets of her work pants. "Coincidentally, the other boy involved was Violet's son, Todd. We took them to lunch. Violet's idea, actually. But I remembered how you used to do that with Alex and Ben when they were in some kind of trouble."

She was talking too much, a sure sign of being nervous. It wasn't easy, but she forced herself to shut up.

Even her compliment didn't coax a smile from her father. "That's good it all worked out."

"What's wrong, Dad?" When he opened his mouth to protest, she held up her hand to stop what she knew was coming. "Save it. I know when something's bothering you, so get it off your chest."

"You're not going to like it."

"Probably not. So let's get this over with."

"I'm uneasy about your relationship with Burke."

"But I thought you wanted me to be involved with someone," she protested.

"He's not from around here."

Even though she and Burke didn't have a real relationship, Syd felt compelled to argue that statement as a cause for concern. "You're nervous because he's an outsider? Seriously?"

"Yes." He leaned back in his chair and linked his fingers, then rested his hands over his flat belly.

She could see stubbornness move across his face and set up camp. "This is where I point out that Alex and Ben both married women who aren't from around here. Jill Beck Stone married a doctor who moved here from Las Vegas. They're all happy couples and starting families. What makes you think that just because Burke is from somewhere else that he's unworthy?"

Syd actually knew the answer. That part about starting a family wasn't going to happen with Burke. But she met her father's gaze, refusing to look away.

"He's temporary, Syd. His business is based somewhere else. He's here to get the resort going and then he'll go back where he came from." He sat forward and rested his forearms on the desk. "Plus he's got a son. Seems like a nice enough boy, but the fighting at school is a concern. He could be trouble."

"Oh, come on, Dad. Alex and Ben were no angels at Liam's age. They had skirmishes at school when they were kids. And you're their father. Does that mean you're not a suitable man to date?"

"We're not talking about me. This is about you settling down, so—"

"So that you can move on with your life and be happy. I get it." She had to tell him the truth and this was the time. "About that, Dad. I have something to say and you're not going to like it."

"Okay."

"Burke isn't really my boyfriend."

Although Burke had kissed her as if he was and she'd kissed him back. She really liked kissing him and had been prepared to sleep with him before he got the call

about his housekeeper. Syd knew her willingness to go
to bed with the man colored everything a murky shade of
gray. Technically he wasn't her boyfriend but he had said
he wanted to date her. Casually. So she wasn't exactly
sure what they were.

Her dad rubbed a hand across his face. "So when he
drove in here and you introduced him as the guy you'd
been seeing, that was a lie?"

"A big, hairy one," she confirmed. "But, in my own
defense—wrong thing, right reason."

"That reason being an attempt to get me to commit to
Loretta?"

"Yes. You have to admit you're practically living with
the mayor. Isn't it about time you get her a ring? Make an
honest woman of her?" Syd hoped now he really was in a
place where he could hear her.

His mouth twitched, evidence that he was trying to
maintain a stern face and failing big-time. "So you think
we should get hitched?"

"Although that term brings to mind a horse attached to a
wagon, if you're as smart as I think you are, you'll propose
and get married as soon as possible." Syd moved closer to
the desk and settled her hip on the corner. "You deserve
to have all the good things in life. I hope you know that.
You have to squeeze the happy out of every single day."

"I do know that."

"Then get off your tush and quit wasting time." Emotion and her passion to make him understand kicked up
the pitch of her voice. "I can take care of myself. And if I
need help, which I won't, isn't it better for me to have you
and Loretta together? The way I see it, you're a twofer."

A slow smile curved his mouth. "That's a nice thing
to say."

"I'm a nice person." She grinned. "So now I have to
come up with your power-couple nickname."

"What in the world?"

"They do that with Hollywood couples. Combine first names. You and Loretta could be Lo-Tom. Or my personal favorite, drumroll please—Tom-Lo."

"Stop." He shook a finger at her, then turned serious. "Syd, thank you for trusting me with the truth."

"Actually, I really hate deceiving you. Too much guilt to carry around."

"And I have to confess that I didn't really buy the act. It was suspicious from the start."

"I guess it's a compliment that I'm not a very good liar." She folded her arms over her chest, not really surprised by his admission. As a kid, she could never pull a fast one without him being wise to it. "And in the spirit of full disclosure, the whole truth is that the day he drove in, I'd never seen him before in my life. But we spent time together pretending to be a couple."

"And you like him." It wasn't a question.

She nodded. "And he says he likes me. That he'd have gotten around to asking me out sooner or later."

Just thinking about the look in his eyes when he'd said that made her quiver all over. The attention, especially from a man like him, was incredibly flattering and that was a problem. It could set her up for a really hard fall.

"I see." Her father nodded thoughtfully. "It goes without saying that he has excellent taste. But, Syd, I can't help having concerns—"

"Objections," she interrupted.

"That's too strong a word. He seems like a nice enough guy. I don't think he would deliberately hurt you, but my concerns about the two of you haven't changed. He's an outsider and unlikely to stay here in Blackwater Lake."

"Understood."

"Syd—" He got to his feet and said her name to stop her from leaving when she straightened away from the desk. "Before you go—I have to apologize. I didn't mean to push you into lying about your personal life. I've only ever wanted to be a good father. Protect you."

"Oh, Dad—" She walked over and gave him a hug. "You're an amazing father."

"I wouldn't go that far."

"I would," she said eagerly. "Watching you with Liam reminded me of when I was a little girl and how much I loved hanging out with you." She stepped back and smiled up at him. "Still do. Thanks for being the best father I could ask for."

"Thank you for loving me enough to do anything for my happiness."

"If you don't ask Loretta soon, I may have to get really creative and wild. Who knows what I'll do?"

"Now you're starting to scare me. I promise I'll take care of it." His voice was teasing, before his expression turned serious. "But do me a favor, Syd. Don't get hurt."

"No need to worry, Dad. I've got it under control." So she'd just told another lie.

The truth was she'd never felt about anyone the way she did about Burke. It was dishonest to say she had everything under control when every time he walked into a room she had less power over her feelings. All she had for sure was a bucketload of doubts.

Chapter Ten

"Thanks for meeting me here, Syd." Burke held out a hand indicating one of the visitor chairs in front of his desk. "I have a favor to ask."

"Another one?" Her smile was teasing.

He really liked that smile. It felt like forever since he'd seen her, but just the day before he'd had lunch at the diner while Sydney, Violet and the boys kept him company. The whole experience had felt so completely normal and fun. He hadn't wanted to go back to the office and that was saying something for a man whose life was his work.

Today he'd asked her to come to the office when she left McKnight Automotive. Since she was busy when he'd called, there wasn't a chance to explain why he wanted to see her. But she wasn't wearing McKnight Automotive standard-issue pants and shirt, which indicated she'd taken the time to change. Her fashion instincts were spot-on. She looked chic and beautiful in straight-leg jeans, a white silk blouse, a navy blazer and low-heeled shoes.

"I hate to impose on you again," he said. "It isn't enough that you helped me out with the fighting incident at school yesterday. Believe me I'm grateful."

"And your way of paying me back is asking for more? You really were born with a silver spoon in your mouth, weren't you?" she teased.

Burke shrugged. It was a blessing and curse. Money didn't make your life perfect. If so, his mother wouldn't have died so young. On paper, a guy who'd grown up without a mom and was raised by his father should have been equipped to parent his own son whose mother had no interest in the job. But Burke's father had never been around and he had no blueprint for how to be a dad. Syd, on the other hand, had never even known her mother but had hit the dad jackpot. From him she'd absorbed great instincts.

"Before I get to the favor, I have to tell you that Liam and I had a greeting-card moment last night. Thanks to you."

"Really? What did I do?"

"You suggested a father-son chat instead of grounding him for eternity."

"Oh, that."

"Yes. That." He leaned forward, forearms on the desk. "I told him I wanted to talk about what happened at school. He was sullen and defensive at first, but eventually he opened up. It was—" He stopped, searching for the right description and finally said, "A first for us."

She looked pleased. "What did he say?"

"That everything's different here and he doesn't like it. He's angry and feeling insecure."

"He said that?" she asked, obviously surprised. "Awfully grown up."

"Not in those exact words, but the message came through. It's not home, not what he's used to."

"How can it be when this is only temporary?" She

shrugged, but that didn't distract from the shadows in her eyes.

Burke had a feeling something was bothering her and didn't like it. He preferred her sunny-side up and wanted to fix any problem. That was new, he realized. Usually when a woman needed something emotional fixed, he headed for the nearest exit.

"What's wrong?" he asked.

Her lips compressed into a tight line. "If you hadn't called me, I was going to call you."

He was glad to hear that, although her expression was a clue that her motivation wasn't necessarily similar to his. The favor he wanted to ask was a thinly veiled excuse to see her. One thing he'd learned since bringing his son to live with him—when a single father didn't have live-in child care, dating was complicated. He had to get creative.

"Why were you going to call me?" he asked.

"To let you know we don't have to fake it any more. Dad knows what I did."

By that Burke was pretty sure she meant that their relationship deal was outed. But the truth was that after the first dinner with Syd and her dad, he hadn't been pretending to like her.

Which begged the question... "How did he find out?"

"I confessed." She shrugged again. "I couldn't keep lying to him."

"How did he take it?" Burke liked Tom McKnight and losing the man's favorable opinion bothered him. "Was he angry?"

"No. And that's the worst part. If he'd gotten mad, I could have been defensive and self-righteous. This was so much worse." She shook her head at the memory. "He said he's just trying to be a good father. Protect me."

Burke shared the man's inclination for that and could understand the motivation for putting off his own life for the sake of his child. But he could also understand Syd's determination to convince her dad she was okay and get him to commit to a new, personal phase.

"Should I talk to him?" he offered.

"Why would you want to?" She seemed surprised by that.

"Because I don't want him to think I make a habit of deceiving people."

She tilted her head to study him. "You actually care what he thinks of you."

"Yes." Now he shrugged.

"It would be very noble of you and I have no objection. For the record, he claims he wasn't fooled for a second." She shifted in the chair. "In the spirit of complete honesty, I did tell him what you said, that you'd have gotten around to asking me out if I hadn't approached you first."

"So you told him everything?"

"Pretty much." Her expression was guarded, indicating she'd held something back.

He decided it best not to push. "So I can make an honest woman of you now?"

"Others have tried and failed," she joked. "So, don't keep me in suspense. What is this favor? Just so you know, I'm keeping a tab."

"I wouldn't have it any other way." He grinned and leaned back in his chair. "The idea actually came from my talk with Liam. It was his anger and insecurity that made me call you today."

"Interesting. My expertise is with a car engine. I'm not a shrink."

"Very funny." This is where he had to sell the idea. "This is much easier than that. You're a local. I have an appointment with a real-estate agent who also manages rentals in and around Blackwater Lake."

"Okay." A puzzled look crossed her face. "I'm not sure how I can help with that."

"The thing is, I think if I can find a house to rent, something more homey than the lodge, it might help Liam to feel settled. I guess it's a dad thing."

"I think it's a good idea. But I still don't know what I can do to make it easier."

"That's where being a local comes in. I need your advice on location, good or bad, and your general impression of the property. From a woman's perspective."

"Well, I'm a woman."

And how. Burke couldn't help it when his gaze dropped from her eyes to the top button on that silky blouse. She *was* a woman and he was the guy who almost had her. If only his cell phone had rung *after* they'd let nature take its course maybe he wouldn't ache to touch her now. And now was a lot more complicated than then.

"All I'm asking for is your educated opinion on what we see today."

She nodded. "No one ever said I don't have opinions. I can do that."

"Great." He stood. "We're picking Liam up at Todd's house on the way to meet the agent at the first property. I have the list he emailed."

She smiled. "Liam had a playdate?"

"Yeah. Progress. And if he's going to reciprocate, it would be nice to have a house to do it in. Not a hotel." He looked at her. "Let's go."

Several hours later, the three of them had racked up more frustration than miles. There hadn't been much to look at and for what they'd seen, the agent had used adjectives and descriptions like *rugged. Rustic. Diamond-in-the-rough.* Something a splash of TLC would fix right up.

After Burke had declined all of the rentals, they'd

gone back to his office so she could pick up her car. The Holdens' collective discouragement was too much. Syd had invited father and son to her house for dinner. She didn't have the heart to send them back to Blackwater Lake Lodge. As nice as her sister-in-law, Cam, made the place, it wasn't a home. The least she could do was not condemn them to another meal in a restaurant. She offered to fix a home-cooked meal for the boys.

And if she was being honest, with her dad spending all his free time with Loretta, Syd was a little lonely eating by herself.

She and Burke were sitting outside in patio chairs at the round table that could accommodate four. They were sipping white wine while Liam kicked around an old soccer ball that had once belonged to one of her brothers. Glancing over, she noted that Burke's expression was troubled. Being unable to make a home happen for his son had to be really hard for a man used to holding power and getting what he wanted. Or making it happen.

"The first place wasn't that bad," she said, trying to cheer him up.

When he met her gaze, his was wry. "If you like sharing your living space with a raccoon family."

"You don't know animals were occupying it. That was the agent's speculation."

"More like an educated guess. Based on the fact that the cabinets were rifled through and the place was trashed. Looked like wolves lived there."

"Maybe Mr. and Mrs. Raccoon had a party and invited friends." She sipped her wine, then said, "I know, maybe it was the kids. The folks were out hunting and gathering while the teenagers threw a kegger without permission."

One corner of his mouth curved up. "Nice try."

"I thought it was pretty good, actually. I can only conclude that you're determined to pout."

"When you put it like that…" He was slumped in the chair, head resting on the thick outdoor pad. His gaze followed his son, running around chasing the black-and-white ball. "Look how much he's enjoying being outside. I don't think Cam would sanction him practicing headers and goal kicks in our suite at the lodge."

"I would put in a good word, but you're probably right about that." Syd laughed. "But it's not the end of the world. You have four walls and a roof over your head. A two-bedroom suite. Best in town."

"And it's lovely." He rolled his head to the side and glanced at her. "Can I just say that this resort can't be built too soon. Blackwater Lake needs more housing options."

"I can see why you'd think so."

"If only I didn't have to be here, but I've found that things go a lot faster and smoother if I'm on site from the beginning, meeting face-to-face with people, keeping everyone accountable for the work. Flying back and forth to troubleshoot really slows things down."

She nodded. "I see your point."

"For the record," he said, "I'm not pouting. Just disappointed."

Liam kicked the ball toward where they were sitting then flopped in the chair beside his father's. He took a sip from the glass of lemonade in front of him. "What are we gonna do, Dad?"

"About what?"

"A place to live."

"It would appear that we have no choice but to stay where we are, son."

"Really? No way. Todd lives in a nice house and has a really big backyard. We played tag today with his little sister. She was 'it' all the time 'cuz we were faster."

Syd wasn't sure how that information was connected

to the current problem, but figured all would be revealed. "Sounds like you had fun today."

"Yeah." He looked at his father. "But you always say when you get invited somewhere you should invite them back. How can I do that? We can't play tag in a hotel."

Burke's mouth pulled tight. "We'll think of some way to reciprocate."

"What?" Liam rubbed a knuckle under his nose.

"Return the favor," Burke explained.

"I don't see how." He slumped in his chair and looked like Burke's Mini-Me. "I'm the only kid in my class who lives in a hotel."

"Technically, it's a lodge," Syd said. "And have you asked everyone in the class where they live?"

"No." Liam thought for a moment. "But I haven't seen any of them at the lodge. And I would have if they lived there."

"Good point." She met Burke's gaze and whispered, "I think he's going to be a lawyer when he grows up."

That got a grin, but it faded fast. Syd could see that it was killing him not to be able to give his son what he wanted most and blamed himself for the fact that he couldn't. She fully expected his next words to be about a trip to the toy store—to buy something to make him feel better. But his comment surprised her.

"I'm bummed about the situation, too, Liam. But there's not really anything I can do to change it. We're lucky to have a nice place to live and enough food to eat. There are a lot of people in the world who don't have that."

"Yeah, I know. That doesn't mean it doesn't stink."

"I hear you, buddy."

"You know, Liam," she said, "if you want to be outside with friends, there's the park. It's brand-new—just opened officially a few weeks ago." One of her first very public "dates" with Burke. "There's lots of room to run and

fun equipment to play on. Or you could come over here."
She held out a hand, indicating all the space available for
running and playing. "This is a big yard and my dad still
has my brothers' basketball and portable hoop, baseball
and mitt. Lots of stuff to use outdoors. You're welcome
to come over anytime."

"Really?" Blue eyes so like his father's glowed with
excitement.

"Really. *Mi casa, su casa.* And, before you ask, that's
Spanish for my house is your house. Just give me a call
before you come over. Okay?"

"Awesome! Thanks, Syd."

"You're welcome."

"I'm going to practice soccer again. It would be more
fun if Todd was here, though."

"We'll work on making that happen," Syd promised.

"Cool." Liam stood, then walked over, leaned down
and hugged her. "Thanks."

"You're welcome." She smiled, marveling at the abundance of youthful energy as he kicked the ball nearly to
the back fence and ran after it.

"Yeah, thanks," Burke echoed. "I owe you. Again. It
seems my debt to you just keeps growing, a helping-hand
tab."

"No big deal. It's like you said about returning favors.
Paying it forward. When my dad needed help, folks were
there. It's the Blackwater Lake way."

"And this town is a great place. But—" He reached over
and linked his fingers with hers. "I can't think of anyone
I would rather be in debt to."

Oh, my. The warmth of his hand made her tingle and the
heated look in his eyes had her wishing they were alone.
This presented her with a dilemma. Her dad knew the truth
about them pretending to be an item. Burke knew her dad

knew so there was no reason for pretense, no need to act as if they were attracted. Unless they really were attracted.

He was voluntarily holding her hand and looking at her as if he wanted to take her upstairs and ravage her. And she would very much like to be ravaged by Burke Holden.

But…how she hated that word. She also felt a swell of contentment. A peek into what it would be like to have a family of her own.

And that was a problem.

Sex was a purely biological need. But if the physical need became an emotional attachment, then things dipped into dangerous territory.

The conversation with her friend Maggie echoed her father's concerns. Burke didn't live in Blackwater Lake. This was all temporary, with very little chance of working out in the long run. She had to keep her heart out of the equation, keep it from getting crushed.

It had happened once and even though that was a long time ago, a girl didn't ever forget how bad it felt. This was not a good time to remember that distance from Burke was what she needed. Unfortunately she'd just offered him her house as a playground.

About five minutes after Burke and Liam left Syd was still putting the finishing touches on cleaning up the kitchen. Hamburgers and paper plates didn't make a big mess, but the sink needed a scrub and the granite counters could use a wiping down. She heard the sound of the front door opening and closing, followed by her father walking into the kitchen. He was holding the soccer ball in his hands.

"Don't tell me. This is a clue that you're leaving the family business to train for the women's World Cup."

"Very funny." She folded up the dishrag and settled it over the hump between the two sinks. "You just missed

Burke and Liam. I invited them over for dinner and got out the ball for the kid. He needed to run around."

"I see."

Syd hated when her father said that. It sounded so relaxed, rational and reasonable, but she knew it really meant he didn't see at all. The words didn't quite take on the impact of disapproval because the tone wasn't there. But it was awfully close.

As always happened, those two one-syllable words goaded her into an attempt to change his attitude. "Burke asked me to go with them to look at rental houses. Now that his son is here with him, he'd like to get out of the lodge and into something more family-oriented."

"How'd that go?" Her dad tucked the ball underneath his arm, then leaned back against the island across from her.

"You know as well as I do that there's very little for lease around here that's decent and available. It was a complete bust."

"You felt bad and asked them to stay for dinner."

She shouldn't be surprised that he knew her so well, but somehow she was. "Yeah. Liam needed to let off some steam, get rid of that energy."

"I see."

There it was again. That response was starting to make her teeth hurt. She might as well put everything out there, including the standing invitation she'd initiated.

"I told them that any time he needed a yard to play in ours was available."

"What about the park?" Her father's voice was pleasant, the tone unchanged. His expression gave no clue about what he was thinking.

"I mentioned it."

Tom nodded thoughtfully. "That's nice of you to offer our yard."

"But?"

He shook his head. "But nothing. It was a really nice gesture on your part."

"But…you're wondering why I would do that."

Instead of confirming, he asked, "How do you feel about Burke?"

"He's a good guy."

"Romantically," her father added.

"There is no romantically. I just think he's down-to-earth and fun. I like him."

"In spite of the fact that he went along with your scheme the first time you met?"

"We already talked about this," she reminded him.

"Not all of it. I see the looks between you two when you think no one is watching. I know how a man looks when he's got ideas about a woman—"

"Dad." She held up her hand for him to stop. They'd had this awkward conversation when she was about twelve and that was an experience she didn't want to repeat. "I get your drift. Enough said. There's no need to discuss this."

"I disagree. You know I'm concerned. Can't help it." He shrugged. "And I'm not so sure you don't have feelings for the guy."

"I told you—"

This time he held up a hand to stop her. "You're acting as if I'm going to chase him off. That's not the case."

She looked at him, eyes narrowing suspiciously. "Then what are you trying to say?"

"If you like him, I'm okay with that."

She wasn't. "Seriously, Dad, I'm not stupid or desperate enough to fall for a guy who isn't staying. And I'm not willing to move to be with him. Blackwater Lake is my home and I love working with you. So, it's settled."

"Look, honey, I know you got pretty banged-up when Violet and Charlie messed you over. Doesn't matter whether or not they meant for it to happen, it still hurt. And Loretta has told me how deeply a teenage girl can feel the pain and hold on to it."

"Loretta said that?"

"She did. A very wise woman." There was a tender expression on his face. "Not that we were talking about you, or anything."

"Of course not," she said drily. But it made her feel a little sad that he'd never had the perspective of a close relationship with a woman when she'd been growing up. "Speaking of Loretta, no offense, but why are you home?"

He shrugged and crossed the space between them, then slung his arm across her shoulders. "I guess I wanted to spend some time with my girl."

"That's nice." She rested her head on his chest for a moment. "Don't worry about me, Dad. I'm fine. Really."

"Of course you are." He sighed. "I guess I just wanted to say that I'm not the best example of getting back on the horse after falling off. And I know that it's hard to do when you've been kicked in the teeth. That sort of thing can shape your life choices."

"Listen to you being all in touch with your feelings."

"This is hard enough without you being a smart aleck." There was a teasing note in his voice. "But seriously, Sydney Marie, do as I say, not as I did. Take a chance. Don't hide from it all."

"Okay, Dad."

But that was easier said than done. She'd been keeping herself isolated for a lot of years and wasn't sure that habit could be broken.

Or that she even wanted to.

Chapter Eleven

"Dad, why can't I go over to Syd's? She said I could go anytime I wanted to run around outside and play ball." Liam's voice had the beginning of a whine.

Burke had just picked him up from school and they were headed back to the office.

"There are a lot of reasons. First, Syd is working and there's no one at the house to supervise you. Don't even say it." He knew what was going through the kid's mind. "I can't stay with you. There's work back at the office. And a surprise for you."

"Me? What is it?" Just like that the whine vanished without a trace.

"If I told you, it wouldn't be a surprise, would it?"

Burke hadn't said anything about family coming to town. Sloan was here with preliminary drawings for the resort. But Burke's father, who had retired from the company, had announced he was coming along, too. In Burke's experience, the man had a way of not showing up and he'd decided not to say anything to Liam and risk disappointing him. If Walker Holden showed up it *would* be a surprise—for Burke, too. But Sloan had texted that the two of them were driving from the airport and given their estimated time of arrival. That would put them at the office when he got there with Liam.

He could hardly blame the boy for wanting to go to Sydney's house. For Burke, though, it wasn't about the house as much as seeing her in it. Or anywhere else for that matter. She was sunshine and flowers. Just looking at her made him feel good. He'd been to some of the fanciest, most expensive restaurants in the world, but hamburgers and wine on her patio had been one of the best meals he'd ever had.

She was a natural with kids, too. Liam really liked her. It was something they both agreed on and that hadn't happened in a long time.

Burke pulled in to the parking lot of the O'Keefe Technology building. Liam jumped out of the car practically before the engine was shut off. After hitting the lock button, Burke hurried after the boy and caught up with him at the lobby elevator. He checked his phone and read Sloan's text. His cousin and father were waiting in Burke's office.

He and Liam rode up together and when the doors opened, the kid was out like a shot, but this time he didn't take off.

"What's the surprise?" he asked. "A new video game? A dog?"

Lydia, his executive assistant, looked up when she heard the boy's voice. "Hey, Liam. How was school?"

"Hi. Okay. What's my surprise?" He marched up to her desk.

"I'm not at liberty to say." Her eyes twinkled when she looked at Burke. "But your afternoon appointment is here."

"Okay. Let's go, son." He put his hand on the boy's shoulder.

"It's just going to be a boring meeting. Do I hafta stay?"

"I'm afraid so. But I'll try to make it quick."

He opened his office door and two men occupied the sofa, coffee in front of them on the table. It took a couple of seconds, then Liam dropped his backpack and raced over.

"Uncle Sloan!" Liam knew the man wasn't an uncle, but Cousin Sloan sounded dumb. When the boy was little they'd settled on the title as a gesture of respect.

"Hey, kid." His cousin grabbed the boy in a bear hug. With Sloan's dark hair and eyes he didn't much look like Burke except for height and body type.

Liam wiggled free and looked at the other man. "Grand-dad!"

"Hello, Liam." Walker Holden embraced his grandson with what looked like genuine affection.

Burke couldn't tell. He didn't recall being on the receiving end of warmth from his father. "Hello, Dad. You're looking well."

The man was about his height and they had the same blue eyes. His father's brown hair was shot with silver. "Burke. It's good to see you."

He shook the offered hand and made sure his grip was firm enough and eye contact held just the right amount of time. Then he met his cousin's gaze and grinned.

"Sloan." Burke grabbed him in a quick hug.

"Is this my surprise?" Liam asked.

"Yes. Uncle Sloan is here on business." He didn't know why his father was there.

"Cool."

"When I told him there was a surprise waiting for him, he was hoping for a video game or a puppy." Burke felt a dash of guilt for not addressing his father's presence, but he didn't know why he'd tagged along.

"A dog sounds like a great idea," Sloan said. "After the meeting we should go to the pet store. This town has one, right?"

Burke shook his head. "I don't know. And it doesn't matter. There's no way we're getting a dog. We're stuck at the lodge for the duration and that's no place for a dog."

"I bet Sydney would keep a dog for me and I could go visit." Liam looked up hopefully.

"That's not something I would even ask her to do." That, Burke thought, was how good she was with kids. Obviously his son trusted her completely.

"Who's Sydney?" Walker asked. "A local contractor?"

"She's awesome," Liam said. "She and her dad have a garage. She let me watch while she did a tune-up. And I got to hand her tools."

"So, Sydney is a she?" Sloan got that expression on his face, as if to say there was something going on.

"Sydney McKnight. She's a friend," Burke explained. "I did her a favor and she returned it. Her uncle runs the county permit office. She told him I'm a nice guy."

"Clearly her judgment is impaired," Sloan joked.

"And you like her?" Walker put a hand on his grandson's shoulder.

"She's cool. So is her dad. She cooked hamburgers for me and Dad the other night. Then she let me play with her brother's old soccer ball. It was fun."

"So, you like it here in Blackwater Lake?" The older man looked as if it really mattered that the boy was happy.

Liam thought for a moment. "I miss Chicago and my house. And Mary. But I have a friend at school now. Todd. His mom is a friend of Syd's."

And her friend's husband was Syd's old boyfriend. Yet somehow she'd found a way to forgive Violet for the past. It still amazed him. "My son is the only kid in his class who lives in a hotel."

"Yeah. That part stinks."

Burke explained that single-family living space was scarce in this town. And rentals were practically nonexistent. The lodge was the best place for visitors to stay. When notified about his cousin's trip with his father, he'd booked rooms right away and fortunately there were vacancies.

"I knew this area was crying for more housing," Sloan declared. "And I'm anxious to show you the preliminary sketches. They're on your desk."

"The architect is an award-winning designer and someone I've worked with before," Walker said. "I'm pleased with what he's done."

Burke held back the urge to say he'd try not to hold that against the man. "Liam, do you have homework?"

"Some math. And reading."

"Why don't you go in the other room with Lydia. It will be quieter there."

"But, I want to hang out with Granddad and Uncle Sloan."

"That's funny." Burke looked down at the boy. "A little while ago you didn't want to be here for a boring meeting."

"That's before I knew it was with them." He looked at the two and grinned when Sloan winked.

"You'll see them later. Get your homework done and we'll do something fun after." They stared at each other for several moments in what was becoming a standoff. Finally Burke said, "This is not negotiable. The sooner you get at it, the sooner you can visit."

"Your father is right, Liam," Walker said.

Burke was surprised his father had backed him up. The feeling of having the man in his corner was weird and suspicious.

"Okay." The single word came out of his son's mouth along with a big sigh.

"This won't take long, kid," Sloan said. "Then I'll spring you."

"Thanks, Uncle Sloan. 'Bye, Granddad."

After Liam had left the office Burke asked, "Why are you here, Dad?"

Some emotion flitted through the man's blue eyes. Defensiveness? Guilt? Sadness? It wasn't clear and then the expression was gone. "I wanted to see how Liam was doing. And you."

Now it was really weird. After his mother died, the man was gone all the time. He'd never shown up much at all, let alone to see how Burke was doing.

"We're fine." *Wary, skeptical, but otherwise all right,* he thought. "I'm really anxious to see the sketches."

"Let's do it." Sloan walked over to the desk and picked up the tube lying on top of it. He opened up one end and shook out the sheaf of papers rolled up inside, then spread them out.

Burke carefully inspected each sketch. There was a condo complex with parking nestled in the mountains near the ski area. A retail multi-use compound with living space above. Restaurants and bars. And all of it was just wrong. It was glass and chrome, modern, cold and impersonal.

He looked at his cousin. "This is an awful monstrosity."

Sloan's eyes narrowed. "Don't sugarcoat it. Tell us how you really feel."

"I'm sorry. But all this glass—"

"To showcase the spectacular views of the lake and mountains," his cousin explained.

"I get that. But there are ways to do it so that a building doesn't look like it was lifted from the skyline of Chicago or New York and plopped down in Montana."

"I disagree, Burke." Walker was flipping through the drawings. "When there's snow on the slopes, these structures will blend in."

"With the ice maybe." Burke shook his head. "What about the trees? Or when it's spring and the ice has melted?"

"I agree with Uncle Walker. I like where the architect is going with this concept."

"That's because you live in the city. But what about when you want to get away from it all? If you were from around here, you'd see where *I'm* going with this. The mayor needs to see and approve of these. And she won't. Because the town is going to hate them."

"Really? The town?" There was sarcasm in Sloan's voice. "I'm sort of surprised you're thinking in terms of what the town will think."

"That's because you haven't spent time here in Blackwater Lake. This is one of those rare places that takes on a character of its own and that's a reflection of the people here. They're supportive, warm and welcoming." He pointed to the drawing of the glass-and-metal structure. "Not icy and aloof. The town will hate that," he said again.

"The town may just have to live with it."

Syd was part of the town and wouldn't like living with it.

"We need new sketches and a different focus from someone who knows and understands the area." Burke looked from one man to the other. "Syd's sister-in-law lives locally and is an architect. She used to work for Hart Industries in Dallas."

"I've heard of them," Sloan said. "Impressive body of work."

"Let's give Ellie a chance to come up with something. If the mayor agrees with me. In the meantime, I'll show you around so you can get a feel for what I'm talking about."

Sloan and his father exchanged glances, then both nodded.

Burke was glad they were open-minded. That was easier than trying to explain the unexplainable. Which was that it wasn't the town's feelings he cared about. Good, bad or indifferent, Sydney McKnight was the one he wanted to please.

Sydney sat beside Burke and across the table from Liam at the Grizzly Bear Diner. She wasn't sure how this seating arrangement happened; she would have been better off looking at the two Holden men, but Liam sat first. Then she'd slid in on the other side of the booth and Burke joined her. Now their thighs and arms were touching and she expected to spontaneously combust any second.

"So when did your father leave town?" she asked, trying to take her mind off what was happening to her body.

"This morning."

She'd met his father and cousin at dinner. Burke had called to invite her and warned that his family would be there. She'd been a little nervous. The reaction meant that she cared what Walker and Sloan Holden thought of her, a clear indication that she wasn't indifferent to Burke. But dinner had gone well as far as she could tell.

And tonight at the diner had been fun. As Burke had once predicted, Liam loved the place.

She took the last bite of her salad, chewed and swallowed. "I like your father."

"Really?" Burke looked skeptical.

"He's very charming." Meeting Walker had been like looking into the future and seeing how his son would look when he was in his sixties. Still outrageously handsome and incredibly distinguished. "You look a lot like him."

"No, I don't."

"Dad, people say that all the time. And that I look like you. Which means I look like Granddad."

Unlike his father, the younger Holden seemed to have a

close relationship with Walker. Syd saw the resemblance between all three.

"Your granddad is a very handsome man. There are a lot worse things than looking like him. And without extensive plastic surgery, there's not much you can do but embrace it and move on."

"Okay. Consider this moving on." Burke set his used paper napkin on the empty plate in front of him. "If we're all finished here, I suggest we go down the street to Potter's Ice Cream Parlor for dessert."

"That's a great idea, Dad."

Syd smiled at the boy. He was so different from the hostile, unhappy child he'd been just a couple weeks ago after being dragged to Blackwater Lake. Making a friend had helped but couldn't completely explain the transformation. Burke must be doing a lot right, though she suspected he wouldn't see it.

"Earth to Syd—"

"Hmm?" She blinked and looked up at him. "What?"

"How do you feel about ice cream?"

"In twenty-five words or less I have a deep and personal bond with it that is both celebratory and therapeutic."

"Huh?" Liam looked at her as if she was speaking in an obscure foreign dialect.

"I think that means she likes it when she's happy and uses it as a coping mechanism when she's sad."

"Very intuitive of you, Mr. Holden," she mused.

"Does that mean we can get some?" Liam demanded.

She and Burke grinned at each other and said, "Yes."

"Okay, I'm finished," the boy said. He crammed the last chicken tender in his mouth and mumbled, "What are we waiting for?"

"The check," Syd reminded him.

"Oh, right."

Burke signaled the server, who brought the bill over, along with a plastic grizzly bear toy and a T-shirt for Liam.

Syd was glad they were finally getting ready to vacate the small booth. She'd been in this place a bazillion times and sat everywhere, always with plenty of room. This was her second time sitting beside Burke with legs, thighs and arms brushing, and her reaction was the same. She was hot all over and ice cream would help cool her off.

Besides, she liked hanging out with Liam and his father. They were friends, but she would breathe easier if she could be his friend with a generous buffer zone around them when hanging out.

After paying the check at the register, they walked outside—Liam first while Burke held the door for her. That was nice. A gentleman as always. Burke clearly didn't like being compared to his father, but Walker was a courtly man and it was likely his son had picked up the trait from him.

They headed down the street past Tonya's Treasures, the town souvenir-and-gift shop. Beyond it was the ice cream parlor and The Harvest Café, which shared a connecting door and were now both Maggie's businesses. The latter had once been a dry cleaning store, but the owners had let the lease run out. They retired and moved to California to be near their grandkids. Maggie Potter and her partner, Lucy Bishop, seemed to have the business under control.

When they reached Maggie's, Burke opened the door and Liam started to go in. He put his hand on the boy's shoulder to stop him and said, "Ladies first, pal."

Syd's heart actually fluttered as she passed without actually brushing up against him. So much for her buffer-zone theory. "Thanks."

"My pleasure." His voice went husky on the last word, giving a hint to his thoughts.

The interior of the ice cream parlor was cheerful and

bright. Pictures on the walls were of ice-cream scoops, sundaes, shakes and cakes. Some with sprinkles, others with whipped cream and a cherry. There were small, round tables filling the center of the room and metal chairs with heart-shaped backs and red padded seats.

Syd walked over to the glass display case, surprised to see Maggie behind it. Her friend had an office upstairs over the café, where she worked keeping the books and ordering supplies. Manning The Harvest Café counter was handled by her partner, and normally a part-time high-school kid was here in the evening on the ice cream side. But not tonight.

"Hi, Maggie. What are you doing here?"

"Taylor broke her wrist at cheerleading practice. It's kind of important to be able to use it when scooping ice cream. Couldn't find anyone to fill in on such short notice. Most important—she'll be fine."

"Where's Danielle?"

"She's with my tenant, Josie."

Syd remembered her friend explaining about renting out one of her upstairs bedrooms to her friend for the extra income. Another bonus, apparently, was child care for emergency situations like this.

"Hi, Maggie. This is my son, Liam." Burke came up behind Syd. She could feel the heat from his body and shivered at the closeness.

"Hi." Maggie bent down and looked through the glass because she couldn't see over it. "Nice to meet you."

The boy waved in response. "Do you get all the ice cream you can eat?"

"Liam," Burke said, "that's not an appropriate question."

"It's okay." Maggie laughed. "If he asked how much I weigh or my age, that would be inappropriate. And the answer is yes, I own the place and can eat as much as I want. But you'd be surprised how fast you get tired of ice cream."

"No way." Father and son spoke together and with great feeling.

Syd laughed and wondered if Burke realized how alike the two of them were, how much they had in common. The father had come a long way since the boy had come to live with him.

"What can I get you?" Maggie asked.

It was obvious that Liam knew exactly what he wanted because he immediately ordered a scoop of cookies-and-cream, and another of chocolate caramel with whipped cream, nuts and a cherry.

"A man who knows his own mind. Coming right up." Maggie put it together and handed over the cup at the low counter by the cash register.

"Thanks," the boy said politely, then took his dessert to a table to start eating before it melted.

"Syd? The usual?" Maggie asked.

"Of course."

Burke arched one eyebrow. "One of the many small-town-living perks is that your ice-cream preference is not a secret. But if you got wild with a scoop of peanut butter and bubble gum, people would talk."

"It's true." She took the waffle cone with vanilla ice cream that Maggie handed her and tasted it. "So good."

When Burke ordered two scoops of rocky road, Syd wondered if there was any deeper psychological meaning in the choice. Then he made sure Maggie knew he wanted it "neat."

She pulled a cup from the stack on the counter. "I'm guessing that means no topping or embellishment of any kind?"

"I'm a simple man."

Syd could have argued that point until hell wouldn't

have it, but decided to keep the thoughts to herself. Again Burke paid and they sat with Liam at a table in the center of the room to eat.

The bell over the door rang and in came her father and Loretta Goodson, hand in hand. They were smiling at each other, clearly in love, and Syd felt a rush of conflicting emotion. She was happy for them, of course, but there was a darker feeling, too, something very close to envy. She felt like a selfish toad.

"Hey," Liam said when he saw who it was. "Over here."

The newcomers tore their gazes from each other and glanced at the table. Tom waved. "Great minds think alike. Can we join you?"

"We'll make room." Liam jumped up and pulled over two chairs from another table.

Burke slid closer to Syd, closer than he'd been at the diner. It was cozy. She'd be lying if she said it wasn't nice. And it was the death blow to her fantasy that a buffer zone would make her attraction to the man harmless.

In a few minutes the older couple sat in the chairs between Burke and Liam.

"Madam Mayor, I don't think you've met my son. Liam, this is Mayor Goodson."

"It's great to meet you." The mayor started to shake his hand, then laughed. "Mine are sticky."

"Me, too." Liam grinned.

"It's becoming a family affair," Loretta said. "It was nice to meet your father and cousin. I hope they feel it was worth the trip here. The unscheduled visit saved a lot of time."

"How so?" Syd asked.

"The resort's overall concept in their rough draft was unacceptable, and the town council agrees." The mayor took a bite of ice cream, then swallowed. "You were right, Burke. The buildings were modern and sleek, which would be fine somewhere else. But we were looking for quaint and charming. Sort of sophisticated mountain getaway."

Burke nodded. "You can thank Syd."

"Me?" She nearly choked on her waffle cone. "What did I do?"

"You tutored me in what's best for Blackwater Lake."

"We never discussed architectural design," she protested.

"True," he agreed. "But you told me what the town stands for and the values of folks who live here. I just knew sleek and modern wasn't it."

"I'm surprised you're that perceptive," Syd commented. "No offense."

"None taken. And, for the record, I'm usually not that astute. But your commitment to this community is inspiring."

"That's my girl." Her father looked proud.

"I'm going to work with Ellie on a new concept. We'll get it right."

Loretta nodded her approval. "Ellie's good. But you have to know we'll keep an eye on everything."

"I'd expect nothing less," he said. "But you can trust me not to mess it up."

Syd wasn't so sure the same could be said of her and she didn't mean building a mountain resort. The misgivings were all about herself. His admission about being perceptive with her had come out of the blue and she didn't want to believe it. If she did, going all in with her heart was a real possibility.

Earlier she'd noticed that he'd come a long way from the stressed-out father who'd been forced by circumstances to bring his son here. But that was no guarantee he'd changed his mind about a family. Or any other commitment.

If she let in the notion of him being different with her,

that opened up a very real possibility of her getting hurt. Something that never occurred to her when she'd started this whole thing.

Chapter Twelve

Sydney walked into the Fireside Restaurant at Blackwater Lake Lodge and Burke thought she was the most beautiful woman he'd ever seen. It wasn't boasting to say that a man in his position had been around some of the most stunning women on the planet, but none of them could hold a candle to Sydney McKnight. Her long dark hair gleamed even in subdued restaurant lighting and fell past her shoulders like silk.

No little black dress tonight—it was sexy black slacks instead. Her top was sheer chiffon with a camisole underneath. Four-inch platform heels made her legs look a mile long, but mostly he couldn't shake the image of them wrapped around his waist.

That thought made him ache with need.

He'd been wanting to have her to himself ever since that night he'd taken her home and nearly ended up in her bed. With Liam here there hadn't been an opportunity for a second chance, but tonight was the night. Hopefully.

There had been a look in her dark eyes that he'd swear was a longing that matched his own and that wasn't ego talking, either, just experience.

When the restaurant hostess pointed out the table where he waited, Syd gave him a big smile, then shook her head at something the woman said before walking over to him.

Burke stood to greet her. He fully intended to give her a friendly peck on the cheek, but somehow his lips found their way to hers. And breaking off the contact took more willpower than he would have imagined.

"Hi." He took her hands in his own and squeezed.

"Hi." She seemed a little winded and it had to be from the kiss. No way could she have run fast enough in those heels to be out of breath.

Burke pulled out the chair at a right angle to his and held it for her to sit. When she was settled, he sat down beside her, wishing they were as close as a few nights ago at the ice cream parlor with her father and the mayor, when their thighs had brushed repeatedly. It was the most intimately he'd been able to touch her for far too long.

"I'm glad you were free for dinner," he said.

"Boy, were you lucky I wasn't tied up," she teased. "My social calendar is just packed. I couldn't get another engagement in if I used a shoehorn."

"Very funny." He signaled the waiter to bring over two glasses and the bottle of wine he'd already ordered. "I bare my soul and look what happens."

"You called because you were at loose ends with Liam sleeping over at Todd's house." She gave him a wry look. "If there was any soul-baring going on, I missed it. And that's a shame. I would have liked some souvenir pictures."

"You mock me. That hurts," he said, trying to look deeply wounded.

After the bottle was uncorked, the waiter poured a small amount for Burke and waited for his approval before filling Syd's wineglass. "I'll bring bread," he said. "Is there anything else I can get for you right now?"

"Not at the moment," Burke answered. "We'll order in a little while."

When they were alone he held up his glass. "What should we drink to?"

"I don't know. You decide."

He thought for a moment then said, "Here's to my good fortune that you had an opening in your busy social calendar for a lonely bachelor."

She looked sympathetic before nodding her approval. "To that."

"How was your day?" He sipped from his glass, then set it down and looked at her.

"Busy. Folks are getting their cars ready for winter. It's already October and before you know it the cold weather will be here. There are a lot of tune-ups and inquiries about snow tires."

He wondered if the winter was more brutal here than in Chicago. Being more rural than urban would pose different weather-related challenges. "It is getting to be that time of the year."

"Yeah. If I had my way, I'd winter in Tahiti."

"You don't like the cold?" he asked.

"If you polled people, I don't think you'd find many checking the 'love it' box on the questionnaire."

"Do you go somewhere tropical to get a break and thaw out?" He would love to take her to Tahiti. Seeing her in a bikini... Now there was a souvenir picture. Or out of it—even better.

"I keep threatening to go to Hawaii or Florida."

"Why haven't you?"

"I didn't want to leave my dad alone." She shrugged.

"Now you know he has...companionship," he said diplomatically.

She gave him a warning look. "Don't even hint about them sleeping together. I don't ever want that thought in my head because I'll never get it out."

"Didn't one of your brothers stop by his house unexpectedly and find them in a compromising situation—"

"Burke—" There was a warning expression in her eyes and the tone in her voice threatened serious consequences.

He would take his chances. "Your brothers must be proud. His…athleticism…bodes well for them as they get older."

"One more word and I'll put my hands over my ears and start humming." The way her full lips twitched hinted that she wasn't as bothered by this topic of conversation as she pretended.

"Okay, I'll be good."

Tilting her head to the side in a little bit of a flirt, she said, "Not too good."

"Time will tell."

There was a look in her eyes that promised heaven. Dear God, she was going to kill him.

"My point in bringing up your father's…situation…is that you don't have to feel as if he needs someone to look out for him."

"It's a difficult habit to break," she admitted.

"A midwinter trip to Bora-Bora would be a good start. You should go with a friend."

"Getting away isn't easy for most people." She toyed with her wineglass. "And the airport is pretty far. It's a particular challenge in a blizzard."

"Pretty soon there will be an airport closer. And those are just excuses." Burke studied her. "You're lonely, too, aren't you?"

Her gaze snapped to his. "I didn't say that."

"You didn't have to. Takes one to know one."

Without conceding the truth of his out-of-the-box statement, she made one of her own. "So, you're pretty hostile to your father."

And he'd been so careful to keep it from showing. "What gave me away?"

"Pretty much everything." She reached beneath the cloth napkin covering the bread and pulled out a crusty roll, then put it on her small plate. After sliding a pat of butter beside it, she met his gaze. "It was little things. The way your eyes got angry when you looked at him. A tone when you talked. Irritated, I guess, at anything he said, no matter how harmless. And body language—your shoulders tensed. Or you almost winced every time Walker opened his mouth."

He wasn't sure which was worse—that he felt antagonistic toward his father or that she was dead-on about it. "Wow."

"You didn't tell me I'm wrong." She broke a piece off the roll, buttered it and popped the morsel into her mouth.

He could dance around it. He usually did. But for some reason, he wanted her to know he had a good reason for feeling the way he did.

"I guess I never got over the way he acted after my mother died," he admitted. "And he wasn't around a whole lot when she was battling breast cancer."

The teasing challenge in her eyes was chased away by sympathy. She reached over and covered his hand with her own. "I'm sorry, Burke. That must have been so difficult."

"That means a lot coming from you. You never even knew your mother." He turned his hand over and linked his fingers with hers.

"It was different for me because she was never part of my life so I didn't feel the emptiness when she was gone. I guess I envied my friends who had moms, but people here in Blackwater Lake filled in."

"How?"

"Maggie's mom took me for my first bra. If I needed a dress for prom, there was always a woman to help. Dad told me about sex and all that." She grinned. "It was an experience. For us both."

"I bet."

"My point is that you can't miss what you didn't have. But you lost your mother at such a vulnerable age." Empathy shimmered in her eyes.

"Yeah." It had been the loneliest time in his life. "My father went right back to work. He was always busy, but after the funeral it was like busy on steroids."

"And you're angry about that."

"Let me count the ways." He tried to smile but it didn't happen. "He never showed up for anything going on in my life. Holidays were hit-and-miss. It was like losing both parents at the same time."

"Oh, Burke—" She sighed and squeezed his hand. "I was too little to remember how dad was after losing my mother. But people who were there say he buried himself in work because he couldn't deal with the grief, but everyone knew he loved her very much. Plus he had to make a living with three mouths to feed. Maybe men handle loss by burying their feelings in something familiar and not talking about it."

"Maybe."

But Burke wasn't ready to let go of the resentment. It hit him again when his own son was born and he had no role model to draw from. Mostly he tried to do the opposite of what his father had done, but somehow he'd fallen into the workaholic pattern.

"I couldn't help noticing that Liam is genuinely fond of his grandfather. And vice versa. There must be a reason. Kids aren't easily fooled." She thought for a moment.

"And here's a radical thought. It might help to talk about your feelings with Walker."

"Maybe," he said again.

But he was thinking hell would freeze over before that happened. And the attitude must have shown in his voice and body language because Syd nodded but didn't say more about that.

"I also noticed that Liam seems to be settling in nicely."

"He's...adjusting." He appreciated the topic change and suspected she'd purposely steered the conversation in a more positive direction. "Better than I thought he would."

"Has it occurred to you that settling in wouldn't have gone so well if you're as bad a father as you seem to think?"

"No, it never did. I think any credit goes to you, your dad and the school."

She shook her head in faux frustration. "For an intelligent man you're not so smart about some stuff."

"Like what?"

"You're a single dad and Liam is a great kid. Work is demanding so others have to fill in, but he spends more time with you than anyone. Something positive you're doing must be rubbing off on him."

Burke wasn't completely convinced, but admitted, if only to himself, that there could be some truth in what she said.

"Are you hungry?" he asked.

"Starved."

He signaled the waiter to bring menus. "Then we should order."

"Sounds good to me."

He planned to do as many courses as possible to keep her here. Saying goodbye after dinner with her always seemed to come too soon and he was never ready. Idly he wondered if that feeling would ever go away.

Syd was having a wonderful time and it felt as if they'd occupied the intimate corner table for two at Fireside for minutes instead of hours. Wine, salad, entrées, dessert and after-dinner drinks had been consumed and Burke was signing the check.

But she wasn't ready for the evening to end.

He put the pen inside the leather holder with the bill, then looked at her. "Are you ready to go?"

"Yes," she lied.

They stood and he waited for her to precede him to the exit. On the way he said good-night to the waiter, server, busboy and hostess, calling each one by their given name. Obviously he'd gotten to know them, but she supposed that happened when one lived in a hotel.

He settled his hand at the small of her back and the contact touched off a chain reaction of nerve endings that sensitized every inch of her skin. She wanted to snuggle in closer but resisted. There was nothing more awkward than being obvious about wanting someone and getting the message that they didn't share your feelings. Burke would have to make the first move.

Just before stepping from the privacy of the long hallway into the lodge's lobby, Burke stopped and looked down. "I had a really good time tonight."

"Me, too."

"Tomorrow is Saturday."

"You're kidding." She pretended shock and surprise. "Really? I had no idea."

"Let me rephrase." He looked down for a moment, then met her gaze. "I don't have to work. Do you?"

"I do, as a matter of fact. Saturday is busy at the garage." Syd's heart beat a little faster as she had a hunch where he was going with this.

"Oh. Then you don't want to be out too late."

"A girl has to get her beauty rest," she agreed.

He put his palm flat on the wall beside her and moved closer, trapping her in the best possible way against his body. "If you were any more beautiful, that face would have to be registered as a lethal weapon with the sheriff's office."

Her heart started to beat even faster as his look went from lazy to lusty in a nanosecond. "So…" She swallowed once. "Wild guess here…you don't want to say good-night yet?"

"You're very perceptive." He gently brushed the hair from her cheek, then traced his index finger along her jaw.

"We should take a walk." She glanced down at her feet. "Although I don't know how far I'd get in these shoes."

"That depends on where you want to go." His voice was a ragged whisper.

Her heart skipped a beat, then kicked in again, hammering harder than ever. "I'd crawl on my hands and knees if necessary. Depending on the destination."

The corners of his mouth curved up as his gaze danced over her face. Then he lowered his head and kissed her. His lips were soft, warm, coaxing and caressing. Pressing his body even closer to hers, he let her know he wanted her.

Tracing her lips with his tongue, he teased her mouth open then slipped inside. He tasted good, she thought, like wine and the chocolate cake they'd just shared. She didn't consciously put her arms around his shoulders, but she suddenly realized they were there. In the blink of an eye she was incredibly turned on and it was a miracle she could think rationally enough to make a point.

Against his mouth she whispered, "Someone is going

to walk by and they might not say it out loud, but you can bet they'll be thinking we should get a room."

His smile was wicked. "As luck would have it, I already have one."

"That is lucky."

He moved back a step, then grabbed her hand. "I don't think we want to go through the lobby. Let's take the back way."

She was trapped in a sensuous haze and let him lead her to an elevator in a more discreet location. He pushed the up button and almost immediately the doors opened. They got in and rode to the top floor of the lodge, where he pointed to the end of the hall and the double-door entry of his suite. It seemed far away, too far, but with him holding tightly to her hand, she matched her steps to his long stride. After inserting his key card, he opened the door and let her go inside first.

Behind her there was the sound of a click and then the entryway's overhead light went on. In front of her was a sitting area with a couch, chairs and tables. A flat-screen TV was mounted on the wall. On the far side of the room was a formal cherrywood dining table and six chairs.

She turned to look up at Burke. "I've never been in a suite before."

"What do you think?"

"Rich people really are different."

"Not that much." He took her hand and they walked to the right, stopping at the double doors.

He opened one to reveal a king-size bed, sitting area with a plush love seat and French doors leading to a balcony that overlooked the mountains. The only light was drifting in from the other room and that made erotic shadows in this one.

"Be it ever so humble…" He took off his suit jacket and tossed it on the tufted, cream-colored bench at the foot of the bed. Then he loosened his silk tie, undid the button at his neck and slid it from under the starched collar of his white dress shirt.

Burke removed her small evening bag from her fingers and gently put it by his coat. Then he looked down at her and said, "Where were we?"

She stepped out of her heels and felt even shorter than usual when looking up at him. "I think this is where we left off."

Moving closer, she started undoing the buttons down the front of his shirt before tugging it from the waistband of his slacks. After spreading wide the sides, she rested her palms on the muscular contours of his chest. The dusting of hair tickled her fingers as she slid them down, exploring the feel of him to her heart's content.

When she reached his rib cage, just above his belt, she must have hit a very sensitive spot judging by his sharp intake of breath.

Burke caught her wrist in a strong yet gentle grip. His breathing was harsh and uneven. "My turn."

There were no buttons on her top, so he gripped the chiffon and camisole together and pulled them up and off as she lifted her arms to assist.

His gaze caught fire when he saw her black bra and he shook his head regretfully. "As much as I like the way you look, that has to come off."

Without a word, she turned her back and let him undo the clasp. His hands settled on her shoulders and brushed the satin straps down until the wispy garment fell at her feet. He circled an arm around her and nestled her back against his front then used both hands to cup her bare breasts.

He kissed his way down her neck and with thumb and forefinger toyed with her nipples. She tried to hold it in, but a moan slipped past her lips as the exquisite torture went on and on until she was sure she wouldn't be able to stand it. While she was occupied by the intense pleasure of his touch, he reached down to her waistband to undo the button and lower the zipper of her slacks. The silky material slid easily down her legs and she stepped out of them.

He splayed one big hand over her middle and slid the other down between her legs, cupping her there. His ragged breathing stirred the hair by her ear and his voice was even more ragged as he whispered to her what he wanted, what he yearned to do with her.

The next thing she knew he'd yanked down the bed's comforter and blanket and bared the sheets beneath. He scooped her up into his arms then settled her in the center of the big mattress. Not taking his eyes off her, he set a world record removing his clothes. The expression in his eyes turned dark and intense as she shimmied out of her black panties. Then he slid into bed beside her, reaching out and pulling her against his warm, bare skin.

He brushed his wide palm over the indentation of her waist, over the swell of her hip, then flattened on her abdomen. This time when he caressed between her legs there was no wisp of lace blocking the touch. He rubbed a thumb over the bundle of feminine nerve endings and she believed it a very real possibility that she could go up in flames.

Before she could tell him what she wanted, what she'd craved for so long, he reached into the nightstand and pulled something out. Through a lovely daze, she realized that he'd opened a condom and put it on. Then he gently eased her to her back, braced his forearms on either side of her to take most of his weight and slowly entered her.

Feminine muscles wrapped around him and nerve endings wept at the glorious intrusion. She pulled her heels up higher on the bed, making the contact even more exquisite. Moments later, pleasure blasted through her in a nearly spontaneous explosion.

Burke pushed into her one more time, then went still and groaned, finding his own release. For a long, lovely moment they just held on to each other as shock waves turned to ripples and their breathing slowed to something resembling normal. Truthfully, the meaning of normal had forever changed for her.

He rested his forehead to hers. "That was…"

"Nice," she said.

He lifted his head and even in the dim light his wry expression was visible. "You couldn't think of a more enthusiastic adjective than *nice?*"

"Awesome? Amazing? Spectacular? Great." She shrugged and the hair on his chest rubbed her breasts, sending tingles up and down her spine. "They're all clichés."

"What we just did rates a better description than *nice,*" he said.

Sex with Burke Holden was so awesome and amazing that she would swear it rocked her soul. And that was a scary thought. She figured he wouldn't appreciate knowing that and she didn't want to make herself that vulnerable by saying it out loud.

"Yes, it was better than nice," she agreed.

"Are you okay, Syd?"

"Of course." But she didn't lift her gaze any higher than his collarbone.

"I'll be right back." He rolled away and the bed dipped and rose as he left it. "Don't move."

Her body felt boneless and she couldn't move if she'd wanted to. Syd put her forearm over her eyes, but still sensed when a light went on nearby and heard running water. How she wished that she was better at hiding her feelings. She had wanted this almost from the first time she'd seen him drive into McKnight Automotive.

And now she couldn't shake the sensation that it had been a mistake because it had been so awesome, amazing, spectacular and great. But the last thing she wanted was to be that type of woman, the one who wanted it until she got it and then played hurt.

Why couldn't a girl know she was going to have second thoughts before jumping into the deep end of the pool?

The light went off and seconds later Burke was back, pulling her into his arms. "Okay. Talk to me. What's going on in that mind of yours? And please don't say you're fine, because I know you're not."

It took several moments for her to figure out what she wanted to say and he let her take the time.

"I guess I want you to know that casual sex isn't what I do. One-night stands aren't my thing."

He nodded his understanding. "And if I thought it was your thing, I wouldn't be here."

She rested her cheek on his chest and settled her arm over his flat belly. "You wouldn't?"

"No." He kissed the top of her head. "I like you, Syd. A lot."

"I feel the same about you." Maybe more than like.

"And that's why I want to be completely honest with you."

"Oh?" This was where he said what she'd been thinking, that it was a mistake they shouldn't make again. She braced herself.

"I want you again."

"You do?" She wished it was possible to see his face, but he'd rested his chin on the top of her head.

"Yes. And I hope you want me. This isn't casual for me, but I also can't make any promises."

"I don't expect any." She knew how he felt about commitment. He'd been completely up front about that.

He raised up on an elbow and looked down, studying her. "Can we take this one day at a time? That's the smart play."

"It is," she agreed.

God help her. She was far gone enough to take whatever he could give, but there was a part of her that longed for a promise of forever.

Chapter Thirteen

"This is fun, Dad."

Liam kicked the soccer ball somewhere in Burke's general direction and he jogged over to get it. They were in Sydney's backyard on a beautiful Sunday afternoon while she was inside cooking dinner for them.

"It is fun." Not in the same league as what he and Syd had done in his bed the other night. But it really wasn't fair to compare the two. Bonding with his son was a blessing he honestly had never expected to have. Physically bonding with Syd had been mind-blowing.

If he was being honest it was more than physical. There was a connection and it was more than he'd anticipated. He liked women; he dated. And he walked away. But there was something about Syd that he couldn't put into words, qualities that drew him. Things that had nothing to do with what she looked like. Not a single woman he'd dated had come close to the wonder that was Sydney McKnight.

It had bothered him a little when she didn't push back

on his declaration that he couldn't make any promises. But then, she'd once expected promises from a guy and he'd made them to someone else. Still, that was a long time ago and he wondered what she wanted now.

Liam stood across the yard, hands on hips. "Hey, Dad. You gonna kick the ball or stand there and think about it?"

It was an interesting experience hearing your own words coming out of your child's mouth. He hadn't even been thinking about kicking the ball. Images of Syd in black bra and panties? Yes. Kicking the ball? No. His concentration was messed up because pretty much what he wanted to focus on was her. But that wasn't fair to his son.

"Okay, kid. Comin' at you. Get ready. Think you can handle it?"

The boy grinned. "No problem."

Burke kicked it pretty hard and Liam concentrated, judging the path, moving a little to his right. He stopped the ball with his foot, nudged it to the side, then sent it back.

"You're getting pretty good, son."

"Thanks. I've been practicing with Todd. He said maybe I could join his soccer team. The season's already started, but there might be an opening. Do you think that would be okay? I know we have to go back to Chicago, but I was thinking maybe in the meantime?"

The kid was making a thorough case for it as if he expected to be turned down. "I don't see why not. I'll get the information from Todd's parents and check in to it. Let's see if we can make that happen."

"Cool."

The ball came to him and Burke stopped it with his foot, then picked it up. "We should probably have something to drink. Syd went to all the trouble to make lemonade and leave it out here for us."

"I am kind of thirsty." Liam ran across the yard to the patio table holding a pitcher and two glasses.

"Here you go." Burke held out a full glass after pouring the sweet, cold liquid into it.

"Thanks, Dad."

They sat down side by side in the padded chairs and guzzled lemonade.

"This is pretty good stuff." He watched his son drag his forearm across his mouth to blot the excess liquid. Then the boy seemed to realize what he'd done and glanced up, waiting to hear what he'd done wrong.

Normally Burke would have called him on the breach of good manners, but two things stopped him. Number one: they were alone and this was a guy moment. No ladies present to be offended. And, number two: he didn't want to spoil this father-son moment with a lecture that usually ended by saying Liam wasn't being raised by wolves. There were teachable situations, but this wasn't one of them.

Syd was the one who'd made him see that you picked your battles. It was a parent's responsibility to make sure his child knew what was and wasn't acceptable in polite society. But the chances were pretty good that someday when he took a girl out for dinner Liam wouldn't use his sleeve for a napkin. Or he would only do it once and get an advanced degree from the school of hard knocks.

"Dad?"

"What, son?"

"I'm sorry I was such a dork when I first got here."

Burke couldn't have been more surprised if an alien ship landed in the yard and an extraterrestrial said "take me to your leader." Finally he was able to say, "Don't worry about it. I understand. It was hard for you, leaving your friends and everything that's familiar."

"Yeah." The boy looked down frowning, as if remembering the experience.

"I'm sorry you had to go through that. The good news is that Mary will be okay after rest and recuperation. She's retiring, but we'll figure things out. At least you'll have your house, yard and friends back."

"Yeah," he said again, a little uncertain. "And I'll have to leave the friends I made here. I thought it was boring at first, but I really like Blackwater Lake."

"Good. It's a nice place. And since work will keep me here for a while, I'm glad you like it."

"You know what the best part is?" The boy looked up, a vulnerable expression in his blue eyes.

"What?"

"I get to hang out with you a lot."

"Really?" Burke felt a tightness in his chest. "You like doing stuff together?"

"It's awesome." Liam nodded eagerly. "We don't even have to do stuff. I like just hanging out or watching TV together."

The tightness in his chest squeezed a little more. This was one of those moments that he wished you could hang on the wall and look at when life kicked you in the teeth. But it also pricked his guilt. For a long time he'd been making excuses to justify pushing off his son on the housekeeper, when the truth was that he could adjust other things in order to spend enough time with his child. And he hadn't. It took Blackwater Lake to make him see that things could be different. He could be different.

"I'm sorry, too, Liam."

"What for?"

"I haven't been a very good father to you. I'm always busy. Not around. Blaming it on work."

"Mary says what you do is important. That a lot of people wouldn't have jobs if not for your company."

Even his housekeeper was making excuses for his parenting—or lack thereof. "The truth is that I could have done better as a dad. I love you and I love spending time with you. And I'm making a promise that from now on we'll hang out a lot more."

"Cross your heart?"

Burke made the sign over his heart and held out a closed fist. His son bumped it with his own. This gesture was more sacred than a handshake and again one of those unspoiled moments that stand out in a father's mind.

"You know, Dad, if you don't keep your promise Syd wouldn't like it."

"No, she wouldn't. I've never seen her mad and don't ever want to."

"Me, either," Liam agreed.

They sat there for a few moments and Burke basked in the glow. Everyone he talked to in town said that it would be winter soon, but so far the only sign was that nights were colder. This Indian summer weather fit his mood perfectly, he thought. If he had to give the feeling a name, he would call it contentment. It was noteworthy that he recognized the sensation since it had been in short supply most of his life.

"Dad, when we go back to Chicago, do you think she can come for a visit?"

The words yanked him back but he wasn't sure which "she" his son meant. "Who?"

"Syd. Do you think she could come and see us?" The boy looked up hopefully and his feelings were there for the world to see. He was going to miss her.

"It's all right with me," Burke said. "I hope she'll visit. I'll ask her."

"Then I'm sure she will."

"Why do you think so, son?"

"Anyone can see that she likes you a lot. Do you like her?" Liam asked.

"I would say we're good friends."

Who slept together. But of course he wasn't about to tell that to his eight-year-old son. If Burke was being honest with himself, he would admit that Syd was more than a friend, but how much more?

"Todd is my friend. Do you think I could ask him to visit in Chicago?"

"Of course. But that's up to his parents."

Burke realized that Liam wasn't the only Holden wearing his emotions in plain sight. He'd grown accustomed to seeing Syd almost every day. The frustrations that were constant in his work on a daily basis didn't seem so bad when he knew that night he would spend time with her and talk about it. She was an excellent listener and often had good advice.

Sydney McKnight was a goodbye he wasn't yet prepared to handle.

Hell, the other night after dinner he hadn't been ready to say good-night. That's one reason he'd taken her up to his room. And making love to her was nice.

The word made him smile as he pictured her saying it. Once wasn't enough; he wanted her again. It was another in a growing list of reasons for not wanting to say goodbye to her.

Part of his job involved solving problems. This one was personal and more delicate. But an idea popped into his mind that could fix everything.

Sydney walked from the service bay to the office, where her father was working, and poked her head in. "Hey, Dad. I'm all caught up."

"So you're done for the day?" He looked at his watch and his eyebrows rose. "Before quitting time. Are you that good? Or just motivated to get out of here early because you have a date with Burke?"

"I'm that good," she said with a grin.

There was no date, but a girl could hope. Still, it was Monday and therefore a school night. She completely respected the restrictions that put on Burke's social life.

Alone time with him was precious, but she'd enjoyed hanging out with father and son yesterday. She liked watching the two interact and Liam was just a sweetie. The sullen child she'd first met had disappeared, thanks to whatever Burke was doing.

Syd heard her father's voice and realized she'd been lost in her own thoughts. "I'm sorry. What was that?"

"I said, Loretta and I are going to the diner for dinner. You and Burke and Liam should join us."

"I'm free, but I don't know about the boys."

That's how she'd started thinking about them. The boys. While in the kitchen cooking, she'd glanced out the window and noted identical serious expressions on their faces, indicating a serious discussion underway. Burke had never mentioned what they'd talked about.

But he'd been really attentive afterward. While eating dinner, he'd caressed her thigh underneath the table and stolen kisses when his son was out of the room. There was something different about him, an intensity and focus that were fine-tuned and firing on all cylinders. It was exciting, if a little unsettling. She didn't know what to think. Was he making the most of every moment because the time was fast approaching for him to leave town?

"If I hear from Burke, I'll let you know."

"You could call him," her dad pointed out.

"Guess I'm a little old-fashioned." And maybe a little insecure. A call from him meant he really wanted to see her. "Are you ready to leave?"

"Not yet," he answered. "I'm going to finish ordering

the parts for Floyd Robinson's truck since I have time to kill before meeting Loretta."

"Okay, then. 'Bye, Dad."

"See you, Syd."

She'd just walked outside when her cell rang, making her heart skip. It was like being a teenager again, waiting to hear from that special boy.

She looked at the caller ID and smiled when she recognized that special boy's number. "Hi, there."

"Hey, Syd. It's Burke."

"I knew that."

"Right." His voice was clipped, distracted. "Where are you?"

"Just left the office." She'd just mention dinner. What the heck? He'd called her. "Dad and Loretta are going to the Grizzly Bear Diner. If you and Liam want—"

"There's something I need to talk to you about. Are you going home?" He sounded weird.

"Yes. On my way there now. Why?"

"I'll meet you."

"Burke, what's wrong?" There was no answer and when she looked at the phone it said, *call ended.*

Suddenly her heart wasn't skipping but her stomach was, and not in a happy way. She didn't want to face him in work clothes and needed time to change. It was a challenge to drive as fast as she could and still be just under the speed limit.

After squealing into her driveway, she parked the car, unlocked the door and raced up to her room. She pulled off work pants and shirt then grabbed black jeans and a long-sleeved pink T-shirt. After brushing out her hair, she left it loose around her shoulders, then put on tinted lip gloss.

As she was considering whether or not to put on makeup, the doorbell rang and she scrapped the idea. How she looked wouldn't matter since what he had to say wasn't going to be good. Being a pessimist was a downer but it was better to be realistic and prepared.

She raced downstairs and opened the door. There he was on the porch and the sight of him made her heart swell to the point of aching. His white dress shirt was rumpled and the sleeves were rolled up to mid-forearm. The expensive gray-and-black silk tie was loosened at his throat. Five-o'clock shadow made him look incredibly sexy. If he hadn't said he needed to talk, she would have grabbed that tie and tugged him upstairs.

"Can I come in?"

"Sure." She shook her head to clear it, then stepped back and pulled the door wider.

"Thanks." He walked past her and stopped in the entryway.

"Would you like a beer?"

"Not now." He dragged his fingers through his hair. "There's something I need to talk to you about."

"So you said." She braced herself for the brush-off. "What's up?"

"I think we should get married."

The words started a roaring in her ears, but his expression was intent and sincere. "I'm sorry. We should do what now?"

"Get married."

She felt as if this was some kind of surreal board game and she'd just jumped to the end after skipping major steps in the process.

"What's wrong?" she finally asked.

"Nothing. It's all good." He smiled at her as if that explained everything.

"I think I need just a little more information than that."

"I've been thinking this over all night, but I can see where you'd need context." He met her gaze with a "trust me" expression in his own eyes. "This makes really good sense."

On what planet? she wanted to ask. With an effort she held back and tried not to make a judgment until hearing him out. "Explain it to me."

"You like me—"

"What makes you so sure about that?" Right this minute she wasn't sure how she felt.

"Because you're not the kind of woman who goes to bed with a man unless she has feelings for him. Positive feelings. And believe me I know the difference." His blue eyes darkened with intensity. "And Liam noticed it, too. He said you like me."

"He did?" What was this? Junior high?

"Yes, he did."

She knew she was bad at hiding her feelings but hadn't figured she was so obvious a kid would notice. She wasn't sure why this conversation and his proposal were putting her on the defensive, but his declaration made her want to push back. Except she couldn't deny she really liked him. That was the truth.

"Okay."

"And I like you," he added.

She had to take his word for that because he wasn't as obvious as she was. "Nice of you to say."

"Liam likes you, too. And you're terrific with him."

"He's a great kid."

"See?" He beamed at her as if she was his star pupil. "We could be a family."

That's what she'd always wanted. And her dad wanted it for her. It's what had made her approach Burke in the first place. But this was weird and was probably the reason he'd been acting differently last night.

"A few days ago we agreed to take it one day at a time."

"And today I'm asking you to marry me."

Skeptical and weird was not how she'd expected to feel when a man she cared very much about proposed to her. "What happened to change your mind? What's the rush, Burke? Are you going back to Chicago?"

"Eventually."

"It's a cliché to say this is so sudden, but— This is so sudden. Why?"

His face took on a stubborn expression, not unlike his son when he didn't get what he wanted, when he wanted it and under the terms he requested.

"Why not?" he answered. "Think about what you'd have."

This was beginning to sound like a business deal and a chill started in her stomach then spread slowly outward. "Spell it out for me."

"First, there's a big house. Cars. I know you'd like that." He thought for a moment. "You talked about traveling to some place warm in the winter."

"Wow."

"Hawaii. Florida." He completely missed the underwhelming tone in her voice so when he went on she didn't interrupt. "Tahiti would work. Would you like to scuba dive? There's a reef on a small island in Micronesia that's supposed to be the best in the world for seeing manta rays." He looked at her. "Have you been to Europe?"

"No."

"I could take you there. It's spectacular. London. Paris. Rome. Venice. Florence. We could lease a private yacht and see them all."

"And the only catch is that I have to marry you."

His brows drew together. Frustration or annoyance? It wasn't clear. "I can take you away from all this…"

She remembered the night he'd surprised her with flowers and dinner. Such a romantic gesture it took her breath away. But it was also the night when he'd said he would never marry again. Followed by the statement that the only commitment he could make was to do what was best for his son.

This was a decent proposal, but it was coming from a place where it was best for Liam, which meant it would never work in the long term.

"If that's your best offer, you don't know me at all."

There was a flash of something in his eyes and this time it was clearly anger. "We could be good together. You. Me. Liam—"

"No thank you, Burke."

"Syd, think about this—"

"It's probably best if you go now."

Since she was so easy to read, Syd turned away before he could see the expression in her eyes that would be a giveaway about how hard it was to turn him down. Without another word he left and she was alone. Alone with the realization that she'd said no because she was in love with him. Hell of a time to realize the truth of her feelings.

Now she understood why she'd been on the defensive when he made his case for marriage. He'd skipped the most important step.

The one where he told her he loved her.

Chapter Fourteen

Syd was in no mood for a family get-together, but a girl didn't always get what she wanted. Thoughts of Burke Holden immediately came to mind along with the scene of his proposal here in her home just the day before. If she'd gotten her wish, he'd have asked her to marry him as if he really meant it. Not because she was his solution to a child-care problem.

Now she was standing in the kitchen with her dad, Loretta Goodson beside him, her brothers and their families gathered around the big, granite-topped island. They were all waiting.

Her father put his arm around the waist of the woman standing next to him. "I have an announcement to make."

"You're pregnant," Ben joked.

His pretty blonde wife, Camille, stared at him in mock horror. "You're a doctor. Remarks like that could start rumors that you skipped anatomy class."

"I've heard that rumor." His older brother, Alex, elbowed him. "There's another one currently circulating that he patched up a broken leg with Super Glue."

"Why don't you guys just stuff a sock in it and let Dad speak," Syd snapped. "Your daughters are more mature than you. I'd call you two-year-olds, but that would be an insult to toddlers."

"Wow." Alex looked at her, one eyebrow raised in surprise. "Someone got up on the wrong side of the bed today."

"That better not be a remark about this being that time of the month." Even as Syd's anger shot into the stratosphere, she knew it was misplaced. Alex wasn't the man she wanted to verbally eviscerate.

"Why don't y'all quiet down and hear what your dad has to say." There was something peacemakerish in Ellie McKnight's soothing Texas drawl. "And Alex, my love, apologize to your sister for that insensitive remark."

"Whatever you want, sweetheart." Alex leaned over and kissed his wife's cheek. "Syd, I'm sorry you're irritable and surly."

"And I'm sorry you're a male chauvinist pig." Somehow she managed to keep her tone teasing and everyone laughed.

"Okay, if you're all finished?" Tom looked around expectantly and everyone nodded. There were no more smart-aleck remarks. He took a deep breath. "I asked Loretta to marry me and she said yes."

There was a moment of silence while the information sank in. No one was really surprised; they'd all known this was coming. And when the hush ended, whistles and words of congratulations started. It was clear that everyone approved. Then there was a lot of hugging and kissing.

Syd did her best to hide her romantic trouble. How ironic that her dalliance with Burke had started because of her determination to convince her dad he could and should move on with his life. The romantic pretense hadn't lasted long because she and Burke had a genuine connection and they never had to work at it. At least for her it was effortless. Her dad just made the announcement about getting married again and Syd couldn't let him know that she and Burke were not now—and never would be—a couple.

She looked around at her family. Her dad and his fiancée tenderly touching and kissing. Alex and Ellie, her arm through his, talking intimately. Ben swinging Cam into his arms for an impromptu dance around the kitchen. Her two little nieces exploring the only cupboard not child-proofed, pulling out the kid-friendly stuff inside as if they were getting away with something. It was crowded, loud, chaotic.

Syd had never felt more alone in her life.

If she didn't do something her dad would see there was a problem. "We need the right kind of liquor for a special toast. I'll run into town and see if I can get some champagne."

"Not necessary." Her father put a hand on her shoulder to stop her from leaving. "I stashed a couple of bottles in the garage refrigerator."

"Then I'll go get it," she offered.

"Let me," Alex said. "You round up some glasses."

"Okay."

Too bad. A couple minutes in the solitude of the garage might have helped with an attitude adjustment. She'd been willing to go the extra mile to get her dad right where he was and didn't want to spoil this lovely memory with her bad mood. It was tough to be hearty when your heart was broken.

"We don't have champagne glasses," she informed them. "Not even the plastic kind from New Year's Eve. Although it will offend my sister-in-law the hotel heiress's five-star sensibilities, I think wineglasses will work. I *propose* we do that."

As intended, there were loud groans at her pun. Cam wrinkled her nose at the idea of champagne in the improper glass but conceded it was the best option. That didn't stop her from mumbling about a little warning and she could have arranged to borrow the right flutes from the lodge.

Ellie and Cam pitched in to help so that when Alex returned and popped the cork on the bottle, an eclectic group of glasses waited on the kitchen island. Seven to be exact. An odd number. Because Syd didn't have anyone.

As her vision blurred with tears, she was nudged aside while her brother poured the bubbly golden liquid. Then the glasses were handed out. The toddler girls got sippy cups with juice even though they were too little to understand what was happening around them.

"As the eldest son, I propose a toast," Alex said. "To Dad and Loretta. Congratulations!"

Everyone sipped.

Then Ben cleared his throat. "As the second son, an heir and a spare," he said, "way to go, Dad. Welcome to the family, Loretta."

Loretta's eyes were suspiciously moist. "Thank you. That means a lot to me. It was important to Tom that you all approve, so I'm glad you do."

"It was never Alex and Ben who worried me."

Syd couldn't meet her father's gaze. He'd said something similar just before Burke had driven into the auto shop for the first time. The pain of that memory sliced clear to her soul and somehow she had to keep them all from seeing. It was her turn to propose a toast.

"Ben and Alex have memories of Dad with Mom, but I don't. To me there was always sadness in his eyes. Until Loretta." She held up her glass. "To the woman who put a twinkle in my father's eyes. Thank you for making him smile again."

Loretta hugged her, too moved to speak. There was a chorus of "aww" and then everyone drank.

When the excitement died down, the conversation turned to wedding plans. "This is going to be a short engagement. A week, maybe two," her father said. "Just long enough to put together a simple ceremony at the church. Family and friends."

"That would be pretty much the whole town of Blackwater Lake," Alex pointed out.

"And we wouldn't have it any other way." Loretta smiled up at the man she clearly adored. "As the mayor of this town, I have resources."

"And she knows how to use them," Tom said proudly. "This woman can delegate. But we're going to need everyone's help."

"Anything you need, Dad." Syd meant that with all her heart. After all, she'd propositioned a perfect stranger in order to move her father's romance along.

"I was hoping you'd say that." Loretta met her gaze. "Because I'd like you to be my maid of honor."

Syd's chest tightened as she reached out to hug the woman who would marry her father. "It would be my… honor."

"Cam, Ellie, will you be co-matrons of honor?"

"Of course," they both said at the same time.

While everyone was oohing and aahing over the engagement ring, Syd slipped quietly out the back door. She drew in a deep breath as the chill in the air cooled her face. The only light was what spilled from the kitchen. She'd never felt so much like she was on the outside with her nose pressed up against the window, wishing she had what everyone else did.

Finally all by herself, the tears she'd been fighting trickled down her cheeks. Her chest hurt from holding everything back and the realization dawned that in all her life she'd never been quite this miserable before.

She never heard the back door open, but suddenly strong arms came around her and pulled her into a comforting hug. Her father's familiar warmth wrapped around her.

"What's wrong, baby?"

The kindness and support just made her cry harder, but her dad silently held on until the sobs quieted.

"Oh, Daddy, you should go back in. I didn't want to spoil the celebration."

"You're not spoiling anything."

"I tried not to let anyone see how upset I am."

"You're my girl." He sighed. "I know you too well. When you snapped at Alex for making a joke, it was a dead giveaway. Usually you're the one leading the smart-aleck attack. You can't hide how you feel from your old man. Consider that a warning."

"Understood."

"Now," he said, snuggling her a little closer, "tell me who made you cry."

"Burke." She sniffled. "He asked me to marry him."

Tom gave her one last quick, hard hug before putting her away from him. Light from the window underscored his puzzled expression. "I'm sure there's a connection between the crying and the proposal, but for the life of me I can't figure it out. Do you want me to take him out back and beat the tar out of him because he *wants* to marry you?"

"Of course not." She took a shuddering breath. "He told me once that he would never marry again. His wife was a selfish witch who doesn't want to be a wife and mother."

"I'd say he chose poorly, but—"

She held up her hand. "And he also said that every decision he makes is based on what's best for his son. So the fact that he asked me to marry him really has nothing to do with me. With us."

"How can you be so sure?"

"He never said he loved me—" An emotional lump in her throat blocked the rest of her words.

"I warned you not to get hurt, but I guess that's not something you can help." Tom shook his head. "I'm really sorry, honey. It's likely you learned to be wary of love from me. And you should know that your mom would be very put out with me for teaching you that."

"You didn't. It goes way back to when Charlie and Violet eloped." She'd vowed not to get hurt again. The circumstances were different, but the result was the same. Her heart was crushed.

"The message your mom would stress is to take life in both hands and live every day as if it were your last." He gently tapped her nose. "That's what you made me see when you concocted that ridiculous scheme to make me think you'd met the man you were going to marry."

"Ironically he did ask. Even though it backfired on me, I stand by my decision to make you see that it's okay to be happy."

"I appreciate that more than you'll ever know."

She brushed away a tear that was rolling down her cheek. "I was afraid if you knew about Burke and me you'd call off the wedding. You're not, are you?"

Her dad shook his head. "That wouldn't fit with my new philosophy. I just want you to be as happy as I am."

"I will be." She gave him a quick hug. "And I want you to know that I don't need a man. I have my family and I know you guys are there for me."

"Absolutely." He glanced over his shoulder. "I have to get back. Do you need another minute by yourself?"

"Yeah. Thanks for understanding, Dad."

"Anytime."

After her meltdown at being the only single McKnight, Syd better understood her father's desire to see her settled. It seemed that for her, settled meant being by herself. What she'd had with Charlie wasn't a deep and lasting emotion; Burke had shown her the difference. She was in love with him and knew that losing him would hurt for the rest of her life.

As with her father, there would always be a sadness in her eyes.

Burke sat alone in a booth at the Grizzly Bear Diner and contemplated his half-eaten Papa Bear burger. The combo wasn't quite as appealing or exciting as the first time he'd ordered it, but everything had changed since then.

Liam was living with him, although tonight he was having dinner with his friend Todd. Burke had taken Syd to bed for amazingly nice sex. More important, the first Papa Bear burger experience had been before Syd fixed a hamburger for him at her house.

He was realizing that it was the company, not the food, that made everything taste better. And if the look on her face the last time he'd seen her was anything to go by, Burke wouldn't be getting another invitation to dinner at her house.

Maybe that was for the best. He'd hurt her and didn't want to do it again.

From his booth in the back he saw Mayor Goodson walk into the diner alone. She stopped at the hostess podium and chatted with Michelle Crawford, the diner owner, who was filling in for Violet Stewart. The two ladies were looking very serious about something, then the mayor smiled and lifted her left hand while Michelle thoroughly examined one of the fingers. The appraisal was followed by a hug.

Burke guessed that Loretta was showing off an engagement ring. If he was right, and he would put money on it,

Tom McKnight had popped the question and his proposal had been accepted.

If Syd was here they could share a high five. Mission accomplished. But she wasn't here. Apparently Loretta was going to be, though. Michelle pointed in his direction and the mayor walked resolutely toward him.

"Hi, Burke."

When she sat down across from him he decided they were apparently going to have a conversation.

He nodded. "Madam Mayor."

"How are you?"

"Fine." He looked at the diamond on her left ring finger. "It would appear that congratulations are in order."

"Tom asked me to marry him." She extended the hand and looked dreamily at the tangible proof of the engagement as if she still couldn't believe it was real. "We told the kids last night."

By "the kids," he was pretty sure she was referring to Alex, Ben and Syd, who had to be ecstatic about this turn of events. Her dad was finally moving forward with his life. If Burke had played any small part in the successful outcome, he was pleased. He would have been more pleased if Syd had personally passed along the news. He missed her.

It had only been a couple of days, but he craved the sight of her.

"How did 'the kids' take the announcement?"

"They were all very happy for their dad. And me," she added.

Don't say it, he warned himself, but the words came out anyway. "How's Syd?"

"She was the most pleased for her father." The mayor's eyes narrowed. "Because she felt responsible for him hesitating on the proposal."

"Right." Not a news flash and not what he really wanted to know.

"In fact she was afraid her dad would call it off when he found out the two of you were over."

"You know?"

"In this town good news travels fast. Bad news spreads at light speed." She shook her head and gave him a pitying look. "Poorly played, Burke. I expected better of a hotshot like yourself."

"I'm not sure what you mean."

"You're not seriously going to make me spell out the pitfalls of what happened, are you?"

"I asked her to marry me," he protested.

"And listed the perks as if a proposal was a job interview." Loretta actually tsked. "And there were no flowers, dinner or grand gestures. This conversation happened just inside the door of her house. While you paced like a caged tiger. A very unhappy one."

"Whatever happened to 'it's the thought that counts'?"

"That's the thing. It didn't sound like you thought it through. Along with the houses, cars and trips, you offered to take her away from all this." She held out her hands, a gesture that included all of Blackwater Lake. "Did it occur to you that she might not want to leave? That someday she'll be taking over the business Tom spent his life building? That she loves this town and it's in her blood?"

No, he hadn't thought about that. But it was a confession he had no intention of sharing. He was a man of action. The business wouldn't have exploded under his leadership if he'd been anything less than that. But apparently when dealing with women, being a man of action had its drawbacks.

As far as he could see, there was only one fallback position here. "I was sincere about wanting her to marry me."

"Really?" There was no anger, frustration or sarcasm

in her tone. Just pity. "You wanted her to marry you. But do you want to marry her?"

"I asked, didn't I?"

"It was the way you asked." She leaned forward, resting her forearms on the table between them. "As if you wanted her to say no."

A man of action never wanted rejection. Now he was starting to get irritated. "How did Tom propose to you? What did he say to get a yes?"

Her look was wry. "He certainly didn't leave out the three most important words. In fact, he led with them."

He knew what she was saying. Those three words were all that stood between him and another failure. "It was a decent proposal."

"Was? You're giving up?"

"What am I supposed to do? She turned me down flat and said don't darken her doorway again."

"She actually said that?" The mayor's tone was skeptical.

He shrugged. "It was more like don't let the door hit you in the backside on the way out."

"Can't say I blame her."

This woman was an expert at sending mixed messages. First he was giving up and now she was validating Syd's reaction. "Whose side are you on?"

"That implies you expect special treatment because of the business your development project will bring to Blackwater Lake."

Sydney was the only thing on his mind and if he could change that he would do it in a heartbeat. "Believe it or not," he said, "I wasn't thinking about business at all."

"I'll have to trust you on that, Burke. And trust me when I say that I'm not taking sides. Both of you are my concern."

"Okay." He met her gaze. "I suppose everyone in town knows about this?"

The mayor smiled. "A person in this town would have to be living under a rock not to. But everyone likes you and wants the best for you and Syd."

"Glad to hear it." If he focused hard enough on Liam and the job he came here to do, maybe he wouldn't miss Syd so much.

"I have to go meet Tom. And for the record he doesn't know I talked to you. I just stopped by to show Michelle my ring and she mentioned you were here."

"So you decided to read me the riot act?"

"That wasn't the riot act. Believe me, you'd know if it was." She met his gaze. "But I'm asking a favor. I'd like you to think about something."

"Okay."

"You don't strike me as the sort of man who gives up easily. It seems out of character."

She was right about that. He was also smart enough to know when not giving up turned into beating your head against the wall.

"Syd made her feelings clear," he said.

"Did she? I wonder. But that's for you to decide. This is my 'buck up' speech." She cleared her throat. "I've been in love with Tom for a number of years now, long before he was ready to move on from losing his wife. If I'd given up, I wouldn't be getting a happy ending now."

"So that's the message? Don't give up?"

"We only fail when we fail to try," she said. "For what it's worth, folks in Blackwater Lake are pulling for you and Syd."

"Why?" he asked skeptically.

"You're good people. And she's one of our own. We want you both to be happy." She slid out of the booth and stood. "Okay. That's all I have to say and worth what you paid for it."

"Thanks, Loretta. I appreciate you talking to me." Then he remembered the question that she'd skirted before. "How's Syd?"

She sighed and there was sympathy written all over her face. "She's as miserable as you."

That information should have given him some satisfaction, but it didn't.

Chapter Fifteen

Burke was sitting on the sofa watching a movie with Liam. On the flat-screen TV stuff was exploding and giant robots were morphing into cars, trucks and helicopters. It was loud and didn't require much concentration. That was fortunate since he couldn't concentrate, at least not on this.

All he could think about was Sydney and the void in his life now that she was gone.

Liam missed her, too. It had been over a week since they'd spent time with her and the boy had been asking questions. When were they going to see Syd? Could they go to her house for dinner? Maybe she and Burke could sit on the patio again while he practiced with his new soccer ball.

Burke was running out of excuses. Pretty soon he was going to have to tell his son that they wouldn't be seeing her anymore. And he knew why he was putting off that conversation. Saying the words out loud would make it final and that was going to hurt like hell.

There was a knock on the door and he looked at his watch. Eight at night was kind of late for a visitor. But he felt a small spurt of hope that maybe Syd had had a change of heart.

"I'll see who's there."

Liam looked at him. "Do you want me to pause the movie?"

"No, that's okay." He didn't know what was going on now and missing a minute to answer the door wouldn't make much difference.

He walked across the suite and looked through the peephole, but Sydney wasn't standing there. It was his father and for some reason that surprised him more.

He unlocked the door and opened it. "Dad. What are you doing here?"

"Granddad!" The TV sound stopped when Liam paused the movie, then ran over to greet the newcomer. "I didn't know you were coming."

"That makes two of us. What's up, Dad?"

"Do you mind if I come inside for a few minutes?"

So he wasn't planning on staying long. Burke figured that was standard operating procedure for his father.

Liam grabbed the older man's hand and tugged him into the suite. "I'm so glad you're here. Aren't you glad to see him, Dad?" The boy looked up and frowned. "You don't look happy."

It was more about not trusting than anything else, he thought. Walker Holden only showed up when it suited him, so there had to be a reason he was here.

"If I'd known you were coming, I'd have picked you up at the airport." He met his father's gaze.

"I rented a car. I'll be very happy when you and Sloan get this resort project going and build an airport close by. It's nearly a hundred miles from the current one."

None of that explained the reason for this visit. Burke

figured he wouldn't know until his dad was ready to say what he wanted.

"Can I get you a drink?"

The other man nodded. "Scotch if you have it."

"Of course."

Burke had cultivated a taste for good Scotch because he knew that was Walker's favorite. It would be something they had in common. Maybe a bond. But that was many years and a lot of crushed expectations ago. He'd finally faced the fact that he would never be at the top of his father's priority list.

Burke walked over to the bar, where several kinds of liquor and glasses were arranged. He took two tumblers and poured a small amount of the amber liquid into each.

"Can I have a soda?" Liam's look was pleading. "You and Granddad are going to toast to something and I need something to drink, too."

"Okay. But nothing with caffeine. You have school tomorrow and it's almost bedtime."

"But Granddad is here. Can't I stay up a little later? It's a special occasion."

Burke knew how he felt. As a kid on those rare occasions when his father had been home it had been special for him, too. "Maybe a few minutes—"

"But, Dad, I don't get to see him a lot now that we don't live in Chicago."

Reading between the lines he would have to guess that at home the two had seen each other frequently. When had Burke missed that?

"I'll be here for a while, Liam. We'll spend a lot of time together."

"O-okay," the boy said grudgingly.

Clearly the old man was uncharacteristically patient and understanding. Even diplomatic. When did that happen?

As soon as everyone had their respective liquid, Liam said, "I think we should drink to Granddad's visit."

"Okay." Burke clinked his glass with theirs. "Where are you staying, Dad?"

"Here at the lodge. But I couldn't get a suite on such short notice."

"When did you decide to come?" Burke thought a round of twenty questions might shed some light on the mystery.

"Two days ago. After using Skype with Liam." He sat on the sofa with his grandson beside him and an arm around the boy's shoulders.

Burke sat across from them. They made an affectionate picture and he had an odd sensation that felt a lot like envy. He didn't remember sitting with his father like that. It was hard to do when the man was gone all the time.

"So, what did you two talk about on Skype?"

"You." His father sipped his Scotch. "How unhappy you are."

Burke looked at his son's expression that was just this side of guilty. "Liam?"

"It's true, Dad. You don't smile. You don't want to play ball. And when I ask if we can go to Syd's house your mouth gets all weird and your eyes are mad. Did Syd do something?"

She said no, he thought, and was taken aback by the way his chest got tight at the memory. More pressing, though, was the fact that the conversation with his son about her absence from their lives was going to happen much sooner than he'd expected.

"Syd didn't do anything," he said.

"Then you must have done something." His father's voice was neutral, not critical or harsh. Just matter-of-fact.

Still, Burke felt defensive. "Why does it have to be my fault?"

"Because that young woman is sensible, practical and straightforward. Salt of the earth. Pretty, too. I like her."

"I don't need your approval." But Burke was annoyed that he still couldn't stop wanting it.

"Your mother would have liked her, too." It was as if the man hadn't heard his son push back. "Sydney reminds me a lot of your mother."

Liam leaned closer to his grandfather. "I wish I could have met her."

"You would have loved her."

There was a tone in the older man's voice, a wistful sadness. And the look in his eyes was an echo of the expression that had been there right after his mom had died. It was a mixture of fear and pain. Burke recognized it because he'd felt the same way.

"I'm sorry you never knew her, Liam." Burke sipped his Scotch and waited for the burn in his throat to subside. "She was sweet and funny. She taught me to be kind, loyal and loving. That's who she was."

"I didn't deserve her," Walker said.

Burke stared at the man who was acting nothing like his father and wondered where the heartless bastard had gone. "Why do you say that?"

Instead of answering he looked at his grandson and smiled proudly at him. "More than anything I'm sorry that your grandmother never knew you. She would have loved you so much and been so proud of you, Liam. You too are kind, loyal and loving. Your father instilled in you all the qualities that his mother made sure he had. Everything he needed to be a good father he learned from her. Not me."

"Dad?" Burke stared at the man whose voice and face were familiar, but the attitude was something new.

His father's eyes were bleak. "I should have been around more after she died. I'm sorry I wasn't. You're raising a terrific young man. In spite of my bad example, you're a wonderful father."

Liam smiled up at him, then looked at Burke. "Yeah. You're pretty cool, but way cooler when Syd's around. Maybe you should apologize to her for what you did."

"First, I think we should hear what he did to alienate the young lady."

"Syd's not young," Liam said.

"She is to me," his grandfather pointed out.

"Why does everyone assume it's my fault?" The two just stared at him and Burke sighed. "Okay. All I did was ask her to marry me."

"Well done." Then his father's smile faded. "Yet the two of you are estranged."

"Dad's not strange." Liam looked confused. "Syd isn't, either."

"It means they're not together," Walker explained. "When Sloan and I were here, I saw for myself that she cares very deeply for you. It surprises me that she didn't accept your proposal."

Burke figured he might as well confess and move on. Maybe even change the subject. "I told her about all the perks of being married to me."

"You mean like a job interview."

That's what the mayor had said to him. Had he actually proposed to her in a way designed to make her refuse?

"Yeah, it was pretty much like that." Burke got up and moved to the bar to pour himself another drink.

His father stood and followed him. Behind them the TV sound came on, meaning Liam had lost interest in the men's conversation.

"Burke, I know I wasn't a very good father to you and I'm sorry. There's something about having a grandchild that makes a man examine the mistakes he's made and try to do better. I can never undo what happened or make it up to you. There's no reason you should hear me out now, except that I'm asking you to."

Burke figured there was nothing left to lose. "Okay, I'm listening."

"When your mom got sick I wanted to fix it because that's what I do. But this was out of my hands and I felt helpless. Then she died and I didn't know what to do with the pain. I had everything money can buy and lost the one thing it couldn't. Love. The day your mother was buried was the day I buried myself in work. I'm very sorry I wasn't there for you, son."

Burke just nodded because there was a lump in his throat the size of Montana.

"I can't help thinking that you learned to run from love and that I'm the one who taught you to do it."

"My ex-wife gets some of the credit."

"Pinhead." His father's voice dripped with loathing. "I knew she was wrong for you, but didn't say anything. Figured you wouldn't listen to me of all people. There's no place in hell low enough for a woman like that."

They both glanced at Liam, who was intently watching the movie and paying no attention to this conversation.

Burke blew out a long breath. "He stopped asking about her a long time ago. But I'm sure at some point he'll want information."

"When he's old enough to handle it, you and I will be there to help him deal with the repercussions." His dad reached out and squeezed his shoulder. "And I hope Sydney will be there with you, son. I didn't say anything to you regarding my doubts about your first marriage. Whether you listen to me or not I won't make that same mistake now. Don't follow in my footsteps and isolate yourself from the people who care about you."

Burke felt years of resentment slip away. "Why did you come all the way to Blackwater Lake, Dad?"

"Because I love you and Liam. In the event that you needed me, I wanted to be here to help."

Burke knew he wasn't just talking about Syd, but everything that happened after his mom died. He could have sworn there was a cracking sound in his chest followed by ice falling away from his heart. His father was warning him that love was everything. If Burke lost the woman he loved while there was a chance of having her, he would turn into a bitter shell of a man.

He pulled his father into a hug and felt the heaviness he'd carried for so long lift from his shoulders. "Thanks, Dad."

"Thank you, son." They stepped away and looked at each other and his father said, "Now, what are you going to do about Sydney?"

"That's a good question."

It was amazing how fast a wedding could be pulled together when the whole town pitched in to help. As promised, Loretta had mobilized and delegated, starting a phone tree to spread the word about when and where, and that the reception would be a potluck in the church multipurpose room right after the ceremony at the church located in Blackwater Lake's town square.

Syd's dad had asked her Uncle John to be his best man while her brothers would be groomsmen. Flowers were ordered, nothing extravagant, just simple and beautiful.

Now Syd stood in the back of the church. Double doors separated this area from the rows of pews. As instructed, she was wearing her favorite dress—a red number with a peplum that hugged her like a second skin and four-inch heels to match. Her heart hurt terribly, but she had to put that aside because nothing was going to spoil her father's big day.

Still, she thought that Liam might have liked to be here.

Then she pictured his eager little freckled face that was so much like his father's. Once was a fluke. Twice was a pattern. It seemed that when she gave away her heart, she lost not one, but two people she cared about.

Fortunately, just then her two sisters-in-law joined her. Cam was wearing a royal blue dress with a draped bodice showing a hint of cleavage. Ellie had on a green number with long sleeves and a flirty skirt. The jewel-toned shade highlighted her beautiful eyes.

Syd looked them over and smiled. "You both look completely stunning."

"Are you sure?" Cam smoothed the front of her dress with the hand not holding a bouquet of white roses and baby's breath. "In my wild heiress days, I was in charge of fundraising and fashion events where a designer's career could be made or marred forever. I even walked the runway on occasion. But I've never been this nervous."

"No one would mistake me for the fashion police," Syd said. "But in my humble opinion you look fantastic. You, too, Ellie."

"That's a relief," she said, her Texas roots strong in her voice. "Alex told me that, but everyone knows we dress for other women and he's a man." Her eyes twinkled. "And then he tried to get me out of this dress."

"*Very* high praise." Cam looked Syd up and down. "I've never seen you look more amazing. Burke Holden is my friend, but he's a complete idiot. He doesn't know what he's missing. I tried to talk to him and make him understand that you two are made for each other, but he's being stubborn and—" The words stopped when Ellie cleared her throat. Cam looked mortified. "I'm so sorry. Me and my big mouth."

Syd desperately wanted to ask for specifics about what he'd said, but this wasn't the time. She had the rest of her life to wonder why he couldn't love her. "It's okay."

"No. I'm usually more sensitive than that, but I guess today I'm more nervous than sensitive."

"Don't worry about it." Syd did her best to smile and hoped she pulled it off. "I'm great. Where do you two have my nieces stashed?"

"Maggie Potter has Amanda," Cam said. "Her mom, brother and his fiancé are watching Leah. So, with Maggie's little girl, Danielle, four adults are keeping track of three toddlers. But the little ones usually play nice and keep each other occupied."

"Okay, then." Syd nodded. "Whatever will be will be and that's how Dad and Loretta want it."

"Did I hear my name?" The mayor had emerged from a room off to the side that was reserved for brides. She was wearing a cream-colored lace-over-silk tea-length dress with a neutral shade high heel.

"You look beautiful," Syd said. "Are you nervous?"

"No. I can't wait to be Mrs. Tom McKnight."

As if that was her signal, Rinda Bartell walked over. The blue-eyed blonde was a church volunteer who coordinated weddings. "We're ready to start, ladies. The gentlemen have taken their places in the front with Pastor Will. Sydney, you'll be last before the bride. Camille and Ellie, who wants to go first?"

"I will," Ellie offered and Cam gave her a grateful look. "One of the first things I did here in Blackwater Lake was break my ankle so everyone knows I'm a klutz. If I fall today, Cam, just go around me. I'll be a distraction. That should take care of your nerves."

"It doesn't," she said. "But let's do this."

"I'll go cue the organist," Rinda said and hurried away.

They had a moment for wishes of happiness before Ellie opened the doors separating the rear of the church from the pews. Then the music started and she headed up the aisle.

Cam waited a few beats then followed. Syd gave Loretta a thumbs-up gesture before starting her walk.

People filled the seats and the ones on the end that she could see smiled broadly and murmured that she looked beautiful. Diane and Norm Schurr gave her a little wave. Jill and Adam Stone, with their son and daughter, were there. She passed Violet, Charlie and their kids. This time she grinned at them and meant it. Finding happiness wasn't easy and she was glad for her friends.

She saw her father with Uncle John beside him. Her brothers were there, too, and all the men looked incredibly handsome in their dark suits. Just before she took her place, her gaze settled on her dad. He nodded his approval, then his expression changed. He looked expectant, or excited. She knew him as well as he knew her and this was something more than a man about to get married.

Before she could wonder what was going on, his expression changed, filled with happiness, and she knew he'd seen his bride walking toward him. Her father took two steps to meet Loretta and held out his arm. She put her hand in the bend of his elbow and they moved in front of the pastor.

"Tom, Loretta, in front of most everyone in Blackwater Lake I have to say—it's about darn time."

The congregation laughed, including the bride and groom, dissipating any lingering nerves. Then the pastor cleared his throat and started the ceremony. "We are gathered here today in the sight of God, family and friends to join Tom McKnight and Loretta Goodson in marriage."

He talked about love being patient, kind and understanding. The obligations of a husband to his wife and vice versa. Her father and Loretta vowed to love, honor and cherish then exchanged rings. The minister said the "I now pronounce you husband and wife" part and it was time for him to announce you may kiss your bride. But that's not what he said.

"Ladies and gentlemen, there's someone here who has requested permission from Tom and Loretta to say a few words."

Syd heard the click of a man's shoes walking down the aisle and glanced in that direction. Her legs started to tremble when she recognized Burke and Liam Holden approaching. The boy looked so handsome and grown up in his suit and tie. And Burke... Seeing him was like a shot of adrenaline to her system. She couldn't believe he was here.

He stopped in front of the wedding party and thanked both the pastor and her father. After that, all his attention was focused on her.

"Syd, you were absolutely right to refuse my proposal. It was decent enough, but not even close to what you deserve. I can do better. Please hear me out."

"I will," she whispered.

He moved closer, stopping about a foot away. When he spoke, his words were clear and loud enough to be heard in the church's far corners. That was partly because in spite of the capacity crowd, it was possible to hear a pin drop.

"When I asked you to marry me, I said I would take you away from all this. It was glib, a cliché. The truth is that Blackwater Lake is part of who you are and I would never change you. I love you and that means never asking you to choose between me and what you care so deeply about. But I'd move heaven and earth for you. That includes my corporate office. I plan to set it up here in Blackwater Lake."

Syd had the ridiculous thought that she hoped whoever her father had asked to video the wedding was still recording because she would want to see it later. Burke was still talking and she was pretty sure it was important but all she could focus on was the "I love you" part.

Then he said, "You would make me the happiest man in the world if you'd marry me."

Before she could even process those words and form a response, Liam spoke. "I love you, too, Syd. And I want you to be my mom."

That's when the tears she'd been struggling to hold back trickled down her cheeks. And judging by some loud sniffling and a chorus of "ohs" she wasn't alone.

She glanced at her father, who stood with an arm around his new bride. "You knew about this?"

"Burke asked for my permission to propose. I gave it without hesitation. He's a good man. He'll take very good care of my little girl."

"Oh, Daddy—" Her voice broke.

And then Burke was holding her and whispered against her hair, "Please don't cry. I wouldn't have crashed the wedding if he hadn't been on board with this."

She nodded. "But why was it so important to do it here? Why now?"

"For one thing I needed a grand gesture." The corners of his mouth turned up. "But it's more than that. Your father's happiness is as important to you as yours is to him. As he takes this step forward in his life, it was necessary for him and everyone in Blackwater Lake to know that I promise to love and protect you as long as I live."

"Oh, Burke. That's so—"

"Please don't say nice." He smiled. "Just say you'll marry me."

"Since that's a much better proposal than the one I made to you—yes." She pulled back just enough to see his face and said in a voice as loud and clear as his had been, "I love you, too. Of course I'll marry you. There's nothing I want more than to be your wife and Liam's mom."

There was spontaneous applause and when everyone settled down, the pastor cleared his throat. "Now it gives me great pleasure to say—I present to you, Mr. and Mrs. McKnight. Tom, you may kiss your bride." His grin was wide when he said, "Burke, you may kiss your fiancée."

Burke didn't waste any time. He cupped her cheek in his hand and smiled tenderly before touching his mouth to hers. She sighed with happiness and felt a soft puff of air on her face, like the caress of a mother's fingers or the brush of an angel's wings.

Suddenly awareness filled her heart and soul that two mothers who couldn't be here in body for their children were here in spirit and signaling their approval of a most decent proposal.

* * * * *

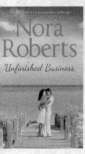
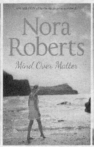
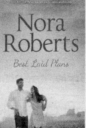
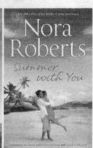

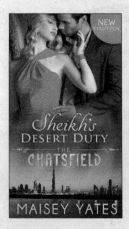